# BAREBACK

*Bareback* is Kit Whitfield's first novel. A graduate of Christ's College, Cambridge, she completed an MA in Creative Writing at the University of East Anglia. She lives in London.

KIT WHITFIELD

# Bareback

**VINTAGE BOOKS**
London

Published by Vintage 2006

2 4 6 8 10 9 7 5 3 1

Copyright © Kit Whitfield 2006

Kit Whitfield has asserted her right under the Copyright, Designs
and Patents Act 1988 to be identified as the author of this work

First published in Great Britain in 2006 by Jonathan Cape

Vintage
Random House, 20 Vauxhall Bridge Road,
London SW1V 2SA

Random House Australia (Pty) Limited
20 Alfred Street, Milsons Point, Sydney,
New South Wales 2061, Australia

Random House New Zealand Limited
18 Poland Road, Glenfield,
Auckland 10, New Zealand

Random House (Pty) Limited
Isle of Houghton, Corner of Boundary Road & Carse O'Gowrie,
Houghton 2198, South Africa

Random House Publishers India Private Limited
301 World Trade Tower, Hotel Intercontinental Grand Complex,
Barakhamba Lane, New Delhi 110 001, India

The Random House Group Limited Reg. No. 954009
www.randomhouse.co.uk/vintage

A CIP catalogue record for this book
is available from the British Library

ISBN 9780099503620 (from Jan 2007)
ISBN 009950362X

Papers used by Random House are natural, recyclable products made from
wood grown in sustainable forests. The manufacturing processes conform to
the environmental regulations of the country of origin

Typeset by Palimpsest Book Production Limited,
Grangemouth, Stirlingshire

Printed and bound in Great Britain by
Cox & Wyman Ltd, Reading, Berkshire

Without Joel, this book would have no beginning;
without Peggy, no middle;
without Gareth, no ending.

With love and thanks to you all.

## From Sunset to Star Rise

Go from me, summer friends, and tarry not
      I am no summer friend but wintry cold,
      A silly sheep benighted from the fold,
A sluggard with a thorn-choked garden plot.
Take counsel, sever from my lot your lot,
      Dwell in your pleasant places, hoard your gold;
      Lest you with me should shiver on the wold,
Athirst and hungering on a barren spot.
For I have hedged me with a thorny hedge,
      I live alone, I look to die alone:
Yet sometimes, when a wind sighs through the sedge
      Ghosts of my buried years and friends come back
My heart goes sighing after swallows flown
      On sometime summer's unreturning track.

Christina Rossetti

Question the lady to see if she will tell you why the beast hates
her. Make her tell you, if she knows!

Marie de France, Bisclavret

In the reading of this story, therefore I do first request reformation of opinion.

'A True Discourse Declaring the Damnable Life of One Stubbe Peeter', George Bores, London Chapbook of 1590

# 1

The story is a simple one. According to Ellaway, his car broke down, he was lost, and was trying to find a shelter when he started furring up. He shouldn't really have failed to find one – there are always government lock-ups within walking distance; you should be able to reach at least one between dusk and moonrise. At least, that's the theory; like most of our theories, it's prettier than the real world. Winos are the biggest problem since they're too drunk to make their way, but this guy's story might be true, manicured nails and all. It happens every month. Then again, it might not. It's not much of a story. And the fact remains that when Johnny tried to round him up, Ellaway bit his hand off at the wrist. Most lunes don't do that. They go for you; of course they do. We've all got scars. There's a deep slash running up the inside of my left forearm from my first dogcatch; a heavy dent in one of my hips from when I was twenty-two; a map of lacerations around my calves – and I'm a good catcher, I get mauled less than most. But breaking bone is something more. Lunes aren't usually savage enough to hurt you that badly before you get them tranked. They all go for you, but they aren't all the same. It depends what kind of person they are. This man has to have something in him to make him capable of mauling my friend.

His face looks like a college kid's, though I know he's a few years older. A City boy, which means he's paid well, better than I am. He'll be paying me himself on this one, and then I can pay my bills. I study him with some hope, and notice how differently he sits from the pro bono cases I usually get. He's crouched forward, watching me. Maybe he'll have better manners than usual. I light a cigarette, offer him one to be polite. To my surprise, he takes it. Lycos don't usually smoke.

'So,' I say, 'you realise the charges are serious. Your best hope is in proving that you tried to get to a lock-up but couldn't.'

'I did.' He says this as if it were obvious. My hopes of a courteous client slip a notch.

I sigh. 'I don't suppose you remember the actual crime?'

He gives me a look: I've asked a foolish question and called what he did a crime. 'Of course not. I can't even identify the man.'

I flip a picture across the desk. 'His name is Johnny Marcos. He's got a wife and three kids, and since you took his hand off he's on restricted pay and worried sick about their education. He's a very decent man.'

'You know him?' My client looks surprised. 'I thought legal advisers weren't meant to take cases where they're personally involved.'

Bright boy. 'This is DORLA, Mr Ellaway. We all know each other. There's only a few thousand of us. It's a small world. And since we all do –' I stop myself from saying dogcatching '– full-moon duties sometimes, that could have been any of us. And since you'll get a

2

non-lyco judge, you're going to have to work hard at convincing us it wasn't your fault.' I don't mention how well I know Johnny; he doesn't need to know that. Three days before Christmas, and this happened to him.

'Why can't I have a normal court? Any bareback judge is going to be prejudiced against me.'

Bareback. Well, there we are. He's no better mannered than any of the tramps I usually get. I give my illusion about the gentlemanliness of the monied classes a little kiss and send it on its way. 'Like I said, Mr Ellaway, this is the Department for the Ongoing Regulation of Lycanthropic Activity, and we handle our own affairs.' I get out a map of the area. 'Now, you say you were round here when your car broke down, yes? And you started walking east. There's two lock-ups within reach.'

He sucks on the cigarette I gave him. 'I told you, I don't know the area.'

'You should know enough to stick to the main roads. You would have come to a shelter if you had.'

He shrugs, and lounges back, his legs asplay. I take out another file. 'I've got your record here. Dangerous driving, twice, driving over the legal limit, and possession of narcotic substances. I have to tell you, Mr Ellaway, it doesn't look good.'

'They dropped the narcotics charge.' He drops ash on my floor.

'Were you using anything that night?'

'Drugs are illegal.' He looks amused at himself.

'How about a little nicotine withdrawal? Cross because you couldn't fit a cigarette in your jaws?'

'Hey, hey.' He sits up, waving his hand. 'I didn't come here to be accused. I'm your client, you know?'

I run my hands through my hair. 'Mr Ellaway, I'm

just trying to tell you the kind of things they'll ask you in court. You've crippled a man for life. If you can prove it wasn't your fault you were out, then you'll get off. And if you can't, then it's negligence, grievous bodily harm, the works, and you are looking at years. Years, Mr Ellaway. Judges don't take kindly to this sort of thing.'

He shrugs again.

The telephone rings. 'Excuse me,' I say, and pick it up. 'Hello?'

'Lola?' It's Josie. She's been working on reception ever since she let two lunes get away in one night. 'Lo, I got a call from your sister. She says she's gone into labour and could you go to the hospital. She's at St Veronica's.'

My throat jumps a little. 'I'll get on it. Thanks, Josie.' I turn to Ellaway, who is still dropping ash on my floor. 'Mr Ellaway, I have to go. I'll see you again tomorrow, and I want you to think about what I've said. I need as many details as possible, so remember everything you can. Now, good morning.'

'Good morning.' His handshake cracks the bones in my knuckles, and he's still sitting in the chair.

'Mr Ellaway, you can go now.'

'Oh. Right. I'll see you tomorrow.' He gets up and swings out of the room.

'And could you close the –' He disappears, leaving the door wide open. I express a few opinions under my breath, and go to close it myself, making myself a promise to bill Ellaway for every possible expense I can think of. I'll bill him for every cup of coffee I drink as long as I'm working for him. I'll get it hand-ground, I'll add cream. The thought cheers me a little.

4

I call my boss and explain. 'Is it all right if I take the day off? I'll work overtime next week.'

'A baby.' His voice sounds reflective, not that it ever sounds any different. 'Well, off you go. You can see if it turns out to be one of ours.'

I can't tell if this is a joke, so I laugh just in case. I get my coat and squeeze out of my little office. On the way past reception, a hand comes down on my shoulder.

'Miss Lola May, you save my life.' It's Jerry, one of my winos, being herded in by my friend Ally. Jerry smells like a dustbin, which means he's fallen off the wagon again. 'Wanna thank you frall your good legal advice, Lola May, you're good legal vice lady.'

'Hey, Jerry,' I say. 'What are you doing here?'

'Got stuck out last moonite. Wasn't my fault, tried to shelter, you know always try. Don't mind shelters, quite like them ashually. Can't always find my way, not my fault if I try, Lola May. This guy says I pissed on him when he tried collar me but would I do that? Wouldn't. You know I'm nice guy, Lola May.' He rocks back and forth, his eyes wide like a kid's. 'Think they'll sue me for cleaning bill, you gotta help me Lola May. Don't wanna pay cleaning bill. Not mon . . . not mada . . . mada money. Tellem I wouldn't ever piss on a guy juss doing his job.'

I've seen him worse than this: he's pretty bad, but his sense of humour hasn't drowned out yet. He's been able to go out and get drunk again, so he can't have been locked up in the cells all this time. Maybe this won't be too rough. 'What's he in for?' I ask Ally, who's standing a little back from his charge.

'Moon loitering. This is the twelfth time, he's not doing well.'

5

'No cleaning bill?' says Jerry, swivelling his head.

'Jerry,' I say, 'what happened to your AA programme?'

'M'wife left me,' he says.

'Yeah? Was that before or after you fell off the wagon?'

'Ohh, Lola May you gon break my heart. You're hard woman, Lola May.'

My feet are starting to itch. 'Look, Ally, I'll take this case if you can hold it over till tomorrow, he's one of my regulars.'

'Lucky you.'

'He's harmless.'

'I,' Jerry declares, 'am a gentleman. Do my best.'

'Can you just put it on hold for a day?'

'I think I'll put him in the lock-ups to dry out,' Ally says, grinning.

'Don't wanna sleep on straw. Lola May, tell him I don wanta sleep on straw!' Jerry wails as Ally hustles him down the corridor.

I turn to head out, and that's when I see there's a man on the chairs who's been watching the whole exchange. His hair sticks up in tufts, his eyebrows are trained into fierce peaks. He sits with his lips a little apart, baring his teeth. The effect is meant to be vulpine, but it looks more like a bad photograph.

'Excuse me,' I say.

The man doesn't take his eyes off me.

'Are you being seen?'

He turns his head aside, slowly, and spits through his teeth onto the floor. Then he looks back at me.

'Fucking skins,' he says.

*

I take the bus to the hospital. Sitting in the back, I catch myself folding a little paper bird out of my ticket: I crumple it and stuff it into my pocket. There's no need to fall back on nervous habits.

My sister Becca and I are not really close.

The baby could be one of two men's, thanks to a DORLA screw-up that's just another wedge between us. Caught between home and work one moon night, Becca presented herself at the nearest lock-up like a good citizen. It happened to be a Friday, and there were a lot of people there; Fridays and Saturdays are always the worst. So some genius put her in a cell with some man she didn't know. Which would probably not have had serious consequences, except that Becca is one of those unlucky women whose menstrual cycle tends to be at mid-point around the full moon. When she furs up, she goes on heat. If I'd known that at the time, I could have told her to take the Pill and knock her cycle out of sync, but I didn't hear about it till later.

It's a government mistake, not hers, so legally neither she nor this anonymous man is responsible. But unfortunately for Becca, her husband didn't see it that way.

Like a good sister, I went with her to the prenatal classes. I helped her with breathing exercises, I held her hand. I got DORLA to certify that the adultery wasn't her fault, which was no joke, but I did it, entitling her to enough of her husband's fortune that she had money to get by on. I even promised to stay with her when she went into labour. Throughout the pregnancy, though, there was a barrier between us, and I could guess what it was. It isn't just that I work for the department that's responsible for her being a single mother, my conservative sister's worst nightmare. It's that she couldn't tell

7

me how much she hoped her baby would be normal, because that would be telling me how much she hoped the baby wouldn't be born the way I was.

More than most people, she has a horror of having a non-lyco baby, and that is because of me. It was only when we were very little that she didn't notice the difference on moon nights. She'd lock up at home with my parents, and spend the night grooming or whatever, while I would be opted out of it and taken to a DORLA creche. She gave me looks like I was refusing to share something. And later, I couldn't join in the excitement of choosing a career, because we all know what happens to barebacks: they get conscripted into DORLA. There's a choice of what you can do within it, but no question, ever, of not working for them. It's too big a job, and being non-lyco is too rare a birth defect: we all double up and do several jobs at once as it is. That is decided for you at birth. Becca never says that I wouldn't get into the spirit of things at home, but I know that's how she thinks. As far as she's concerned, the Department for the Ongoing Regulation of Lycanthropic Activity stole her little sister. If it steals her baby, I don't know what she's going to do.

Becca is in the middle of a white bed, her dark hair in a mess that in other circumstances she would be ashamed of. She gives me a polite smile as I come in, that just about covers the disappointment that I'm not her husband. 'How's it going, sis?' I say.

Her voice has a different accent than mine, because of the lyco schooling: even when she's this tired and stressed, she sounds classier. 'The doctor

8

says everything is going fine, it should only be a few more hours.'

A few more hours sounds like quite a while to me, but then Becca always said I have no patience. I settle myself down in the chair by the bed. Becca appears to go into a contraction, and I let her have my hand. Her grip is harder than Ellaway's.

'Breathe,' I remind her.

I want a cigarette, but if I lit one in this place they'd have me arrested, DORLA agent or not. Becca pants on the bed, and I inhale the sterile air, trying to imagine it is ash-grey. It tastes of disinfectant.

A man with a green paper hat comes in with a purposeful stride and examines my sister without making any comment. After a couple of minutes, Becca releases my hand and I flex it, trying to get the flesh back to where it was before. The green-capped gentleman nods to himself and says something about dilations to the nurse. He turns to the door.

'Hello,' I say to him before he can reach it.

'Hello. I'm Dr Parkinson, the consultant – I assume you're a friend of hers?'

'I'm her sister.' Becca flops her head back on the bed, and doesn't say anything.

'Well, she's doing just fine,' he says in a soothing voice. 'I'll make a few more calls, but there should be no problem.'

Becca's face creases for a moment with anxiety, then she turns away from me. Evidently she hasn't asked him what's uppermost in her mind. She would have done better to ask behind my back before I got here. Since she hasn't, she's not going to say it to my face. She isn't fooling me, but I appreciate the gesture.

Though I'd appreciate it more if she didn't need to ask him so badly.

'Is it going to be all right?' I say.

'Pardon?'

'Is it going to come out feet first like it should?'

He makes the beginnings of a deprecating sound, and I cut across him. 'Only I was born head-on, you see, and my sister and I agree that one non-lyco in the family is enough.'

'Ah. You're from DORLA?'

'Yep.' Becca is silent, not looking at me.

'Well, there's nothing to worry about. I'll see that everything turns out just fine.' And out he swans. It's no kind of an answer, really. Sonograms have shown the baby often enough, feet tucked together, poised for the descent, and from the way he's laid, there should be no question of a problem. Things can go wrong at the last minute, though. The baby jams, the neck bends, or not enough oxygen goes to his brain at the wrong moment, or too much happens before he's ready. Being laid wrong is the indicator, not the cause. I was born head first like every other non I know, but even with an ultrasound photograph nestling in her wallet, Becca isn't going to stop fretting until she sees her lyco baby in the flesh and blood. The doctor hasn't reassured her.

'There you go.' I pat Becca's hand. 'No need to worry.'

She speaks without looking at me. 'That isn't fair, May. You know I never said anything about not wanting it to be . . . to . . .'

This is true. She didn't.

I have a choice here. I can lie, and say it was just me who was worried, and I only brought you into it to give my worries weight; or I can tell the truth and say, yes, but I know that's what you were thinking. I'm quite relieved when another contraction starts up and takes away the need to answer.

My sister toils on the bed. I sit and watch. No doubt she is in great pain, but she was probably right. I can't get into the spirit of things.

The consultant returns at intervals. I wonder how she's affording him: money drips off him instead of sweat. I sit on my plastic chair and let him ignore me.

Becca lies on the bed and speaks to me once or twice every hour.

Finally we come to it. I tilt my head round and find that the desired end is coming to pass. Tiny feet appear, then tiny knees, by which time it's perfectly clear that the infant is going to be a lyco.

The doctor produces him with a subdued flourish, and there he is: a little baby boy, smeared with fluid and trying his best to move his brand-new limbs in the scalding light. His face is funny-looking, folded over and pressed bright red; he looks like a skinned rabbit. He's terrified.

Parkinson picks him up, examines him, puts him through a few moments of tests. Becca's hands fidget on her chest; I sit very still. 'Perfectly sound in every way,' Parkinson finally pronounces, and he hands the little mite over for the nurses to excoriate. The boy's puckered face contorts as they set to work swabbing him.

Becca's face is running with sweat; she's almost sobbing. 'Oh thank God. Oh thank God, oh thank –'

Then she remembers that her bareback sister is listening.

'Don't worry about it,' I say, and shrug. 'At least you get to keep him.'

Another contraction comes along, this one for the

afterbirth. I give her my hand and squeeze back as hard as I can. This is to stop her from crushing it altogether. Perhaps it feels like fellowship from the outside.

By the time I get home, I have three separate backaches. I swipe card my way through the door, get in the lift and go all the way up to the seventh floor. The building is a little scuzzy. There are dust mice under the radiators and peeling paint on the windows; when I take a bath, I've been known to get bits of plaster in my hair. All of this means that it's cheap, which means I can afford it. And also, lycos don't live here, not adult ones anyway. It started out with nons moving in because of the low rent. The flats are undersized anyway, and lycos prefer to have at least one biggish room for a lock-up. After a while, the lycos moved out because there were too many damn barebacks around, and now it's pretty much lyco-free. We tend to have lyco children, as the condition's not inherited, and some of us, a very few of us, marry lycos, but there's a non in every flat. This has its advantages, the biggest being that no one acts like I'm about to arrest them.

I get to my apartment. I've painted the rooms red and blue, trying for cosy, but really they're just small. The bedroom consists of a double bed where I sleep alone, and about an inch of space each side. The kitchen is narrow, and has some food in it, enough for dinner. I haven't thought about food for a few hours, so I'm not yet hungry, but I will be in a while; I need to work myself up to it. What I've been looking forward to is a hot bath, the first major consolation of the evening.

My feet hurt. I kick off my scary-lady shoes, and

hobble towards this goal. When I open the door, I find that there's a big wet patch on the ceiling, pouring a narrow stream of grey water down into a minor flood on my bathroom floor.

This is a disappointment I do not want to have to deal with, but I cannot have a bath with the room in this state. I make my way upstairs, shoeless, and knock on the door of the Cherry family, the people responsible for this misfortune. The kids, I discover – lycos both – are babysitting themselves tonight and have forgotten to turn off the tap.

'Could you turn it off now?' I say. 'My bathroom is full of water.'

The boy giggles; the girl says, 'We're sorry, Miss Galley, really we are.' She looks so worried I'm half inclined to apologise – except that she has a giggling brother who flooded my ceiling, so I don't. They take off to repair the damage, and I head back downstairs, wondering if my ceiling might dry by itself.

I'm at my door when I'm caught by my neighbour opposite, Mrs Kitney. Mrs Kitney is an old biddy from Personnel who somehow manages to make everything she says sound like she's sympathising about some intimate medical complaint.

'You're back late, Lola,' she says.

'No, I'm fine,' I say. This is not the most apt of answers, but the way she talks, I can't help myself.

'You don't have any shoes on,' she confides.

'I was just going upstairs for a minute. The Cherry kids forgot to turn a tap off.'

'Ohh, but it's terrible news about poor Johnny Marcos, isn't it?' she says, shaking her head at me.

I don't think she knew him well, but she's bound to

13

have heard. 'Bad lune. I'm advising him, but he doesn't have much of a case. The judge isn't going to go easy on him.'

She frowns. It's possible she's surprised that I'm betraying client confidentiality like this, but only in the same way it's possible I'll win the lottery and be a millionaire.

'You're advising him?'

'Yeah, the man who took his hand off. Someone's got to do it. I always get the no-hopers.'

'Oh, you haven't heard!' She claps her hands to her mouth, then leans towards me. 'It's not his hand, Lola. It's him. Someone shot him tonight.'


Back in my apartment, I lock and bolt the door. I don't know whether I'm frightened or whether I want to be alone. I don't know anything. Closing my eyes, I try to bring up Johnny Marcos's face, but all I can think of now is his brown eyes.

The sound of a slap makes me jump. I must be nervous. I go to see what's wrong, and see, through my bathroom window, a body of water fall through the air. It lands with a smack seven storeys down, and another one follows it. It takes me a minute to put together that the Cherry children are throwing water out of their bathroom window.

I can't stand this. Johnny Marcos is gone beyond hope of retrieval and I can't listen to any sharp sounds. I go through to my sitting room. The walls cramp in on me, and I switch on the television to block them out with noise.

The news headlines fill my flat. There's a war in

Africa. There are earthquake warnings in San Francisco. There's a move to lower inflation rates. There's an inquiry into the health service. There's a new toy invented that sold out within an hour of shops opening.

Some of this is local, but there's nothing about us. Johnny didn't make the news.

# 2

I remember the last time I saw Johnny. I was on my way from a legals' meeting, one of those tombola affairs where they dole out who gets which lawbreaker. His arm was still in a bandage, layered over the stump at the wrist. In his remaining hand was a mop.

'Hi, Lo,' he said. His face, going on forty years, had always had a puppy-dog look, big old eyes and friendly looking jowls. It wasn't so long since the attack, but it seemed like he'd gained weight; his face was sinking. He looked more kicked than anyone I'd ever seen.

'Johnny. How are you?' I said.

He shrugged. 'Guess we won't be playing squash again.'

I tried to smile. 'Where am I going to find another partner who's such a good loser? You've just got to learn to play left-handed.'

'I'd be a better loser then,' he said. 'But I didn't always lose, did I?'

'No,' I said. 'You were good.'

He looked at his mop; it had an old, battered handle. 'Lo, I –' He stopped. 'Listen –'

I thought I knew what he was trying to say. 'Look,

Johnny, you've probably heard I'm advising the guy who did this to you.'

He didn't look at me. 'That's your job, Lola girl.'

'I've –' I wanted to tell him that I'd seen Ellaway's record and it would set any judge dead against him, but Johnny was one of those types who actually cared if you told him things you shouldn't. The grapevine in DORLA has tendrils in every room and we all know everything, but it bothered Johnny. I shrugged instead. 'As his adviser, I'll do the best I can for him. As your friend, I hope they make him into a rug.'

'Lo.' He looked up at me. His eyelashes were going grey. 'Can we meet some time?'

'Sure, Johnny,' I said.

'Thanks,' he said, and nodded. 'I'd like to see you.'

I thought at the time he was forgiving me for representing Ellaway. It's only now it occurs to me he might have wanted to tell me something.


As soon as I get to work next morning, I'm stopped at reception by Josie. 'Ellaway's yours, isn't he?' she says. I open my mouth to say that if he was actually mine I'd dispose of him humanely; she goes on before I can. 'He's in the cells. He keeps saying he wants a lawyer.'

'We've arrested him?' He had an appointment with me this morning; they must have pounced on him and locked him up the second he walked in. That will have given him a shock.

'Yes. Gus Greenham and Ally are down there with him.'

'Ah.' I'm not sure how much they can have put the

screws on him so early in the day, but it's as well to have a good cop down there too. 'I'll be right down.'

Ellaway is in one of the lock-ups, with only straw and a water bowl. He's sitting on a chair they've moved in, his suit mussed, his hair tangled. Greenham and Ally are in there with him. I don't go in to join them. I can't do what they're doing. I've no love for this bad lune, though. Let him sweat a little more if his own lawyer's out of reach.

'Galley,' he says. 'Where the hell have you been? Tell these bastards I want a lawyer.'

There's a chair by the bars, and I sit in it. 'You've got one. Me.'

'I want a proper lawyer. I've got a right to a proper lawyer.'

Greenham cuffs him, not too hard. 'Watch how you speak to the lady, boy.'

'I've got my fucking rights. Why can't I have a lawyer, Galley, why aren't you doing anything?'

I cross my legs. 'As I've been trying to tell you for two days, Mr Ellaway, you're in DORLA now.'

Greenham wrenches his head back, and Ally paces in front of him. 'Let us hear your alibi, Ellaway. It's going hard with you if you don't have an alibi.'

Ellaway makes a choking sound. 'Lower his head a bit, Gus, you're compressing his voice box,' I say. Greenham is a thug, but we can get on when we have to and what I've said is practical. He lets Ellaway's head down an inch.

'Galley! Why aren't you stopping them?'

'Stopping what, Ellaway? We haven't done anything to you yet,' says Ally. The murder has hit Ally badly, I think; his voice is hard.

18

I find I'm rocking to and fro in my chair. This yuppie shooting Johnny Marcos when he was already facing trial for maiming him does not, in cold daylight, seem that likely. There could be other reasons, though, and with Johnny lying dead because some piece of fur took a gun to him, I'm not feeling sympathetic. 'Mr Ellaway. As you probably have heard, your victim, Johnny Marcos, was shot last night. If God loves you, you've got an alibi, and if you have, I must advise you to produce it now.'

'I was at home.'

'Can anyone verify that?'

'I live alone. I've got a right to a lawyer, I can't just be left here.'

'I'm your lawyer, Mr Ellaway.'

He starts struggling, and I see he's been handcuffed to the chair. 'I don't want a fucking bareback lawyer, you'll string me up, I've got to get out into the real fucking world.'

'This is the real world,' says Ally. 'And you, Ellaway, are not getting out of it.'


My professional conscience gets to me, and I have him shown up to my office. He wasn't down there long enough to get really scared – instead, he is furious with me: it has begun to dawn on him that he's not going to be handed over to mainstream justice. I could get him a lyco lawyer, in theory, but I did that a few times when I was a rookie, and I grew out of it pretty fast. Lawyers are fine on their own patch with their own people. On our patch, dealing with us, they're something else. They don't come out and say, Fucking skins.

Not quite. It's remarkable how close someone can get to saying it without using vulgar language – and most lawyers practically build their cases on it. Ally promised a few years back that he'd shave his head every time a lyco lawyer managed not to mention 'public opinion' or 'the majority of citizens' within ten minutes of arriving. His hair's halfway down his back and still growing.

'Mr Ellaway,' I say. 'You'd better start talking to me, because I'm more on your side than anyone else in this building.'

'Fuck you, Galley. I saw how on my side you are.' He isn't just angry. I think his feelings are actually hurt. The world isn't his in here, and no one's helping.

'Look,' I tell him. 'You're a big suspect, and you're a big suspect in a serious crime. A DORLA official has been killed, do you understand the seriousness of that?'

He glares at me.

'Whatever you think of DORLA, Mr Ellaway, it's not going away. And every man and woman in this building is part of it. That wasn't just Marcos, that was a shot at all of us. So if you expect me to sit and hold your hand while my people interrogate you, then you're going to be disappointed. But you are my client, and I will represent you. And since no lyco lawyer is coming to help you, I'm the best you'll get. So, for your own good, I suggest you try to get along with me, because there is no one else who will help you.'

It's important that I get as much out of him as I can now. I don't like the sight of blood, and everyone here hates Ellaway. Me included, of course. But soon as we release him, he'll go straight to a lyco firm and then he will have a lawyer. Hell, he's probably got one already;

all his offences and all his money make this a good chance. This is a DORLA case, the first crime was a moon-night offence and that puts him in our territory, but he's allowed to bring in his own lawyer to work with me if he wants to. And once we've got a lawyer on the scene, then that's it. Ninety-nine point six per cent of the population at the last count will rise to protect him, and Johnny can go to hell because God is a lyco.

'Mr Ellaway. You're not making this easy on yourself. You can be held here a long time. It's not me who decides that, it's my job to put you up for bail. Tell me something that gives you an alibi and I can apply for your release.'

'I told you, I was at home.'

'What were you doing?'

'Watching TV.'

'What was on?'

'Some old black-and-white movie about airmen.'

'What channel?'

'Two.' His answers fire right back at me, but this doesn't mean they're true; he could have just looked at a paper.

'Did anyone visit you at that time?'

'No.'

'Any phone calls?'

'Yes. Yes, I made a call.' He leans forward.

'Who to?'

He chews his lip a moment, then opens his mouth. I've never seen anyone before whose lips can shrug, but that's what they're doing. 'Lewis Albin. A man I know called Lewis Albin.' He writes down a number and address.

'What time was this?'

'About nine o'clock.'

Johnny was shot between eight-thirty and ten, the doc says. I don't think we've told Ellaway that, but then he'd know it if he shot him. 'Right, well, we can check your telephone bill; what company are you with?'

'It's a mobile. It won't be on the bill, it's pay-as-you-go.'

The bastard is an idiot. 'Mr Ellaway, that's not much of an alibi, then, is it? You could have called from anywhere.'

'I called from home.' There's tenacity here. It isn't just stupidity, or not ordinary stupidity. He's not even trying: he's just waiting for us to let him out, because he's certain that nothing can really happen to him.

'This Lewis Albin, who is he, a workmate?'

'No.'

'An acquaintance?'

He shrugs.

'Tell me, do your employers know you're facing criminal charges?'

He shrugs. 'Kind of. Some of the people at work know, but it's not a big deal, I mean, we didn't talk about it much. I don't know if my boss knows or not.'

For a moment I stare at him while he toys with my cigarette. He doesn't even know what he's said. He actually looks surprised when I put a stop to the interview and send him back to the cells.


Lewis Albin is not a name I'm familiar with. I check his address: it's a classy area on the other side of town, bordered by a shabby area. Artistic. It's in the Five Wounds district – his house is near enough the park itself to put the price up. The next thing to do is check with him; maybe he heard the TV in the background or something, which would clear Ellaway and leave us free to find someone else to swing.

An answerphone clicks on after two rings. 'Hello, this is Lewis. Let me know, and I'll call you back . . .' The voice is young, healthy, with good lungs behind it, almost like an actor's. He doesn't have a non accent, which I could have guessed straight off: it's a bit more regional than Ellaway's, but still middle-class lyco. I think I'll pay a call on this Mr Albin.

Jerry is hauled up from downstairs, and I have to deal with him before I can leave. They've put the hoses on him; he stinks less, and he's quieted down. Moon loitering is an awkward one, because of course he's guilty as hell, and what are you supposed to do about it? Imprison him for a few months, and he'll only be that much more of a nuisance.

'Jerry,' I say. 'You know you could do six months for this.'

Even sobered up, he leans on his consonants like they were a bar table. It's something he's done more and more over the years; most people pressure him less when he acts drunk. He knows I don't fall for it, but habits are hard to break. He's got to stop if he wants to help himself now, though. 'I don want to go to jail, Lola. What'd I do in there?'

'Time, Jerry. I don't see you liking it.'

'You're a hard woman. I tell you that before?'

'Every time, Jerry. What, you want me to be nice to you and let you fall around town and get dogcaught every month? You're slipping, you need telling that.'

He slumps in his chair. His clothes hang off him, his

23

hair straggles in greasy sheets. I can see why he prefers himself in his cups.

'Look, Jerry. You go back on your AA programme, and I can maybe, and I mean maybe, get the judge to go easy on you.'

'I don't wanna go to jail,' he mumbles. 'Why do I have to get hauled in?'

'Are you listening? You stick with your rehab, and you've got a chance. You break it, and you're counting bars, ones that don't serve you whisky. Prison or the pledge, Jerry. It's your choice.' With Jerry, it's usually worth saying things several times: your chances of at least part of it sinking in are better.

'I been on the wagon.'

'You've been out in the moon twelve times.'

'Twelve times.' He blinks at me. 'Why'd they haul me in on this one?'

'Probably because you pissed on the catcher. That kind of thing gets on people's nerves, you know? And cute though your face is, Jerry, we're getting sick of the sight of it.'

'Don't remember pissing on anyone.'

'You wouldn't, would you? You were luning at the time. Between your drinking and your furring up, it's a wonder you remember anything.'

He stays scowling, which is a relief of sorts. Anyone else would probably tell me to keep my bareback insults to myself: Jerry's still half a minute behind. 'Don't remember pissing on anyone. Would I do that?'

'Yes. You would. Jerry, I've got good news for you.'

He looks up at me, hopeful despite his hangover.

'You are going back through the system. AA, your social worker, the works. As of now, you're on the dry.'

His face falls, but I harden my heart. I don't want him in jail. He's one of my less ungrateful clients, but right now he's the least of my worries.

'Hard woman,' he mutters, quiet enough so I can pretend not to hear.

I almost like him, but I don't care to be blamed for speaking the truth. 'Jerry, a few short centuries ago you would have gone to the stake. I'm an angel of mercy.'


I had two years to learn it all, how to be a legal adviser for the Department for the Ongoing Regulation of Lycanthropic Activity. That's our name nowadays, in this country; it changes from time to time, according to the era. Two years to learn the laws. It didn't seem long at the time.

They're old, our laws, they've bent and twisted under the weight of history, and nobody but us studies them much. Everyone's used to the curfew, most citizens are willing to lock themselves up. It's less trouble than thinking up an alternative. Every now and again someone mutters that if we hate lunes so much, maybe we should just lock ourselves up and let normal people get on with it. I can't disagree with that, it would be better for us, if not for them. Mostly.

We used to be the Order of St Giles; that was where we started. Giles, Aegidus, patron saint of cripples, protector of rams, saint of woods and forests and fear of the night. Patron saint of barebacks, though Judas Thaddeus, St Jude Saint of Hopeless Cases, probably gets most of our prayers. St Giles is our saint, Giles and the Dominicans.

This is what I learned in two years, in the gaps between

classes in administration, animal handling and marks-manship. Before the fourteenth century, the laws and curfews relating to moon nights were what I've been taught to call ad hoc: you made them up as you went along. If people lived in a village with livestock, they locked themselves up and got any nons that happened to live in the area to keep watch so they didn't attack their own flocks. If they lived in a city, there was probably a nightly curfew anyway, so not much changed when the moon was full. If they lived somewhere remote, they did whatever seemed sensible. If they were beggars, they roamed and slaughtered and were hanged for it later.

Then the plague came. It was a bad time to be alive, back then, a hard time to stay alive. There were wars, mercenaries roaming; there were famines, starvation, ergot in the crops and people living on poisoned bread, and the Black Death swept across Europe like an Angel of the Apocalypse. The Book of Revelations was coming true: Plague, War, Famine and Death were riding out. It was the end of the world.

A bad time for roamers. Lunes don't understand words like 'quarantine'. Surrounded by death every day, watching their neighbours rotting alive and never knowing if they'd be next, there can't have been a man or woman who wasn't fearful. People were killed for wiping their dirty hands on walls by fellow townsmen who thought they might be putting on curses; Jews were killed for supposedly poisoning wells. And people who got out of their houses at night were declared plague-spreaders, and wracked citizens who'd seen half the population die spitting blood built pyres in the middle of towns and burned them alive.

That was early, before the Inquisition really got under

26

way. Some of my teaching at school I had from nuns, who weren't eager to share these details with us: it was DORLA-appointed teachers who were prepared to tell us about history. The Church identified a new enemy: witches. Satanists, people who were prepared to turn their backs on God and all things pure and sacred for the sake of a little temporal power to work harm against their neighbours. It would have been a pretty terrible crime, if it had actually existed, and witches were declaring their wicked deeds on every rack in the continent. It was a legalistic process, the witch hunt, there were degrees of torment imposed in regular sequence and forms of confession to be gone through, and it worked with an efficiency that seemed like divine justice.

Incubi, succubi. Demons that came and made love to you in your sleep, seduced you into giving your soul to Satan. The trouble is, you don't remember too well what you were doing when you were asleep, so it's a hard accusation to defend yourself against. The same applied to luning. No one remembers it all that well. It was hard, then, to deny you'd had commerce with the Devil while you were luning, that he hadn't come to you in the form of a man and called you to heel, in the form of a dog and had sex with you, in the form of a rat and made you eat him in a black Communion. Certainly hard to deny it when you were hanging by your arms in the strappado.

People were losing themselves. Even to read old library books about it was enough to give me bad dreams, years ago when I was a girl. It was as if the world had lost its soul. People carried away non children who weren't guarded by luning parents, lunes killed other lunes every moon night. Hungry enough to eat each other, desperate enough to run wild on moon nights, that's what apologists say about them now. At the time, all anyone thought was that they were evil. Luning, already regarded by the Church with the suspicion that sex, childbirth and all the other carnal upheavals the human frame fell prey to, became a matter of panic. The Inquisition came down hard, they went on the hunt. The Dominicans, the founders of it all, took up their nickname like a banner: *Domini Canes*, the Hounds of God, appointed to run down Satan's wolves. Protestants, who by then were killing Catholics with equal fervour, declared luning to be an unregenerate state, because you were incapable of faith while under its influence. Pious citizens who feared temptation to sin, or frightened citizens who didn't want to find themselves at the stake, take your pick, people began locking themselves away. They hammered bars across their windows, they called in priests to bless a room in their house and anointed the thresholds with holy water and nailed crosses to the doors, and went inside to wait out moon nights in the hope of Christ's protection.

And for the most part, it was granted. The odd person slipped through the net, but by that time, the curfew had done its work, and while witches were still dying in the flames, people began to breathe again about moon nights.

We were useful, back then. People needed us.

It was a Papal Bull that settled it. We were marked out by the affliction God had laid upon us, we were to be his guards. We were created. It wasn't a monastic order, the Order of St Giles Aegidus: we were lay brothers and sisters, allied to God's law. It was voluntary, officially, no one need join who had no vocation, but of course, we joined. There were liable to be some serious questions asked, questions involving shackles and thumbscrews, if we didn't. And we'd suffered, we'd been suffering more than most, with lunes roaming the highways starving from the famines, with accusations of witchcraft flying and liable to land on those who didn't fit in. Aegidans did not get accused of witchery. We listened to the accusations, we bore witness in the trials, we patrolled and inspected the lock-ups people were creating for themselves. Initiates didn't starve, we were paid out of the tithes and had enough to eat and some security in the world and were the new guardians of laws that, in those days of famine and plague, were useful enough to seem holy, divinely ordained. We began in the Catholic countries, the deaths and trials began to fall back, and soon enough even the Calvinists set aside their dislike of Papal authority and created Aegidan orders of their own, different in name but identical in role. Christendom was, miraculously, almost united on an issue. On the first of September, St Giles's Day, everyone gathered at church, lycos and nons alike, to pray for protection and to give thanks.

Quite a few of the churches in the city have shrines to St Giles, even now. I used to go and pray at them, sometimes, when I was little, and I thought no one was watching me. They're a monument to an earlier, bloodier age, that's what some people think. Certainly it's the older churches that have them. Nowadays, of course, we have social benefits and atheists, and St Giles doesn't get as many prayers as he did.

*

I catch a bus over to Albin's part of town. When I sit down, I'm careless. There's a welt on my palm, a deep slash from the last moon night. The lune ran at me and forced the pole into my hand. As I sit there, I'm studying it, prodding it with my thumb, testing the edges for pain. The inside of my hand is visible. The man I sit down next to sees it, and gets up to move to another part of the bus. Nons don't have calluses on their palms like lycos build up after a few years of nights on all fours. Our hands are smooth, pale inside: it doesn't show that much unless you're sharp-eyed. When it comes to spotting nons, people are. Most of us get into the habit of curling up our fingers to hide it, so our habitual hand position is a fist. The man settles himself on another seat, watching me out of the corner of his eye. My hand moves to my pocket to get my gloves out, but I stop it. I'm damned if I'll put them on in front of him.

I put them on for the walk to Albin's place, and when I get there I take them off. There are bay windows and a front yard full of evergreen plants; it's a detached house. Lots of garden. It's not unlike the area I grew up in. Very unlike the area I live in now. I rap the polished doorknocker, and then see there's an intercom: I'm about to ring it when a voice sounds from it. 'Hello?' It's a woman's voice.

'Hello. Is Mr Lewis Albin at home?'

'Just a moment.' The intercom clicks off. I wait just long enough to get impatient, then Albin's voice sounds.

'This is Lewis Albin.'

'Mr Albin, my name is Lola Galley. I'm from DORLA. May I speak to you?'

There's a silence. 'DORLA? What do you want to talk about?'

'Mr Albin, I'd like to come in.'

The intercom clicks off. I study the ivy that's climbing all over the façade; it's got a grip on the house with little tentacles. Just as I'm wondering whether he's going to make me ring again, the door opens.

Albin is in his early thirties, I'd say, about average height with broad shoulders. Smart-casual clothes: the kind that you wear for years because they're too well-made to fall apart and too expensive to go out of fashion. His face isn't handsome. It's quite ordinary of feature, but with good skin and an intelligent expression: he's brighter than the dull-eyed lost souls I'm used to dealing with. What you notice about him is how little you notice the scar that runs from eye to mouth on his left cheek. An ugly thing, yet somehow, with his manner, it barely shows; on another man, it would stand out a foot.

His hand rasps against mine as he shakes it. 'I'm Lewis Albin,' he says. 'Won't you come in?'

Plants in the hallway, muted colours, sanded floorboards, sub-rustic decor. Taste. I am escorted to an upstairs living room and seated on a sofa. A woman in floaty clothes sits cross-legged on the matching one.

'Would you like some coffee?' Albin says. When I accept, he nods to the woman. 'Sarah, would you mind?' Sarah unfolds her legs and goes into a connecting room.

He sits himself on a chair. 'Now, how can I help you, Ms Galley?'

He's remembered my name first time round. 'Mr Albin, I'm advising Mr Richard Thomas Ellaway on charges of assault and murder. According –'

'Murder?' He interrupts as if I've hit him. The shock

sounds genuine, though a bit theatrical in his modulated voice.

'The murder of John Marcos. You may or may not know that Mr Ellaway has already confessed to assaulting John Marcos last moon night. And yesterday afternoon, he was murdered.' Albin rubs his hand across his mouth. 'Now, according to Mr Ellaway, you spoke to him on the telephone at about nine p.m. yesterday. Can you verify that?'

In the silence that follows, I can hear the ivy on the façade tapping on the window.

'Jesus.' Albin puts his head in his hands. 'Jesus.' It comes out like a sigh.

I frown at him. 'Were you a close friend of Mr Ellaway, would you say?'

He looks up at me, pale. 'No.'

'Can you verify that he called you?'

'Yes. Yes, he did.'

Sarah comes in with a tray. There's a coffee pot, three cups, milk in one jug and cream in another. She serves me, and brings the tray over to Albin and pours his coffee black as I sip my own. Toasted velvet fills my mouth.

He takes her hand. 'Sarah,' he says. 'This lady's got some bad news. You remember Dick Ellaway? It seems he's been accused of murder.'

Her eyes grow big in her face. Albin looks at me to explain myself, but I want to see how he's going to say it. She sits down and rests her head on the back of the sofa, and he gives her her hand back. 'Dick Ellaway attacked a man, you remember? And it seems someone shot the man yesterday, and he's been accused. Ms Galley's advising him.'

Skilful. Very skilful. Or else innocent. There's nothing in what he's said that tells me anything about Ellaway, their relationship, or how much he knows. Sarah's breath hisses out through her teeth, and she wraps her arms around a cushion. 'I remember Dick Ellaway,' she says.

First things first. 'Mr Ellaway says that he called you on a mobile phone. Do you remember hearing any noise in the background?'

Albin rubs his face; his hand doesn't linger on the scar. 'Voices, I think, slightly tinny. It sounded like he had the television on.'

'Anything else?'

'Not that I remember offhand. I wasn't really paying attention to the background noise.'

'But it sounded like he was inside?'

'Yes.'

'How was the line? Clear? Interrupted?'

'It was clear. No break-ups.'

'And what time was this?'

'Nine for nine-thirty, I'd say.'

I don't feel good about this. What Albin says will probably stand up in court. I doubt Albin and Ellaway are in league: there's a sobriety about Albin that's as different from Ellaway as I can imagine, and I can't see them getting along well under pressure. My client is saved. So like I say, I don't feel great.

'How do you know Mr Ellaway?'

Albin rubs the back of his hand against his chin. 'We met at a party a couple of months ago. Met for drinks a few more times since. I deal in antique furniture; he was interested in buying some pieces.'

'And did he?'

'I sold him an old coffee table – would you like to

33

see the invoice? I can post it to you. Nothing more. He wasn't really an antiques enthusiast.' His voice is neutral, giving away little of how he feels about this: he's just telling me.

'I would like to see it, thank you. What did you talk about when he called you?'

Albin frowns and taps his foot for a moment. He looks over at Sarah, who's leaning back against the sofa, then turns his head towards me. 'Is that relevant to your case?'

'If your account and his tally, it would help confirm his alibi.'

'I see. But there's no law that says I have to tell you, is there?'

'Not at this time, no, Mr Albin. But it would be doing everyone a favour.'

He sighs; his face is apologetic. 'I'd rather not tell you. Seeing that he's a client, I'd prefer not to discuss our conversations.'

'It was a business call?'

'I'm sorry, Ms Galley.'

I turn my attention to Sarah. 'Were you there when this phone call was made?'

She shakes her head.

'May I ask how you and Mr Albin know each other?'

'We're friends.'

'You say you know my client.'

She shrugs. 'We've met.' For all her wispy clothes, there's a vibrancy about her voice, like Albin's, that speaks of class.

'May I ask when?'

'Once when Lewis and he were doing the deal.'

'Is that relevant?' Albin puts in.

I fold my hands in my lap. 'Only so far as I'm defending him. Character witnesses might help.'

'But I've told you we spoke on the phone. Doesn't that give you an alibi?'

'Yes. But I've still got to defend him for the assault.'

He bends his hands around his cup. 'As I've said, I don't know him very well.'

I take another sip of the delicious coffee, and keep my eyes on him. He meets them for several moments. I keep the gaze up; when he starts talking, he doesn't look away. 'Ms Galley, I don't think I could stand as a character witness for him. I'd have to testify to his prudence or his responsibility, or to other qualities that in truth I don't think he possesses. I'm unwilling to perjure myself, and from your point of view, I don't think I'd make a very convincing witness. You'd be better served by somebody else.'

A drip of coffee runs down the side of my cup, and I stop it with my finger. 'You don't like him?'

'I don't dislike him. But if you want me to testify that I don't think the incident was his fault, I can't.' He turns his head away from me. It's just a fraction of a turn, but it's enough to signal that he considers the matter closed.

There is a silence. Sarah keeps looking at me, the neutral stare of one who can look as long as she likes. A cat may look at a king, my mother used to say, but it's easier for a king to look at a cat. I look back through my whiskers and let the silence hang. I'm getting more and more uncomfortable, but I will not break it first.

Albin leans forward; then he picks up the coffee jug, comes over to my chair and pours me another cup. It's an oddly gentle gesture.

'How long have you been working in DORLA, Miss Galley?' he says.

The cup warms in my hands and I set it down. 'Since I was eighteen. With training and preparation for it beforehand at school. Same as everyone else.'

'Do you like working there?'

I open my mouth to say Yes, thank you, translating as, Why would I answer a personal question? Once I get there, though, I find I don't feel like it. If he's smart, let him hear a straighter answer. 'It's not a question of like or dislike. I could dislike it all my life and still have to go into work the next day.' This is truthful, though it's not the only truth; it's as close to it as I'm getting with some stranger lyco.

'It doesn't sound like you work for the love of it.'

'That's luxury thinking. I work. No one else would be allowed to employ me.' He raises his eyebrows, and I find I'm annoyed that I'm talking this way to him. 'I like it like I like having a trank gun, because it keeps people off my back.'

As soon as I hear myself say this, I regret it. I turn into a child scuffing my heels against the elegant sofa, and he's sitting there, smooth as ever and giving nothing away. The look on his face is one of puzzlement and sympathy, and I do not want that.

I tuck Ellaway's alibi under my arm and leave.


As I'm heading for the bus stop, something strikes me. The run-down area to the south of here is Johnny's part of town. I could go and visit his family. Johnny married a lyco, a woman called Susan who always showed up to non gatherings and made conversation. They used to

36

have me over for dinner. I'm not sure I can bear it if she's grieving, but she was always nice to me.

When I knock on the door, it's their eldest, Debbie, who answers. She's quite thickset for her twelve years; that's how I thought of her anyway. Today, something has shrunk her. Adolescence is just kicking in, and it looks like it's going to keep kicking: her skin is starting to blur, her teeth and elbows are way ahead of her. She's still wide-shouldered and thick-wristed, but I'm starting to notice that she only comes up to my chest.

'Hey, Debbie.' I have an urge to crouch down to talk to her, and stop myself. She's too old for that.

She smears her fingers across her face. 'Hi, Lola.'

'How are you doing?'

'All right, I guess.' Her head hangs down, she doesn't bother to shrug.

'Yeah?'

'I'm cooking for everyone. I cooked spaghetti last night. And I tidied the living room.'

I can't smile. 'I bet your mum was grateful.'

'I dunno.' She tugs the door back a bit. 'You want to come in?'

'Thanks, Debbie.' I touch her arm as I walk into the hall, and she flinches away. I squash down the impulse to pick her up; she can't go on coping unless I let her.

Susan is sitting in the living room. Debbie creeps in behind me and rights two chairs that lie on their sides next to Susan: the gesture is furtive, and I pretend not to notice.

Susan's blonde hair straggles across her face. Her hands have always been pink and battered; now they look bad. Her nails are bitten down to stubs. She turns her head with a slow gesture as I come in, as if she were under water, and her expression doesn't change.

'Lola,' she says.

I clench and unclench my hands. 'I was in the area,' I say. 'How are you doing, Sue?'

Her eyes go back into space. 'I don't know.'

'Susan, I'm so sorry.'

'Yes.'

Sue was always a brave woman. It's brave to marry a non, and braver to stick with him. No non earns a good living. Mixed marriages are rare: even liberal lycos don't usually meet nons; we work together, socialise together, carry scars that few lycos would want to deal with, not when there are so many people in the world with smooth, unscored flesh and the world before them to choose from. People treat her differently. She must have thought he was worth it. I see her sitting in her cramped, unkempt room, scrawny and exhausted, and I want to tell her she's brave, I want to remind her she's brave so she can start being so again. I don't know how.

'Look, you know where I live. Anything I can do . . .'

'Thank you.' She stares at her hands.

'Would you like me to stick around, help out for a few days?' I pray as I say this that she won't accept, but if she does then I'll do it.

'No thanks.' She lifts up her head. 'Would you like some coffee?'

I don't want any, but it'll get her out of the chair. 'Yes please. Thanks.'

She stands up with the same underwater weight, and I see that it's worse than I'd thought. Because she's pregnant. It doesn't show much on her little hips, but she's pregnant.

'Sue? How many months till the baby comes?'

'Four.' Her voice is dull. 'We weren't going to tell people till a few weeks from now, I've had stillbirths. We thought it'd be okay.'

She's stopped in the middle of the room. I go over to her and put an arm around her. She stays weighted to the spot, staring at the wall.

# 3

From: pkelsey@soc.gov
To: lmgalley@dorla.gov
Subject: Jerry Farnham

Dear Lola Galley,

Hello. I'm Jerry Farnham's new social worker, and I see from his records that you're his legal adviser at DORLA. And that he's up for moon loitering – which isn't such good news.

Anyway, I hear you're in favour of putting him back on the AA programme? I'm with you on that one if you are – in any case, we should get in touch, see what we can do about it. Drop me a byte and let me know.

Best wishes,
Paul Kelsey

I frown at my computer screen. This is Jerry the wino, my old friend. If he's got a new social worker, it's news to me – although it would have been news to me if his old one had got in touch with me either, she was the invisible woman. No one in the social service wants to work with us. So now I've got a mainstream guy on my back, someone else to deal with. Wonderful.

Mind you, I reflect, the e-mail itself isn't too bad. In fact, by lyco standards it's pretty courteous. Best wishes, indeed. Thinking of how to answer it, I go to my pigeon-hole and pick up my mail. There's a heavy, smooth envelope waiting for me, and when I open it, I find something that takes my mind off Jerry.

This is very bad news. I've discovered who Ellaway's lawyer is. The envelope discloses a creamy, headed, embossed letter, asking for an appointment, and I read the signature three times before I take it in. His name is Adnan Franklin, a man I never thought I'd meet. People who have legal training know him, at least by reputation. You can read about him in the newspapers several times a year – although you don't see him on television, he's too refined or something. Some of his defence cases are seminal, others merely exemplary. He costs more per case than I make in a year, and if he's against you, there's nothing you can do. Nothing.

I have a forlorn hope that it might turn out all right, after all, we are representing the same client. When I remember Ellaway's face, though, the way he looked at me, the hope turns into a wish, and the wish into a plaintive murmur that sits at the back of the class and knows its place. Ellaway hates me. I sat back and watched my colleagues hit him. I held him in detention and refused to allow him to call his regular lawyer. Never mind a bad lawyer, to Ellaway I'm practically a criminal. That I haven't done anything unusual by DORLA standards is not something Franklin is going to see.

I fold the letter with a sigh and rub my forehead,

cradling my temples. In the old days, Aegidans didn't let suspects have outside lawyers. There was a manual for witch hunters, the *Malleus Maleficarum*, that insisted on it. Witches' lawyers couldn't be told who the accusers were in case their clients decided to witch them. It must have been easier to pursue cases. We kept it to ourselves, we dealt with it on our own terms. We're too enlightened to take that line in public now. I'm going to have a bad time with this one.

I shake my head, try hard not to dwell on it. Instead, I type a reply to the new social worker, typing fast without really thinking about it.

From: lmgalley@dorla.gov
To: pkelsey@soc.gov
Subject: Re: Jerry Farnham

Dear Paul Kelsey,

Yes, I'm trying to make Jerry take the pledge. If you've met him, you'll probably have a sense of how likely that is, if not then the answer is – not very. He's a hopeless drinker and has been since I've known him. He's been on the wagon five times, and fallen off each time. He's like a walking advert for the Prohibition. But I agree with you, prison is only going to make him worse, he drinks more when he's depressed – though so do I and everybody else too – and if we lock him up he'll just get depressed and be that much more of a pest. So mostly it comes down to you putting him on a programme and me trying to sweet-talk the judge into thinking that he means it this time.

Sound fun? He's still in our cells, by the way, have you been to see him?

Lola Galley

About three seconds after I've clicked on SEND, I realise what kind of letter I've just sent to a total stranger. A lyco total stranger. A lyco total stranger from the social services whose interests are going to be focused on protecting his client, and if he's anything like some of the social workers I've met, then the only thing to do now is shoot myself.

Becca sits with her baby cradled to her, swathed in a woolly blue blanket, and gives me a cautious look. I sit opposite, carefully not looking at the mess that surrounds us. Some medic I was whiling away a moon-night watch with once told me that's a good sign, it means she's spending her time bonding rather than cleaning. She certainly has a good grip on the infant. Leo. She holds him as if he was the last piece of the world.

'How are you feeling?'

She glances down at him. 'A bit tired. All right. The doctor said it was a healthy birth.'

'What, that very elegant one I met?'

'Dr Parkinson. Yes. He's supposed to be very good.'

'He certainly thought so.'

A little smile flickers on Becca's face, then she checks it. 'I thought you'd be more approving.'

'Approving?' She can't have said approving. My approval has never been something she even wondered about. I must have misheard.

'Didn't you fix him for me?'

43

Leo struggles in his blanket, and she turns her attention to resettling him, which gives me time to think. It must be that someone arranged it for her, someone in DORLA hired a high-calibre doctor in exchange for losing her husband. Now I think of it, it fits in with DORLA's general habit of compensating you in kind rather than parting with any of its finite stock of pennies and actually making reparation. Oh, God. Does she think I organised this?

'Me DORLA or me me?'

'I – I don't know. Never mind.' This translates as me DORLA, I think. Nice to know where my identity lies.

I change the subject. 'How's the baby getting along?'

'He's fine. He only wakes up once each night,' says Becca, and goes into some details about what proportion of time he spends asleep, which doesn't mean much to me as I haven't been around enough babies. Her face is quite relaxed as she tells me. Though I'm not sure what she's on about, it's a relief to me to see her that way: her eyes are on the bundle in her arms, it absorbs all her attention, and it seems to be keeping her content. She tells me about feeding and weighing, and it sounds like a very peaceful life.

'Do you want to hold him?' she concludes. She gathers him up and carries him over. I'm not sure how to arrange my arms. Becca lowers him to me, watching me out of one eye in the wary certainty that I'll let his head fall back, or drop him, or drown him in my cup of tea. This is a little unjust, and to prove it, I fix my arms in a good stable position, brace myself, and take his head in my hand. The little skull rolls in my palm like an orange. I take a good hold on him, and then have a look.

The crumpled face I saw in the hospital has unfolded, the scarlet forehead has settled into pink. In the centre of his top lip there's a round blister from sucking. I touch his face, which is smoother than anything I've ever felt, and he opens one eye to wheeze at me. His mouth is working, so I offer him a finger and he seizes on it in great good faith. I am very interested to know whether he'll cry when he finds that no milk comes out of it, in which case I'll return him straight to his mother and apologise to him. He doesn't. Instead, he sets about flaying my fingertip, grinding it against his palate and sucking the skin off with unrelenting determination. His eyes are open, crossed, they're smudgy blue like most white babies'; later on, I think, they're going to go brown, like Becca's, like mine, and they look straight at me, they don't flicker at all. He's hurting my finger. He's the best baby I've ever seen.

'He's lovely,' I say.

Becca smiles. There's weariness in her face.

'Are you okay?'

She tidies her hair. 'I'm all right. Just a little worn out. He's quite a handful.'

I try to pitch my voice, but there's no tactful way of saying this. 'Has Lionel been in touch?'

She shakes her head, her eyes looking out of the window.

'Does he know the baby's born?' Or that you named him Leo? That's a question I don't have the courage to ask. When Becca told me she was calling him Leo, all I said was, that's a nice name. Not, are you naming him after his father?

'Would you like some more tea, May?' Becca picks up my cup and takes it into the kitchen. There's neither

45

anger nor sorrow in her voice: it's polite, distant and dead.

She goes into the kitchen; from the sound of it, she's unpacking the groceries I brought for her by way of a care package. Looking through the door, I can see how little there is in the fridge. I wonder if she's even been outside since the birth.

Leo stirs, and proves himself an intelligent boy by figuring out that I'm not his mother. He opens his mouth and yells, his face going redder with each breath. I can see his point. He's working on very little information here; for all he knows, she might never be coming back.

Becca hurries out of the kitchen, stops in the doorway. 'Is he all right?' she says, breathless.

'He's fine.' I lay him over my shoulder and walk to and fro. 'Shush, little cub,' I say, soft enough that Becca doesn't hear me. 'Shh . . . I know I'm not your mum, but I haven't stolen her, she'll be back. She'll be back. Oh, that's a big noise. It's no good, you don't fool me, I'm not going to get all worried. We're just going to be nice and calm . . .' My training, I think it's my training, is coming to the fore. Babies, like other animals, can sense fear. Leo cries for a bit, and then, when he realises I'm not going to get agitated, calms down.

Becca returns with a cup of tea. I don't rub it in that I've proved her wrong and that I can handle a baby without killing him. Instead, I sit, and play with Leo's fingers.

Becca brushes her fringe out of her eyes. It's an old gesture that she's used all her life, I haven't seen it for a while. 'How are things with you, May?' she manages to say. She's now letting herself in for the risk of my talking about DORLA. I can see she's going to be polite about it.

'Not much. Lots of work, that's really about it.'

'That's all?'

I look down at Leo. I think he's fallen asleep. A little crust sits on his eyelids, and he lies quite peaceful, not criticising me.

Possibilities open. I could visit him a lot, I could play with him and give him attention and spoil him. The vision lasts for a brief moment. I look up and see Becca watching me with that held-back look. Perhaps she just doesn't believe that my life could contain nothing but work, that I'm hiding something. Perhaps she thinks I'm holding back on her. Leo wakes again, I look away from his mother down to my nephew. His eyes are unfocused. He can't see me. I stroke the side of his face, and his fist unbends and relaxes. This makes me so happy for a second that when I remember reality again it bites so deep and cold that I know it isn't letting me go.

Leo is all right with me now. If I'm nice to him, he'll like me when he's one, when he's two. He will. He'll love me until the day he gets old enough to ask my sister, What's wrong with Auntie May?

Why does Auntie May work when the moon's full? Why does Auntie May work for a bad place? Mummy, what does bareback mean? I can hear it now. And I can't feel safe, I can't place any trust on what Becca's going to say.

Normally I like them a little older before they start breaking my heart. But this one's going to do it at four or five, and it's going to be worse than anything before.

I tighten my grip on him and lay his face against mine.

*

I worry and worry about Franklin.

I worry about Jerry's new social worker, too, and it's a surprise when he replies.

From: pkelsey@soc.gov
To: lmgalley@dorla.gov
Subject: reality bites

Dear Lola,

Yep, you're right. I met him before he got arrested, and he's unpromising, to say the least. Burn this letter. Though I did like him. I reckon if I pick on him enough, I can keep him on the dry for a while at least, and who knows – hope springs eternal in the human breast . . . Short term, though, do you know what judge he'll be up against? And if so, do you think the judge's innocence can be preserved?

Anyway, I know a good AA group for him, so you don't have to worry about that end of it. Let me know when the trial date is, and I'll see what I can do about character references and so on.

Thanks for your e-mail.

Paul

It doesn't make sense. By all accounts, he should have sent me a stiff lecture, maybe even lodged a complaint with my superiors about my unprofessional attitude. Instead – 'Thanks for your e-mail'?

It's a piece of good fortune I dwell on, to distract myself from the thought of Franklin coming to get me.

*

The appointed hour comes sooner than I expect; time flies by while I worry about it. Then, right on schedule, there's a knock on my door, and I rise to meet my fate. The door opens, and ushers in Adnan Franklin, the man who's going to crush me. There's been no communication between us since the appointment was made. A few times, I've caught myself scanning the paper for mentions of his name; on the whole, I've been trying not to think about it. Now, finally, my hour has come. The door closes behind him with a respectful click, and I shake the great man's hand, trying to take in as much as I can.

He's smaller than I'd expected, though I ought to have allowed for the shock that goes with meeting a famous man in the flesh; there's no way he could have been as big as his reputation. He's under average height for a man, though still taller than me, and slenderly built; something about his movements suggest compactness of muscle, rather than slightness of bone. His dark hair is glossy and well cut, his tan skin doesn't bear signs of ageing – he must be fifteen years older than me at the very least, but it doesn't really show. His suit is made of a grey fabric that almost glows, it's so well-woven. The hand that shakes mine has a light, steady grip, and he nods to me, swift, courteous, and assured.

I gesture him into a chair and get back to my desk as fast as possible, hiding my cheap knock-off trouser suit and worn shoes behind it. 'I'm glad you could come to see me,' I say, telling myself that it's true in a way – I might have had to brave his offices.

'I'm glad to meet you, Ms Galley, since we have a client in common.' His voice is not loud: rather, it's quick and clear, you have to pay attention to it. I rest my chin in my hand, taking possession of the desk.

'Richard Ellaway. Yes. I understand you've been his lawyer for some time.'

'I have indeed.' Franklin gives me a beady look. 'I must ask you, if you'll forgive me – have you never considered passing up this case?'

The man has barely sat down yet! This comes so suddenly that I blink at him, astonished into forgetting who he is. 'It's a bit early in the meeting for you to be suggesting that, isn't it?'

He looks at me, puzzled, then gives a little laugh. It's a perfect laugh, urbane and restrained. It's so good that I wonder how it can be natural. Then I take another look at him, and feel obscurely sympathetic. I don't think it's his fault that he's so refined-looking – well, he chooses his clothes, I suppose, but his manner doesn't seem forced. He's so much what I expected, cultured, well-dressed, confident, and so different – I mean, he's actually flesh and blood – that I'm at a sudden loss. I'm supposed to have an opinion on this man, that was how I was planning to get through this interview. Actually, I just don't know what to make of him.

'I mean no reflection on your abilities, Ms Galley.' Franklin sits back in his chair. His hands, broader than his wrists would suggest, rest peacefully in his lap. 'Only that I believe you have a personal interest in this case.'

'You mean I knew the victim?' I say. 'Well, if you can find me a DORLA adviser in this city who didn't know him, then maybe I will pass it on.'

Franklin frowns. 'I don't doubt that many of them knew this John Marcos by sight. You, however, were well acquainted with him. He was your friend. Do you really think you can be impartial?'

I shrug. 'Maybe not, but I hope I can be professional.'

'Hm.' Franklin nods; it's almost as if he's conceding me a point. Then he leans forwards. 'And in your definition, professional involves sitting back and watching two men assault your client?'

'Assault?'

'The day of his arrest, Ms Galley, and please let's not pretend you don't know what I'm talking about.'

I feel a little pulse of nerves inside my chest, and then it goes away. My bread and butter is winos and derelicts, so I'm not used to proper, expensive lawyers, but this must happen to people higher up the ladder than me all the time. 'I'm not pretending anything, Mr Franklin. You'll find the records show it was me who ended that interrogation. You can check it.'

'I have. And you did. Fifteen minutes after you entered. I have the testimony of my client, too, which is not favourable to you in the least.'

I smile. 'Well, he doesn't like me.'

'My client states that not only did you fail to intervene when he was assaulted, but you refused to allow him to call me, although he specifically asked to. You arrested him on suspicion of murder, held him without charge, during which time he was subjected to actual bodily harm and denied access to a lawyer. I assume you know how many human and civil rights decrees this contravenes? If you were responsible to the Bar Council, Ms Galley, you would be disbarred. Is that your definition of professional?'

He does it awfully well. Some kind of protective detachment has taken hold of me. By rights I should probably be cowering: after all, without even mentioning the Middle Ages, he's just accused me of breaking the laws of the land, the continent and the democratic world, betraying the principles of my profession, and being a disgrace to civilisation in general. It's quite possible I'll find I'm shaking after he's gone. Right now, though, all that's left in me is an impersonal admiration for his delivery. Really, he's very good.

'I'm not responsible to the Bar Council, Mr Franklin. I'm not a member.'

'I know. I'm familiar with DORLA legal practices. How many years of training did you have – two? It seems you qualified at twenty with only a basic grounding in the laws that apply to your narrow field of interest. That's less than an undergraduate degree. I'd hardly say you were qualified to represent my client.'

'That's a little hard, Mr Franklin. I had the standard DORLA training – I know it's not up to mainstream standards, but it's better than you imply. It's only short because we're so understaffed, we just haven't time to train for a full term. And *our* client violated laws that put him within DORLA jurisdiction. He was always going to be given an adviser with my qualifications.'

Franklin puts his head on one side and considers me.

'Would you like some coffee?' I say.

'Coffee? Oh. Yes, please.'

I stand up and switch on my baby kettle. 'It's only ersatz, I'm afraid.'

'Thank you.'

I turn around and lean against the wall. He can't do anything to me. I say this to myself several times, and then try an experiment. 'Mr Franklin, we do have a client in common. He may not like the way I've handled things, in fact I'm sure he doesn't. And I doubt you do either. It isn't the way I would have handled things if I had the resources. But in answer to your question, I think I have to say, yes. By the standards of my profession, by the standards of the Department for the Ongoing Regulation of Lycanthropic Activity, my behaviour was professional.' I pour water into his cup.

'You really believe that it was fit behaviour for a member of a government institution?'

I hand him the coffee. 'DORLA's an odd place, Mr Franklin.'

'Not that odd, Ms Galley. I've noted numerous cases where DORLA operatives were successfully sued. As I understand it, there are almost monthly demotions within your ranks. Please let's not pretend DORLA isn't accountable; I can produce a great many instances where your members were held responsible for their actions.'

My heart sinks a little; I manage not to sigh. 'That does make us look accountable, doesn't it. Mr Franklin, I admire you, so I'm telling you this because it's useful, not because I'm trying to get round you: those demotions are part of the system. People do get publicly punished here, it's good for the government to make sure it happens. But they'll never overhaul us. That would be too close to backing us up. Moon night's too insoluble a problem, and we're too good a scapegoat. It's easier to punish us at intervals than to make us properly accountable.'

Franklin raises an eyebrow. 'You're telling me straight out that you can't be held responsible?'

I shake my head. 'I can. Personally; you can go after me. But if you're thinking of making this a landmark, shake-up-the-system case . . . well, I'd advise you to do it with a better client. Because Mr Ellaway did maul someone. Look, the point is, I have no doubt your client has much to complain of. If I was in his position I'd be no happier than he is now. But the thing is, he needs a DORLA representative. You can speak at his trial if you want to, I'm quite happy for that to happen. But I have to as well. You could get him another adviser within DORLA, but truthfully, I doubt they'd be any more . . . aggressive in protecting him than I have been.'

'Then God help the country, Ms Galley, because DORLA is the most unethical, inconsistent and unprofessional institution I can imagine.'

I sit back down, and prop my chin up again. 'Maybe. But we have our own problems. Look, Mr Franklin, I can't compete with you. I'm laying my cards on the table here. We have a client in common, and you can pursue his grievance against me, or we can both focus on acquitting him. Personally, I'd just like to get this case over with. Does Ellaway want to sue me?'

Franklin looks at me with canny eyes. 'He has talked of it, yes.'

I'm starting to feel tired. I can't keep this up much longer. 'Please don't let him.'

'Ms Galley, why should I feel any obligation to be dissuaded, by you, from the interests of my client?'

'I don't think it will be in his interests. He can sue me, and it'll go through a lyco court and they'll hang me from the yardarm. It won't do him much good. I don't have any money he can sue me for, and if he wants to ruin me, then – well, I don't think he needs to prove anything. I know my place. Outside of this office, it's nowhere. But inside it – ruining me won't change

DORLA's practices. It'll just prejudice the court against him when he comes up for trial. And he's looking at life imprisonment as it is. DORLA's a bottomless pit, Mr Franklin, and injustices slip into it without trace . . .' I trail off. I don't want to be ruined. As I'm talking, I hear what I'm saying, and I realise more and more that Ellaway can destroy me if he wants to, and he probably does. And since I want him to spend his life in jail, I can't pretend he doesn't have justification. I'm lost. I shouldn't have messed with a rich man.

I look up, and find that Franklin is still regarding me. 'It is your opinion that suing you would be bad for our client's case?'

'Undoubtedly. And I can't change that, so please don't blame me.'

'You don't think that his chances of appeal might not be better if he could claim he was improperly represented?'

'What, with you on his side?' Franklin almost laughs. I raise my head. Is he going to let me off? 'That's how it would work in a lyco – excuse me, in a mainstream court. But even so, the fact remains that all the . . . incidents . . . he wants to sue me for happened after he was arrested for the original crime, after I had already had one session advising him, and given him no cause to complain of my conduct. I don't think he killed Johnny Marcos. I don't think so. But he doesn't deny he maimed him, and we have the victim's statement, medical evidence, and the testimony of Marcos's partner that night to back that up. That's the case I'm representing him on. Not that that makes it any better from his point of view, but my behaviour on the case of DORLA versus Ellaway for GBH and attempted murder has been perfectly adequate. So suing me for his interrogation on another charge might not stick.'

'I think it would, Ms Galley. In the normal world. But I believe we have to negotiate certain – prejudices is not too strong a word, I think – which make for a rather extraordinary way of handling this case.'

'Mr Franklin, you're dead right. So – by your leave – are you going to sue me?'

Franklin puts his hands together. 'No. Purely on the grounds that this is an unaccountable judiciary, that must be handled as carefully as possible.'

'Ohh.' I let out a breath that I didn't know I was holding. I throw a quick, nervous look across the table, but either Franklin hasn't noticed, or he has and he's too well-bred to let on.

'Ms Galley,' Franklin says. 'I have to inform you, I find your legal ethics incomprehensible.'

I should come up with a dignified response. I spend a little time searching, and find that I can't think of one. In the end, I just shrug. 'I don't blame you.'

'Your attitude is a little cavalier, for one who is responsible for a man's freedom.'

'Yes.' I uncross my legs and sit up. 'Yes, I can see why you say that.'

The expression on Franklin's face is almost quizzical. 'You're a rather strange young woman.'

'No, not really. Not if you look at it through my eyes.'

Unbelievably, Franklin shrugs. I didn't know that chess-player's body could make such a movement. 'However, I suppose we shall have to work together as best we can. I have another appointment now. May we meet later on to discuss our client's case?'

And he reaches across the table to shake my hand.

After he's gone, I sit down and laugh in sheer relief. Somehow I've escaped. I've met Adnan Franklin and I'm still alive to tell the tale. How I escaped, I don't understand.

# 4

This moon night it's my turn. Standing in a queue for equipment, already suited up, I stretch myself as best I can in the protective clothing and try not to think. The collar stick weighs heavy in my right hand. I'm loaded up like a fisherman. Maybe if I concentrate on feeling ridiculous, I won't get the fear.

I spot my trainee across the room, leaning against the wall. Sean Martin, his name is, though everyone calls him Marty; I've been teaching him for a few months. His shoes are usually undone, but he remembers everything I say.

I raise my hand to get his attention. He waves back, and I manage to get through the crowd that fills the room. As he straightens up, I am surprised, as I always am, at his height. He's a slight boy, narrow across, with a way of stooping a little to one side so his cowlick falls into his eyes. You forget he's tall, unless you're right up next to him.

'Do I get to drive?' he says. His hopeful smile upsets me. I don't want to have to watch it disappear.

'I don't think so. Come on,' I say. We set out; it's a lot easier to get through the crowd with Marty's six foot one moving in front of me.

We've been assigned van thirty-two, which is the one with the crack across the windscreen. Marty jostles my shoulder as we head for it; his breath billows in the cold.

'Ready to round up?' he says.

'Fight any lune in the house.' I say this mock-tough. My voice doesn't shake at all.

'You can take them. Any lune messes with us is going to end up lining your gloves.' His voice is reassuring, which irritates me: no stripling gets to reassure me, however smart. I'm also disturbed that he sees through my joking that easily. At his age, it's not natural.

'Keep my dainty fingers warm,' I say.

'I'll cure the pelt. No sweat.'

His voice stretches tighter as he speaks. I toss the keys in the air to distract him, and miss them on the way down. Marty crouches and hands them back to me; once down, he stays crouched. I watch him for a few moments, then tug on his shoulder. 'On your feet, kiddo. We've got dogs to catch.'

He rights himself. 'Bring them on.' He says this without looking at me.

We settle into the van. Marty produces a flask of coffee; I take a pack of Pro-Plus out of my pocket, and use a swig from his Thermos to knock one back. Marty shakes his head at the packet when I proffer it.

'You'll be sleepy,' I warn.

He looks at me. An apologetic expression is on his face; the catching hood has squeezed it at the corners so it's flushed. 'I don't need stringing out any further,' he says.

*

There's a silence on these nights like nothing you ever hear. It's so quiet it's almost musical. We sit in our van, the flood lamps on top giving us a small circle of light. Lycos never see this. No one to run the power, no one to run the water, the gas, the telephones, the city. It all shuts down, the electricity grids go off, the world is black. Lycos lock their doors with bolts instead of coded security pads and hope nothing catches fire until morning. We run our shelters on generators and stock up on water and supplies, and the darkness outside lays siege. Our radios and tracking systems keep us reminded that there are other people in the world. We need reminding. First-aid workers at the shelters, skeletal staff at the DORLA offices. And no one else, no one else awake or tame. We dwell on the shelters, think about them a lot. It's like knowing that down under the deep sea there is a bottom somewhere.

Our patrol tonight takes in Spiritus Sanctus Park and the area around it. Last time we had to do Kings, which wasn't so bad; Kings is less densely wooded, so there's a better chance there of finding a lune that's kept out of the forest. Though not as much as any of us would like. Sanctus is small, forested, impenetrable. Too many trees, not enough open spaces. No one likes getting assigned there; it's early in Marty's training to get given somewhere so difficult. I wonder if that's a token of official approval of him, or of me.

Marty is biting his fingernails; I reach over and pull his hand out of his mouth without taking my eyes off the tracker. 'Bad habit,' I say. 'Light me a cigarette, will you?'

He makes a noise like one fragment of a laugh, and

gets out the pack for me. 'Nothing much on the tracker,' he says.

'Not yet. Best not to worry about it, though. Could just be a quiet night.' I turn the van left along the patrol route. As I do this, I wonder how I've become the grown-up. I've been catching since I was eighteen, and I still don't know a damn thing about doing it safely. I think about the woman who taught me catching, my friend Bride Reilly, a big jolly woman with blonde-by-choice hair who showed me all there is to know about a right hook. I share cases with her sometimes. She's got a new trainee: a boy shorter than I am who boxes as well as she does, probably to make up for his lack of height. Bride used to sing dirty songs as we cruised, tell jokes and make me forget my fears. Poor Marty's stuck with me, and I can't think of any way to make him forget.

'How many –' Marty's voice clicks in his throat. 'You never told me – how many catches does this make it for you?'

I keep my hands on the wheel. 'I can't remember. You lose track after a while.' I am lying. I remember every single one.

Marty takes my lighter out of the pack, and as he does so, there's a soft wail from the left. His hand jumps, and my lighter falls on the floor.

'Cool it,' I say, my voice snapping. This is tough enough if your partner's calm, there's no way I can keep my head if Marty starts panicking on me. 'Check the tracker, will you?' I swing the wheel in the direction of the voice, and slow down.

Marty draws a deep breath, and lets it go. 'About eleven o'clock,' he says. 'Just one.'

He's making an effort to brace himself. 'Atta boy.' I say this very softly, and turn my attention to the road.

I stop the van and take a look: it's small, smaller than it should be. 'Might just be a stray dog,' I say. My nails dig into the steering wheel as I say this. There are days when I dream of driving around all night, ignoring all pick-ups and just staying snug inside my own van. My fantasies are going to have to wait, though.

This one is outside a park. Less common, more risky. We'll have to fight it in the streets. I look at the map, and try to plan a route.

'Maybe it's a juvenile,' says Marty over the sound of the engine re-starting.

'You don't miss much,' I tell him. 'Or it could just be showing up smaller than it is, of course, that happens often enough. Or it really could be a stray. In which case, I'll go to church tomorrow. You awake?'

He rubs his eyes. 'Yes.'

'It's past your bedtime, kid. Sure you don't want any Pro-Plus?'

'No, thank you anyway.' His manners do him credit.

I look at the street ahead of us. Grey in the head-lights, with no streetlamps burning, it looks rainswept, war-torn, faded. I turn at the junction, and try to stop imagining things.

'Okay,' I say. 'I want you to do this collar. I'll be right behind you. Remember, if this is a juvenile, it'll be more likely to be panicking, so you need to be effi-cient. No missing its head and swatting it with the collar or anything like that, I don't want to be chasing it till sunrise. Clear?'

'Yes.' He fingers his catcher. 'What if I do miss?'

I think he's just covering all his bases, but the thought

still chills me. There was a time when I wanted to do every collar for him, to spare him the dangers of being bitten and me the risk of him missing. I can't, I'd be doing him no favours. He has to learn sometime. 'Then we trank it and take the consequences.'

'Is that bad? I mean, worse?' Marty chews his finger-nail.

'It's not good.' They ought to teach him this kind of thing in school classes. I'm not too surprised they don't, though – they usually leave the worse facts to be found out by experience. 'People don't like the idea of tranking children. So they don't make child-sized darts. It would be like admitting we might use them.' No one thinks baby lunes can possibly be dangerous. No one who hasn't seen them. 'If we trank it, we'll just have to drag it to the nearest shelter that's got someone who knows a damn thing about First Aid.' As I say this, I find we're nearly at the right street.

I turn the corner and something sinks inside me. Not my heart, I think, that's tethered into place, yet it still gives me a long second of dismay when I see that Marty was right. It's a juvenile. A small one, not much bigger than a German shepherd, and it's doing its best to dig through a pile of black bin bags. Withered lettuce leaves and wet cereal boxes are scattered across the street; the smell of rot hits us at the same time as the sound of whimpering.

I take my trank gun out and watch how Marty handles the pole. When he first started, he looked like he was conducting an orchestra for some slapstick number; I didn't dare let him carry it outside. I was impressed, though: two catches along, and he'd progressed to just awkward, and now he's managed some perfectly competent collars. He's a quick learner. And he'd better be as able as I think he is on this one, or we'll end up rushing the juvenile to a shelter with a sedative overdose.

The yellow light of the van has turned everything pale, and the shadow of the pole looms black against the pile of trash. Then Marty's foot comes down on a grey leaf. It only makes a little splashing sound: that little sound, then silence. The juvenile stops digging. It pulls its head out of the pile, and a waterfall of bags tumble down around it. It looks up, and it sees the pole.

The sound it makes is like something falling from a great height to smash at the bottom. A whimper, and the whimper rises to a screaming snarl, and then it leaps bare-toothed into the air. There's a dull gleam as its jaws snap together just under the pole, and it circles round on the pavement preparing for another leap.

'Marty, hurry,' I mutter. 'Catch it while you still can.'

The juvenile leaps again, up against the wall and back towards us, it's fast as a cat. Marty swings the pole and misses, it knocks against the side of a building and it's way out of line. The juvenile gives a high, grinding wail. In a minute, the whole street will start howling. Already there are several voices coming down, they blend and rise, coming down on us, and I press my hands against my head because I cannot afford to panic, whatever the noise I cannot afford to panic. Marty wrestles with the pole and swings again, way off-balance: the collar brushes the juvenile's head and doesn't catch it.

'Marty, in a minute it's going to attack you.' My voice is as quiet as I can make it. 'Catch it now.'

Marty reaches the pole out. It hangs in the air above

the juvenile, and the juvenile cringes down, snarling at it. There's a moment where there's nothing but howling voices and the snarls below us, and then the juvenile springs. Marty makes another swing just as it leaves the ground.

There's a thud and a shriek, and I see what's happened. He hit it with the stick. Bad luck, bad timing, he missed and he hit this under-age stray on the head with a heavy ten-foot pole. The juvenile cowers on the ground, its head between its feet and its tail between its legs. Its howls shouldn't make sense to me, every howl should sound the same. They don't, though. This pitched, shaking wail may be lune-talk, and I don't know how lunes think: all of that is true. It doesn't matter, not just this minute. I know crying when I hear it.

I take the pole out of Marty's hands and collar the weeping juvenile in one shot. Once it's collared it fights, and we shove it, still sobbing, into the van, bruising its neck as we go. It lands a bite on my calf as we get it up the ramp, but its teeth don't go through the suit. I'll just have a mark there tomorrow. Marty holds it pressed against the wall.

'Hold it there for a bit,' I say. Lycos have chips in their necks inserted at birth, to help us ID: I scan the microchip in his neck with the chipper as I pass, and yank open a cage door. Marty harries him in, and I slam the door and lock it.

'Check this reading, will you?' I say.

'Toby McInley,' says Marty. 'Seven years old.' Toby McInley curls up in the middle of the cage, shivering.

'What have we got?' I go to look over Marty's shoulder. What we've got on him is nothing surprising. He's on the at-risk list: a social worker, neglect, suspected abuse. They're always the ones we find out on the streets.

I leave Toby sitting huddled on the floor and start the van up again.

'That wasn't good, Marty.' This is a matter of fact.

Marty rubs his fists together and doesn't say anything.

'Marty. You have to be quicker than that. You can't just catch them a clout with the pole, you could get done backwards and forwards for that. You're lucky it's a neglected child whose folks probably won't sue.'

'I didn't mean to,' he mutters.

'I know you didn't mean to, it doesn't matter that you didn't mean to. You did. You've got to be more careful.'

'I know.' Marty glares at his fists and slouches down in his seat. I could go on in this vein for a while, and I probably should. There's no excuse for that kind of mistake. The trouble is, it was a mistake. We all make them. There's just no good way of doing this job.

'Anyway,' Marty mutters. 'It worked.'

'What?' I turn to look at him, and he sits glowering at his feet. 'Marty, did you do that on purpose?'

'No.'

'Did you do that on purpose?'

'No.'

Toby is silent in the back. There's only the sound of the engine and Marty kicking his feet on the floor, and nothing else. I open my mouth to tell him to stop it, then decide against it and change gears instead. The thud of the gear stick is the loudest thing for a mile around.

'It won't do, Marty,' I say.

'It was an accident,' he says. He sounds upset.

'I know. But parents can sue over injured juveniles. It'll mar your record just as you're starting out. Next one, we do absolutely by the book, okay?' I think of the wailing as the pole knocked the boy's head.

I see Marty come close to saying, Whatever. He doesn't. He stretches out his fingers for a moment, then says, 'Yes. I'll be careful.'

'Good for you.' I half-smile at him, nod. He's a smart boy.

We drive for an hour in silence, back into Sanctus. Toby doesn't howl in the back. He crouches, silent, calling no attention to himself. Marty taps his feet in a regular rhythm and stares out ahead of us at the blank road. Whenever I look at him, I see the wall of trees behind him, the woods. The first layer is visible, with monochrome bark and ragged branches: they quiver a little at the edges and make no sound. The shadows they cast in our head beam twist and slice by us as the light passes them. After the first layer, nothing. A few shapes are visible, branches and ivy, braided into each other so you can't judge distance, and shadow overlays shadow in a deep tangle so I can't see more than five feet in.

For a while, we have rain, a few heavy drops that trickle down the windscreen and then stop, leaving the air chilly and close.

I'm beginning to think it might be a quiet night when there's a bleep from the tracker and we both look towards it. An ugly, shining clump has appeared on the screen. It doesn't have the appearance of a single figure: its shape is amorphous, like two, three, four objects close together. It's in the park, it's near us. It shows up left of centre on the screen. Which means that I've got to turn the van around, head into the woods and make a careful way through the black and grey trees.

'Two,' I say. 'Maybe more.' Marty bites his lip; his hand drops to his gun with the motion of the van swinging round. I don't think he's noticed he's doing it.

The way the woods are planted, you can just about drive between the trees, at least most of the time, if you go at a crawl. Twigs crush under the slow-turning wheels as I drive forward, barely at walking pace, the van rocks to and fro on the uneven ground. When it rocks, I can hear it grate at the joints, make sounds of wear: it turns into a machine, just a mechanism that's liable to damage. The wheels creak as I tug the steering wheel to and fro, jostling our way around the trees. It chills my fingers, and I find I'm staring down at them. I might not have them all in the morning.

'Marty.' My voice crackles in my mouth. 'Listen, this is going to be a tough one.'

'I know.' His head is ducked away from me.

Stopping the car, I unfurl my still whole hand and reach out for the radio. 'This is Galley, car thirty-two; Galley, car thirty-two, calling from Sanctus Park, Sanctus Park.'

'Yes?' Josie's voice comes over. She must have been sitting at the switchboard all this time. She's so hurried she's panting.

'We've sighted a group, size unknown. Is there any back-up available?'

'Just a moment . . . No.'

'None?'

'No. Everyone's miles away, and it's a heavy night. You'll have to handle this alone.'

I hadn't expected anything else, not really, but this is still shattering. 'Thank you.'

'Sorry, Lo,' says Josie's voice, and then the radio clicks off.

'Lola?' Marty's voice sounds in my ear, very softly. 'How are we going to handle this?'

I count my fingers. I don't know. 'We've just got to round them up.' He draws breath, and I keep talking before he can start. 'It depends on the size of the group. Now, we can leave most of the cages open because we've only got one of them occupied, so that's one thing working for us. If there's only two of them, then we can go for one each. And it's possible that the group may scatter when they see us, I've seen that happen.' I have. I hold this thought.

'What if there's more than two and they stick together?'

I inhale. 'Then I'll do the catching and you cover me. No, listen to me. I go for one, and if the others close in, you fire your silver gun into the air. It makes a lot of noise, and they'll probably back down. Two bullets, so you can do it twice if need be. If there's more than two, one of us needs to stand guard the whole time.'

'Will we – will we be able to see them?'

I look at him, seeing the narrowness of his shoulders, his height lost as he sits down. 'You mean because of the trees? Well, they – they sometimes provide cover for us too, Marty.'

'Can't we just trank them?' It's soft, plaintive like a bird's song. I close my eyes briefly before answering.

'Not to start with. We can't. Not unless we're in serious danger.' He gives a strangled laugh. I try to scowl at him. I want to laugh too, I really do, but if I start laughing I'm afraid of not being able to stop. 'That's the law. You read it at school, you've done exams in it, I know you know the drill. Tranking is a last resort. We may well have to take it, but not until we have to.'

'Oh.' Marty makes no complaint. He hangs his head.

'Listen,' I try to soften my voice, 'normally we could. But after that first mistake tonight, you could lose a lot if we bend the rules on this one. I know it's hard, but we've just got to try.'

'I thought the bullets were the last resort,' Marty says quietly.

I shake my head at him. 'Don't let a lyco hear you say that. As far as the rest of the world wants to know, they're not a resort at all.'

'Have you ever fired the bullets?' Marty wants to know. He's picking at his fingernails.

I swallow. 'Not so you'd want to know about.'

I start up the engine again, and we roll over the ground. The branches are unreal in the artificial light, they loom around me and I have to remember that they're solid. The dark, the quiet, the figure on the tracker, they're making me light-headed, and if I'm not careful, I might try to drive through the trees.

The tracker glows red in the darkness, with the white cluster of light still there. It's very close to the centre. The lines across the tracker cross in the middle, there's a point of convergence which is us; and just a few millimetres away from it is this foreign, multiple shape. I drive forward just a little more, and the shape breaks open, splits like an amoeba into three separate circles. I look out through the cracked glass of our windscreen, and see nothing but textured, receding shadows.

'Okay,' I whisper. 'Now we've got to be very quiet. Don't knock the windows, don't rattle your seat belt, just keep still.' There are three separate shapes on the scanner, ten metres from us. I press the accelerator, and the shapes move. They can hear us.

Ten metres, fifteen. The van moves forward, and I check again. It's the same reading. They've moved with us, they're keeping out of reach, they're not running away. Ten metres. We've got to walk.

'Marty,' I say. 'We're getting out here.'

'They're still in the dark.'

'We're not going to get any closer. Okay, remember: I catch, you guard. Fire your silver if you –'

'I know, I know,' he hisses.

'– but God help you if you hit one of them. Are you all right?'

He shakes himself. 'Yeah. Yeah, I'm all right.'

'Let's go.'

I can smell gunpowder as I step down onto the grass, gunpowder and wet earth. The cold bites at my lips. My breathing is loud enough to hear a mile away.

The van casts a tall shadow, and there's an oval of light; I can see nothing outside it. I put on my torch and step forward: the scanner showed one shape directly ahead of us. There are two trees close together, monumental in my torch beam. A little smear of light spreads around me, and I listen. I hear nothing in the dark.

Then the impact hits my back and I'm crushed down on the ground with my mouth full of grass. My head hits a fallen branch, skin splits on my forehead, and there's a great weight on my back pressing my lungs down into the ground. Cloth rips between my shoulder blades and heavy teeth batter against me, trying to get

71

through. Wet breath burns my neck. I try to shriek to Marty and grass chokes me.

Another blow slams me and I'm rolled onto my back with two lunes over me. I see black gums, I see the glint of pink from four eyes, I see teeth longer than my finger-nails up against my face. I jab upwards with my catcher and knock one of them in the throat; its jaws snap together and it backs off with a roar, and I roll away. The sound of Marty's gun goes off, and the second lune flinches for only a second before coming back at me. My catching arm is pinned to the ground and I only have time to throw my other arm up over my throat and scream.

There's another blast, and some impact kicks the lune sideways. It hits a tree as it falls then tumbles down and snuffles on the ground, wailing, some blood is slick on the grass because Marty's shot it in the leg. I'm on my feet with my catcher and trying to get the other one and the collar swings wide as the lune runs by me and heads for Marty.

Marty has shot both his bullets and he doesn't have a catcher and his trank gun is still on his belt. His hands are empty as the lune leaps for him. I grab for my trank gun and as I do another lune comes out of the dark behind a tree and they both pin Marty to the ground and slash.

My trank dart hits the first one in the shoulder. There are several seconds of tearing flesh before the dope takes effect. The other lune looks up, sees the dart, and whips round. It runs straight for me. There are three seconds in which I know with bright cold certainty that I'm going to die, and then the lune is past me, through the forest and away into the night. I look after it. It's gone into the dark beyond where I can see it. After a moment I remember the wounded one, and when I look for it, it's gone too; it must have got up on three legs and run.

The ten steps across to where Marty is lying are among the worst I've ever taken. Marty's lying on the ground because he was empty-handed and couldn't defend himself, and he was empty-handed because he did what I told him. The little walk I take, around a tall horse chestnut, over some leaf litter and across a fallen branch to where he lies, will last me a lifetime and beyond.

Under the yellow light, blood looks almost black. Marty lies on the ground with a strip of tar across his throat. Oil trickles out of him, his face is smeared with charcoal, and his eyes are moving. I can hear his breathing dragging over his shredded throat like metal over stone.


I load the tranked lune myself, I tug a bandaged Marty into the van and drive him to a shelter. The medic keeps him alive till morning and then puts him into a hospital. They transfuse blood into him, inject chemicals into him, lace up his throat with catgut. He might not be able to speak again, they aren't sure.

This is our life, or a part of it. Bad night. Bad night.

# 5

'This could go on your record, Ms Galley.'

My superior, Hugo, is a big man. Well over six foot, heavy-shouldered with a blunt-boned peasant face, soft spoken. He'd be called imposing, if he worked in the outside world. I'd always known it, but this afternoon when I see him, I remember as if for the first time just how big he is. Sitting leaned back in his chair, not even doing very much, he takes up a lot of space without really bothering. I am a small woman at the best of times, and today, I've had a night without sleep chasing the wolves, and a stay at the hospital waiting to hear if Marty would live, which have left my eyes stinging with fatigue. There are deep, dark bruises from the night's batterings on my back, legs, arms and head. It's an effort of will to meet Hugo's eyes.

'Your trainee, Sean Martin, isn't able to tell us what happened, and we only have your testimony and the physical evidence. Which,' he sighs, 'is not in your favour. Do you have anything to say for yourself?'

Even sitting as straight as I can, he towers over me. I look up at him. 'Only what I've told you. We requested back-up, which we were refused, and found ourselves outnumbered by a group of really – very savage lunes.

They came at us from all sides. No two-man team could have handled it.'

'So you shot one of them with a bullet before you remembered your tranquilliser gun?' He almost sounds gentle.

I close my eyes for a moment and cover my mouth. 'I told Marty to use the sleeper only as a last resort. Policy.'

'Policy also to use the tranquilliser before the bullets, I think.'

'Yes, sir.'

He gives me a ruminative glance. 'Can you account for it?'

'I –' Marty should have shot with the trank. I know that. He's lying in a coma with his voice torn out, and anything I say could get us both strung up. At least, I think so. It's never possible to know what Hugo's thinking. I bite my lip and look at my hands.

Hugo sighs again. 'Let me make a suggestion. Firing the .36 to make a noise would account for it being in his hand. Which, being a technique you are known to use, makes it the likeliest explanation, yes? And we can understand that the boy may have panicked on seeing you attacked, and fired with whatever he had. Why he did not also have his tranquilliser gun at the ready, though, is harder to account for. I must assume he was acting on your orders.'

'Yes, sir.' My hands try to hide themselves in the fabric of my trousers.

'The incompetence of a recent recruit has to be taken into account, I think. Particularly as the individual he shot cannot accuse him without laying himself open to an accusation of the attempted murder of two DORLA agents. The fact remains that our young Martin was armed with the wrong weapon, in the company of a more experienced operative.' His eyes come to rest on me, and his face is impassive. I was wrong. It's me that's in trouble, me and me alone.

'Would you care to tell me how this came about?'

'I – I wanted to make sure he could do a round-up by the book. Marty had already made one mistake that night, I was trying to protect his record.'

'At the cost of his life?'

The mild question makes me jump up. 'Is he dead? Has he died?

'No. For which we have the doctors to thank. The doctors, and no one else, Ms Galley. This has been mismanaged.'

'I know.' It bothers me that all I can do is stare into my lap, but my fund of fine speeches has run dry.

'You let yourself be attacked, and left your trainee unattended with no weapons and no defences against what sounds, from what you say, like a coordinated attack. I know they aren't common, but you have to allow for them. You did not take adequate precautions, Ms Galley. Sean Martin was your responsibility, and he remains your responsibility if he is injured through your carelessness. And your preparations were inadequate for a coordinated attack.' He turns over a piece of paper and leans towards me. 'I know you didn't expect to be ambushed. If this had been a more normal situation, your actions would probably not have been wrong. But I have to go on what happened, Lola. The boy was injured and two out of the three perpetrators got away, all because he did what you told him. There isn't much I can do for you.'

He leaves a pause for me to say something. If there was anything to say, I might say it now, but there just isn't. Maybe I meant well; it doesn't matter. What mattered was keeping Marty from the teeth of the lunes. The bruises on my back and legs are beating out of time with one another as I lift my head.

'Lola.' Hugo lays his blunt hands flat on the table. 'This will be raised at the next meeting. I shall have to raise it myself. There's no way not to with an incident this serious.' We call it the short-straw party. Every disciplinary board meeting, somebody gets punished, just to show people like Franklin we're answerable, some of the time. I'm about to get strawed. My hands start to shake, and I clamp them between my knees. 'I'll try to speak for you,' Hugo continues. 'In your favour, you're a steady operative, and while you have your injury rate like everyone else, it's uncommon for you to mismanage to this extent. And also,' he adds quite noncommittally, 'the injured party in this case is not a member of the public, but one of our own, so the press won't be able to claim DORLA brutality. That is fortunate for you, I think. Though, of course, there's his family to think of, and families are seldom cooperative when one of their conscripted relations comes to harm. I believe some of them are coming in today to pick up his belongings and arrange a representative for him – it might be best if you are careful how you act around them.' He studies my white face with mild interest, and goes on. 'In any case, I will speak in your favour, but you should prepare yourself for the possibility that you will be disciplined. Given our workload, of course, I cannot put you under any restricted duty in the meantime, but I will advise you, be careful. Are we clear?'

'Yes. Yes, we're clear,' I manage to say.

He keeps his impassive eyes on me. He could finish

this either way: a comment to show he's on my side, or a further rebuke to put me in my place. He does neither.

I get to the door and find my way through it. Once on the other side, what I want to do is hit the foetal position and stay like that for the rest of my life, but I'm confronted with a full office of hectic people running to and fro, telephones ringing in the new year, voices shouting over each other, and a whole building trying to sort order from chaos. Everyone can see me. I balance my way all across the room and down the hall to my little office. It's only once I'm there that I bury my head in my arms.

A memory comes to me. I was about four, I think, half Becca's age, and sitting in the bathroom, perched on top of the laundry hamper. There was blood trickling down my leg. Even back then, I wasn't much of a crier. The idea that I might be bleeding to death had occurred to me, and I had a sense that I ought to be worried about it; really, I was more worried that the blood would get to my white sock and stain it. Be careful with your things, my mother would say to me, I was already saying it to myself, rocking to and fro and making the basket creak under me. To prevent this, I tried to stop the blood with my hand, and smeared red across my shin. It was stickier than I had expected. I scratched my smudged palm with my other hand, getting blood on that, too, and then realised that I was stuck: on top of a basket with a knee that hurt and two hands that couldn't touch anything and no way of getting down.

I don't know why I was so afraid of my mother finding out. From the moment I was born, she had scolded me less than she should. There was a kind of resignation about the way she handled me. Instead, she scolded Becca for not watching me, as if I couldn't be expected to do any better.

I leaned out and called in a furtive whisper, 'Becca? Becca?'

Becca came out of her room with a doll in her hands, then saw me and marched into the bathroom.

'I'll get blood on my sock,' I said.

'Socks don't grow on trees.' Becca frowned at me, and sat her doll neatly against the wall. The idea of a sock tree made me giggle. 'It's not funny, May!' Becca said.

'I can't get down.'

'So don't you laugh at me.'

'I can't get down. I'm not laughing at you. Can you help me?'

'You should be more careful,' Becca said, and took hold of my foot. I whimpered as she unbent my leg, and she gave it a little tug before wetting a face cloth and cleaning the blood away. She washed in neat strokes, working from the foot upwards, and when she reached the knee, she dabbed around it with a very gentle touch. I told her I didn't want disinfectant and she put some on anyway, and pressed a plaster down with her whole palm. Then she pulled me off the hamper and washed my hands under the tap, and I wriggled because I wanted to wash them myself.

'You're being silly,' she said.

'Let go my hands.'

'I'm helping. Aren't you going to say thank you?'

*

The phone rings, and I answer it, glad to have someone to talk to. I've got to work. I was wool-gathering, and anyway, I don't think that memory really went anywhere. Except that it was the first time I remember having to deal with blood, and the stickiness and traps of getting hurt, I don't know why I was thinking about it. Except that once you're injured, it takes patience to get out of it. I say 'Thank you' quickly, quietly, to finish things off, and turn my attention to the call.

'Lola Galley.'

'Hello, this is Nick Jarrold. We've met a few times.'

'Yes, I remember.' Nick Jarrold is a gaunt man with a number three buzz cut, a misfortune that makes his head look huge on his bent neck, like a baby's. He started working forensics and police liaison fifteen years ago, and has been killing himself with fifty cigarettes a day ever since. Tobacco leaves grow in his throat; I can hear them rustling together when he speaks. It's the expense of it that gets me the most, three packs a day on our wages. There are cheaper ways to die.

And he used to be Johnny's partner. That's the other thing. Johnny used to laugh about him, comment on his cigarette habit, but they'd been working together for over a year when – just don't let him mention Johnny. 'How are you, Nick?'

'All right,' he lies in a wheeze. 'How's things with you?'

'Things. Are just. Lovely,' I say through my teeth. 'I'm. In wonderful. Spirits. I love my life. What can I do for you, Nick?'

'Listen.' He sounds like he has laryngitis; I clear my

throat in sympathy. 'I'm in the shelter you brought your fighter into last night, I'm doing the morning shift.'

'I've made a statement,' I interrupt. 'It should be on its way to you.'

'We've got it, thanks. But since he ricked this morning, he's been – he's kind of unusual. We thought you might want to have a look.'

'Unusual? Who is he?'

'Well, his name's Seligmann, if that helps. Not someone I've run into before. I don't know what to make of him. You might want to take an interest in him, seeing that he's yours.' 'Take an interest' is one of those euphemisms that can mean anything; it's unlike Nick to talk round like this.

I rest my hand in my hair. 'Thanks, but I'm up for a short-straw party. I could lose my job.' This shouldn't be easy to say, but to a man living on maybe three table-spoons of lung, it can't sound that pathetic. 'I don't know if it's worth the time.'

'They won't straw you when they read our report of him,' he rasps. 'No one's going to blame you for this one. Come and have a look. It doesn't have to be today, we're not letting this one go. We'll send him to your cells. You can look at him there.'

'What's his name again?'

'Darryl Seligmann.'

'Are we charging him?'

'Kendalling, maybe attempted murder. I don't know. That's your area, you can make something up if he insists on a charge. You will see him, though?' The Kendall statute lays down that it's illegal to resist arrest more than a reasonable person who was luning would be expected to do. Kendalling is putting up too much of a fight. It's one of the vaguest laws on the books.

'Oh, God, Nick, I don't know. All right. I'll see him when he's brought in. Thanks for telling me, now listen, I've got to go.'

'Okay. Good luck.'

'Thanks.'

'Lola?'

'Yeah?'

'Look out for yourself.'

Heading back to my office from the coffee machine, I see my old teacher Bride coming across the room with a big ironic grin across her tarty mug. 'I hear you're for the axe, love,' she says.

'Mm-hm.' I succeed in grinning back at her.

She pats my arm, and then her face sobers up. 'How's poor little Marty?'

It takes a few seconds to pull myself together enough to answer. 'He'll live. Whether he'll talk again or not is another matter.'

'Oh, pet.' Bride puts her arm around me. I start to shrug it off, until I realise that if I did, it wouldn't be there any more. My face crumbles at the edges.

'Some teacher I am, huh?' I say.

'What happened?' she says, giving my shoulder a shake.

'I told him to fire his .36 in the air and not use his sleeper unless he had to. He was unarmed when they charged him.'

'Poor boy,' she sighs.

'He's just a kid. I've messed him up for good and all.'

'He might be all right. Kids heal up pretty well.'

'Maybe,' I say into her shoulder. Bride fluffs my hair. 'Hey,' I say. 'I spent money on that haircut.'

'Good for you. Haircuts, shoes, and bras. They're the three things you've got to spend money on.' She gives her heavy bust a rueful glance, then casts a critical eye over me, my narrow chest and square, childish hips. I pull my jacket tighter. 'Or maybe it's just me. Anyway, what about this attack you had last night? Marty aside, I mean.'

'What about it?' I'm tired of talking about it.

'Chit-chat says it looked coordinated. We haven't had one of those for a while. Want me to look into it?' No one's going to promote her, but she's still an okay investigator, she's taught me enough tricks to show me that her help might be worth having.

'Nick Jarrold called me. He wouldn't tell me any details. You could look into that.'

'I will. You should too, though, Lolie. He's your catch.'

'I will, I will.'

'Hmph.' Bride lets go of me and dusts off her hands. 'Sub-Kendal next time if I were you.'

'I know, I should have.' Sub-Kendalling means tranking a fighter, then pleading the Kendal statute whether it was life or death or not. Word against word, yours against the lyco who's waking up with a trank hangover. It's a pretty fine distinction. If you stop to read the rule book, you aren't around to plead the law the next morning.

'You can't trust them an inch, Lo, you know that. Balls to what the law says.'

'Yeah. Balls. How's your trainee?'

'Nate? He's a bit slow. Doesn't laugh at my jokes.'

'Oh, then he must be bad.' I'm starting to feel a bit

better; quite a few people find Bride annoying, I think, but she has a good effect on me.

'He wants to go into finances, can you imagine?'

I can, if I make a lot of effort. 'Masochist. Is he into whips and leather as well?'

'Oh no, he's a very good boy. You were much more fun. I have the feeling he's into the military end too.' She shrugs. 'Can't ask him, of course.' The military connection is the closest DORLA gets to top secret. Moon nights aren't synchronised across the globe because time zones vary: different countries begin and end a few hours ahead of or behind each other. Soldiers lock up in barracks; military scientists and supreme commanders fur up and stop watching the skies. If your enemy is luning and you aren't, they're wide open. It wasn't a problem until someone invented long-range missiles. A few too many massacres some decades ago produced a UN resolution: during full moon nights, any countries at war with each other are under an enforced truce. Break the moon night ceasefire and the whole of the UN goes to war with you. In theory. If it's not against a powerful nation's interests. No country is quite prepared to risk its life on it, so bases get built, underground bunkers at hidden locations, with launch codes for retaliatory nuclear bombs that can be accessed the minute a ricking general is back on his feet. Specially trained DORLA volunteers staff them; no one else knows where they are, or even who the volunteers are. Young men form the majority, it's known. And why not? You get to feel like a soldier while staying indoors, away from lunes roaming the night with teeth bared.

Marty wasn't interested in joining up, I knew that. He took his chances outside with the rest of us.

'So,' says Bride, 'have you broken any hearts lately? Been around the lads yet?' She takes my arm and steers me through the office.

'No.' We've been over this ground before, and well though she means, I'm running out of humour about it.

'You need to get out more, pet.' Bride used to be out a lot of nights; not since her husband Jim's heart attack, though. The doctors said he could live for years if he didn't strain himself. Most nights, I know, she just stays in and tries her best to rob him at poker. I could mention something of this to get her out of my eventless love life, if I wanted to lose my best friend, that is.

'Thanks, Bride. I'll put it in my in-tray.'

'Wasting yourself in an office,' she mutters. She opens her mouth to say something else, then stops in her tracks.

'Come on, Bride.'

'Ohh.' Bride has stopped looking at me. I follow where she's staring: there's two women coming into the reception area, one old and one young. They're huddled together.

'What? Unaccompanied lycos?'

'Lolie – don't they look like someone?'

I try to see it.

Then I see it, and I pull my arm out of Bride's to grip my hands together. They look like each other, they can only be mother and daughter. They look like family. They look like Marty.

The younger one glances about her. She's surrounded by bustling people: it's Day One, the first day after moon night, and no one has the time of day to give her.

She sees us, and we're standing still, so she makes her way over. 'Can you help us?' she says. I've seldom heard a lyco speak softer.

I open my mouth, close it. Bride has a look at me, and takes over. 'What can I do for you?'

'We're trying to find room 45A.' They're looking for the liaison section. Someone's going to meet them to talk them out of suing us.

'You're on the right floor. You need to go out the door you came in, turn left and follow the corridor round, you'll see it.'

'Thank you, Mrs –?' The young woman looks at Bride for her name. She's younger than I am. If she just leaves it at Bride, if she doesn't start talking socially, I won't have to speak to her.

'Reilly. Bride Reilly.'

'Mary Martin.' She shakes Bride's hand. Her mother doesn't move. Mary Martin stands still for a moment, her face drawn, then she opens her mouth. 'My brother worked here.'

'Yes, I know,' says Bride. 'We're all sorry for you. He's a good boy.'

'You know about it.' Mrs Martin speaks for the first time, saying this very quietly, as if it confirms something. She looks at me.

The silence stays. Finally Bride clears her throat and introduces me. 'This is Lola Galley, Mrs Martin.'

'How do you do, Mrs Martin?' I hold out my hand. She takes hold of it for less time than it takes to blink, then takes her own hand back and cradles it in the depths of her cardigan.

'You worked with Sean?' she says.

'Yes. Yes, I did.' If I walk the world for ten years,

maybe I'll find something comforting to say to this woman.

Marty's sister looks at me with her mother's face. 'Sean told us about you. It was you he went out on – on full moon nights with, wasn't it?'

I swallow. 'Yes. It was.'

'Oh.' His mother says this from a thousand miles away, and it's the quietest beating I've ever had.

'Mrs Martin, I'm sorry –'

She turns her head aside, and her eyelids come down like blinds to keep me out.

Her daughter takes hold of her arm. 'Well,' she says. 'We should be getting on so we can get back to the hospital sooner. We just came by to see someone and pick up some things. It was a pleasure to meet you, Mrs Reilly. Miss Galley.' A little expression comes onto her face as she turns to her mother. 'Come on, Mum,' she says, and she steers her round towards the exit. At the door Mrs Martin turns her head as if to look back, and her daughter puts an arm around her and whispers to her. Both of them are hunched like refugees as they leave.

'Well,' Bride's voice bounces off my ear and scares me. 'That could have been worse.'

I can't take my eyes off the door. 'I've fucked up their son.'

'They didn't scream or spit at you, love, count your blessings. I remember when I was younger, this man whose wife got hurt in a catch came in, yelling and screaming, carrying on. Tried to stab me with a pen, the fool. Poor bastard.' She takes hold of my arm. 'Leave it be, Lo.'

\*

The first drink was for Marty. The second for Johnny. The third is for me.

I need more people to drink to.

The Scotch is like rainwater, it clings to me as I knock it back, and the smoke in the bar is making my eyes sting. It's just the smoke. It's just the drink. I give a dull glare to the bar, which is brown and dirty, there are pools of drink on it and piles of black ash. I'm dropping my cigarette ash down with the rest of the mess. I down another drink and gesture to the barman. He gives me a kind look as he pours for me, and my face contorts. I turn away. Just because he sells me drink doesn't mean he can look at me.

I raise the glass, and I can't think of who to drink to; there's enough people to put me in hospital with alcohol poisoning who need a toast. I count them in taps on the glass. Marty lying in hospital so hurt the sound of a footfall might damage him, Johnny rotting in his grave, Susan Marcos who hasn't called me, Jim who can't go outside because his heart's no good for him . . . This is making me worse. I tap against the glass, not even trying to think of people who need it. We all do.

I think I'm bad, because I want the mauls and deaths and pain to happen to other people in DORLA, people I don't know. I'm tired of it happening to my friends, and I can't imagine it not happening at all. Just a few strangers, I ask fate, just for a while.

This toast is to fate.

I want another cigarette. My movement is going, the barman has to light it for me. He's a skinny grey-haired man with crossed eyes and natural courtesy. His courtesy is going to make me start crying. It's getting more important to think of people to drink to, I can't have my Scotch until I think of someone. I stare into it, pulling at my hair to pull an answer out. What I come up with is Leo. My little nephew Leo. I want to see him again. I'm going to call Becca and go round to see him. He's going to be all right, he's got me drinking to him and he's got all his arms and legs, and he's not going to lose them chasing wolves.

If Johnny heard me talking like that, he'd make me stop. Johnny could see things in our life that he thought were worth it. He believed in fate. Johnny could take the world as it was, he played by the rules and found meaning in them that was never there.

I want him back alive.

My head weighs down towards the bar, and I set my drink down before I drop it. Beer soaks into my sleeves as I lean forward, and it's when I'm leaning forward, elbow-deep in mess, that I see the man next to me tip his head.

I turn to look, and find myself gazing into something that stops me dead. The eyes are breathtaking, my breath actually snags in my throat for a moment before I catch it: deep blue lights fanned out around a wide black pupil, dark lashes curling like fern leaves. He gestures towards my half-empty glass and then towards the bar with a star-white smile. An angel is trying to buy me a drink. I set down my glass and remind myself to mistrust him.

'Evening,' he says.

'Yes, it is.'

'What are you drinking?'

'Alcohol. It makes me drunk. You can get it almost anywhere.'

He grins, and takes my glass out from under me. The whisky swirls as he moves it under his nose, smelling it; little trickles of the drink cling for their lives to the sides of the glass.

'Scotch, single malt,' he says to the barman, raising his hand and pointing towards a bottle. I find there's a new glass in front of me, cosying up to my old one.

'For you, sir?' says the barman.

'A red wine, please.'

'Oh, one of those,' I say, and the man laughs and raises his glass to me.

I raise my hands to him, flashing smooth skin.

'What's your name?' he asks me.

'You're wasting your time, Adonis. See the pads?'

'Adonis?' He leans forward, laughing in puzzlement, and I see he's deceived me already: apart from those eyes, his face is pretty normal. It's perfectly nice, but nothing extraordinary, just a pleasant face with two searchlights in the middle.

I shrug, and sip the ice dregs of my old drink. 'You know, you had me fooled. For a moment there I thought you looked like a Greek god.'

'You surprise me,' he says. 'What is your name?'

'Look, you see my hands? See this?' I yank my sleeve up, and lay bare the scar that runs from wrist to elbow inside my left arm. 'Thanks for the drink, but you may as well back out now while it's still half polite.'

'What, because you're from DORLA? Give me some credit,' he says.

'Credit for what?'

'Can't I buy you a drink?' he says. There's a little crinkle on his forehead. What anyone so beautiful thinks he's doing pretending anything can disturb him I don't know, but still – it's not likely, really it's not, but he might just be genuinely worried.

'Sure.'

'Your health,' he says, and raises his drink.

I push away my drink and pick up the one he's bought me. Little coils and spirals twist around the ice cubes, and when I sip it, the heat spreads down my throat. It's a better malt than the one I had before.

'Do people often do that?' he asks me.

'Do what?'

'Run for cover when they see you're a non.'

I scowl at my drink. 'What's to run from? You all run things twenty-seven days out of twenty-eight. I can't do a thing to you.'

He rubs his forehead thoughtfully. 'That's not quite true.' He isn't contradicting me, just trying to think of the right answer. 'There are stories about what happens in DORLA, most of them made up, of course, but it's no joke if you arrest someone. And your conviction rate's way higher than the regular judicial system.'

Regular, he said. It's better than normal. 'Maybe we're just efficient.'

He laughs. 'Maybe. I don't know. Anyway, I don't suppose you came here to talk about work.'

'No.' I take another sip. 'I came here to get drunk.'

'All on your own?'

'Yeah, what's a pretty girl like me doing drinking alone? Answer, I'm keeping company with this glass. We're getting along very well, he and I. And while you're at it, what's a nice girl like me doing in a place like this?'

He laughs again, then puts his drink down; it makes

91

almost no noise as it touches the counter. 'You are pretty, you know.'

I open my mouth to say something, and find it empty of words. My drink is heavy in my hand, and I set it down with a thud and bury my fingers in my hair. 'Look,' I say. 'I don't know if I'm drunk enough to let you pick me up. You seem like a nice guy, but I'm hard work even when I'm sober, and I've had a bad day.'

'You're not that hard work,' he says. 'What went wrong?'

I close my eyes, open them. Still in one piece. 'Someone's injured, and it's my fault. I should have kept a better eye out for him, and I didn't, and now he's in hospital.'

'That's hard,' he says.

I look up at him. 'Aren't you going to say you're sure it wasn't my fault?'

He has a nice look on his face, sympathetic but not dead-weight. 'I wasn't there. It might even have been. But so what, we all make mistakes.'

'Yeah,' I mumble, 'but your mistakes make you late for appointments. Mine put people in intensive care.'

'I'm sorry.' He pushes my drink towards me, and then makes a little gesture with his fingers. I look towards where he's pointing, and see that I must really be drunk. I've left my sleeve rolled up, and the scar is uncovered for the world to see.

'Oh God,' I say. My hand flies to cover it, and he reaches out to pull my sleeve down. I let him. His fingers skim my wrist. He stops with the sleeve pulled halfway down, and then runs his fingers over the scar.

'Poor girl,' he says. 'That must have hurt.'

I clench my fist. 'You're wasting your time, lover boy,' I say. 'It's scar tissue. It's dead flesh. I can't feel it.'

His hand opens, and cups around my wrist.

'Don't,' I say.

'Are you all right?'

'No. I'm not all right. Look, whatever your name is. I think you're trying to pick me up. I'd like to. But you'd start hating me two minutes afterwards, and I don't want to have to watch your face when you try to work out a way to get rid of me. So if you're looking to get laid, I really think you should try someone else.'

He gives half a laugh, then stops. 'I'm just talking to you,' he says, and his hand comes gently off my arm. 'Anyway, my name's Paul, Paul Kelsey.'

I jolt in my chair, just manage to stop myself spitting out my whisky. The amount I've drunk suddenly becomes a problem. 'Since when?' is what I come out with.

'Since I was baptised . . . What's the matter?'

'I know you.' My voice is tripping over its words. 'You're the guy sent me that e-mail about my wino, you're a social worker. What you doing in my bar?'

He leans his head around to get a look at me. 'Are you Lola Galley?'

'Yeah. Oh God.' I put my head on my arms, letting the mess on the bar stain my sleeves. 'We're s'posed to work together.'

'You sent me that funny e-mail, didn't you?' he says, removing my drink to a safe distance where I can't knock it over.

'Funny? It was dreadful. It was – unprofessional.' I

get the word out. 'Why didn't you write back and put me in my place, eh?'

'Are you kidding? It's the first time I've ever heard of anyone getting a message from anyone in DORLA who assumed they were on the same side.'

'Oh.' I can't figure that out. 'Well, we're not.'

He drinks some of his wine. 'Why not?'

'Dunno. Just not. Probably.'

'Can I suggest that you drink some water?'

'No. I'm researching our case. Looking at it from our client's point of view. Please let me be drunk, I don't want to be sober just now.'

'Really, I couldn't tell. What's the matter?' He's stopped smiling. The look on his face ought to be disapproval or something, but it's not, it's just – interest.

'My pupil got hurt because of me. And before that, my friend got killed and left behind three kids and a pregnant wife, and we don't know who killed him. And my job's on the line. And I miss my sister, and I know if I see her it won't make things any better.' I'm speaking to the bar. 'Aren't you sorry you started talking to me?'

He grins. 'No. Not really.'

'Why the hell not?'

'Can we meet socially some time? I mean, maybe without the whisky,' he says.

'We're working together. You can reach me through DORLA,' I succeed in saying.

'Like that, is it?'

'Yeah. Look. Oh, God –' I put my face in my hands. 'Kelsey, I'm drunk. I'm tired. I've had an awful, awful day. I'm not making any sense. I think I'd better go.' I stand up. The room takes a slow spin to the right, and I put a hand to my head as I stumble towards the door.

Outside the bar, I look back through the window. The bartender shrugs, and pours Paul Kelsey another drink.

# 6

I spend the next evening with the Marcos family. It's Debbie who lets me in and shows me into the living room. It's not in much of a state. Susan sits in the same chair as before, and Debbie comes up behind her and puts her arms around her mother. Susan puts a hand on Debbie's arm without turning her head. There's a vacancy about Sue's expression that frightens me. Little Debbie nestles her head against her mother's, and her eyes are continually flitting to Susan's face. It's as if she's trying to nudge her into life.

The two boys, Peter and Julio, tumble into the room. Debbie jumps at the noise, and turns around. 'Have you laid the table?' she says. Her voice is edgy. I'd forgotten how quickly children get angry.

'No,' says Peter, the youngest, and gives Julio a shove.

'You've got to lay the table. I cooked the dinner, you've got to lay the table, it's your turn to do it.'

Peter gives her a glare, and stamps at her. Debbie stands between her brothers and her mother and half-shouts, 'You've got to do your share!'

Peter shouts back, 'Go to hell, you're not my mother!'

'Hey, hey, hey.' I get between them. 'It's okay, take it easy.'

Debbie talks to me in an aside, not quietly enough. 'I'm sorry you should see this.'

'Suppose I lay the table?' I say.

'Peter should do it.'

I check on Peter, who's only just this side of smashing something. 'Yeah, but let's let him off, eh? I bet I can do it faster.'

She gives me an angry look as I steer her into the kitchen. Together, we find plates and lay them out, pull chairs in line. Sausages are sitting in the pan, potatoes and frozen peas have been cooked. I'm impressed: for a girl Debbie's age, this is a pretty good meal. There's a mug in the middle of the table, with some thin, bare branches in it that she's picked from somewhere. I look at her bend her head over the table, frowning as she lays the forks in line. All this, and her family is still lying in pieces around her.

'This looks terrific, Debbie,' I say.

'Mm.' She doesn't look at me.

I go back to the living room. The boys are simmering: Peter is kicking things, and Julio is brooding on the sofa. I sit beside him and give his arm a light punch. 'You okay, kid?' I say.

He glowers at his feet.

'Debbie's cooked a great dinner.'

'I'm sick of her cooking.'

'Well, she's trying to be nice.'

He kicks the sofa. 'You going to try to talk me round? Do the shrink bit like my school nurse? You going to do that?'

'Me? Hardly. I wouldn't know a shrink if he came up and bit me,' I say. He fidgets, his face twitches. He shuffles to and fro, opens his mouth, closes it. 'I remember my school nurse. All she ever did was give us aspirin. You came in with a broken leg, she'd ask if you wanted one or two aspirin. Course, my school was pretty poor.'

Julio's face works and he doesn't look at me. 'She just makes me so mad,' he says.

'Debbie? Why?'

'She thinks if she does all this stuff and bosses us around, it's like it'll all be okay.'

I pat his leg and he moves away. 'I'm really sorry,' I say. He rolls his eyes and frowns to get the misery out of his features; even to me, it sounds like a pathetic thing to say. 'That doesn't help, does it?' I add.

He shrugs.

'Debbie is trying to help, though,' I go on. 'After all, can you cook?' He scowls, he thinks I'm mocking him. I manage a grin. 'I'm not much of a cook myself,' I tell him. 'Come on, kiddo, let's go and eat dinner.'

During the meal, Debbie makes efforts at conversation that founder, Julio is terse, Peter bad-mannered and Sue silent. A dispute arises about who's going to clear the table, which ends with me doing all the washing up while the children retreat to their various bedrooms. Debbie hasn't learned yet about cleaning up after yourself as you go, and the kitchen is a mess. I rummage around, looking for cleaning agents: nobody has bought any for some time, and there are only a few containers with dregs in them under the sink. These I water down as best I can, and scrub respect for Johnny into every corner.

Back in the living room, Sue sits inert. I come in, say, 'How are you doing?'

She turns her head away. There has got to be some

better way to help a grieving widow. I'd give a great deal to know it.

'Have you thought of asking the neighbours for help?'

'For what?' she mutters into her lap.

I pause. This is a non building, bigger flats but otherwise much like mine. With Johnny dead, their staple is gone: they're a lyco family in the midst of a nest of nons. She's cut off. Her best bet would be to rely on Johnny's memory – there can't be a man or woman in this building who doesn't know what happened to him. She could put herself in the way of a lot of casseroles and babysitting if she could just get herself together to ask. 'Lots of people would be happy to do things for you, Sue. Cook meals for you, help out with the kids – look, I don't know everyone here, but I bet they would.'

'I don't know.'

'Listen.' I feel desperate, I want to shake her and shake her until she's happy. 'Look, would you like me to ask around? I'm sure I could find some people willing to help, just to tide you over until you're – feeling up to it. Shall I do that?'

She sighs, puts a hand over her face. 'I don't know what's going on any more, Lola,' she says, and her shoulders shake.

I go over to her, lay my hand on hers. 'It's okay, Sue.'

Her face contorts. 'I don't know what's going on, I just can't take it, I –' No sound comes out of her as she sobs.

I don't know what's going on either. I squeeze her hand and crouch by her, mute. She keeps on shaking, and I tell her that I'll call people, I'll phone around and get people to help her out. I'm still bent double over her unresponsive hand when Peter comes in.

He flies at me, shoves me backwards, stands between me and his mother like a tiger. 'What are you doing? You made her cry, don't you make her cry!' he wails at me.

'It's okay, Peter –' I start towards him, and he knocks my outstretched hand away.

'Get out of here!'

'Peter –'

Debbie comes into the room. She runs to her mother and wraps her arms around her, glaring at me. 'It's okay, Mum, it's okay,' she says in a tone of accusation. I look to the doorway and see Julio is standing there too, watching the scene with smouldering eyes. What part of it is putting that look on his eleven-year-old face I can't tell; it may very probably be me.

'It's okay,' I say, and my voice echoes off the walls.

Peter looks from me to his mother and back again, then gathers all his strength into a shriek. 'Go *away*!'

A better woman would have handled this better, a better woman would know what to do now. All I can do is listen to Peter. It's advice of a sort, and I take it. I gather my coat, my bag, myself, and leave without a word.


I go into work the next morning, and I fix it. I need a back-up man, I need authorisation, I need strength of will, and my bare hands. I get clearance without even a question. My first thought is to ask Bride to back me up; she's busy and gives me Nate instead, her little trainee. I brace myself. Downstairs is my man, the man I want some answers from. Today, if there is to be justice, I am to be a dangerous woman.

'I'll lead the interrogation,' I tell Nate. We walk down the steps to the cells as I brief him; our feet clatter and the stairs get dimmer and narrower the deeper we go. 'You hang back. Don't say too much. Back me up.' The thought of bright, damaged Marty comes over me as I'm saying this, it leans on me so hard that I actually stop for a second to rest my hand against the wall. Nate rattles on ahead and I shout. He turns, surprised. I wouldn't have to shout at Marty, I only needed to say things to him once. He listened to me, God damn it, he listened so well it put him in hospital from ignoring his common sense. I wouldn't have to brief him to hang back, Marty was smart. Marty was smart. This sentence claws at me as I stand facing Nate's blank stare, and I shake myself. Marty is smart. And they may yet mend his voice. And I'm about to have some words with the lune who drank his blood.

'Which part of "hang back" did you not understand?' I say to Nate, and walk on past him, pulling rank to override his offended start.

Darryl Seligmann crouches in a corner of his cell. There's a bench at the back he could sit on, and a couple of chairs bolted to the floor; instead, he's back on his heels. Both his thumbs are pressed up against his mouth. His hair hangs down around his face, screening it. He doesn't look up as I turn the key in the lock. It's only when I stalk in and bang the door behind me that he raises his head with a jerk.

I stop in mid-stride. I recognise this man. I've seen him before, just a few weeks ago. It was – that's right, it was the day Leo was born. This man spat at me as I was leaving the building. The spiked hair is trailing down, matted, the fierce eyebrows straggle, but it's the same man.

'What do you want?' he rasps, and it's the same voice I heard before saying 'fucking skins'.

I pocket the keys, and take a seat. Here, in my power, is the man who tore up Marty. And me. I remember feet on my chest, teeth over my face. My fist clenches. 'My friend, you are in so much trouble.'

'What the fuck you got on me?'

He speaks through his teeth, his voice is low. I lower my voice to match it. He's incommunicado, he's spoken to no one on the outside, not even the police. I can do anything to him, anything. 'Why don't we start where it starts. What were you doing out in the moon that night?'

His eyes are black. He hunches under the bench and glares at me. There's something adolescent about his posture, the strained wolfishness of it, knees folded up around his ribs, elbows drawn back, lips in a half-snarl. Other children, lyco children, used to make similar stances at me. His mouth is lacklustre, a stage-growl pulled over crooked teeth, but the lines around his eyes burn. I don't know what he's saying, I just know that by God he means it.

I speak slowly, softly, my back straightens out like a dancer's as I lean towards him. 'What were you doing out on a moon night?'

His lips barely move. 'Fuck you.'

Nate twitches behind me, and I snap my fingers at him to make him stand still. I mustn't look away.

'No. Not me, my friend. You. You are not getting out of here. You want a phone call?' He looks up. 'You can't have one. You want a lawyer? You can't have one. Not till we know what we want to know. And you can stay here for your whole life, if we want you to. So fuck me? I don't think so. You are staying with us, and

102

we are going back to the beginning. Why were you out on a moon night?'

'That's your song, isn't it? Sing another,' he mutters.

'Nate, help me get him into that chair.'

I have my hands on him. Seligmann struggles and kicks, but he's thin, his muscles aren't bulked up like a luning man's, and there's two of us. He isn't luning now, and he can't outfight us both. I cover him with a sleeper gun as Nate cuffs his hands to the chair. 'This'll give you a hell of a headache,' I tell Seligmann. 'Don't make me dope you. You'll fall asleep and we'll just have to do this again some time. And I'd rather have you awake.' He lashes against the cuffs. 'Hold still. You see over there?' I point. There's a dogcatcher pole hanging on the wall just outside the cell. 'We can keep you still with a collar if you prefer. What would you prefer?'

His eyes stay on me and he doesn't answer.

I stand up. There's something black inside me, something coiled. The thought that I can hurt him makes me shake. Do I want to? So much of me does. I draw my hand back, I can feel the cold prison air stroking it, feel every hair on my arm, my hand is bright with life as I swing it hard and slap him.

Cold judders up my arm. Even as my palm touches his face, I freeze in horror at what I'm doing. His head jolts to one side, I did that to him. My palm stings, itches, tingles, what I've done is being branded into it.

Seligmann turns his face back to me and bares his teeth. 'Weak, pussy,' he says. 'You hit like a girl.'

I hit him again before I realise what I'm doing, hook him with a closed fist. Bones in my knuckles knock bones in his jaw, there's so little skin between our bones to protect him. His head snaps back a little way, only a little, as if a rubber band held it in place. 'Better?' I say. I don't recognise this shaking voice as my own.

The eyes blaze, his voice is steadier, stronger than mine. 'Go on,' he says.

I'm shivering, I've never been warm in my life. There's a place on the hand, under the thumb, that never heals if you damage it, an area of almost unprotected nerve. I lean down, half-crouched, almost straddling him. I'm very close to his face as I dig my nail into his hand.

His face clenches, little pants escape him. I lean forward, press my shoulder forward, but I can't make myself dig hard enough to damage him. Seligmann rolls his head like an animal, trying to move himself out of the path of the pain, and it hits me again what I'm doing. I snatch my hand away, grip it, leaving a white dent in him, white dent that floods with red. Healing blood. The bruise I've given him will fade in a day.

I hear him again, a hoarse half-whisper that's lowered for menace. It should be theatrical, I should be able to see through it. 'That's all you can do, kitten,' he says.

My stomach twists, I'm dizzy. Through an effort of will that almost collapses me, I hit him again, flat-handed, three times, left right left. My arm as it jerks around is stiff, awkward, graceless, the fall of his head as it reels from my blows looks assured and steady in comparison.

Seligmann looks at me again. My hand is raised, and I can't hit him, I can't, I physically can't. I have to do something with my hand, so I place it on his head to turn his face towards me. My fingers twitch at the texture of his greasy hair, I can feel the heat of his scalp through it. All I can see is a human being that I'm hurting, and what I want to do is cradle his head, leave my hand there, stroke him, make him better. I hate him. I push

104

his head back a little, and speak into his face. 'Tell me,' I say. 'Tell me what you're doing.'

He doesn't speak. It's my own weakness that's doing this to me, it must be. He can see into me, he can see I can't do this. How can a man tied to a chair still beat me?

'Answer her.' A voice comes from behind me, and I nearly shriek in shock. It's Nate, I'd forgotten about Nate, my world had shrunk to me and Seligmann and nothing else alive. Anger at Nate fills me, the graceless oaf, the idiot, the boy who made me jump. He can see me, he can see the impotence that Seligmann has pulled out of me. My weakness lies on the floor at my feet, pink and spidery and twitching, a raw nerve pulled out for the world to see. I'm hulled out, exposed, filthy.

Seligmann leans his head away from my touch. 'Go on, baby,' he says, 'let's see what you can do.'

I choke. Nausea overwhelms me, there's a terrible moment in which I think I may actually be sick, which recedes and leaves me thankful to the point of desperation for my body's lack of drama. I can't go on. I turn my back on Seligmann, sit in the chair facing him, and focus all my strength on sounding calm. 'You're not doing yourself any good. What are you expecting? Branding irons? Racks? This isn't the Inquisition. You can stop dramatising yourself.' All of this is true, it has to be. He is dramatising himself. It's just me that can't cope with what's going on, that thinks it's real and terrible. 'Why don't you drop the hero mask, it's going to get boring. We're keeping you till we get some sense out of you. And believe me, martyrdom isn't exciting. Whatever you think you're martyring yourself for. Or maybe you just think you're tough. It doesn't matter.'

I have to cut him down to size. He's got to just turn into an ordinary man. That I've hurt him mustn't give him power over me. I focus on his stagey snarl, the melodrama of it, the contrivance, and I can almost look down on him. 'You can be as tough as you like. But you'd be free sooner and save us a lot of trouble if you'd try to make sense.'

He laughs. 'Oh, I make sense,' he says. 'I make sense.' He tips his head on one side. It almost looks comic as he starts the soft chant.

> I caught a little catcher man
> Who tried to collar me.
> He chased me with his silver gun,
> He chased me with his pole,
> I jumped on him, and sat on him,
> And bit him full of holes.

I recognise this, and my muscles pull tight, tension runs up my spine in a wave. I heard it as a child. It should bounce off, but it doesn't, it's like hearing an old joke for the thousandth time when it wasn't funny the first, it's like the fiftieth punch on an already bruised arm. That he would dare be so stupid. And that this time round, it's true.

I look at Nate. Nate steps forward. He shifts on the balls of his feet, he moves into boxing mode. The first three punches hit Seligmann over the solar plexus, a place I never even thought of hitting, all I could think of was his face, but Nate's going in close. His body is inches away from Seligmann's. My hands pulse, and I remind myself that this is nothing I haven't seen before. It's just that I haven't beaten a detainee before, not

106

really. Breaking my cherry. Nate's swiftly-moving body blocks Seligmann's view of me, and I bless Nate for that. Now Seligmann can't see the sickness on my face. I stare hard at Nate's moving back, and try to keep my mind straight on the reasons why this is all right.

All I can come up with is a memory.

> I caught a little rabbit,
> I caught a little flea,
> I caught a little catcher man
> Who tried to collar me.
> He chased me with his silver gun,
> He chased me with his pole,
> I jumped on him, and sat on him,
> And bit him full of holes.
> My mama says I'm naughty,
> I should have let him be –
> But Mama, I was hungry, so –
> *Don't*
> *Blame*
> *Me!*
> They showed me to the jury,
> They showed me to the court,
> They showed me to the bareback judge
> And this is what he thought:
> He'll lock me up for ever,
> He'll throw away the key
> Your Honour, I was hungry, so –
> *Don't*
> *Blame*
> *Me!*

They'll hit me with a catching pole,
They'll chain me in a pit,
They'll push me off the courthouse roof,
They'll chop me into bits,
They'll skin my pretty fur coat off,
They'll drown me in the sea,
But catcher, catcher, I am hungry –
*Can't*
*Catch*
*Me!*

\*

Becca had to pick me up after school. 'It's your job in the family,' my mother would say, which we both knew meant no arguments allowed. My job in the family was less tangible. My mother hardly ever said the phrase to me. It was as if I wasn't part of the contract.

However, it was part of the contract that I had to wait for Becca to pick me up. Her school was a few minutes walk from mine, and finished a quarter of an hour later. I first heard that rhyme on one of those days. Becca had arrived fairly early, before I'd had time to scuff more than the tips of my shoes kicking the desk, and we walked home in a good mood. I was trying to tell her about my piano teacher, I think, who wore long scarves and had red nails that clicked on the keys. Piano lessons were one of the things that my mother insisted on me taking, also insisting that Becca oversee me to make sure I practised. While at first I had resented this effort to turn me into a lady, I was in the process of discovering a liking for it. That I had enjoyed the pretty sounds I could get out of the white keys was, on that day, something of a revelation, and I was trying to communicate it to Becca, while

Becca was trying to explain to me what an octave really meant. I said it was eight notes, and she, from the height of her ten years, had explained that there were different musical scales, and even semitones weren't the only way to measure things.

It's funny how clearly I remember that day.

'I know what an octave is,' I said, 'Miss Dencham showed me, look, it's like this.' I pulled my hand out of her grip and stretched my fingers wide.

'That's not an octave, May, your hand's too small.'

'Is not.'

We rounded a corner. I could feel the warm pavement through my shoes, and there was a summer smell of cut grass from somewhere. Ahead of us was another school, one that neither of us attended. Becca frowned and took my hand in what I thought was an officious grip. 'Come on.'

I pulled my hand away. 'Look, this is an octave, I *can* do one.'

Becca grabbed my hand again. There was a yellow plastic watch on her wrist. 'Come *on*, May, we've got to get past this school.'

'Will they throw stones?' I said – I had just been reading a book in which that happened.

Becca gave me a brief glance of puzzlement, then threw a nervous one at the school. 'No. Come on.'

I don't know why I hadn't heard it. They were chanting. 'Don't Blame Me' is a clapping rhyme, I learned later: you sing it, and whoever's It chases you at the end. As we got nearer, I was able to make out what they were saying.

They were going to eat me.

They didn't know I was a non. Becca took my hand

and yanked me forwards, her head held high and her face scarlet. From a distance, it probably just looked like a girl trying to make her little sister behave.

Becca kept walking, pulling me, with the rhyme going on in the background. The blush on her face was one that I was to see a great deal in the future. Even when I wasn't around, I think she was uncomfortable when people called attention to how different nons are, and there she was in public, with people out-and-out *singing* it, and she was stuck with her non little sister. She marched forward, saying to me, 'Just keep going, May.'

If she hadn't pulled me, I might have walked by. Gone home and cried. But Becca's tugs on my arm infuriated me, and between her trying to jerk me into pretending it didn't matter, and the children behind the fence chanting, I lost control of myself.

I gave a mighty pull and freed my hand from Becca's. The clapping children stopped their rhyme to see the drama that my mad dash was promising, and I ran up against the fence, shouting at them. And then, of course, they cottoned on. I was shouting, 'I'll catch you! I'll catch you!' It crazed me that I could think of nothing to shout at them that was as bad as the jokes they'd been throwing around, quite casually, about me. I was in that state of fury that only children feel, fury that can crack you in half, fury that you know will never go away, that no more thinks of calming down than of considering the devil's point of view.

They started laughing, pointing. 'Bareback! Bareback!' I shook the fence and someone shouted, 'Look at her soft little hands! Come and get us, bareback!' Another started up a new rhyme, and they all took it up.

I shrieked, and Becca came up behind me. She grabbed

me around the waist, and pulled me, struggling, all the way past the playground into the next street.

The horror doesn't leave me. I don't understand how it is that a nursery rhyme enables me to sit back and watch one man beat another. But a childish slur is a hard one to deal with. It seems so immense at the time, the fact that it maddens you and no one cares is something that can never be understood. I stare at Nate's back because it is not in itself a violent thing.

I am ashamed of myself. I am holding a nursery rhyme as a talisman against torture.

There is no excuse for what we do to him.

Nate steps back, a little winded, and cracks his knuckles. I look at him, and although he's of my kind, I'm almost more frightened of him than I am of Seligmann. It strikes me that I've been pretending to myself that he was performing a task, going through a series of motions, and that the nature and quality of those motions was not important. And he was. That's what it was to him. His face is almost undisturbed.

I think he's damaged Seligmann's ribs. There's blood around his lips, his spine strains against the chair, bending inwards. His posture is crouched for real now. I can hear every breath he takes.

I open my mouth, but Seligmann speaks first. 'Best you can do?' There's cancer in his voice, gravel, hours of shouting, only he hasn't screamed once. He spits through his teeth, pink liquid. It may be that he's only bitten his tongue.

111

I ask him the question that I've been wanting to ask all my life, of every wolf in man's clothing that I've ever known. Even as I ask him, I'm cold, heavy, because I know he won't give me an answer that'll satisfy me.

'Why did you try to kill us?'

I want the answer to this with every fibre of me. Nate leans against the door, not that interested. He becomes almost unreal in my sight, a man of straw. It's Seligmann who knows what's at stake.

Seligmann grins, panting; blood rims his teeth. 'Tasty girl. Wouldn't you take a bite?'

'Stop it.' My voice is soft, as if speaking through a headache. 'I'm not asking you for jokes. I want to know. Why did you attack us? We wouldn't have hurt you.'

The irony of me saying this to a man I've just watched beaten with hard and exact science doesn't even occur to him. 'You couldn't of.'

'Why then?'

'Shit.' He dabs his tongue against a bright wet cut on his lip, one that I put there. 'If you've got to ask, you wouldn't understand.'

I almost laugh, it's such a ridiculous thing, such a sharp thing to say. My throat hurts. Every inch of him must hurt. 'Enlighten me.'

I get up and walk towards him. I don't know why. That I can hit him, twist him, compress him, is something that I've almost forgotten. He turns his head up towards me, and flinches away. 'Bitch,' he says. 'Go on, I don't fucking care. I've got you going. I should've slashed your face off when I had the chance.'

I shrug hard, and force a tough answer out of myself. 'Maybe so. But I've got you by the balls now, haven't I?'

He grimaces, moves his arms against the handcuffs.

'You don't have me, bitch. You can't get me. You and your kind, you think you're worth something? No chance. Just freaks, that's all you are. Soulless. Cripples. You're not even alive. You're going down.'

'Soulless?' Soulless? That's not a word he'd use. It can't be. Insults, curses, rhymes, these I've heard before, and from him, they make sense. They don't account for why he scares me, but they make sense. And now he's talking about souls? It should sound weird in his mouth, like he was quoting someone else, only it doesn't. He spoke with force and conviction, his beliefs alive on every battered inch of him.

Seligmann looks at me for a moment, a clear straight look, and for just that moment there's nothing posed or contrived on his face. He looks at me like he might look at a fish gasping out of water, with distaste and distance and no feeling at all. Then he drops his head. Hair hides his face again, and what I see is a man, a hurt, injured, tired man slumped in a chair. He doesn't look up when I try to talk to him. Nate stays leaning against the wall, a little frustrated by how the interrogation's going, a little annoyed at being out of things. And I stand over Seligmann, boneless, exposed, and bereft, with no answers to my questions.

# 7

Something has happened to my fingers, they won't fan out, they won't stay straight. They're concussed. They stumble over each other as I try to type.

> Recommended action: suspect should be held in detention. His behaviour may or may not indicate

What could it indicate? He never said he was up to anything.

> His behaviour may be general hostility, or indicative of a more serious problem.

My bones are hollow, there's cold air inside them. Something's eating at me. A death-watch beetle, chipping away, leaving white mazes of cold air behind it till my skeleton is light as a bird's. It's going to keep mining me till I'm shredded into a dried-out honeycomb, then flex its wings and fly out of my mouth. I can hear it chipping.

'That's your watch, Galley,' I mutter, and push my mouth against my wrist. My fingers are dancing, rippling as if in a strong wind. I suppose I must be shaking.

The reasons for his behaviour are unclear, but his hostility appeared unusual, and it may be best to monitor him for a while. Subject has made no request for visitors or legal counsel.

I look out of the window and there's a storm coming in; the sky is the colour of an over-boiled egg yolk, green and sulphurous.

I want this report finished. If I could finish it, I could have some coffee and warm up. I'd like very much to dash through it and do a slack job, but I can't dash if I can think of nothing to say.

In the light of these facts, it would seem that detaining him here is feasible.

What made me want to be a lawyer? I don't think I ever believed I'd set the world to rights. I've ended up sitting at a desk using words like 'feasible', and there must be some good reason why I got here.

There's a knock at my door. I don't want to answer it, really, I don't want anyone to see me sitting here with my veins showing through my skin, but another person might bring some heat into the room.

'Come in.'

A head comes round the door, and the cold spills out of my bones and into my flesh. 'Is this a bad time?' says the face.

'No,' I say before I have time to think of a truthful answer. 'It's all right. Paul Kelsey, yes?'

'That's right,' says Paul Kelsey, and the next thing I know he's sitting opposite me. 'How are you?'

'Fine. I'm fine. Sorry, I –' My voice sticks in my mouth.

'Are you okay?' He puts his head on one side and frowns at me.

'I —' I touch my forehead, blink hard, my hands won't keep still. 'Sorry, I'm having a bit of a day.'

'Mm.' He nods, perfectly pleasant.

'Are you here to talk about Jerry Farnham?' This is practical, this I think I can handle.

'Well, I was passing.' He's just sitting there looking happy. He's bigger than I remembered, a tall man. What's he doing bringing his happy self into my cramped-up office?

'You could have made an appointment, you know. My telephone works very well.'

He ducks his head for a moment, then shrugs. 'I could. You're right.' I haven't made a dent in his good mood. 'But then, I thought I'd just say hello.'

'Don't you say hello on the phone?'

'No,' he says reflectively, 'I say, social services, how may I help you. Or I say my name. Are you too busy? Because I can always come back another time.'

'No.' I run my hand through my hair. 'No, I'm sorry. Look . . .' I shake my head, trying to clear it; my brain knocks to and fro against my skull and I give myself a headache. This is no good. 'We seem to have got off to rather an odd start. It's mostly my fault, but can we just take it from here? Because we do need to sort out Jerry's case.'

'Yes, we do.' He gives me a look of amusement.

'Well, don't look at me,' I hear myself say. 'I'm trying to sort this out as much as you are, pal.'

'I'm sure.' The amused look lingers, then his face sobers up. 'How's your sister, by the way?'

'What?'

'Your . . .' He sketches in the air. 'That night in the bar, you were talking about your sister.'

'Oh, Christ.' I bury my face in my hands. 'Do we have to do this? I'm trying to be a professional.'

'Have to do what?' He gives me a wounded glance, still looking entertained.

'I was halfway out of my skull, I was off duty. You don't have to rub it in.'

'You were pretty interesting, really.' His face is dangerously close to a grin. 'Anyway, who's talking? I was coming on to you. I was pretty off duty myself.'

'Oh.' My head comes off my hands and we look at each other. The room goes quiet. 'Were you?'

I wait for him to answer, wait seconds and seconds. A pulse is beating in my throat. He draws a breath. The silence stays between us, thickens, goes solid.

'Was I what?' he says, too late.

I look back down at my desk. 'Never mind.'

I glance through my fringe at him. He doesn't look amused any more. His mouth chews itself, and then he raises his eyebrows. His face is talking to itself, and I can't understand what it's saying. He sits still in the chair.

One of us has to say something.

My hands rest on the table, inert. I flex my fingers, drum them against the surface, and look up at him. With a tug of self-control, I even manage something like a wry grin. 'Well. If we leave aside my drunk ramblings and your kerb crawling, we can still talk about Jerry Farnham.'

'Jerry Farnham. Yes.' He slaps his palm against his leg and sits up. It's an arresting mixture of gestures, the slap like a middle-aged man, then his shoulders shifting

117

like a boy's as he straightens. I stop myself wondering about his age, and put my eyes back on his face, his black-lashed eyes.

'Yes, Jerry.' I push my hair off my forehead. 'Now. Have you found him an AA group yet?'

'Yes, though that doesn't guarantee that he'll go there. I mean,' he leans his elbows on the table, so far forward that he's almost lying down, 'it's going to be hard to get him to make any real commitment to helping himself. It's not exactly relaxing, what he's going through with the loitering charge. I mean, my problem is his general welfare.'

'Your problem?' I say.

'Mm?'

'I just thought I heard you say you were going to take some work off my back.'

He looks pleased. 'Well, you shouldn't have to take away his whisky.'

'No, I'd just drink it myself. You were saying?'

'That as far as we're concerned, it's the short-term problem, which is getting him off the loitering charge. Do you think you can do that?' His tone has gone professional. It sits oddly with his casual posture. He scrubs a hand against his head, looking up at me and waiting for an answer.

'Well.' I tap the table, think about it. This is my area. 'Do you want it in detail?'

'Do you have time?'

I think about what I'll have to go back to if he leaves. 'Yes. Hold on.' I talk to him over my shoulder as I get out the file. My hands are a little steadier than they were. 'It could go either way. Clearly he did what he's charged with, the best we can hope for is a suspended sentence. And whether I can get that or not depends on how world-weary the judge is.'

Probably that's an improper thing to say to an outsider, but he doesn't seem to mind. 'As in, I've seen too many like him, send him down?'

I turn. 'Hell, no. As in, why bother looking after him in prison.' I look at him. 'Have you worked with DORLA before?'

He shakes his head. 'No. My first time. Any advice welcome.'

He's new to this, new to everything about us. No scars. DORLA people don't get government services when they have problems; we have to take care of our own. Social workers only get involved when there's a lyco client. It occurs to me that it's just possible I'm the first non he's ever had a conversation with.

I sit down, lay the file on my lap, trying to sort what I want to say into words. If I was talking to Bride, I wouldn't have to, I could just pull a face and leave it unsaid and she'd know what I was talking about. And I've never tried explaining it to a lyco before. For some reason, it seems important. 'What we want is an exhausted man who can't be bothered to follow through with the law. It's one of those laws that a lot of us would ignore if we could. I mean, not every case, there's a lot of people cause us a lot of trouble loitering, but the screw-ups like Jerry . . . The thing is, none of us make the laws, and they don't always work. I'm sorry, I'm not saying this right.'

He's studying me. 'Go on.'

I slip my hand inside the file, feel cool smooth paper. 'We just have to carry out the laws. I mean, if you work for DORLA you can't be a politician, a civil servant, any of those types, so none of us get to make the laws, we just have to carry them out. Even if they don't really stick. And – and with Jerry, the law isn't going to help at all. It's just a rule we've got to do something with if someone breaks it. We – we – everyone has feelings about it. We just need a judge who can't face following through with the whole business.'

I can't believe I've said all that to a stranger. I just said all that to a lyco.

'Why?' he says.

'Why what?'

'Why do you have to do something with the rules?'

'Instead of ignoring them?' My voice sounds quiet in my own ears. 'Look, Kelsey, you just get to share my client. You don't get to come in here and question my career.'

'No,' he says, just as quietly. 'I guess not.'

I look at him again, but he's looking at my arms, my wrist buried in the file.

The telephone rings, making me jump.

'I –' I make some gestures, grasping air, and turn to the phone. 'Excuse me.'

The receiver is chilly against my ear. 'Lola?' It's Josie.

'Speaking.' I keep my eyes down, aimed at my in-tray.

'Lo, I've got some good news. You know Marty?'

'Marty?' Do I know Marty? I clutch the phone with both hands.

'We've just got a call from the hospital. The doctors said he said something today.'

'He –' I swallow. 'He said – ?'

'His voice came back, Lo.' Josie sounds a little

hoarse. So do I. It's the news we've all been waiting for. 'Now, the doctors said it's not definite, he could have a relapse, or get an infection or something, I don't know, but –'

She hastens on, and the phone goes loose in my grip. 'Ohh . . .' It's all I can say. 'Ohh . . .'

'Are you all right?' Kelsey is on his feet, all ready to fetch me a glass of water or open a window for me, and I wave him back into his chair. All I can feel is relief, a great cool wave of relief like a waterfall washing down my back.

'Josie, that's great,' I manage. 'Thanks.' And I set the phone down in its cradle, gently so as not to break it, not to damage the news. My arms are weightless and clumsy, as if a great load had just been taken out of them. A smile is coming out of my mouth, spreading across me.

'Are you all right? Can I get you some coffee or something?' A voice sounds in front of me. I open my eyes and smile at its beautiful owner.

'Coffee,' I say, 'would be lovely.'

I sit back and enjoy watching him make it. He leaves the jar out of its box, and I don't suppose it really matters. He's even quite tidy, for a man, I reflect cheerfully. I watch him as he frowns with concentration, screwing the top back onto the jar, and then puts it down on the table and forgets about it as he turns his attention to the kettle. He passes me the mug and I wrap my hand around it, hold it against my face. I'm warm.

'Have you had good news?' he says. The idea seems to please him.

'Yes. Yes, I have.' I touch my heated cheek and hold

121

the cup against the other one. 'A friend of mine has been in hospital, but I've just heard he's going to be okay. Or they think so, anyway.'

'Lola, that's wonderful.' What's he doing saying my name, I wonder, and then lie back in my chair again. The coffee is as bad as you'd expect cheap instant to be. I'm enjoying it.

'What was wrong with him?' Kelsey says. I think he's trying to decide whether to look polite or curious.

'A maul.'

'A mall? Like a shopping mall? Was he in an accident?'

I put down my coffee. Really I should know this for what it is, cosseted ignorance, but I'm too relieved to hold it against him. Instead, I grin. 'You really haven't worked here before, have you?' And I move my nails in a clawing motion across my throat.

His eyes widen and he shifts in his chair. He puts his fingernails in his mouth, a gesture that makes him look younger. 'Oh,' he says. 'Well, I'm sorry.'

'No point in fidgeting about it, it wasn't you,' I say, and shrug. 'And he didn't die in the end.' I suppose it's wrong of me to rub it into him like that. I think it's upsetting him. He's just so different. He doesn't turn his head with a flinch like a horse twitching off a fly. I've seen that so often, and it's not what he's doing. He moves his shoulders to and fro, it's a fly he's not shaking off. I don't want him to suffer, really I don't, but I have just a little power sitting in my hand, just a little piece that's dropped into it without warning, and it's hard not to feel it.

Finally he looks up at me, and the power slips through my fingers. 'Does that happen a lot?' he says.

I lay my hands together; my voice is quite light. 'It happens to all of us sometimes.'

'Sorry,' he says. His face is talking again. If he was tiptoeing or offering condolences I don't think I could take it; but this look is much better. He really does look sorry, in an innocent sort of way. It's almost like a kid offering me a biscuit, convinced that it will solve my problems.

I let the air out of my lungs. I'm about to reply when I remember that Marty is going to be all right again, and the smile comes back onto my face and goes through me. I get to my feet, walk across the office. 'I think I'm going to visit him,' I say. 'You don't mind, do you? Only we could do this another day, and I'd really like to see him, I haven't seen him since – since he got hurt, and being that it was my fault and all,' I unhook my coat from the door, 'I'd like to see him, even if it means braving his relatives again.'

Kelsey's also on his feet. 'Sure, sure. How are you getting there?'

'How am I –? By bus, why?'

'Well, I could drive you.' He raises an eyebrow, gives me an enquiring look.

'Oh.' I pause in draping my coat over my arm.

'Or are you worried about the planet?'

'Hell no.' I laugh. 'I just don't have a car. Yes, thanks, a lift would be great.'

Getting past reception without being caught leaving before quitting time turns into a little adventure. We pull it off by having Kelsey talk to the girl on the desk – not Josie, some new rookie we haven't settled yet – while I sneak by, my attention apparently on some papers in my hand. We get the lift to ourselves and grin to each other in silence, then walk through the downstairs lobby with the guiltless stride of people who have other matters on their minds.

'If there's anything I've learned in an ill-spent life,' I remark as I settle into the seat of his car, 'it's that the best way to avoid getting caught is to look like you're doing it on purpose.' His car is an old green hatchback, I notice with the critical eye of a woman who can't afford her own vehicle; it's clean, except for having muddy wheels. Something knocks my feet as he starts the engine, and I pick it up: a large rubber ball. 'What's this?'

'What's what?' he says, his eyes on the road.

'This ball.'

'It's a ball. I use it when I'm visiting very young kids sometimes.'

'Mm. Do you have anatomically correct dolls in the back seat?'

He takes his eyes off the road and looks at me.

I cover my mouth. 'Sorry. I don't know where that came from.'

He looks at me a moment longer, then his mouth twitches and he laughs. 'No big deal. At least you said it.'

'Oh, I'm kind of thinking it would have been better if I'd *not* said it.'

'I don't know. I reckon you're better at coming out with things.'

'In the five minutes you've known me,' I risk saying. 'And I don't know where you got that idea.'

He grins to himself and looks at the road. Being pleased by my odd remarks is something he has no business doing, but I'm still too relieved to care. There's another silence, less tense than the ones in my office. We're driving past Abbots Park, one of my favourites in the daytime. The road around it is a little raised, and the outer circle is ringed with trees. The park turns under my eye as we follow the curve of the road round it.

'Can I ask?' he says.

I take my eyes off the bare, clean branches. 'Ask?'

'Your friend. You said it was your fault.'

As I lean my head back against the car seat, it comes to me that I haven't really explained it to anyone. I've written reports and justified myself here and there; putting it into words is something else.

'It was, I guess. He's my trainee. We were out on a – patrol –'

'You may as well say dogcatch. I know that's what you say.' He doesn't look at me. His voice is expressionless.

I frown. 'It's no worse a word than bareback.'

He glances at me. 'No, you're right. But that's not a word I say.'

'Oh.' I push my hair off my face. I should answer this, only I can't think of anything to say, so I carry on. 'Well, he'd messed up before, so I told him we had to go by the book. And that meant that when we ran into a group of bad lunes, he wasn't carrying his tranquilliser gun, because we're not supposed to use them except in a real crisis. So –' I speak quietly, 'they attacked him, and he didn't have his gun out. And they mauled him.'

There's a moment of quiet before he replies, only the noise of the engine. 'Is that what you were drowning out when I met you that night in the bar?' he says.

I close my eyes, trying not to feel disappointed. I had no reason to expect him to say something comforting. 'That was it. Mostly.'

'You shouldn't feel guilty.' This isn't said in a consoling tone, it's said deadpan.

I make a very quiet noise, turn to stare out of the window. We're past Abbots Park.

'You shouldn't.' His tone is flat, yet for some reason it doesn't match the drabness of the streets. 'Of course it was your fault. Nobody could go through life doing what you do and make no mistakes. Look at that scar on your arm.'

'I –' I make a gesture, push against the air. 'Maybe I should walk.'

'I'm not trying to insult you. Please calm down.' He actually says please, like he was asking for something. I keep my head turned away, fighting what he's just said.

He talked about my arm. He remembers the scar there. Oh, God. Ten years, ten years of long sleeves and keeping my arm to my side if I wear a pretty dress, one misjudged moment when I was a girl of eighteen and now I have a great worm dug into my flesh that'll never go away. That's what he remembers about me.

He doesn't even sound too upset. 'Lola, I don't mean you're to blame, all I was saying was that your job's dangerous. If you hunt lunes, people are going to get hurt. It's not your fault if it happens sometimes. You were just –'

He trails off and his mouth chews itself.

'– within the margin of error,' I finish for him softly. 'Yeah.'

I hang my head. I'm sulking like a child, that must

126

be what it looks like from the outside. It's just too hard to pull myself together.

'But he's going to be all right,' Paul Kelsey says.

'Yeah,' I say. 'Yeah, he is.'

'Are you all right? Look, I didn't mean to offend you.' He taps the steering wheel, making an ironic mouth. 'I just think aloud sometimes.' He shrugs. 'Ask anyone.'

'You think aloud? In your job?'

'Well, no. Off duty.'

'So you're – off duty?' I say the phrase carefully. It's what he said about coming on to me in the bar. It weighs in my mouth, heavy with potential and danger.

He turns his head, looks at me. I can't read his face, I don't know his face, there's nothing I know about him. I have to find some way of reading his face –

The car swerves, jolting me out of my panic. Some careless driver cut across him, he's only just seen it.

I look away. The moment's past, we're safe again. 'Didn't know I'd be dicing with death when I accepted this lift,' I tell him. It's an easy thing to say.

He shrugs. 'What can I say? I'm just a bad driver. No help for it.' He steadies the car. 'Look, I didn't mean to offend you, what I said about –'

'Kelsey,' I say. 'Spade. Hole. Digging. Stop.'

He smiles. The truth is, it's a few minutes since he said it, and once the shock's worn off, I feel almost good about it. It's a change from struggling against all the well-meant lies about how it wasn't my fault. It's almost peaceful. Like the buzz in your mouth after the first burn of a spice wears off.

*

This does not, however, prepare me for the fact that when we get to St Veronica's, he doesn't drop me off in the car park but escorts me right the way inside. We're halfway down the corridor and he's still there, shoes squeaking on the shiny linoleum. I keep almost asking him why he's following me, and then not doing it.

'I'm here to see Sean Martin,' I tell the receptionist. 'Can you tell me what ward he's on?'

'Visiting doesn't start for another half hour,' she says, without looking up from her computer. Kelsey looks around, looking for somewhere to sit, I think, and I undergo a brief conflict. I could sit down with him, or I could get in to see Marty. It won't be hard to force my way in. The thought makes me lose strength, because he'll see me for what I am, a non, I'll turn from a person to a frozen-skinned freak in front of his eyes. It's a bad idea. So I decide to do it, already angry with him for judging me.

'This is a business matter,' I say hard enough to drag her eyes off the screen, and put my DORLA card in front of her face.

She looks at the card, and then at me. Her smoothly powdered face unsettles, shows itself. If she were luning, she'd be pacing the cage, baring her teeth and worrying the bars. 'I'll phone you through,' she mutters.

This is the hospital Leo was born in. The two of us pass the labour ward, and indeed, I see the man who delivered him, the elegant Dr Parkinson, sauntering down the corridor. He looks even sleeker without his green paper hat.

128

'Dr Parkinson,' I hail him.

'Good morning, Miss . . .' he looks at me, trying to place me.

'Galley, May Galley. You delivered my nephew last month.'

'Ah yes.' He looks genuinely pleased. 'Have you named him yet?'

'Leo.'

'A good name, that. I had an uncle called Leo.' His smile is impressive. Strong teeth, well-kept skin, assurance. He looks like my father, like my father's friends. The relaxed, nourished look, the look of people who don't worry about paying their rent, people who walk down the streets and watch other people defer to them. Or hate them for what they have. It's still regard of a sort.

It's a look I never had. A year ago, before that stupid ruinous night, before Leo's conception and her husband's desertion, Becca used to look like that. Looking at the man who delivered my nephew somehow brings home to me how the gloss has faded from Becca's skin.

'He's a bonny boy,' I say.

'Excellent,' says Parkinson, looking at his watch.

I make the excuse to keep walking before he can do it.

'That man doesn't appreciate my nephew,' I whisper to Kelsey. For some reason I don't try to fathom, this is only half a joke.

'May?' says Kelsey.

'Yes?' I respond automatically.

'I thought you said your name was Lola.'

'Oh . . .' I shrug. 'May's my middle name. My family call me May.'

129

'How come?'

'Just do. It says Lola May on my birth certificate. They called me Lola at the creches.' I say the word, creches, almost without a flinch.

'Creches?'

For a social worker, he's not very well informed. 'DORLA creches.'

'Oh.' He nods to himself. I tense, waiting for him to go awkward, sympathetic, but instead he just takes it on board. I guess he hasn't heard the stories. Or else he's seen worse.

'You know, for a social worker, you're not very well informed.'

'For a lawyer, you're not very diplomatic,' he bats back at me.

'I'm not a lawyer, I haven't the training.'

'Fair enough.'

Being rude to him doesn't seem to get a rise, and for a moment I have the urge to be ruder. Probably I'm curious, or I just want someone to take things out on. Then we get to Marty's floor. I clutch my hands together as we reach the ward door.

There are rows of beds in here, all with curtains hanging around them, off-cuts of some cheap printed fabric on metal frames. I can feel the thinness of the mattresses from where I'm standing. Falling back a little, I hang closer to Paul Kelsey. To my annoyance, and also unsettlement, I feel his hand on my arm in a brief touch. 'It's okay,' he mouths at me.

I scowl at him, clear my throat. 'Thank you, Mr Kelsey,' I say in as stern a voice as I can produce.

'I'll wait,' he says.

I see the bed, Marty's bed. Kelsey sits himself down

a little distance from it, and I unclasp my hands, and walk towards it to pull back the curtain.

There he lies. Marty turns his head at the scrape of curtain-ring on rail, and his eyes widen a bit at the sight of me, surprised. I look at him. I can't get my face to move. Bandages, a drip, hospital sheets. They've trussed his throat, buried it under white cloth. They've pinned a bag of water to his arm, and laid him flat on an ironed white bed with salt water going drop by drop into the pale fragile flesh inside his elbow.

I stand and watch this, and I have to reconcile it with the expressions on Marty's face. He isn't looking at the end of the world, there are no burning cities or toppled towers in what he sees. He looks so ordinary. A little look of surprise to see me, and then his face crinkles up in a smile. It's a young smile, rather gauche, not quite relaxed and full of hope that life may yet turn out well.

The boy is actually pleased to see me.

'Marty,' I say.

I'm not prepared for his voice. 'Hi Lola,' it says, and it's hoarse, scoured, as if someone took a tool and scraped and scraped it dry. They said he could talk again, the doctors said he had his voice back. They lied. This isn't his voice.

'How are you?' Marty says.

Marty thinks I'm a grown-up. I have no business showing him a weak face.

'Well enough, kiddo,' I say. 'Good to see you sitting up again.'

He smiles back. I wish I'd brought flowers. 'Doctor

131

says my voice come back fine.' He chokes on the C of come, swallowing the previous word.

'How are you bearing up, kid?' I say. I say *bearing up* rather than *how are you*. Bearing up is what he's going to have to do.

Marty shrugs. 'Okay.' His face is pale, his eyes don't quite meet mine when he says this.

'Managing okay? I mean, apart from the injuries and the nightmares?'

He gives me a startled, caught-out look.

'We all have nightmares, Marty.' I lay my hand on his foot. It's as close as I can get to gentleness.

Marty bites his lip. If he had his voice, I think he'd say something. There's nothing he can say, though, not really. What they did to his throat is keeping him from filling the air with polite chit-chat.

'This is just what happens,' I say into the silence. 'You learn to live with it.'

He plucks at the blanket.

'I know,' I say, 'the last thing you want is some patronising woman telling you your life's going to be no good.'

Marty makes a whispering sound, non-committal.

I draw hospital air into my lungs. 'I'm sorry about what happened,' I say. 'It was mostly my fault.'

'S'okay,' Marty croaks. 'Mine too.'

'Well,' I grip his foot, 'you'd have been better armed if you hadn't listened to me. Except you hadn't much choice in that either.'

'Nor did you,' Marty says. He speaks quietly. He could just be being friendly, or it could be he's already resigning himself. With so few words, it's hard to know.

I breathe in again. 'We've got one of the prowlers

who did it,' I say. 'Not the other ones. We're checking hospitals for people coming in with a silver-bullet injury, the one you shot in the leg, but nothing yet.'

Marty doesn't say anything. It's quiet as a moon night in here.

'I'm sorry,' I say. 'Your throat will heal up, and you'll be okay. You'll just have a few scars. Maybe you can grow a beard.'

Marty feels his face. He has such a sweet smile.

'I'm sorry.' I keep on saying it.

The hand feeling his young-skinned, beardless face shivers in the air. Marty gives it a hunted look, clenches it and drops it by his side. He gives me a look to see if I noticed.

I'm sitting right here, I can't pretend I didn't. 'Don't worry about it,' I tell him. 'It's just catcher's twitch.' I try to make it sound minor.

'I'm going to have that?' Marty's voice comes out in a thin wail.

I pat him, cursing myself. I should have ignored it. 'Everyone gets it. It passes. Anyway, it's not such a bad thing. If a shrink objects to it, then you just get some moon nights off. That can't be bad, right, kiddo?'

Marty bites his lip. I shouldn't have said anything. There are twitchers in every building. You see them, restless, contorting, their faces rippling constantly like a puddle when it rains. Most of us are nice to them, most of us know it's one way we could end up, but they're not popular. Talking to them feels ill-fated. And Marty's not out of his teens, he's a baby, still not sure of his looks, his manner, his luck. I don't see him getting many dates if he gets the twitch.

'Everyone gets it sometimes,' I tell him. 'Ask around.

Me included, one time. It passes.' It was only for a few hours I had it.

I remember hospital sheets, a thin pillow too small for its case. Mouldings around the light fitting in the ceiling, and no light bulb in it. I stared at those mouldings for hours. The pain was hanging over me, threatening, just an inch away from my flesh, and if I moved, I knew it might settle back in. I kept almost moving, and then stopping. Then my face contracted and I felt it setting in. The left-hand side of my face was tugging, buzzing. Twitching. I pulled myself out of bed, bandages trailing, and stared at myself in the mirror, watching my left eye jump, standing straight-backed. I stood there for three hours, breathing in, breathing out, breathing in, staring at the eye. My stitched-up flesh pulsed, and my legs went numb, but I did not go back to bed, I stood on my cold feet, watching. I don't let myself remember any other pain. Three hours, and I made it go away.

'Yeah?' says Marty, and I re-enter the hospital, the present day.

I can't look at such hope. 'Yeah,' I say, with as much firmness as I can invoke. 'You're going to be just dandy.'

It isn't long before a nurse comes along and ushers me out. I get halfway down the ward before I remember that Paul Kelsey is waiting for me.

The nurse gives me a look as I go back for him. I let him. Of the things I could feel right now, feeling ridiculous is the easiest.

Kelsey is waiting patiently at the end of Marty's bed. The curtains have been drawn again. 'Sorry,' I say, and we go out together, the nurse hanging over us until we get out into the corridor.

We stand in the lift. I don't have a thing to say.

'What's catcher's twitch?' It's a shock to hear a healthy male voice after Marty's husked-out croak and my subdued alto.

'You were bloody listening?' I snap before I can stop myself.

Kelsey bites a fingernail. 'Well, I was right on the other side of the room.'

'And you can't bother to pretend you didn't hear?'

'Oh.' This seems to clear the matter up for him. I can't believe I said anything so stupid. 'Sorry.'

I glare at him, and he keeps looking at me. He shrugs, looking helpless.

I steady myself on the lift wall. I may as well tell him. 'What it sounds like,' I say. 'We get worked over by lyco shrinks once a year to see if we've got it. It isn't always much, just a twitching eye or a shaking hand. It's not that uncommon, really. No one deals well with dogcatching, at least, no one you can trust. The ones who don't get bothered by it, they're the people you should be worried about. And it passes.' I hold on to that thought. 'It does pass.'

'That's okay then, isn't it?'

I can't have him think Marty's making a fuss about nothing. I lower my voice a little, speaking carefully. 'It's not good if it gets into your brain. You can get paranoid, unreliable. Not so useful any more. I guess you'd call it post-traumatic syndrome or something like that. There . . . There have been incidents.'

'Oh.'

The bell rings, and the lift door opens. We step out,

head towards the exit. I can feel my heart beating all through my chest and stomach.

We get as far as the foyer, and then stop. I lean against the ochre-painted wall, next to a plastic-coated sign warning me about the dangers of meningitis. There's a picture on it of someone cradling their head in their hands.

I lean against the wall, rest my head against it.

'He'll be okay,' says Paul Kelsey. I hear him through my closed eyes. At the sound of his voice, I lift my head up and look at him.

'Kelsey,' I say. 'Do you have any scars?'

'Scars?'

All I can do is say it again. 'Do you have any scars?'

He keeps looking at me. 'I've got one on my head, I guess. Under my hair. Hit my head on a window frame . . . it's not a very interesting story. Look.' He bends his head, parts his hair. There's just a little glimmer of white amongst the black locks.

'Big ones? Any scars over two inches long?'

'No.' He shakes his head, looking at me. Curious.

I inhale, draw a deep, long breath, and look back at him. 'Why don't you ask me out to dinner?'

# 8

We're huddled into a little alcove, white-painted bricks and red-cushioned seats. It's dark in the restaurant. Mood lighting, or just forty-watt bulbs. There's a candle on the table, a red one stuck into a wine bottle already thick with trickles of melted wax, and we actually need it to see. As I pull out a cigarette, Paul reaches out and picks up the bottle to light it for me.

'Thank you.' I find that as I say this, my shoulders untense a little. It's been so long since I was polite.

'You're welcome.'

'Want one?' I proffer the pack.

He shakes his head.

'Please don't tell me you're a non-smoker.' Lyco or not, I hope he smokes. He has to have vices. I can't get along with someone who doesn't have vices.

'I . . .' He plays with the wax on the bottle. He isn't fidgeting; for some reason it really does interest him. 'I used to smoke. Just about everyone I work with does, after a while. But I kept waking up in the night.' He detaches a little red stalactite and fingers it.

'Craving or coughing?' Both of these are situations I know.

'Craving, mostly. It was more that if I woke up,

rather than just going back to sleep like a sensible man, I'd decide that I wanted a cigarette instead.' He looks rueful, as if this habit of his is beyond his understanding.

'So you quit?' I blow the smoke away from him.

'No.' He sighs. 'That would have been making a production of it. I would have got fed up with not being allowed any cigarettes, I would have just ended up smoking again. I made a pact with myself. I could smoke, but I was only allowed to smoke Gauloise brand.'

I cough, a giggle entangling itself in my mouthful of smoke. I don't know why this seems so funny. 'Gauloise? They go with artistic temperament and iron lungs, don't they?'

'Yeah.' He smiles, like he's achieved something. 'They're not very nice. And I feel like a prat smoking them. It kind of discouraged me.'

I let myself laugh, pressing back against the hard, smooth wall. I'm still shaky but it feels good to laugh. Some of the cold starts to leave me.

He's still toying with his little piece of wax. He turns it round, rolling it to and fro. His fingertips are a little weathered, flat at the ends like a workman's.

'Enjoying your piece of wax?' I say.

He looks at me. There's something ingenuous about his expression, and I wish I hadn't said that. Why am I bothering him about the wax? He can play with it if he wants to.

Then he lifts it up and shows it to me. 'Look how wavy it is,' he says. It's a bumpy piece of wax, uneven on one side because it's set in droplets. I suppose it's kind of pretty, if you're determined to find things to be pleased about.

'It's a nice shape,' I say. It's as easy to say something nice about it as something sarcastic.

'Here, feel how smooth.' He takes my hand and touches it to the surface. A little nub of wax presses into my skin, and his fingertips are resting lightly on my thumb. Our hands stop. Both of us sit and look out, not at each other but at our touching hands, raised high in front of us, holding onto a scrap of red candle.

One of us has to pull away. I'm about to lower my hand, because if someone has to break the moment I'd rather it was me, when he takes hold of my fingers. He picks up the index finger, then releases it and takes the middle one, handling it as if it were candle wax, studying it. Then he spreads my hand over his like a palm-reader.

I look away. 'Don't tell me you've never seen a non's hands before,' I say. Because my palm is lying open across his, smooth-skinned, a tenderfoot palm, unmistakably bareback.

'I've seen this one,' he says, playing with it. 'You showed it to me the first time you saw me, remember?'

I stare into my lap. I showed him my hands to make him go away. Is he reminding me of that?

He bends the fingers back a little. 'You're double-jointed,' he says. His voice is quiet.

My heart speeds up. How can I be so exposed when it's only my hand? 'Only my fingers,' I say. 'My thumb doesn't bend at all.'

Paul tests it, finds it straight, and lays his own next to it. His thumb bends back at the joint. Hitch-hiker's thumb, I've heard it called.

I touch his hand, turn it over. It's callused at the edges, the palm is tough-skinned. A lyco's hand. I see hardened palms at a distance on every stranger in

139

the world. At a distance. He has a funny-shaped hand, this man, the palm narrows at the top so it's a sort of spade-shape. A callused hand. A funny-shaped hand. He's letting me touch it. Faintly, cautiously, I run a finger across it.

Skin. Dry and warm, a little ridged. My fingertip slips easily across it as across a polished surface. I reach the end of it, and at the edges of his palm it softens. There's a crease in between his thumb and index finger where it folds, a wrinkle of flexible skin, and my fingertip sinks into it, immersed in fine, pliable flesh.

I'm shaking again. My eyes are unfocusing, my eyelids weigh down and I can feel my lips pressing against each other. This is too much closeness. I take hold of his hand, grasp it to stop it from searching my own any further, to stop me from searching his. And I'm sitting in a cheap restaurant, holding hands with a man.

He studies our hands for a moment. He can do anything here. He could keep hold of me, could push me away, pull me closer. I don't know what I want him to do.

What he does, I would not have been able to guess. He raises my hand to his mouth, kisses it. Just a light kiss, like a gentleman kissing a lady's hand in greeting. And then he gives it back to me.

I take my hand back into my lap, shield it. My head is full of silence.

Risking a sideways glance at Paul, I see him bite his lip, then rub his forehead. 'Well,' he says. 'I guess that's a start.'

Of what, I want to say, but there's no way I can say it. If you're walking over a frozen lake, you don't strike the ice to see if it's stable.

I sit without saying anything, hands folded in my lap. Symmetrical.

After a minute of no speech, Paul elbows me. 'Hello?'

I jump. 'Yes.'

'I haven't killed the conversation, have I?'

He doesn't look embarrassed. If he went all shy and inhibited now, that would be bad, because I can't handle someone more awkward than me, but his expression reassures me. I think he just wants to know.

'No.' I shake myself. 'Just – taking a pause.'

'Okay.' This seems to make sense to him, which is more than it does to me.

'Okay,' I say. I can't think of anything to talk about.

'Do you think that's the waiter?' He's distracted by a little man in a red shirt carrying some plates by us.

That's good. I can talk about the waiter. 'What, the one carrying the plates? Give him the benefit of the doubt.'

'I don't think they're in a hurry to feed us.'

'Are you hungry?'

He tilts his head to one side as if listening. 'I'm thinking about it. Yeah, I am.'

'Thinking about it?'

He raises his hands in the air. 'I haven't eaten today, I think. At least, I don't remember eating. I'm hungry now I think about it.'

He says that, and I find I'm hungry too. 'I didn't either. I had an apple for breakfast, I think.' What I did in the cells this morning comes back to me, and I know why I lost my appetite. I push it out of my mind and look back at Paul. Yes, I'm hungry. Suddenly I'm really hungry.

'I've got a friend,' he informs me with a rather wide-eyed sincerity, 'who says you have to eat bananas if you don't have time to eat proper food.'

141

This is easy talk, this I can handle. My body slackens in a rush. 'Fond of bananas, is he?'

'He says they're slow-release energy. You get less hungry.' The look on his face suggests that he's been told that several times, quite forcefully.

'Oh. I've got a friend like that.' Though Bride will often make me share her chocolate bar to stop herself from eating it all, every now and again she gets an idea for my improvement in her head. 'A few months ago she decided that I should eat porridge for breakfast, for basically the same reasons as your banana man,' I tell Paul. 'She kept getting me samples in the hopes I'd find a brand I liked. She thought I was unhappy because –' Dear God, how did I come to say that? I back-pedal with cautious haste. 'If – if I was in a bad mood or wasn't lively, she thought I must be hungry. It got so that I couldn't tell her I was feeling run-down, or she'd tell me to eat porridge.'

'Mm.' Paul leans his head back against the wall. Up close, he's a little scruffier than I thought he was at first. There are rough patches on his neck where he hasn't managed to shave properly. 'You know,' he says, 'I always thought I'd like bananas more if I wasn't supposed to eat them. Hmp. You should have told her you'd eaten the porridge and you felt worse.'

'You think that would have worked?'

'Well, it did for me.' He gives a half-laugh. 'This friend of mine kept on at me about bananas, so I thought I'd try it. I made a three-course meal. Salad with bananas, and then banana curry –'

'Banana *curry*?'

'It's nicer than it sounds. You fry onions and spice and add bananas and then yoghurt – anyway. I had banana curry for a main course, and then a banana crumble for desert.'

'Your greengrocer must have thought it was his birthday.'

'He did give me kind of a funny look. I think he thought there was no honest purpose that could need that many bananas.'

I giggle again. I sound like a schoolgirl.

'I think I thought I'd better make up for my banana-less life and have loads.'

'So what happened?'

He looks abashed. 'I felt very sick.'

I cover my mouth, laughing. It isn't that funny, really, but I'm laughing anyway.

'Seriously, I felt awful. Lou came round to see me – that's my friend, the one who'd told me to eat all those bananas in the first place – and I was just curled up on the sofa feeling terrible.'

He gives me an almost shy glance. I say the thing that's uppermost in my mind, which is, 'So he laid off you about the bananas?' He raises his eyebrows, gives me a look of pleasure and surprise. I guess he was expecting me to say he'd been stupid, or something like that, but really, I'm on his side in this. A grown man shouldn't have people ordering him what to eat. I sit back and wait for an answer.

Paul shrugs. 'Yeah. I think he decided I couldn't be trusted to handle advice.'

He looks at me for a moment, then gives me a questioning, one-sided smile.

And just like that, we're friends.

\*

The waiter brings our food and our wine in one go. We're both having goulash in little white bowls, the sauce burnt at the rim, and a bottle of some red stuff. I don't know anything about wine, but the waiter just unloads it on the table without comment, so I don't have to pretend to know whether I like it or not. Not that the waiter would care: he pulls the cork out with a gesture like a teenage shrug, and looks at the clock three times while he's giving us our dinner. Paul sniffs at the bottle, then pours me some.

I drink half a glass, trying to steady myself. The inside of my mouth turns to crêpe.

Paul sips it, makes a face and sets it down without comment. Taking a glance at my glass, he sees that it's half-empty and tops it up for me.

'Trying to get me drunk?'

He shakes his head. 'I've already seen you drunk.' He swirls the wine around in his glass, tilting it to and fro and examining the dark liquid from different angles. In this dim room, wine looks almost black, the candle flame and overhead lights forming slippery reflections on the surface.

I nurse my glass, tapping my fingers against the sides. Paul studies his for a moment more, then raises it to me in a salute.

The glass weighs heavy in my hand as I try to lift it in response. 'What – what are we drinking to?' My throat hurts with the effort of speaking.

'How about your friend in the hospital?'

My fingers tighten on the stem. 'To – to Marty.'

'Marty.'

I take another mouthful of the wine, and as I try to set the glass back on the table, it falls sideways in my hand. Red fluid splashes over the side, spatters my hand and soaks into a red wet pool on the white tablecloth below. 'Ohh . . .' I can think of nothing to say. I'm clumsy, stupid, making a numb-handed mess on the clean cloth.

'Never mind,' says Paul, putting a napkin over the stain. It hasn't bothered him, he just thinks the glass is still half-full.

'I –' I'm still holding my drink. Before anything else can happen to it, I try to put it down.

'Hold on.' There's a light hand around my wrist, and Paul is cleaning the wine-stained base, wiping away dark, clinging droplets. 'There you go.' He guides my hand down to the table and I release the glass, let my hand fall beside it. Turning my head aside, I find I've reached up to touch my left eye. I turn my head again, flinching away from my sticky, red-stained fingers.

'Here.' Paul offers me another napkin, and I can't do anything with it, I clutch it in a dull hold and just sit there. He takes it back, freeing it from my grasp, and wipes my hand clean. Cloth encircles each of my fingers, slides off them, thick-woven white cloth smoothes over the back of my hand.

There's a gleam of pain as he touches one of my knuckles, and I see a bruise. It wasn't there yesterday. I flinch, my hand bucks under his, and he picks it up, stroking the damaged area.

'How did you get that?'

I close my fist inside his. 'I hit someone.'

His clasp loosens around mine. He doesn't let go. I don't look at him, but I hear him draw breath, and when he speaks, his voice is very quiet. 'Why?'

I don't move my arm, neither of us moves. 'He bit Marty.'

Quiet.

'And he tried to kill me.'

Paul says nothing. I desperately want to know, but I can't, can't look at his face.

I close my eyes, bow my head. 'That's what happened.'

Paul says something I would not have expected. His tone is level. 'What did you hit him with?'

My head comes up with a start. 'Nothing. With my hands.'

'Your hands?' He's heard the plural.

I look at him. He's so beautiful.

There must be things to say. I've said them so many times. What do you think I'd hit him with, a lead pipe? Though I've even heard of that being done. If you don't like my kind, why are you having dinner with me? If you had at your mercy a man who'd been harming you all your life, who'd have killed you, killed your people if he'd had the chance, who sat there and told you to your face that he hated you, and you could do anything to him – *you could do anything to him* – can you look me in the eyes and say that you wouldn't have hurt him?

I say nothing. There's such an ache in my head. My face contracts, my eyes crush shut and my mouth pulls tight at the corners, and I take my hand out of Paul's to cover it. I won't cry. I won't cry.

'Lola?' It's a question. I turn my head away from him. 'Lola –'

I raise a hand, stave him off. 'Give me a minute.' My voice comes out hoarse and weak, but I just keep it from shaking.

He's touching my hair, trying to get to my face. I

146

don't turn my head back towards him, but I let him touch my hair, for just a minute I let him.

I press my hands over my eyes, steady my mouth, put my face back together. If I speak soft enough, it won't crack. 'Please, don't be nice to me. I'll only start being pathetic.'

He laughs, just a quiet, sad laugh. 'Do you not like being pathetic?'

I shield the side of my face and say nothing.

'Bet I've seen worse than you.'

'Worse –' I have to distract myself, I have to get myself off the subject. 'Worse sights than I've seen, or worse people than me?'

'Oh.' He takes his hand away, brushing my shoulder briefly, and then we're not touching any more. 'Well, I meant worse people. Sights, I don't know.'

'No offence –' I put my hands out in front of me, stare at them, 'but if you haven't, then you're a very bad social worker or I'm a very bad person.'

'No,' he declares. 'I'm quite a good social worker.'

I take a deep breath. 'Yes. You probably are.'

'My God, was that a compliment?'

Flashing a hasty look at him, I see the face of a man who's delighted with a novelty. 'Yeah,' I say, 'make a note of the date and time, because you won't be getting another one for quite a while.'

While he's laughing at that, I take another look at my hands. They're trembling.

Paul sits back, rests his head against the wall. I think he's about to say something when he sees me staring at my hands.

'Um –' he says, meaning something, I'm not sure what.

147

I clench my fists, unclench them, and they haven't steadied.

'As in catcher's twitch?' says Paul.

I look at him, look away. 'It –' It can be catching. Sympathy pains. I won't have it, I can't have it. 'No,' I say, sounding fiercer than I mean to. 'Just a bad day. Look, I'm just going to the bathroom, I'll be back in a minute.'

He rises as I get up, standing when a lady leaves the room.

The bathroom has scruffy tiles and little circles of light fall on the floor from the bulbs overhead. I stand at the edge of one of them and watch myself in the mirror. My eye is steady. My face isn't twitching. I fill up the tiny basin with hot water and bury my hands in it. They curl, the basin is that small, and heat encloses my skin. When I was still little, my first school, there was a teacher, a greasy-haired man with a pink, shabby face, who'd hit us on the back of the hands with a ruler. Not supposed to happen, thoroughly illegal in lyco schools, but the safeguards Becca had didn't apply to me. 'Stay in the real *world*,' he'd say, bringing the stiff wood down. 'This is *life* I'm trying to teach you. You think staring out the window is going to prepare you for the *world*?' He taught us history, some of the worse facts. He was a twitcher. Probably he wouldn't have been teaching if he hadn't got the twitch. I think he knew that the freakishness of it, the little right-ward jerk of his head, frightened our seven-year-old minds as much as the ruler. On days when his head pulled hard on his neck, jumping inches out of line, we knew we were in for a bad time, we'd keep our hands under the desk and hope he wouldn't pull them out by the wrists. 'Think

148

you're too young to deal with *reality*?' Always on the key words. Say 'reality' or 'cope' to any of us, and we'd flinch. This is where I learned this trick. We'd take a vote before each class, and someone would excuse themselves five minutes before the lesson ended, go to the bathroom and fill the basins with hot water. Whoever had come under the fire of his disillusionment would have a bowl full of healing warmth to run to as soon as the class ended.

I'm standing here in this poky little room, remembering Mr Davis, and it isn't what I want to be doing. It's silent in here. I dabble the water to make some noise and it's as quiet as a sound heard from a great distance.

The trouble is, while no one can see me in this small, white bathroom, while it's as good a hide-out as any, it's lonely in here. I want to be back at the table talking to Paul.


He's sitting in his chair, quite placid. I walk soft, watching him from a distance, and he's just sitting there and looking at the table. He isn't even fidgeting. The candle seems to be holding his interest.

As I approach, Paul starts absently passing his fingers through the flame.

'What are you doing?' I hurry up to the table, trying to stop him from mutilating himself.

'Mm?' Paul turns his attention from the candle to me, and the next second burns himself because he hasn't managed to get out of the flame before forgetting about it.

Paul's hurt.

'Ohh . . .' I sit down, scoop some ice out of my water

glass and press it to his scorched finger. 'Dear God, that was silly. What on earth are you singeing yourself for?'

'I'm okay,' he says, 'really.'

'Really. Actually sticking your hand into a fire and waiting for it to catch light.' He winces as I turn the cube over, scraping the ridged edge against the burn. 'Oh, don't do that, I'm sorry. You poor bloody simpleton. No, hold still . . .'

Ice melts in my grasp, and water drips down, rivulets running over my palm, into my sleeve, drenching me. He sits there, letting me press ice against him, droplets soaking into the fabric of his jeans as they fall from our knotted hands through the air.

'It doesn't hurt,' he says. Too soft to be casual.

'This is me being nice,' I tell him. 'Don't pass up the opportunity.'

# 9

When I woke in the dark, it was midnight, and he was awake and looking at me. He lay still, the stillness of a man who needs little sleep and has no need to toss and turn if he finds himself wakeful, and his eyes gleamed in the dim room. Rested but not fully alert, I stretched my arm across the few inches between us, to find him.

'How is it that you've only got cereal?' Paul says, coming back to bed with two bowls balanced on my chopping board in place of a tray. The tiny room is taken up entirely by my dishevelled double bed, and he has to start crawling to get into it.

'I accept no criticism from a man in a hula skirt,' I mumble, making a half-hearted gesture at the two jumpers he's wearing around his waist. He's wider awake than I am. 'I think there's a tomato in the fridge.'

He disappears, and comes back with it.

Later he asks me to come out with him. I don't want to leave the warm room, but I am hungry. The first thing that comes into my mind is, 'You've already had dinner with me.'

This, I do not say.

Once outside the restaurant, we kissed without the waiter's eye on us. We found an alley, light from a street-lamp slanting through it and casting cold shadows in the corners, and we pressed together for warmth as the brick wall pushed into my back. His coat baffled my touch, and all I wanted to do was pull aside these layers of fabric that were keeping him from me. He had the same taste I did, the burnt stew and cheap red wine, but softened and fluid in his mouth, and I dipped in, trying to take some of it with me. His hand traced the back of my neck, and I balanced his head in my palms.

Disengaging, it was hard to talk through the shape he'd left on my mouth, and my lips bumped up against each other as I said, 'Come home with me.'

If he was surprised, he didn't show it for more than a moment. He touched my face.

Inside my flat, I took him into my blue, dark bedroom and unloosed the blinds. I had put no lights on, and all I could make of him was a warm silhouette. I was pulling him down onto the bed when he laid his hands on my shoulders and moved me a little distance away from him.

I leaned towards him, reaching through the space between us, and he said, 'Wait a moment, Lola.'

'What?' I didn't want to stop. I couldn't even think of reasons why he might.

'Why not sleep a little first?'

'No.' I was out of words, couldn't hold more than one thought at a time.

'There isn't any deadline, is there?' I was straining to see his face in the dusk. 'It's Friday.'

'Friday?' I grasped his shirt, close to the skin beneath. He sighed, stroked my hair out of my eyes. His tone was almost apologetic. 'It's just that – to an onlooker, it might seem that you've had a bad day and you're running on autopilot. I don't feel like I have your full attention.'

'You have my full attention.' My head was rocking on its neck, I was sleepwalking, but it was a sensual dream I was sleepwalking through.

He sat on the bed beside me, put an arm around me and lay down. Outside, rain sighed against the streets. His fingers played around my ear, and though my heart was beating in my stomach, I let the stroking action lull me. I was sure I wouldn't sleep, but my eyes closed nonetheless.

It was dark when I woke. His face was close to mine, and a little light coming through the blinds showed that his eyes were open. I stretched, shifted, reached out and touched flesh. I didn't know where his clothes had gone, but his arm was bare, his shoulder, and I ran my hand over him wordless, reacquainting myself with this stranger in my bed.

There was barely light enough to see by. My hands became eyes and searched, my skin became hands and grasped. I lay back to be shaken awake. We turned and plunged like swimmers, drowning in air, and in my narrow room full to the corners with a mattress, the bed rocked like a raft, and the sea opened under me, miles deep. And I sank.

*

I did not mistake any of this for love, but I've been alone a long time.

Sleep with a man and you lose him. That's what my mother would have said if I had asked, what her mother would have said, all those certain armies of older women. They had the world laid out in neat rows, they had topiary shears that trimmed human nature into clear and defined outlines that they understood and tried to teach us, me and girls like me, back when we were still girls. Of course, we scorned them for it. I lay in bed, thinking about older women, while Paul slept, his eyes finally closed and his head buried in the pillow, unable to see me.

I think they meant that he wouldn't respect me. I think even Becca thought that, in some ways. Sleep with a man and you lose him. When I grew up, I tried it. They were right.

It isn't that he won't respect you. But in all the world, nothing isolates you more than sex. It locks you in your own body. The more aroused a man is, the further he retreats from you, because all he needs of you can be felt on the skin, and at the moment of climax, you disappear. I didn't lose men like I'd lose friendships, keys, or faith. They vanished from me as the moon vanishes when the rising sun throws out so much light that it blocks whatever is beyond it. Dazzled, they lost sight of me, and unseen, I lost them, over and over.

I knew I was going to sleep with Paul. I knew I wanted to, anyway. Perhaps I should have waited until after we finished working together so that he could leave more easily.

When he wakes, though, he pulls me to him again,

and afterwards he wants to talk, and the clock moves from eleven to twelve, from noon to afternoon, and he hasn't gone away.

'You don't have any food in this place,' says Paul.

I point at the cereal, and he takes a flake out of the bowl and sticks it on my forehead.

'That's not food,' he says. 'That's sustenance.' He leans across, his lips and tongue brush me as he cleans the cereal off my face.

'You don't have to eat it.' I get all the words in the right order, distracted but still coping.

'Yes I do, I'm starving.'

I take a spoonful out of his bowl. 'Well then.'

'Well, I could have cooked you breakfast if there'd been food.'

His sexual etiquette includes staying the night, I suppose, and serving me in the morning. He's been well brought up.

'Did you know,' he says, playing with my hair, 'that you finger the bedclothes when you sleep?'

'What?' I cover my face, uncomfortable. 'Do I do anything embarrassing?'

'No, no, it's quite sweet. Like this.' He lays his hands flat on the sheet, and starts running them to and fro, tapping out rhythms. 'It's dainty. I like it.'

I look at his hands, and realise what he's doing. 'Ohh . . .'

'Oh? Does it mean anything? I figured maybe you were typing or something.'

'No.' I lay my head down on the mattress, and he pets it. 'I'm playing the piano.'

'You play the piano?' He bounces up at the thought of this, looking enchanted.

'No,' I sigh. 'I used to. I don't have room for one here.'

He lies down, scoops me onto his chest. There's a moment of vertigo. He's stronger than he looks. 'There's a piano in one of our occupational rooms quite near here, it's open access. Like a library. You could play that.'

I make a noise of disagreement, knocking my head lightly against him. 'You've only known me a few days. You aren't allowed to certify me yet.'

He laughs, puts an arm around me. We could argue, heckle each other, or set about renewing foreplay, or he could get up and leave. None of these happen. I lie still, and listen to his heartbeat, a soft double stroke pressed against my ear.

It's dark again, and he suggests we go out. What he wants to do is go and have dinner. I am hungry. Neither of us has had anything but cereal all day. The trouble is, it's cold outside, icy cold.

The trouble is, I don't want him to leave.

'Come on, I'm starving.' He jostles me, trying to persuade. 'Don't tell me I don't get a second date.'

'What?'

'Anyway, we're all out of condoms . . .'

'Thought that was encouraging our invention.'

'Yeah, but we could be even more inventive if we had some. Look, I think we should shift venues. There's actually food at my place.'

'Your place?' I look at him, try not to look away. I don't know what he sees in my face.

156

'Yeah, look. Let's go and get some dinner, then go back to mine.' He's drawing patterns on my forehead with his fingers.

You've already had dinner with me, I think. Why aren't you making an exit? Do you just want another day of this?

We shower, dress, and go out. We eat again, and I'm hungry, I eat like I haven't eaten in months. Then we go back to his flat.


And on Sunday, he asks to see me during the week.

How have I got into this, part of me wants to know. I didn't do anything clever. I didn't do anything good. Yet somehow, here I am, lying in the arms of a man named Paul, who laughs at my jokes, who likes my hair and who doesn't want to escape from me.

I want to ask him why, but I don't. I don't want to do anything that might change his mind.

# 10

Skinless, I walk into work. Air brushes against me, sounds print themselves indelibly inside my ears, and everything impresses me. I keep my balance. I tell myself that I'm only unsteady because I've spent two days horizontal. When I woke this morning I felt good, light-bodied, air flowed easily into my chest. I move with a cautious step, fearful of breaking this.

Bride trundles into my office as I'm filing. 'Morning,' she breezes. By this time it's early afternoon, but I don't bother to point this out.

'Hi, Bride.' I smile at her in a surge of fondness, only mixed with a little trepidation that she may be bringing bad news.

'I see you're terribly busy, love.'

'I can't work in a mess,' I say, rather than explain that I'm trying to keep a good mood and at least heavy boxes of paper don't tangle my mind into a thorn bush.

'You weren't answering your phone.' Bride settles herself in a chair and helps herself to one of my cigarettes, giving me an accusing look.

'Have a cigarette. No really, don't be shy, take one. Anyway, you haven't called me this morning, have you?'

'I mean, over the weekend.'

I keep my eyes on the files. 'Why, were you trying to call?'

'Might have been. Where were you?'

'Home.' I shrug. 'Guess you called when I was in the bath or something.'

Bride bends a look of suspicion on me.

'What?' I try to look innocent. If Bride wants to know something, she will find it out, she's like a dog that won't let go of the ball, able to understand 'fetch' but not 'drop'. And if she guesses anything like the truth, she'll be delighted. She's always nagging me to get myself male company. The trouble is, if she knows then she'll want to know what happened, and what will happen next, and what will happen after that, and I don't want to have to deal with the fact that I haven't any answers. This weekend . . . it would be unlucky to speak of it aloud.

Bride uncrosses her legs, sits up. 'Right, love, out with it. What were you up to?'

'Nothing.'

'If you won't tell me, then I won't tell you my news.'

'If it's news worth hearing, you'll tell me anyway.'

'Don't be mean, Lolie. Where else can I get my thrills?' She's still grinning at me, cigarette burning in her hard-knuckled, boxer's hand, but the grin doesn't quite work. I know she's had a lot of evenings at home lately. A lot of hours behind a shut door, watching her husband's health, avoiding excitement, keeping him cheerful, staving off death with a pack of cards and some low-fat cooking. Too many hushed nights.

I take my cigarette packet away from her so I can

159

touch her hand in passing. 'I'll just let you imagine it. I'm sure you can come up with something more exciting than I did.'

Her eyes waver, and for just a moment her face goes dead. Then she settles deeper into her chair, finds her grin, takes a deep drag on the cigarette, cupping her hands around it as if a wind was blowing through this airless room to snuff it out.

I sit down, rest my head on my hand. 'Marty's better,' I say. 'I went to see him on Friday.'

Bride sits up, looking healthier. 'I heard he was better,' she says. 'How was he?'

I shrug. 'Quiet. Injured. Fighting the twitch.' I stop. Bride wants to hear that he's well, she wants to hear the bright side. We could all do with a little good news. 'But he was still himself, you know, polite as could be, all friendly, good boy that he is.' I keep my mind on my hand, buried in my hair next to the consoling warmth of my scalp. He's a good boy. I remember his soft-spoken mother, and try not to think how much she must love him. 'He's shaping well,' I tell Bride. 'The boy's going to be fine.'

'There's a relief.' She takes hold of this bit of happiness with both hands. 'And it's not so bad for you, either. You can tell the brass that he's recovering. Unless he's going to stand up and blame you.'

'No.' I lift my head off my hands. 'No, he won't do that.'

'Well, there you go.'

I sit up. Maybe it'll be okay. Maybe that good boy who should be out in the bright healthy world will patch together and get over his nightmares and make it through his life more or less unscathed. I think about Paul, how whole he is, how scarless. I'd like that for Marty, but it isn't mine to give.

'Nate said you didn't have much luck with our man downstairs.' Bride cuts into my thoughts.

'What?' I disentangle my mind from my senses.

'Darryl Seligmann, that one.' Bride's face darkens and goes still. 'He says you grilled him but he didn't say much.'

I'm angry with myself for shivering, with Bride for bringing Seligmann into my day. I liked the world this morning. 'Nothing repeatable, anyway,' I say, my voice harder than I expected, more useful. 'He's yours, isn't he?'

'My very own.'

Since she's investigating his case, she has say-so over him, about more or less everything. 'You letting him make calls?'

'No. And I don't plan to, either.'

'You talked to him?'

'This morning.' Bride flexes her hands. I lay my own together, side by side, as if to pray. 'Nothing out of him. I say we just let him sit for a while. I shifted him to Block C. He can wait it out down there.'

I could probably talk her out of this if I wanted to. I don't. When Bride leaves, I close my eyes, listen to the quiet. I check my e-mail. There's a note from Paul, saying nice things, and this is something to be glad of. I read it over, and if I breathe evenly, Seligmann and Marty and Bride's lifeless face will settle into the silt at the bottom of my mind and nothing violent will stir them up to muddy the pool. Just for a while, I'd like a little clear water.

*

At the end of the day, I am calm. I step out into the dark streets, feel cold air on my face, and pull my gloves on, quietly. My flat awaits, my little hideout, where I could go home, sit down, have a bath, remake my bed, sit on my own and listen to the silence. Me and my TV, me and my radio.

I think about it. Then I take a bus and go to visit Becca.

When I knock on the door, I'm all smiles as she answers. I've been thinking about her on the way, the times we played as children, the look on her face when she knew she was pregnant, and by the time I get there I'm actually looking forward to seeing her. She lets me in, and something's wrong. Her face doesn't change as she sees me. She admits me without much comment, and gestures to a chair, sitting down by Leo's cot.

I offer to make tea. She gives me half a smile, and I go into the kitchen. This is when I find her without food. There is the remnants of a sliced loaf in the house, some scrapings of butter, a blackened banana.

Going back into the sitting room, I look at Becca. Her face, still puffy from the pregnancy, has somehow managed to shrink.

'Aren't you hungry?' I say.

She closes her eyes, shrugs. 'Yes.' Her voice with its pretty accent is dry, unused. She doesn't even try to explain the situation.

I sit her down and make her dictate a list for me. She doesn't demur, and this scares me, that my wary sister hardly puts up a polite protest before telling me what she needs. I go to the supermarket, and she hardly protests either when I offer to take Leo along for the ride. Some fresh air will do him good, I tell her, without looking at the piles of unwashed plates or sniffing at the stale smell in the room, and it's true, it will. It will also be nice to be able to see him without her influence, her eyes on me.

I take him shopping. He's fractious, then worried, then good as gold as he gets used to me again, and when I bring him home, I find Becca asleep on the floor.

This is terrifying. Becca who scolded me for letting my socks slide down, who always carried a handkerchief and brushed my hair and made me make my bed neatly has slumped in a heap on her untidy floor, not even curled up gracefully but collapsed in a heap of sticky, child-bloated flesh.

'Exhausted,' she says when she wakes up. Her eyes skitter like a suspect's under questioning, she's confused, confounded with the weight of her fatigue. I make an offer I wouldn't have ventured with a healthy, trim, real Becca.

And she accepts. And through this, unexpectedly, a little more goodness comes into my life.

What I do is take Leo for walks. Over the next few days I reorganise myself, rise early and work late, so I can walk him at lunchtime while Becca sleeps. I could walk him in the evenings, but I don't want that. It isn't that I'm afraid of muggers and tripping in the dark. It's something to do with his serene, intent face, his footie pyjamas, the way the spokes of the pram glint in the light. A woman who pushes a pram gets to craving the sun on her face. I don't know what advert or poster I've been taken in by.

We go to the parks, Leo and I. We like the parks. Daytime, there's nothing in them but people walking two-footed and safe. Considering that this city, like most, is built around its parks, each circular expanse ringed with houses, I haven't been in them very much. Not in the light. My flat is in a cheap area, which means it's far away from the parks; actually it's at an intersection, where the districts around Queens and Abbots meet, which is about as cheap as you can get, and parks have not been part of my daytime life. Until now. Leo and I enjoy the parks, we stride through them and admire the glistening grass. Some days I even think of taking him into the woods, watching the watery winter sun cut through the bare-fingered branches, although I never quite do it. Instead, we walk the paths, and I sing to him.

> Dance for your daddy
> My little laddy
> Dance for your daddy
> My little man.

Then I think I shouldn't sing that. Leo has learned to focus his eyes, and his daddy wasn't there, any day now he will learn to smile, and his daddy isn't here. I change it to something I like better.

> Dance for your auntie
> My little laddy
> Dance for your auntie
> My little man.
> You shall have a fishy
> On a little dishy
> You shall have a fishy
> When the boat comes in.

I sing, and we dance. I take his soft hands and move them, gently so as not to hurt his shoulders, and dance with his arms. One potato, two potato. Seventies disco. Locomotion. Flamenco, even, curling his little wrists back and forth. We can dance anything.

I tell him when he's older I'll buy him ice cream. I tell him I'll let him chase the pigeons and never ask him to stop. I tell him I'll carry him on my shoulders, my back, and he'll see how high the world goes. I steal paper from work, coloured paper meant to write memos on, and fold it, doing origami patterns I first learned to while away the cold hours of moon night in the creches. For Leo, I make tiny aeroplanes as long as my little finger, whirly star shapes, birdies, and string them from the hood of his pram, where they jump and spin in the wind. I tap them as I sing the words. 'You shall have a *fishy*, on a little *dishy*, you shall have a *fishy* when the *boat* comes in.' He and I, we roll through the parks together, and I pull his blankets up around him when the wind bites my face, and promise him fishies.

# 11

Ellaway claims to have been driving home when his car broke down. Checking the map, I see that he was on the road from north-east to central. He works north, he lives central. His apartment is on the east side of Kings, a lovely area and an expensive one.

If his car broke down, then he would have abandoned it and gone to look for a shelter. That's what he claims to have done, and it makes sense: no one would stay in their car if they started furring up, not unless they wanted to destroy it. Every now and again you get some fool trying to claim insurance that way, sitting in their cars and waiting for the moon to rise so they can claim it wasn't their fault they demolished the inside. Usually you find them collapsed on some road, stunned and bleeding from a dozen glass cuts.

So the car would have been there the next morning. If it was on a main road, DORLA agents would have towed it away; if it was on a side road, they'd have left it to the daytime shift, lycos who will have ricked and recovered. Ellaway left it on a B-road, which is touch and go; DORLA towers might have picked it up, or they might have left it, depending on how tired they were.

And what happened then? Ellaway would have been informed where his car was, and would have arranged to have it fixed. I don't see him doing without his car for more than a few days. It would have been fixed, and he would have had it back. What I need to do is dig out the mechanic who mended it, to testify if it was broken down.

Then there's the other question: why didn't he reach a shelter? There were two nearby. Even if he didn't know the area, or didn't know where the shelters in it were, he should have known what to do; they're set out logically, and kids get what-to-do-if-you-get-stuck-outside talks from about eight years old. He crippled Johnny. Pleading carelessness would be tantamount to walking him to the prison myself. Franklin won't have it. I need honest error. If he really didn't know the area, it's possible he got lost, underestimated how long it takes to walk places because he's used to driving, tried to find a shelter by trial and error rather than following the drill. Stupid, but not criminal. It's possible.

It just isn't likely.


I do some hacking, some hunting. The details of Ellaway's car are easy enough to find: blue Maserati, two years old, registration E99 PRM4. Two hours turn up nothing more useful. Internet searches have never been my strong point, and by the end of the afternoon, I'm seeing green flashes every time I turn my eyes.

I telephone Paul. He picks up within a couple of rings, and I grip the phone with both hands. 'Listen,' I say, 'I think I may have to work late.'

'Oh, don't do that.' We were going to meet tonight.

I so want to. If I keep working efficiently, I ought to be able to make it.

'I don't think I can, Kelsey. I have to – I have to . . .' My voice rattles like a stick dragged along rough ground.

'Don't panic,' he says amiably. 'Take a breath, tell the nice man what you have to do.'

I rest my head on my hand. 'Turn water into wine. I want to go home.'

'Yes, do that. That's a better idea.'

'I can't. I have to stay here and turn water into wine.'

'Aha,' says Paul, sounding almost excited. 'Now, this is a splendid opportunity for an object lesson I had in mind. Are you sitting comfortably?'

'I – I'm sitting.' I've had a few of Paul's object lessons before now. They're one of the reasons I want to see him tonight.

'Now, for this you will need a packet of bubblegum.'

'Paul, I'm in the DORLA tower block. We're grown-ups. Nobody has bubblegum. You have to pass through a bubblegum detector at the door.'

'You do have bubblegum. I put some in your brief-case the other day.'

'You were going through my briefcase?'

'You really should tidy that thing up, you know. No wonder you didn't spot the bubblegum under all that mess.'

'Paul, I can't believe you went through my briefcase.'

'I didn't go through it,' he says, like a perfect inno-cent. 'I just put some bubblegum in it.'

'You –' I give up. The man is not going to feel guilty about this. 'Well, I just hope you didn't unwrap it first. And don't do it again.'

'Actually I believe in English it's pronounced "thank you".'

'Ohh . . . thank you.' I glare at the phone and drag my briefcase onto my lap. Sure enough, right at the bottom there's a narrow package, virulent green with big chunky letters, informing me that I'm the owner of a packet of Apple Bomb. 'I'm dating a man who puts gum in my bag,' I say, pushing my luck, just a little push, because I'd so love to see it right itself.

'I'm dating a woman who calls me by my surname half the time. You got it?' he carries on, as if nothing unusual was happening. 'Right, now what I want you to do is this. Put a piece in your mouth and start chewing.'

'That's eccentric,' I comment. Unwrapping a fluorescent segment, I put it in my mouth and bite. 'It tastes like an alcopop,' I mutter, trying to pulp it down.

'You know, most people would say that alcopops taste like bubblegum,' Paul points out. 'I see where your priorities lie.'

'Well, that's what makes me so damn special,' I spit.

'That it does, beautiful Lola.' He calls me beautiful without breaking stride. 'Now, what I want you to do is blow a bubble.'

'Paul, I think your imagination's failing you.' I say it more gently than I normally would. It's a concession.

'I don't hear any bubbles.'

'All right, all right.' I rub the elastic mass against my palate, trying to flatten it, and straddle it across my tongue. It's tougher than I expected. My jaws are starting to tire, an ache mixing in with the taste of mock apple. With a convulsion of the lips, I blow, and plastic stretches

169

out of my mouth for perhaps a second, before a tiny little balloon explodes off-centre.

'That sounded pretty pathetic.'

'Oh, are you an expert?' I say. 'If you are, I wouldn't admit it. It's not to your credit.'

'You wait till tonight. I'll impress you so much.' He laughs. 'It's surprising what you can do with some bubblegum and a bit of imagination.'

'Oh.' My chest loosens. His imagination is well ahead of mine. Damn it, now I want to meet him all the more. 'Told you, I have to work late.'

He ignores that. 'Now, what I want you to do is this. You're stressed, and we can't have that. So I want you to concentrate on your bubblegum. Blow bubbles. And you're not allowed to go back to work until you've blown a bubble at least two inches in diameter. And I'll see you tonight, I'll come by and pick you up. Oh hang on – gotta go.' The phone clicks and he disappears.

It must be a tribute to something that I spend a full ten minutes, stiff-jawed and soaked up to the eyes in the taste of apples, trying to fill a bubble with two inches of air.


Afterwards I phone Franklin. It's a once-in-a-lifetime opportunity: I'm put through to his assistant, she says things like, 'certainly, Ms Galley', and an appointment is scheduled for tomorrow. I tell Leo about it on our next afternoon walk.

'She was even polite to me,' I say, crouching down to adjust his hat.

Leo turns his head and opens his mouth to chew my wrist. Hoisting my sleeve out of his way, I let him have my knuckles to rub his gums over. He's too young to be teething, unless he's a prodigy. I think he's just being pensive. Leo takes a thoughtful munch at me, and I stroke his face while he sucks, soft-tongued, at my fist.

'It's never going to happen again,' I tell him. 'This is my one brush with the high life.'

He nips me. It doesn't hurt, he's too little.

'He's bringing Ellaway with him.' I sit myself on a bench. Leo whimpers as I take away my hand, and I lift him onto my lap, settling his head in the crook of my elbow. 'I've got to meet the man again. I don't know if I can face both of them at once.'

My baby nephew is a good listener, he keeps his eyes on me and lies quiet in my arms. His feet squirm together on my thigh as I tell him about the case, though, and he does that when he's bored. I stop talking about work, and sing him a song instead, giving him my best happy face. His mouth quirks at the corners, and then it's open, a pink little cove, gumless and clean. He's smiling at me.

I lift him onto my shoulder, rest his head against mine. 'Such a clever boy,' I whisper. 'I'll tell your mummy how well you smile. Such a good boy.'


So when Franklin does appear, bringing his client to see me, my first thought is that I wish Leo was here. I could do with a warm armful of someone on my side. I remind myself that I'll see him soon, pat the pack of bubblegum in my pocket and think about last night with Paul, and tell myself that I'm a professional.

Franklin enters the room softly, the air around him doesn't move. His palm is lacquered against mine as he

171

shakes my hand. Ellaway strides in after him and sits down without being asked. I remain on my feet for a moment, standing very still, looking at him.

He sits back in his chair, stretches out his long legs. Seeing me watch him, he shifts sideways a little, rocks his ankles to and fro. His eyes take a long, slow sweep up and down my body. It isn't a lustful look, not more than ten per cent. It's more an appraisal, he knows he can stare at me if he feels like it. 'You're looking good, Miss Galley,' he says.

'Good morning, Mr Ellaway. Mr Franklin, won't you sit down?' I stand up straight. He can stare if he wants. It doesn't touch me.

'Thank you.' Franklin seats himself, sets his briefcase down, a neat parallel beside his chair.

'Thank you for coming to see me.' I seat myself, fold my hands in front of me, take possession of my desk. 'Mr Ellaway, you understand this is just a preliminary meeting to discuss your defence?'

'Well, yeah.' He gives a surprised shrug. That was me reading him his rights, telling him something for the sake of form. All the trouble he's been in before, I guess he hardly needs telling.

'Now, Ms Galley, you've had a chance to read the briefs I sent you?' Franklin says. Ellaway's voice rings in the little room, buzzes hard in my ears, but Franklin's tone is lowered, fits cleanly into the space.

'Of course. Am I right in thinking that you want to present the case straight, attack the prosecution on the grounds of insufficient evidence?' According to the seminars and textbooks, I ought to be paying attention to my client, but I'm not a rookie any more, and I like Franklin better.

172

Franklin makes a small, tidy gesture with his hands. 'I think it's certainly to be considered.' I wait for him to go on. 'If we look at the evidence, there is nothing that proves our client was negligent. The incidents that followed moonrise were certainly violent, but there's nothing that indicates it was more than an unfortunate accident.'

Hey, he said 'our' client. 'There's plenty the prosecution can say,' I counter. 'He was within reach of a shelter. He should have been able to get to one. I've been going over it, Mr Franklin, but whichever way up I turn the map I really can't find a reason good enough for a judge why he didn't.'

'That isn't conclusive proof.'

'No, but it's not in his favour. And we have to remember –' I stop myself from saying, you have to remember; this is my field and he knows it '– that the system works differently here. The burden of proof may technically be on the prosecution, but there's no jury to work on, just a judge, and he's not going to look kindly on our client, whatever we say about it. He won't jump through legal loopholes.' Franklin raises an eyebrow at this. 'What I'm saying is, to convince a judge, the finer points of the law aren't the issue. We have to build a case that sounds likely.'

'That is our intention, I believe, Ms Galley.' Franklin's voice is neutral; there's just a tiny edge. He sounds almost dry.

'Undoubtedly.' I turn. 'Mr Ellaway.' He glances up from picking at the arms of his chair. 'Are you determined to stick to the story you told me the first time we met?'

Ellaway looks idly at his hands on the chair. 'I told

you, I got lost, I didn't know the area.' His posture is sprawled, his head inclined carelessly away from me. I follow where he's gazing, look at his fingers playing with the armrest. The elbow sits comfortably, but there are tendons on the back of his hand, flicking under the skin. I see them twitch and strain as his nails dig into the wood of my chair, cording under the pressure.

I straighten my back, shift in my chair without making a sound. 'Very well,' I say, my voice so soft it wouldn't wake a baby. 'Let's look at the details.'

Within half an hour, I understand Franklin's reputation. I put up objections, he takes them down. Before I met him, I'd have expected him to smash me, bludgeon away the prosecution's arguments. What he does is a lot better: he chips, takes a little sculptor's chisel to whatever I say, until I almost think he has a case. I still doubt we'll win, but we'll put up a good fight. It's the best solution I could have hoped for. Looking over some notes while Franklin settles Ellaway down for the fifth time, I hear myself give a pleased sigh.

Finally Franklin clears his throat. 'Ms Galley, I have a conference in an hour. Would it be all right with you if we continued this discussion in a few days?'

'Very well.' I haven't raised the issue of the car yet, but making him late isn't going to help. 'I'll see you out.'

The two of them stand up. 'Can I give you a lift, Adnan?' Ellaway says. I see in that moment how he is, outside this building, away from this world. He speaks with the comfortable manners of a man who has good things and won't diminish his stock if he shares them, because he has plenty more.

'Thank you,' says Franklin.

I walk them out. It's only when we get to Ellaway's car that I see something. He gets out a ring with half a dozen different keys, adorned with a heavy silver pendant whose every aerodynamic curve breathes design and which probably cost more than my winter coat, and he doesn't see me staring.

It's wrong. All the records say Ellaway owns one car, a blue Maserati, E99 PRM4 on the plate. I know very little about cars. This one is sleek enough to be a Maserati. It just isn't blue.

Ellaway and Franklin climb in from their different sides. I stand a little out of their way where they can't knock me down, and scrawl the new car's number on the back of my hand. Its engine croons as it pulls past me, and I lean against a pillar, my head against the concrete, and the dull yellow lights ripple over gleaming silver paint as the car glides away.

# 12

'Circle,' Paul says.

'I haven't finished it yet.' We're some hours into the evening. I'm getting better at speaking without watching my every word.

We're playing the ice game. I lean over Paul, the ice cube in my hand, using it to draw an image on his back. If he can't guess what it is, he has to perform a forfeit; if he can, I do. We play for best of five. Paul is a better draughtsman than me, his pictures more elaborate. I don't mind. I'm keeping my sketches as simple as possible, making it easy for him: his forfeits are more inventive than mine.

'How did you come up with this game?' My voice is growing softer, unstrung. I rest my free hand against his shoulder blade, it sits curved in my palm, palpable and shapely as an apple. I can't get used to the sensation of his body against mine, the warmth of it, at once alien and familiar. Flesh of my flesh.

'Your idea . . .' He speaks quietly, not flinching under the ice. 'In the restaurant, remember? When I burnt my fingers. We've just improved on it.' He sighs. 'It's a smiley face.'

'Well done.' One out of five. I lick the running water

from the cube, and smooth my hand up and down his back to dry it. 'Not just this game, though. Where do you get your ideas?'

He crinkles his nose and grins. 'Spent a lot of time alone in my room when I was a teenager.'

I think of that, Paul as a boy, the cube slipping like a fish between my fingers. 'What were you like?'

'I was a very nice boy.' I set the ice to him and he takes a breath, closes his eyes.

My hand spiders across his neck, testing the heat and resilience of the muscles. Closing my eyes, I picture a younger Paul, sitting alone in his room, waiting to grow up. Brushing the hair from the nape of his neck, I set the ice down and rest my face against him, my fingertips settled at the warm furrow where spine locks into place with skull, and inhale. The warm smell of the air and the solid muscle beneath my cheek are adult, male. This is what children wait for.

'It's another face,' Paul says, his voice vibrating against my ear. 'A brown-eyed and lovely one.' I lay a light kiss against his spine, just a brief taste. He smiles. 'Two out of five.'

'Not fair.' I sit up. 'That wasn't an ice picture.'

'It was a print. It counts. I'm winning.'

'No such thing.' I drop the ice cube on his back, and he tumbles over trying to remove it. 'You're a cheat.'

Paul reaches the ice cube before I do, but I grab his hand before he can press it against me. We scuffle and I tighten my grip, wrestling his arm away from my face, knowing I'm outmatched. 'Jesus, she's strong for a little 'un,' Paul laughs, and seizes my foot, pulling me down out of harm's way. We lie on the bed, face to face, and look at each other. Paul grazes his fingertips against my lips, and I open my mouth, curling one leg around him to hold him in place. I lean my head up, trying to reach him, but he covers my eyes and holds back.

I flinch as the ice touches my collarbone, draws a slow, stinging path downwards. A circle, small and slippery, and I shiver, images prickling across my skin. He slides it down, cold and sweet against me. Drawing a deep breath, I hold myself still. I want this. There's a triangle, a sweep of something that settles over my beating heart, and then the ice glides high, around one breast, then the other, some symmetry that ends in a rippling line underneath on each side where flesh gives way to ribs. He draws down, a three-sided figure that ends in a line across my stomach, and as my back arches I tangle my fingers in the sheet, holding steady, water chasing in droplets down my waist. Then the ice lifts away, and I nestle my face against his covering hand, an icon glowing against my frosted, shuddering skin. He holds my eyes closed, and my voice catches in my mouth as he draws again, a tiny, wet oval inside the hollow of my throat.

I lie still, eyes shut, trying to keep this, but a tremor shakes me and I crush up against Paul, burrowing for warmth. His hand comes off my eyes and cups my jaw, and I find my teeth are chattering. He runs his thumb across my face. 'Are you okay?'

I nod, catching him by the back of the neck and pressing myself against him. He kisses my neck, touches his forehead against mine and smiles at me, his eyes sleepy with heat. 'Any guesses, pretty girl?'

'I – I don't know.' Only lines on my skin. Only someone's arms around me. I mumble 'What?' into his enclosing hand.

'An angel.' His hand slides into my hair, cradling my head. 'Don't you know an angel when you see one?'

There isn't any answer.


Later, he finds more ice, and I try my hand at art, calling up round-edged images from my childhood books. For Paul, I will do my best at pretty pictures. I begin on a car, then wipe it out and start again, because I was thinking about cars all day. Nothing must get into this room from the outside. I draw apples, I draw a tree and let him mistake it for a lollypop, I draw cats and fish and leaves. My pictures are open and guessable. I invoke the brightest colours and most innocent lines I have seen in all my twenty-eight years, and sketch them out in melting water, playing to lose.


There's a weightlessness to my body today, a suffusion. I perform my tasks slowly, watch my drowsy hands drift about their business as if there was a soft mist between my arms and my eyes. The day is close and chilly, threatening rain, but I'm warm inside my shirt. Finding no seat on the bus, I lean up against a pole and let it dig into my back, thinking about Paul's goodbye kiss, wondering how anyone can sleep so little and yet not wake me. We talked about adolescence, told each other things all weekend. My adolescence did not make me inventive, and when I said this to him, Paul talked about lying awake at night. He sleeps maybe four hours to my eight, he said, and can lie still for another four untroubled by restlessness or unease. He teased me, saying it gave him ideas, four hours of lying motionless

179

with nothing to do but think what we could be doing if I was awake. Then he told me about the glow of the streetlamps through the blinds, the sound of my breathing half-echoing in my tiny bedroom, my hands playing piano on the bedclothes and the arias rustled into the sheets, the voices he hears in the streets and the colour of the walls in the darkness. I wasn't awake for it, so he saved it to give me when I opened my eyes.

At work, I settle into my office and open my files, my hands still lazy on the pages. What I take in is the cool grain of the paper under my fingertips, the texture making it hard for me to pay attention to the words written on to it. When I check my e-mail, I'm more enchanted at the antics of the cute little cursor on the screen than interested in my messages. I shake myself, stretch my fingers out.

I return, once again, to Ellaway's case. Checking up on the car I saw him in, I find that it's a courtesy car provided by his employers. He hasn't reclaimed his old one. The DORLA car patrollers didn't pick it up. Some serious hacking has located it, and it's at a small mechanic's in the Benedict Park district. Benedict, the edge of town, the oldest park. It used to be the village centre before we became a city and sprawled westwards, building backwards from the river. The colleges and schools are around Benedict Park, the bookshops and delicatessens. Scholars must need their cars fixed as often as anyone else, I suppose, but it's not the district you'd take your broken vehicle to. Ellaway lives in east Kings, he broke down east of Foundling Park. It would have made more sense to take it to north Sanctus.

It only takes a little record-checking to find out which shelter Ellaway was taken to, after Johnny's partner managed to collar him. If he wanted his car taken to a favourite mechanic, it's possible he called from the lock-up; for that I'll need a witness. I close the cabinet with some good news: it was my friend Ally in charge that night.

Everyone makes exceptions sometimes. Ally is one of mine.

No one talks about the creches. Lycos know little about them; to a lyco, the word means a plastic box full of toys and some young woman looking out over a floor-full of crawling children. The mummy comes round in her suit and picks up whichever child is hers, saying, hello darling, have you been good? Sunlight comes through the windows.

My first night in a creche, I was two weeks old. My last night, I was a few counted days short of eighteen years and admittance to basic duties in DORLA. They try to break up the age groups, but can't spare the staff to do it properly.

The babies scream. Under cheap bulbs, the light on those nights is synthetic, tainted like the world seen through a fever. Often they're faulty, and strobe and buzz till our eyeballs burn, the cracks in the paint leap and shake. Little cots muster along the walls, plastic-sheeted mattresses for the older ones. There are blinds on the windows and broken toys no one plays with. Toddlers sometimes pound the infants. Teenagers huddle under blankets in the corners.

There were nights when I let no one near me, when I knew that the boys who came to try their luck were just taking an opportunity, and I'd fight them, kick and

181

scratch in a silent battle under the harsh fabric coverings. There were nights when I hadn't the strength to fight and would reach down, moving my hands fast to get the encounter over with as quickly as I could. There were nights when I'd lie unresisting and close my eyes, slipping my fingers under boys' clothing in case I might find succour there. Sometimes the young ones would watch the stirring blankets, sometimes I watched, when I was young. There were nights when the supervisors could stop any of this happening, and nights when they couldn't, and nights when they didn't. Sometimes the children would play, and sometimes attack each other, and mostly everyone lay or sat speechless. In eighteen years, I cannot remember a night where there was more than an hour free from the sound of babies crying.

They thought it would be traumatic to stay at home and listen to our parents moan and snarl. Until we were old enough to work, we had to be taken away. Some children would ask to be taken home, the very young ones, the ones who had just learned how to speak. Whatever adult was asked would usually stiffen and ignore them. If they were young enough to ask, they were too young to understand. How do you explain to an eighteen-month-old child? If your mummy saw you tonight, she'd kill you.

Until I was eighteen years old, I never saw a lune.

The day I signed the lease on my flat and walked into my own place, I sat down, leaned my head against the door and cried with relief.

Few friendships come out of the creches. We do too much to one another within them. Sometimes you recognise a face, but there are no reunions. We have nothing to say to each other.

Ally and I are friends more in spite of meeting in the creches than because of it. Once upon a time I would pull myself up to the cots, heave a crying baby out and sit down with it on my lap, trying to sing to it. Red skin and knotted flesh, a baby more intent on screaming than breathing. Ally would rattle the cots, shouting for them to be quiet. We didn't talk. Later, I stopped singing, and Ally stopped shouting. I knew by the time I was six that that I would never sleep in a creche. I experimented. Reading didn't work: it meant sitting still, holding the pages steady, and unless I could move there was nothing to stop me flying apart altogether. I couldn't bring in a toy I liked better than the creche ones: things got broken in there. Cat's cradle; patience, the cards lined up in rows and complicated shuffles that took me months to learn; jacks on the grimy linoleum. On my eighth birthday Becca gave me a crafts book she'd found about origami. I never asked if she'd seen me looping string and shuffling decks, rehearsing, improving on ways of wasting time. She gave it cautiously and stood away from me when I opened it.

Paper: light and easy, if a foot comes down on your work you start again, with nothing lost but the time you were trying to fold down into small pieces in the first place. Pleasant colours, and sharp, precise edges. I couldn't tell her what it meant, not without telling her how jagged the nights were away from home, but over a few months I made her a whole houseful of paper dolls, paper cats and dogs for their pets, paper rooms to put them in.

Ally was building with matches then; many of us have some habit or other that we learned to fill the hours. He wanted me to teach him how to make aeroplanes. I wasn't kind, but there was so much time to compress. Given something to think about, I devised Spitfires, Concordes, tanks. We didn't talk much, but we knew we'd found something to keep our eyes off the dark-edged windows and the wailing babies in the dazed, hectic light. When we were older he would sometimes creep under my blanket and reach into my shirt, but I didn't know how to resent it. We all wanted some consolation. Sometimes he let me kick and bite him, sometimes I let him clutch paltry handfuls of my flesh. We were in our twenties before we were able to mention it. We seldom talk about it, only a passing joke here and there, never for more than a few seconds. He never laid a finger on me outside the creches. None of the boys did. I never laid a finger on or raised a hand against them. More often, we'd cut our eyes away from each other. I couldn't feel wronged by them, didn't have any sense of how to begrudge what was done. I might not have wanted it – as much as you ever know what you want when you're fourteen – but we all knew it wasn't personal. Even looking back, I don't know what I wanted. Except to be some other girl that things like this didn't happen to.

Ally's the only one I know from the creches that I'm in much contact with, and we don't talk about any of it.


Ally and I first met as adults when we were training. He came in a few months after I did, but was well ahead of me in dogcatching skills before the year was out. He's a technical boy. I never understand why people want to go into Weapons, but Ally loves it. He gets a big kick out of the fact that they have to put up with his unmilitary appearance because he's so good at it. Every now and again someone tells him to get his hair cut. He reminds them of his bet with me – that he'll shave his head when a lawyer manages not to mention public opinion or the word 'majority' within ten minutes of arriving. Though now I come to think of it, Franklin hasn't said any of those words, not once.

I pick up a pair of scissors and head down to Weapons.

Ally's sitting resting his feet against the stockroom wall, his head buried in *Sleepers Monthly*. I knock on the door as I go in. The fluorescent lighting makes the sleeper guns and silver guns stand out from their racks like cardboard cut-outs. Without searching my memory, I know it's an unhealthy light. 'How can you not get a headache in here?' I say.

'Mm? Oh, hi Lo.' Ally takes his feet off the wall and kicks another chair towards me. 'God, you should see this. They've got a new design coming out, they say you can sight up to four hundred yards with it.' He pushes an article under my nose.

'Fat lot of good that'll be, sighting in the dark, is what I think, but then I'm just a girl.' I stand against the wall, a few feet away.

Ally takes his magazine away so I can't insult it, ignores the second part of what I've said. He opens his mouth to explain why I ought to take this new technological advance seriously, but if I wanted to know about beauty in design then I'd look at pictures.

'You,' I interrupt, 'owe me a haircut. I had a lawyer in here who didn't mention public opinion once.'

'Who's that?' Ally's hand makes a protective pass by his head.

185

'Adnan Franklin. He didn't mention the majority of citizens at all.'

'Shit. What did he say?'

I shrug, holding the scissors. They're a pleasant shape in my hand. 'That I'd contravened my client's human rights and broken national and international humanitarian treaties, and let civilisation down.'

'That doesn't count.' Ally leans forward and snatches the scissors. 'He talked about civilisation. That's public opinion. He just used bigger words.'

'Bullshit. Where did you learn philosophy?'

'He said most people wouldn't like you. Same deal, I reckon.'

'No . . .' Franklin didn't say that. That wouldn't have been – 'I think he did like me.'

'Did he now?' Ally isn't a particular gossip, but he likes to hear something first. He likes his information pristine. 'What's going on there, then?'

I sit down. 'No, Ally. Work. Nothing going on. Anyway, I'm seeing someone.'

'Hey.' He sits up, alert. 'Who?'

I wave my hand. I wasn't planning on telling him. 'Just some social worker I met.'

'A lyco? God, Lo, you don't date lycos.' Ally considers that he has the goods on my love life, that he knows about me. I don't want to know about his.

'I don't date, Ally.'

He gestures with the magazine. 'You think they just believe what people say about bareback girls.'

People say that bareback girls are sluts. Or that bareback women are frigid. Fucking a cripple. 'I'm no girl, Ally. And nobody worth listening to says it. Listen, I wanted to ask you about a shelter case you had.'

186

'Who is this guy?'

He's right, nons do usually date each other. He's way too curious. I won't have this. 'The case, Ally, or I'm walking out the door.'

Ally rolls up the magazine and slaps it against his palm. 'Which case?'

'And don't tell anyone I said I was seeing anyone. If Bride Reilly finds out I didn't tell her, she'll put salt in my coffee jar.'

He shrugs. 'Whatever. What's the case?'

'Moon night before last. Someone brought in a bad lune, he'd mauled the first catcher. Johnny Marcos.'

Ally doesn't like to sit still. He doesn't fidget or twitch, and he's fit, smooth-jointed, but he's always on the move, like liquid in an unstable container. His shoulders stop in mid-roll when I say Johnny's name, and he settles in his chair. 'That's the Ellaway case.' His voice is flat. 'I heard you were doing that.'

'I am. I need to know about what happened in the shelter.'

He exhales a deep breath, pushes a hand through his hair. 'Johnny came in mauled, the bastard who bit him was tranked.' He tugs at his lip. 'We had a proper medic, so they took him in the back and patched him up. There was blood all over the floor.'

I raise my hand fast, like a reflex. 'I'm not asking about Johnny, Ally, I need to know about Ellaway.'

He glances at me, starts to say something and changes his mind. 'The trank didn't last long. He came round after a couple of hours. Didn't settle him down.'

I shrug. 'He's a user, cocaine, probably other stuff. Smoker. Probably takes sleeping pills. His resistance is way up there.'

187

'Well, whatever.' Ally leans forward, bounces his hands off his knees. 'Kept coming at the bars. Kept at it, right up until sunrise.' Most lunes slow down a little as the morning gets near.

'How was he when he ricked?'

'Swearing. Angry at the pain, you know the type?'

'Bad lune.'

'Yeah. Started swearing before most of the others started crying, though. They were still just making noises, but he was right there, knew what was going on. Cussing as soon as he had a daytime tongue. Wouldn't lie still for the cramps, either, he was pacing around, crouching down, hitting the wall. Guy doesn't like hurting.'

'You were watching?'

'Yeah, he was making a noise. Threatened to get a shock prod if he didn't shut up.' Ally's eyes are dark, each pupil hidden in a black iris, and shadowed even when he's rested. Strands of shaggy russet hair hang over his face, and his expression doesn't change when he says this.

'Did he?'

He shrugs, rubs his hands together. 'Demanded a telephone. Said it was his right, he wanted a phone.'

'Yeah, I can hear him saying that.' It's cold in here. I tuck my hands into my jacket sleeves. 'Did you give him one?'

'Yeah,' Ally sighs. 'Yeah, I did.'

'How come?'

'Couldn't face hearing him argue. He was a determined one, I could tell, I mean he was demanding a phone before he'd even put the overalls on. You ever try arguing with a naked man?'

'Well –' No. I'm making no jokes about that one. 'He hadn't even dressed?'

'Guess he didn't think the overalls suited his style. And,' Ally puts a hand to his face, 'and there was a juvenile in another cell, fourteen-year-old crying her eyes out. I just gave him a phone and went to try and get *her* to put some clothes on. I mean, she was just sitting crying for her grandma without a stitch on her. Kind of hard to work with a naked girl sitting around.'

'Jesus, Ally, a fourteen-year-old?' My hands tighten around my wrists.

'No.' He looks away from me, bites his lip and glances back. 'For God's sake. Just hard to know where to look, that's all. You've got a sick mind, Lola.'

'*I* have?' I remember what I looked like at fourteen.

'Yeah, you.'

'So, so –' I reach out my hand to pull the conversation back to the point, 'you weren't listening to Ellaway when he made his call?'

'No.' Ally pulls a face. 'Sorry, Lo. I don't know who he called. Someone came to pick him up, though.'

'Who?'

'A man.' He shrugs. 'I wasn't – He signed himself out. And, and the hospital hadn't come round, the ambulance wasn't there yet and Johnny was still in the shelter. I didn't get a name.'

'What did he look like?' I fire the question to blot the word *Johnny* out of my mind.

Ally spreads his hands out, shaking his head, turning from one palm to the other as if they might hold an answer. 'I don't know. Dark hair, fair skin, tallish. I don't know. I don't do faces. I can't tell you anything that wouldn't have you questioning every other man in town. I wasn't looking.'

He sounds helpless, but this doesn't relax me. 'How could you not look? He'd just mauled one of us. Why weren't you looking?'

Ally stands up, fends me off and paces round the back of his chair. 'Lay off, okay? I thought it was clear-cut. I thought your department would handle it. I didn't stare because I wasn't in the mood, it was seven-thirty in the morning and I'd been up all night, and there was blood all over the floor. Just lay off.' He slumps back down and rubs his knees.

I say nothing.

Ally speaks first. 'Look, the number will be on the shelter's phone bill. You can run it through the police and find out who he called if you want to know. It'll just take a few weeks, that's all.' He sounds like he's trying to make amends.

'Yeah. Look, I'm sorry.' He's right. A policeman once told me to my face that we're less of a priority when our suspects can't re-offend for a whole month. Still, I can get it started. 'I'm sorry, I know it's not your fault. And it's probably not important, anyway. Thanks, Ally.'

'Yeah. It's okay. No sweat.'

'That's everything, right? I mean, nothing else happened with Ellaway?' I rub my forehead, remember something else. 'Hang on, you got a look at him before he ricked. Was he clean?'

'Clean?' Ally blinks at me.

'Yeah, I mean did he look like he'd been rolling in the mud or anything? You know, he says he was trying to find a shelter when he started furring up. Says he broke down near Foundling, so he probably would have gone straight there, and there's records of what the plants are in different parks. If there were brambles in the hair he shed or anything, it'd back his story up. I don't suppose anyone saved it when they swept the floor?'

'No.' He presses his hands together between his legs. 'No, the blood. A sweeper came in, disinfected the place, incinerated stuff. Don't you remember? It's a new reg.'

'What new reg?'

Ally screws his face up. 'God bless our government. You know the one. If a catcher is bleeding, everything has to be sterilised. You remember it, last year someone got AIDS from the guy who collared her?'

I frown, shade my eyes. I think I do remember it. Someone had forgotten to put overalls in the cell. The woman was halfway through ricking when the attendant went in to put some out for her. Figured he'd be safe if she was halfway there. She sank her teeth into him, his blood got onto her half-changed gums. He lost a piece out of his arm, and she's dying. Voters were outraged or terrified; it was a scandal. Another notch tightened on protocol, more discipline promised for us. Now HIV-positive nons can't dogcatch or do shelter work at all. They man the switchboards, I guess, earn that little bit less money to spend on medicine. I noticed they'd introduced blood tests along with the shrink evaluations, but it's a while since I've done shelter. I'm clean, I won't let a man touch me without a condom or a test, ever. But I guess it's all come through now, more paperwork, more examinations, more promises to the public that we are their servants. If they tear our flesh from our bones, we won't presume to bleed on them.

My back aches, and my voice is hoarse. 'Johnny didn't have AIDS.'

191

'I guess not.' Ally speaks softly, his eyes on the ground. 'But they made us burn everything anyway.'

'God.' I want to go home. 'So there's nothing?'

Ally shakes his head. 'I – There was a mark on his shoulder. A couple.'

'Marks?'

'I don't know. They could have been old scars playing up, I guess.' He looks down. 'Or maybe someone scored him with the catching pole.'

That would make sense. Smaller cuts heal when they rick; it's a bad injury that doesn't at least half-close. Apart from silver, the terrible allergy that makes even a small cut swell and fester, that makes them wake with open necrotic wounds instead of pink new scars. Looking away from Ally, I make myself think it: if Johnny injured him during the collar, then that might have pushed him to attack. I could claim self-defence, or provocation . . . I could say it was Johnny's fault. 'I – I'll have to look into it.'

'Sure.' Ally makes no sound as he sits in the chair.

I steady my head with my hand as I rise. 'Listen, I'd better go and get the enquiries about that call he made in order, you know how long that'll take. Thanks, Ally. You will testify if I call you, won't you?'

'Sure, Lo. Whatever.'

I turn towards the door. We shouldn't have had this conversation.

'Lola.' Ally's voice makes me look back.

'Yeah?'

'You forgot your scissors.' He holds them up, studies them. His shoulders hunch, and suddenly he gives me half a crooked smile. 'You said your lawyer friend only mentioned civilisation, yeah?'

'Yeah.' My voice is as quiet as his. 'Only civilisation.'

'Well, what the hell.' He raises the scissors before I can stop him, takes his long ragged hair in his fist. 'We'll call it a draw.'

There's a grind as the scissors close, and then Ally is shorn, his hair hanging in uneven tassels to his shoulders. He throws the scissors across the room, and holds up his hand, clutching a sheaf of hair like a trophy.

# 13

There's a handwritten sign taped to the garage door that says 'Please knock loud as our bell is broken'. Ally waits behind me, kicking at stones.

'Ally,' I say, and then stop. This isn't Marty, this isn't Nate, I don't need to tell him to let the lawyer do the talking. Ally's my age, after all.

I must send Marty a card. I sent some flowers, but that was a week ago, they'll have faded by now. They still haven't let him out of hospital.

'Yeah?' Ally's voice cuts across my thoughts. He puts his hand on the door, leaning on it, and drums his fingers. Turned towards me, he takes up a lot of space.

'Do you reckon you can find something?'

He shrugs. 'Find what?'

'Something to back up his claims,' I say, hitching my bag on my shoulder and straightening my coat. 'Ellaway says he broke down. Do you reckon you can confirm it?'

Ally takes his hand off the door and pushes his hair out of his face. He hasn't tidied it since he took the scissors to it in the stockroom, and it tumbles in lank tails around his fingers. 'If they haven't fixed it,' he says, 'I'll see what I can do.'

I wasn't asking for a favour, just an opinion, but I don't say this. We stand without speaking for a few more seconds, and then the door swings up.

A man in a clean white T-shirt and stained jeans stands under it. His face is youngish, in his thirties perhaps, and he's shaved his head to allow for the fact that his hair is already receding. His scalp is dented-looking; the planes and dips of his skull show through the brown stubble of his hair. The posture is assertive, wiry arms poised, shoulders sloping, but his face is amiable enough. 'Yes?' he says.

I can start this friendly, at least. 'Good morning,' I say. 'Do you run the garage?'

He cocks his head and nods. He isn't going to waste time elaborating, the nod suggests, but he's happy enough to let me know.

I hold out my hand and he looks at it for a moment and then shakes it. His hand is bony with a firm grip; lyco calluses and others beside them from holding spanners and screwdrivers. 'My name is Lola Galley, and this is my colleague, Alan Gregory.'

'Kevin White.'

I hand him my card rather than flashing it at him. 'How do you do. I'm here on behalf of a client of mine, Richard Ellaway. He left his car at your garage a few weeks ago?'

White looks at the card, looks at me.

'I'm investigating his case,' I say. 'He got stuck outside on a moon night and assaulted someone. I'd like to have a look at his car.'

Ally taps his fingers against his legs beside me, and I stand still, settle all movements down and hold myself quietly.

White shrugs and gestures with the card. 'You got any proof you've come from him?'

'We don't need proof,' I say, trying to sound like I'm just reminding him of a fact: something about this man tells me that if he digs his heels in, there'll be no shifting him. 'But I have some letters he's sent me about the case.' Neutral ones, from early on, before Ellaway got to know me. I take them out of a folder in my bag and hold them in front of White. 'I take it you recognise the signature?'

White studies it. There's a pause; Ally shifts on his heels, and I hold out the letter for White to see. I doubt he does recognise the signature unless he has a photographic memory, but the letter's genuine and White seems to have some sense. If he'll just accept the letter and decide not to throw his weight around, we'll be in without a fight. I keep silent, unthreatening, and let him read.

'All right,' he says, looking up. 'I'll show you to it.' He turns and walks into the garage. When he can't see, I let my head rock back and smile, just for a second. We're in.

'You've had his car since his arrest, haven't you?' I say to his back.

'When's that?'

I give him the date.

'Yeah, that's right.' Our footsteps echo against the concrete walls. There are a few men here and there, under or over cars; they don't look up as we pass. Black tyres loom at the corners of my vision.

'And what would you say was the trouble?'

'Trouble?'

'When you had a look at the engine.'

White slows down and looks over his shoulder. 'You say you're from Mr Ellaway, right?'

'Yes. Yes, we are.'

He gives us a measuring look. 'Only I have to be careful, you know, I run a good business here, my clients put their faith in me.'

'I'm sure they do.' I mean this. His place is clean, his men are concentrating on their job. He could fix my car, if I had one.

He stops. 'It's just, he was out after curfew, right? So I figured it might be evidence and I shouldn't mess with it. Isn't there a law about that?'

I'm almost taken aback: an actual good citizen. 'So you told him you couldn't work on it?'

White shrugs. 'Yeah. But I didn't do anything unusual, I mean, no one fixes a car unless they get a go-ahead from DORLA or some proof that the case is closed. No offence, I mean, but I don't want to get into trouble with you all.'

I raise my hands. I mustn't look too surprised; this should have occurred to me. I just never thought that mechanics would be scared of us. I should have been chasing up the car sooner than this, even. I'm just used to alcoholics and homeless loiterers. Most of my clients don't have cars. 'Of course. So, where are you keeping it?'

'At the back.' White keeps walking. Ally looks at me, and I glare him into silence.

We reach the car. Here it is, the blue Maserati: even in the dark, it gleams. Ally puts his hand on it, strokes the curve. He's going to love this.

'Mr White,' I say, 'if it's all right with you, I'd like to leave my colleague to have a look at it while I ask

197

you a couple more questions, would you be happy with that?'

'I've got a busy morning.'

'I'll keep this as quick as I can.'

Ally opens the bonnet and nestles inside, and I turn and follow White.

We sit on plastic chairs and I sip coffee from a stained mug. 'Did you know Mr Ellaway before he sent you his car?' I ask.

'No.'

'You didn't?'

White just looks at me.

I blow on the watery coffee. 'So he just brought it in that day?'

'He didn't bring it in. He called and told us where to get it, he offered a collection fee and I accepted. We went and picked it up, and we've had it since then.'

'Called when?' Did he call from the shelter? Was that the call he made on his mobile, the one I'm waiting for the phone company to trace?

'About eleven a.m.'

Too late. The call from the shelter was not to Kevin White.

'Anyway, I sent someone to pick it up, and we brought it back here. And it's still here.'

'Just like that?' I grip the mug to stop myself staring and sit still.

White grins. 'I don't mind. Nice car like that, it raises the tone of the place.'

I flash a smile and push on. 'Mm, but has he been in to check on it since then?'

'Nah.' White shrugs. 'Up to him, he's paying me for the space.'

'Does he come in to pay the bill, check on the car?'

He shakes his head. 'Sends a cheque.'

Ellaway hasn't notified us about the car. He's left it here instead, not telling me where it is. I had to spend some time researching to find this place. He hasn't lied to me, he hasn't broken the law and got the engine fixed before I could look at it, but he hasn't given me the routine information either. White seems to know his job, but I think again what I thought earlier: Ellaway has left his car a long way off the beaten track.

'So –' I put the cup down on the concrete floor. 'So he's not been in at all?'

White dusts his hands together and smiles. 'Nope. Doesn't bother me. Wish all my customers were that little trouble.'


I go over to Ally. He's practically crooning over the engine, tinkering and touching with the fascination of a true devotee. 'Hope you're enjoying yourself, Ally,' I say, making him flinch inside the bonnet. 'It's the closest we'll ever get to a car like this.'

Ally emerges, dishevelled and with a smear of grease on his nose. 'You've got –' I gesture at him.

'Where?' His hand passes across his face.

'There. On your –' I stand back and point. 'Left. Down.' I point again. He gets some of it off, rubbing it off onto the heel of his hand, leaving a trace behind.

'So,' I say, 'did you find anything?'

Ally stops cleaning himself and beckons me to the

car. He dives into it from the front, and I lean over one of the sides. 'See that?'

'Yeah. It's a car.'

The bonnet overshadows us, and our voices echo back at each other in the confined space. Ally's head is too near mine. I look down at his grimy hand, which is pointing at parts of the engine.

'In words of one syllable, Ally,' I warn. I'm leaning hard against the side; sculpted metal presses into my hands.

Ally draws a breath; it sounds louder than my own under the hood. 'Your man – is right when he says the car is – broke. There's a – flaw in the part that makes it go. You can't drive this. But I'm not sure how the flaw got there. He could be wrong to act all – shocked.'

'Ally, what the hell?'

Ally points to the engine. 'This car's in a good state. That's all. And the damage, well – it doesn't look like wear and tear.'

'For God's sake, spit it out. I can't stand it when you hedge.'

Ally looks at me, opens his mouth, closes it, looks back at the engine. 'I could be wrong. But what I'm saying is that he could have done the damage himself.'

I pull myself out of the cramped space and walk to the wall. 'You're saying he trashed his own car?'

'I'm not saying anything,' Ally says. His fingers flex in and out, and he paces. 'I'm not messing with this guy, Lola. You can deal with him, you're the lawyer, but I don't want him after me for saying the wrong thing.'

'Ally, stop it.' I can't watch him fidgeting to and fro, I just can't stand it. In a minute I'm going to slap him.

He turns, runs his hands through his hair. I stand at the wall and watch him. 'I just don't know, Lo,' he says. 'I just don't know what to think.'

# 14

I mutter in my sleep, slap the blankets, and in the end I sit up in the dark. Paul lies beside me. After a while he reaches out and drapes his arm over my leg. Finding me upright wakes him. It isn't until he takes hold of my hand that I realise he's been fingering the scar on my foot.

He looks for a moment, then says, 'How did you get that?'

'I was twenty-five. A caged juvenile with a small head stuck his face through the bars.' I shake my hair out of my face. 'I was lucky compared to Marty. It doesn't show when I'm dressed.'

He lies quiet. Then his hand moves to the slash on my arm. 'What about that?' He speaks softly.

I don't move. 'When I was eighteen, my second catch. It was a hot night and I didn't fasten my sleeve properly. I'd collared a woman, and she ran at me and drove the pole back in my hands. She got up close. And she did that to me before my trainer could stop her.'

His fingers settle into the hollow in my hip, and I freeze. 'How did you get that?'

'I don't want to talk about it.' I roll over and put my arms up around my face.

Paul sits up, leans against the wall. 'Lola?' His tone is cautious. My hands clench against whatever he's about to ask me. 'What does a lune look like?'

'Oh no.' I sit up and pull a blanket around myself. 'No, you don't get to ask me the questions.'

'What do you mean?' He sits very still.

'You don't get to hear what I did in the creches. You don't get to hear if tenderfoot skin has more erogenous zones. You don't get to hear if I like rough sex because shiftless flesh needs a good workout. If we're trained to get off on pain. You don't ask me those things!'

'Hey! Calm down.' Paul's voice cuts across me. There's an edge to it I haven't heard before. 'Don't get paranoid on me. Look, people are stupid. I'm not. It's not fair, Lola. I asked you something else. It's not fair to go off on one just because other people are stupider than me.' The edge has gone; he sounds almost helpless.

I slide off the bed and sit on the floor, wrapped in his blanket, and bury my head in the covers. There's a long silence.

Paul lies back down. He can stare at the wall forever, absorbed as a child, without even wondering if he should be bored.

'They're big,' I say. The voice I hear is hoarse and tentative, I hardly recognise it as my own. 'They come up to your chest, just standing there. They have huge heads, big as watermelons.' I look up. 'Why are you asking? You must know.'

There are three feet between us. My room is on the seventh floor, many feet above the ground. We're sitting over a canyon. 'I've seen pictures,' Paul says. 'And I remember. But it's different.'

'You remember?'

'Some. I don't know. It's different.'

He'll see if I close my eyes. The sheets are forest green, and I stare down at them. 'How?'

Paul sighs, rumples his hair. 'It's hard to describe. I'd say atavistic, I guess, but it's a long word and long academic words are no good for describing it. But I don't think you ever really understand it. Not this way, anyway.' He gestures, two hands, two feet, upright spine. 'It'd be like interpreting dreams. You can say this means that, you can do logic, but you aren't – analytical in the state of mind you're trying to analyse. It doesn't work very well.'

'Their eyes are green,' I say. I can't answer what he's said. 'Not normally; they're grey with a round black pupil. But you know how if you take a picture of someone you get red-eye, the retina reflects back pink. Different receptors come forward in a lune's eye. If you catch one in the headlamps, their eyes flash green.'

'When you change states – you stop understanding what's happening to you. The pain gets harder to deal with the further you go. But once it's over, the pain and the analysis – they don't matter. You don't need to understand it.'

'It's the size of them. The weight. And they're so fast.'

'The pictures I've seen –' Paul turns his head and looks at me. 'They looked beautiful.'

'Anyone who had their hands free to work a camera was catching the lune in a tranquil moment. You can't see beauty when it's poised above your throat.'

'Isn't that just – I don't know – your feelings rather than what you see?'

My feelings. 'Eye of the beholder.' He says nothing. 'I can't help it, Paul. Yes, they're graceful. That means they aim well when they leap at you. Yes, they're – they're beautifully proportioned. So they run fast, and they run towards you. A long smooth muzzle crackles up when it snarls, and as far as grey and white fur goes – well, I just know that if we tried to bite each other, I'd come off worst.'

'So you're afraid?'

'Yes.' I look at him, and he's watching me. 'I'm afraid. I see them day to day and I know I can match them. But at night – there's nothing I can do. Imagine it. Imagine facing someone who can tear you apart if they want to, who can't understand why they shouldn't. Who doesn't have it in them, who's flat-out *lost* how to understand why they shouldn't. And often, they aren't sorry the next day.'

'That's not so.' Paul shakes his head, more to himself than to me. 'That can't be so.'

'I've seen what I've seen, Paul.'

He sighs. I feel rather than see him take a quick glance at me, and then he speaks again. 'I'm lyco too. It's what I am. And I can't – wish I wasn't. You're right in a way. I can't wish I never luned. I don't.'

A field stretches between us in the few inches across the bed, a winter field. Spiders weave their traps across the ground like hammocks, frost grains the grass blades, the air is cold and empty. A footfall, and the ice will crush and snap.

'I'm scared of lunes, Paul.' I close my eyes. This is weakness. I'm laying myself open and handing him a knife.

'I don't want anything to hurt you,' he says.

I feel my eyes sting. The rest of my body is numb, chilled, lost in a winter field.

'I don't wish I didn't lune. If I could give it up, I wouldn't. But I don't want anything to hurt you.'

'Animals run away from them,' I say. 'Every animal. They're all afraid.'

'Wild animals run from people,' he says. 'And it's natural to avoid a predator.'

'A predator?' My voice is very small.

'It's worth it, angel. It breaks your mind open. You can't be so sure of things any more.'

'The lycos I meet are sure. They know God is for them and the world is theirs and the cripples are – are –' My words twist in my throat.

'You've seen things I'll never see, Lola.' His hand slides up my back and rests at the base of my skull.

'You've seen pictures of them.' My voice is quiet. 'It isn't worth it.'

Paul turns over, strokes my head. 'If you could, would you be lyco?'

His hand is on my nape, and I laugh. 'What, be one of those bastards? Not in a million years.'

We sleep again. He lies with his arm over my waist. I'm warm and comfortable at midnight when the phone rings.

Paul gets to it first. 'Hello?' he says, picking up the phone and setting it down on the bed. 'It's for you, Lola. Some woman called Bride?'

I moan, and take the receiver in a limp hand. 'You've got the wrong number, Bride. You don't know anyone who'd answer the phone at this hour.'

'Who was that?' Bride's question is light, friendly, but there's tension in her tone.

Well, she had to find out some time. This is not how I wanted to tell her. 'That,' I say, rubbing my eyes, 'was Paul. He's a nice young government employee who's been taking me out to dinner lately.' Government employee could mean DORLA. I don't feel like handling her interest that I'm going out with a lyco, not right now.

I brace myself for a tirade, or possibly jubilant triumph that for once I wasn't sleeping alone. Instead there's a silence, and it's then that I hear there's other voices than Bride's on the line, people are shouting and hustling in the background.

'Bride? What's wrong?'

'Listen, love, you'd better prepare yourself. Are you sitting down?'

I'm awake. 'No, I'm lying in bed. Bride, tell me, what's happened?'

'It's about Darryl Seligmann,' she says.

I'm sitting up, holding onto Paul's arm. 'What? What's happened?'

'It happened this afternoon, pet. He'd been quiet for days. Nobody was watching him.'

'Bride, tell me. Don't hedge, I need to know now.'

I hear her swallow, and then she tells me. 'He bit his wrist when no one was looking. By the time someone checked on him, he'd lost so much blood that we had to take him to a hospital. They stitched him up and gave him a quick transfusion. He was due to be sent back this evening. But when we went to escort him, he was gone.'

'Gone.' My voice echoes in the cramped room.

'He's escaped, love. Some time this afternoon, someone took their eyes off him, and he just stood up and walked out of there.'

# 15

I'm here. It's dark and cold outside, the gutters are wet and the air is full of mist, there are globes shining around the streetlamps, soft fat spheres with rainbow spectrums at their edges. I'm swathed in a thick coat, my hands tucked away into gloves, and as I stride into the hospital car park the group around the entrance is silhouetted against the bright plastic light coming through the door. Bride sees me, detaches herself from the others and trots across to take my arm.

'He's been gone a couple of hours,' she pants before I can greet her. 'He didn't take a car, but no one saw him. He could be anywhere by now.'

The city has buses and wide streets. In two hours, he could have crossed it.

'Why did you release him?' I say. 'Now everyone will know where he's been these past two weeks.' Because he didn't get a phone call, we alerted no next-of-kin, the police were not informed. As far as the world is concerned, Darryl Seligmann just vanished.

And now he's back.

'We couldn't fix him up on our own.' I've joined the people at the door by now; this comes from Lydia Harlan, one of our medics. About forty, with peachstone brown

209

skin, hair braided into long plaits that she wears in a swinging ponytail, plump and comely with soft, capable hands, Lydia knows as much doctoring as anyone can learn in two years' training and twenty years' practice. Almost every time I see her, she has a medical journal in her hand. 'He did it cleverly. We gave him a mattress when we moved him to block C, he was curled up with his back to us. He ruined the mattress.'

'Who found him?'

'I did.' I turn at the sound of the hoarse, crumpled voice.

'Nick.' Nick Jarrold. Johnny's partner, the man who first had custody of Seligmann. 'Why were you down there?'

'Taking him food,' says Nick.

That's menial work. It's the injured, the restricted-pay workers who do such jobs. If Nick was doing it, we're either under-staffed even beyond what I thought, or he's getting sicker.

'I was doing the rounds,' he husks. 'Bastard knew what he was doing. Took me about five minutes, and all the time he just lay there. Then he turned around when I was about halfway through. He timed it.'

'He turned around?'

'Yeah. Pushed himself to his feet, wobbled on over to the bars, and held out his wrist.' Nick looks at me out of round eyes set in a greying, haggard face, and I see it. The swaying man, arm and hand and side caked and soaked and sticky with blood. 'He still had blood on his mouth,' Nick says. 'He was smiling.'

'Didn't you – Couldn't you smell the blood?' I ask a question fast to close the smeared, smiling face out of my mind.

210

Nick shrugs his shoulders. 'No, I didn't.' Ash rustles in his voice, and I silence myself. Nick doesn't smell anything.

'Who's talked to security?' I huddle into the doorway and look around. Bride, the investigator on Seligmann's case; Nick, the police liaison officer; Lydia, the medic. And me.

'They're not saying anything.' Nick coughs. 'Shall we go inside?' The four of us push through the door and hang together as we stand in the corridor. St Veronica's, the city hospital. Leo's birthplace, Marty's ward, rooms and rooms full of crisis and change.

I lower my voice. 'Why not? Weren't they supposed to be watching him?' We're heading towards the ward now, the scene of the crime, the sterile white room Seligmann got up and left.

'They say he walked out when they were changing shift.'

'Christ.' We walk on in silence, our steps creaking on the shiny linoleum.

We all know what this is. This is a dying man hustled in by DORLA out of nowhere, a pack of freaks with blood on their fists showing up with a real man and handing him over. There will have been bruises on Seligmann when we brought him in, sprains, damage. The doctors received a man who bit into the pale flesh of his wrist with loosened teeth.

Seligmann is a fearsome man. They won't have seen that. They wouldn't have smuggled him out in the laundry, no one will have risked their career for him. But they didn't watch him. Not closely. For them, there was nothing in him to fear.

This is a busy place. As we pass through the wards,

211

the occupied medics and the sick, quiet citizens, I see a face I recognise. There's no help to be had, but I have to try.

'Dr Parkinson,' I hail him.

He stops, turns a civil face my way.

'Lola May Galley,' I say before he can once again not recognise this cheaply dressed, wan woman who's claiming a moment of his expensive time. 'I'm investigating the disappearance of Darryl Seligmann. He escaped from your hospital earlier this evening.'

'Ah.' His sleek skin doesn't flush. 'Good evening, Miss Galley. How's your sister?'

'As you'd expect,' I say. 'Dr Parkinson, we're looking into how he managed to escape, what time, where he's likely to have gone.'

'Hadn't you better talk to security?' He gives a slow, measured glance at the people surrounding me. I put my hand back, just a little, held out at hip level; he doesn't notice until they all step out of his line of vision.

'We have. It's just – hard to understand, Dr Parkinson.' I smile, I don't threaten, I hide my smooth palms by my sides. 'I'd always thought this was a well-ordered hospital.'

The man smiles right back at me. 'Well, I would have said so. But then, I'm on the medical side.' His genial chuckle echoes back off the synthetic walls. 'If you asked me how security was run, I'm afraid I couldn't tell you much.'

'You aren't acquainted with any of the security staff, then? Not even by name, or by sight?'

He backs down without losing grace. 'I wouldn't say that. But personal acquaintance is one thing. All I meant was that the mechanics of their business, I leave in their capable hands. My attention is on my patients.'

I don't take him up on 'capable'. It's too tired a shot. 'Has this happened before?'

'Not to my knowledge.' He lowers his head to me, careful as an elephant. 'As I've said, I have little do with security. But I think I'd remember a serious breach. I think we may have had occasional trouble containing a mental patient now and again, but nothing I'd call serious. The staff have always struck me as capable men.' He smiles at me, bows down over folded hands as if to emphasise the difference in our height. 'Now if you'll excuse me, Miss Galley, I have patients to see.'

I hold out my hand so he has to shake it, and his calluses rub smooth as polish over my bare tender skin. 'Thank you for your help, doctor,' I say, and turn away so he doesn't have to see my face.

The room Seligmann left has mouldings around the ceiling, a plaster rose in the centre. My eye jumps, once, at the sight of it. It's just like every other hospital room. There's nothing in here to explain why the capable men of this institution neglected all our warnings and let a wild, bloody man take a short, untroubled walk out to the streets and freedom.

# 16

Day after day, the rain rattles my window. Day after day, I reach the office with wet shoes, the smell of dust and fresh water soaking into my scarf. Day after day, I work, and I go home, and every door I enter, I feel a heavy saddle lift from my shoulders as I stop watching the streets for Seligmann.

I don't go out much. Becca thinks I don't want to take Leo out in the rain. In her untidy, well-appointed rooms, I sit behind a locked door and hold Leo on my lap, let him squirm, too small to crawl away; I shake bright toys in front of his face and applaud him when he reaches out and grabs them; I coax him to sit up. Against Becca's double-glazing the rain is muffled; it makes a soft noise like paper crumpling.

Paul visits me. When the rain set in, he tried to persuade me to walk in it, but after a couple of tries I stopped. It's too hard to see things far away. The roof of my flat-block is leaking. In my little hideaway ten floors down, there's just a few trickles round the edges of the window frames. We wake to pools on the ledge, bubbles and buckles appearing in my careful paintwork. When the rain patters down, we bet on droplets, make them race, watch the world upended in each little lens of water.

I work. Uneventful cases drift through my hands. Ally sweet-talks Kevin White and gets another look at Ellaway's engine, comes back more sure than before that someone's been tampering. The phone company takes its time and every day fails to come up with the address Ellaway called at the shelter. The police don't find Seligmann.

When he savaged Marty, he and the others, I shot one of them in the leg. We asked the hospital, we hacked into their records, we kept watch. The wounded man never appeared.

Day after day, I hurry through the streets and lock doors behind me, and Seligmann is nowhere to be found.


Am I being punished? Last year I did five dogcatches. This month I've got to do another one, two in a row, and it's only February. My strawing takes place next month. I tell Bride that either they're not planning to straw me and are showing their faith in my abilities, or they're hoping I'll get killed and save them the trouble. She laughs. Neither of us says that it's a bad time, that prowlers and accidents are on the rise, that we're calling everyone young and healthy onto patrol. I don't say that I don't want to patrol without Marty.

'You know what you can do?' she says.

'What?'

'Take Nate.'

'Are you punishing me too?'

She pulls out a pack of cigarettes and offers me one. I take it.

'You got anything against him?' I can't say yes. Bride lights up and sighs out a mouthful of smoke. 'I wasn't scheduled this month. He's standing idle. I won't be going

215

out. Listen,' she lays her hand on my wrist, 'Lolie, I'm getting old.'

I shrug her hand away, not wanting to hear her talk about mortality.

'I'm serious, pet, I'm not first-choice stock any more. Not against lunes.'

She can throw a punch still, we still box sometimes in the gym, I don't always win. She can interrogate a man cuffed to a chair. Not against lunes, she says, and I believe her. They're so fast. Age hasn't started seeping through my muscles yet, not really. I can't bounce back from a sleepless night as I could ten years ago, that's all. Hardly anything. But if Bride's slowing down, she needs to get her pupils trained quickly, because she won't be able to lead the collars much longer. DORLA's seldom tactful about telling you you're past it.

'Old, hell,' I say. 'I thought you said he wanted to be military. You don't have to train to dogcatch for that, do you?'

'You do if you want to keep it a secret you're going in for it. Anyway, I was only guessing.'

'Do you really want me to take him?'

Bride taps ash into her coffee cup. 'He's a pretty good catcher. For a boy his age. He won't get you into trouble.'

'You inspire me with confidence.'

'Well, what do you want, the Olympics?'

I shrug, something stiff in my shoulders. 'I – I don't know. Guess I'm wishing Marty was back.'

Which is true, but not the reason. I'm a sorry woman to use such an excuse.

\*

As I stretch and press my flesh into the tight-fitting gear, I think about the moon. I always liked it when it was crescent, the sanctuary moon, a slender curl of light around the ghostly, shaded disk. When I was a little girl, I used to stare out of the window and watch it. If my mother saw me, often she'd scold in a tired way: 'Come away from the window, May, you'll only make a smudge.' Never, 'Come away from the window, stop dwelling on your future.' On clear nights, I could swear I saw craters and mountains, the textures and patterns on the surface of that grey sphere that stood poised in the sky, waiting to fill out with light.

Paul says that in Middle English there was a word meaning moonlight bright enough to see by. Loten, or some such thing. It got used by poets: a silver fish glinting through the water was loten, a lovely melancholy girl had loten eyes. Paul himself only brought it up because we were listening to choral music and he wanted a word to describe the mood of Allegri's *Miserere*; it's possible he was trying to impress me. He says people stopped using the word when they discovered gas lighting. I don't think it can have been that simple. He asked me what I meant — a zip catches on my leg, I will not think about this night — and I couldn't answer. Maybe the Victorians didn't think loten was a proper expression to use, I said. Maybe people prefer to pretend that we can't see in the dark.

It's a loten night tonight. Another woman might think it was beautiful.


Nate already has the keys to the van when we meet. As I take them off him, look at his young, bony face, it sinks in that we're going to be spending a night together, for hours we'll be alone in a van with the city a waste-land around us and no one within miles. We have to talk, we have to work together, we must make something out of this desolate, lethal night.

I lift the keys from his palm, hooking my finger through the ring, and I don't touch him at all.

He turns and walks ahead of me, slouching in the way that fit boys sometimes do, one shoulder dipping down, then the other. The vans wait in rows for us, couples break off from the crowd at the door and trail across the lot. Some of them say things, and their voices are thin in the open air. Nobody says much.

As we wait in the convoy, queuing to get out into the night, I turn to Nate. 'How many catches has Bride taken you on?' I keep my hands on the wheel as I ask.

He shrugs one shoulder. It's an odd gesture, as if he was straining against something. 'Six.'

'That's quite a few, you're – how old?' My question sounds louder with the van doors closed upon us, more personal.

'Nineteen.'

I could ask how many months, it makes a difference. Marty's nineteen, nineteen years and four months old. If I think of him and try to compare him with Nate, sitting here beside me, they seem irreconcilable. Courteous, soft-spoken Marty, tall and slight, the kind of height that's lankiness when you're a kid and becomes leanness when you grow up; a quick boy, an innocent, a fast learner, with whatever he feels glowing clear through his skin. Small, muscular Nate seems dense and lustreless as lead, he's heavy metal. I can't see past his surface.

'How many collars have you done?' The van reaches the head of the convoy and turns left. There's still a column of vans ahead of us. Something about the reflection of my headlamps on their surfaces makes me think of bent-backed creatures, beasts of burden, a whole troop of them trudging silent into the distance.

'Just one.' Nate says this deadpan, no apology or boast in his tone.

'On the last catch?'

'Yeah.'

'How did it go?'

'Okay.'

'Who was the offender?'

'A homeless woman.'

I turn the van, keep my eyes on the road. The moon shines down, casting a faint, crystal light on the city beyond my headlamps. 'Was she charged?'

'No.'

He isn't being hostile. There's a density to the conversation, a dragging sense that he might talk freely if I could only get it started. He's just answering my questions, that's all. I don't know what it would take to get him talking.

'Bride tells me you want to go into the financial department.' Outside, the world gapes around me and my tiny bid for conversation.

'That's right.'

'How come?'

He shrugs again. Why does he only shrug one shoulder? 'The money's better. I'm good with figures.'

'You enjoy accounting?'

'It's okay.'

Somewhere out in the night, people are roaming baretoothed.

*

Five Wounds Park. This is our area tonight, the west side of it. I review my knowledge of the city's history, to keep the word *alone* out of my head. It's the second oldest park, the first to be built after Benedict. If you're a lyco, the name just sounds pious, traditional. Some people who work in DORLA call it Fifty, but it's a lame joke. The injury rate isn't as bad as Sanctus; the trees in the wooded parts aren't as narrow and closely planted. Instead they're massive, old, trunks you can't put your arms around with heavy, jagged bark. Daylight, it's cool and green, spacious. Tonight, all I can think is that there are immense trees for people to hide behind, trees to be slammed into. Knotted bark cuts a brief, phantom impression into my face, and I shake my head. Nothing can happen to me tonight.

The tracker glows, empty. If Marty was here, he'd be asking about it, he'd need to know if we were in for a quiet night or if we were just in an unoccupied patch. 'We might be lucky,' I say, keeping the van at a steady forty miles per hour and not looking at Nate. 'It might be a quiet night.'

'You think so?' His tone is neutral.

'It's Tuesday. We're on the right side of the weekend.'

'Oh.' Nate says nothing, looks out of the window at the cool silver streets. Five Wounds Park is on my side, narrow iron bars cutting across the occasional tree. It isn't bright enough to make out any details; the trunks, half-hidden by the fence, wait in the background, solid, patient, opaque.

I turn around. 'Nate, are you nervous about this?'

He glances at me, a quick flicker. His shoulder pulls round a little as if shielding himself, and for just a moment I think I see something hunted in his expression. Then

220

his face is static again, unreadable. 'Are you?' He says it as if he thought I was hinting. I can't tell if that's what he really thinks.

I give up on conversation and turn through the main west entrance into Five Wounds. A colonnade of trees, great towering beeches, looms either side of us. I can see the lumps and bulges and irregularities on each trunk like ageing flesh slipping down.

The light beyond our headlamps is watery and pure, and what I'd like to do is switch off the van's lights and just look at it. Five Wounds is so carefully designed, so stately. I took Leo for walks here, before last week, before Seligmann escaped and I locked myself away. In the daytime it was on a human scale, there were people near us and the park didn't seem to extend that far, but now that it's empty and moonlit something has happened to the distance; it stretches on and on, boundless. I could watch it forever.

I brake the van, pulling to a halt in an open space. 'Why are we stopping?' Nate says.

Does he see the night outside? 'I'm just going to take some Pro-Plus,' I tell him. 'You want some?'

'Yeah.'

I break open the packet, dole out the little white pills. Nate dry-swallows his before I can offer him coffee, and I start to say something about it then stop. Instead, I pour myself a half-cup and drink. The sound of myself swallowing rushes over my ears, and I wonder if he hears it.

My head lolls back against the seat, and I look out at the park. I want to sleep. I want to go home, go back to my tiny flat and find Paul napping in my bed, ready to talk to me when I come in. I want things I can't have.

Paul isn't in bed tonight. Fatigue presses down on me, and what I want to do is sit quietly in this car and look out at the empty silver night.

'Are we going?' Nate's voice digs into me.

'In a minute.'

I hear him twitch and shuffle in his seat. The sound pricks me, it's wire wool at the nape of my neck. The scanner is dull red and blank. Nate settles in his seat, still and tense.

Yanking back the gear stick, I gun the engine and start up the patrol again. Maybe the motion of the van will steady him down.


At midnight, the tracker sounds, a sharp electrical cheep. Our mechanical canary. Nate and I come out of our separate worlds and study the image. My glance flicks over it and clocks it, and I open my mouth, then remind myself that Nate's a trainee and needs practice.

'What can you tell me about that?' I say.

Nate looks at me, just for an instant, then looks back at the tracker. 'It's a single lune,' he says. He's taken his feet off the dash, his hands rest in his lap, shifting a little as if he'd like to drum his fingers and is stopping himself. His voice doesn't shake, but it's slightly breathier than usual, just slightly. He sits straight, his legs braced, his head high and alert. 'It's on the move. It's at the edge of our area.'

I check, and I agree; it's right on the edge of the tracker, and when I look at where we are I see I've already driven further east than I'd thought. We've been wandering. 'Tell me about it being on the move. What do you think the situation is?'

Nate frowns, says nothing.

'Why do you think it's moving? How do you think it affects how we deal with it?' I keep the van on the path and head east.

'Well, it'll be harder to collar,' Nate says blankly.

'How so?'

'. . . Because we'll never outrun it, and if it keeps going when we get out of the van we can't catch it up.' The questions seem to assault him, though his answers are right enough.

'Which brings us back to the first question I asked you: why do you think it's running? We need to anticipate.'

Nate shrugs, again the one-sided, jerky movement. For a moment the sight of it goads me, and I press myself back in the seat. 'It could be hunting.'

'Yes. In which case?' The precision of my voice almost drowns out the image of blood soaking through this subtle moonlit grass.

'We wait for it to catch its rabbit or squirrel. Or we shoot the rabbit ourselves.'

A man tied to a chair, spitting out blood. 'Yes. Or use it to anticipate where it's going.' I close my eyes, open them. 'But we're careful. I don't know about you, but I don't feel brave enough tonight to come between this lune and its prey.'

He looks up, and I tell myself I can't get angry at him for hearing me talk of my weakness. I can't.

'Why else might it be running?' The little point of light disappears off the scanner, and I speed up the van to bring it back.

I'm so tired.

Nate raises his hands an inch, sets them down. 'It – might just be running. I don't know.'

223

Chasing another lune, injured and trying to flee the pain, trying to find somewhere familiar. Just running. There's no one here I can ask why lunes sometimes just run. 'They do, sometimes,' I say.

'So what do we do?' Nate picks up his pole. His grip is good, he holds it well. I've got to stop thinking about myself alone, I've got to start thinking of us as a unit. Just for tonight, just for tonight. It's too dangerous out there.

'Well . . .' The lune is getting closer, we're reaching it. I don't want this boy to see me bleed. 'I've heard stories of people doing collars out of the windows of pursuing vans, but I don't believe them. What we do is see if we can figure out what it's doing.'

Nate says nothing. There's no satisfaction in his silence.

'And if we can't,' I say, 'we trank it.'

Next month I face the short straw. Next month Marty should be on his feet and back at work. I should be thinking about caution, orthodoxy, the rulebook. Outside, the night is cold glass and perfect, and I can't stop to watch it.

I press on the accelerator and say, 'So have your sleeper ready.'


Our first sight of the lune is an instant, the sight of a massive grey flank that flies in front of the van and is away again. Nate jumps, knocks his catcher against the door, and I inhale in a hiss and swing round. Trees block our path and I swerve, jolting us both, to follow. It comes into view again, narrow white legs and a great fringed tail, heading away from us at an effortless, bounding run. The back flexes, the long, snaking neck balances, and the lune covers ground with swift, absolute ease while I tug the wheel and chase with our clumsy, rattling van. A man, it has to be, he's four and a half feet at the shoulder, double my weight, immense. He weaves fast as a horse in and out of the trees.

'We won't catch him,' Nate says, both hands wrapped tight around his catching pole.

'Not running,' I say, not daring to take my eyes off him. If he tires, he might stop, but lunes run easy as breathing, they can run for hours. 'Nate, look around, see if he's chasing something.'

'He's not.' Nate glares into the distance, keeps looking. There's nothing there. This man isn't after something. He's just – running.

We reel in our seats as I wrench the wheel again, just avoiding a great oak. Ahead of us, the lune runs on, his white legs flash in the light of the van.

'He's heading for the woods,' Nate says, his voice hardening. I draw a quick breath, because the woods are upon us and this is final. A few hundred yards, and the trees gather together in a mass. We could go through them at a crawl, rolling our careful route round each one, but at this pace we'll die, and it won't even be death by tearing teeth and heavy claws, it'll be a smash of metal and scattered glass and our skulls cracking under the blows of our own vehicle. We can't follow him into the woods.

'Nate, I'm going to do this,' I hear myself say. 'Watch my back.'

And I slam the van to a halt and shove open the door, a brief tussle and then I leap down, land hard on my feet and stagger to right myself and then I'm running,

225

gun in hand, I'm running for my life after him. The ground smacks against my soles, my arms are shaken by the rhythm and my knees are unstable and I'm so slow, my bare soft shiftless flesh in the moonlight is pushed to its limits and weak and no use to me against the fleet, huge, vanishing man before me.

I fire a dart, the gun kicks in my hand and I've missed, my pounding feet are rattling my arm as I run. I fire again, and still he's up, sure-footed, further and further away.

I clasp both my hands around the gun and raise it to take aim.

I fire twice. The first dart flies and stabs into his thigh, he breaks stride and his shot leg scuffles so that the second dart misses but it's all right, it's going to be all right because he can run a few more paces but the trank is in his bloodstream and soon he's going to stumble.

He slows, lopes, covering ten yards, twenty, his left leg cautious on the ground, lifting up and pointing the foot with an injured, balletic grace. Then he stops, raises a leg to scratch at the dart and his head droops, his body folds under its own weight and he's rolled over onto his side, and asleep.

My breath sears my chest and my heart is pounding, my feet ache from the beating they've taken against the ground. I stand, armed, gasping for air, the wide green space open around me and the sky looming above, deep black and clear. I look up. There are so many stars tonight, thick as milk, the sky is cloudy with them. Something could come at me from any side, but the world is empty, soundless, infinite around me. I breathe, and the air feels like a benediction.

The sound of an engine startles me, and I turn to see

Nate driving the van, trundling up to the tranked lune, ready to load. I look down and see that I'm still holding the gun, and I sigh in the cold and remember that this is not the time to stargaze and wonder at creation. So I reload, take four fresh darts off my belt and snap them into place, and follow the van.

This is a stretcher job; the lune is heavy and we have to bowl him onto a stretcher to get him into the van. It can be done alone, but not easily. As Nate unloads him, locks the cage and gets out the chipper to read his details, I take the metal detector and go out to look for the darts. In a crisis you can get away with not doing this, but there are no lunes nearby. It's a quiet night. Junkies trawl the parks every Day One, looking for darts that missed their targets, each loaded with enough sedative to knock out two people in the daytime. It's illegal to use them, to touch them, even – you're supposed to report them to the park staff and get DORLA to send out some menial with latex gloves to pick them up – but there have been cases where people OD'd. No lawsuits against us for leaving the darts behind have succeeded yet, but the day will come.

The metal detector is dull and awkward work. Another night, I'd send my subordinate to do it. This night, though, an unreality has taken hold of me, I can't stand to be in the van. Claustrophobia sucks at me as long as I'm in there, and while it's crazy to linger out in the moon night, still, as I pull on latex gloves of my own, a precaution against picking up a discarded syringe by mistake, all I can feel is frustration that they block the air on my hands.

*

Another circuit, another half hour, and there's nothing out there but transparent moonlight carving shadows in among the grass blades. The man we have in our cages is one Peter Seadon, a home owner, a first offender. He was a runner, not a fighter, which suggests a more peaceful nature. The trank will hold him for hours.

I drive around the edge of our area. The tracker will still tell us if anything comes up, so we can stay where we are. Thoughts keep occurring to me, things I could be thinking about, and they don't hold my interest. I just keep looking back outside.

Close by us, I know there's a lake. Leo and I have sat by it sometimes, while I cradled him and told him that when he learned to sit up we'd take bread and feed the birds. It's outside our patrol, some few hundred yards beyond our designated route, but it's a quiet night. It's Tuesday, Wednesday, there's been one lune all night, and I'd so love to see the lake. I've never seen it by moonlight, and I may never see such a lucid night again.

What I feel when I turn the wheel of the van and go looking for this lake of mine is safe. It may be that I've had too much adrenaline, that the capture of this man Peter Seadon has gone to my head. Post-hazard euphoria, they call it. Now I'm out here, marooned in a great silk-grey expanse, nobody can come at me without being seen. I have a tracker, I have guns, tonight I can fight. There's so much space around me, and whoever I find there won't recognise me, can't talk or chant rhymes or curse me down. It's freedom of a sort.

'Aren't we going off track?' says Nate as we near the lake.

'A little.' I won't tell him I'm looking for something

228

pretty. 'Our area's more or less dead at the moment. There's no harm in sweeping a little.'

'Isn't it, like, punishable by six months' imprisonment?' Nate says. His voice is harsh rather than scared, and I keep my head turned away, trying for unconcerned.

'Settle down, kid. Nobody's going to waste time on a detour we make on a quiet night that doesn't have consequences. If there were lunes in our area, yeah, but nothing's happening. There's no opening for a negligence suit here. Relax.' I'm out of the real world, far away.

The lake is slate-black, barely dimpled by the wind in this calm night. The moon shimmers on its surface, broken by the moving water into a row of crescents, each shifting a little with the waves. It's hard to believe that if I touched the surface of the water it would break, my hand would go through and find itself wet and cold and meet no resistance. It looks so tangible and constant, smooth as velvet. It could be a dip in the world. I thought it would be clear like the sky, but here in the dark, it's a soft, glimmering blank.

'What are we doing here?' Nate's voice is edgy. Looking at a lake, I could say. My eyes could rest here for a long time. I turn my head and make my eyes follow, and I see Nate's legs are curled up in his seat, he's gripping his knees. A woman he barely knows is bringing him wandering through the night, putting him at risk from superiors he hasn't met. He wants this to be prosaic, real, he wants a learning experience. He's on duty.

I'm about to resign myself, turn the van and leave the lake behind and go back on route, when I notice something odd. The tracker has a ring inside it that marks out a certain area, lets us know what's in reasonable range, and it bleeps when an object moves within the ring. The area outside is only a few millimetres of screen. Something is glowing in that area, right at the edge, a smudge to the north-east. It isn't close enough for the tracker to sound and alert us, but it's there. It doesn't look like a single speck.

'Do you see that?' I say.

Nate looks and says nothing.

A coordinated attack. A pack of dogs. A misread signal. This could be anything.

I want to see it.

'Excuse me,' says Nate as I start off north-west, 'but aren't we going way out of our area now?'

'We can get away with it,' I say, focused on my driving, 'if we're going to avert a crisis.'

'Yeah, but shouldn't we get on the radio, ask if anyone's checked it out first?'

'It'll save the switchboard time if we can verify that it's worth checking first.' The words come out of my mouth before I've had time to think of reasons, and I don't believe them.

'What if it's a pack?'

'Then we're within our rights to request back-up, and we're likelier to get it if we're in someone else's area.' The grey path unwinds under the wheels, and I keep driving.

'Won't we get in trouble for this? It's not in our area and no one's asked us to go there.' The tension in his voice scratches at me.

'You won't,' I say. I sit up straight, my voice is clipped. 'I'm exercising my own judgement here, you won't be held accountable for doing as you're told.'

The tracker bleeps as the patch of light gets within our perimeter. It's still shapeless, inexplicable.

'Yeah, but –'

'Nate.' I don't look at him. 'I'm exercising my judgement on this. That's enough.'

Nate sits back in his seat, legs apart, hands clamped against them, and doesn't say another word.

If the committee hears of this, I'll be strawed for sure. If Hugo hears of this, he'd tell me he couldn't approve. If we get there and find another pack of prowlers ready to run us down, I could be killed.

None of this is real to me. I'm beyond tired; the caffeine crackles inside me and my nerves jump, but inside I'm inert, like bright wrapping paper around a soft, dull core. I'm in danger from every side, and I'm exhausted, and just for tonight I'm all out of fear.


We cross Five Wounds, and still the creature on the tracker is ahead of us. It's when we reach the perimeter that I realise I was wrong. This thing I'm seeking isn't inside the park. It isn't far away, I can see that now, but it's outside in the city streets. We're going to have to move on.

The west gate is open for us, and we drive through.

'Why don't they shut the gates?' It's the first time Nate's spoken since I started this trek.

'Why should they?' Puzzlement takes me over; the very houses in front of us have an air of mystery.

'Keep the lunes out, so they don't get into the forests.'

'Open-space catches are easier than streets.' My voice trails along the ground. 'And lunes can jump walls.'

We're back in the streets. Five Wounds is an elegant

231

place to live. The buildings nearest the park aren't even tower blocks, they're houses. House after house, with high-fenced gardens and steps leading up the their own front doors. In this part of town, people can live alone.

Fenced-off gardens, paving stones. The engine makes a low whirr as I drive the last thirty yards, steady myself and turn the corner.

There's nothing here. The street's empty. The tracker shows us to be in the right place, but the road is deserted, grey in the glow of our headlamps, and we're alone.

'Lola?' Nate holds on to his catcher. 'What's up?'

'Hold on.' I pick up my gun and unlock the door.

'Where are you going?'

'I'll just be a minute.'

The door opens and my shoes make little clicks as I step down into the street. I slam the door behind me and stand against the van.

No one here.

I stand still, taut, and wait. I've only stood for a few moments when I hear a noise, a scuffle, coming from in front of me.

What's in front of me is a garden wall, a high and solid one with metal bars at the top. Looking to the side, I can see a house, a biggish one of red brick, and the garden must be tremendous because the wall around it runs on and on. I can hear movements inside it.

Possibly someone's luning in his garden. I've heard of it happening; people fail to lock their windows properly or have faulty bars, and then at night they leap out. If that's happened here, maybe we should caution them tomorrow, but it's not worth a scene because this wall is sturdy. A lune could leap it, but probably

232

wouldn't, not unless he was a real roamer. It's not quite legal, but it's contained enough. Or maybe someone's just keeping goats in his garden, or has locked the dogs out.

I can't see. The wall towers over me, and something's behind it and I can't see. I'm leaning against the van in frustration, hand tight around my gun, when I hear something else.

Someone's howling. It's low-pitched, not loud but penetrating as the ring of struck glass.

Without saying anything to Nate, I go round the back of the van. There's a step above the bumper. Tucking my gun into my waist, I set my foot up. I reach above me and grip the frame that protects us from a rooftop attack, and place my other foot onto the door handle. It digs through my shoe and I grit my teeth, catch hold of the roof-frame with both hands and pull myself up. And balanced on the grid like a battery hen, I'm so close to the wall that I can reach across and grip the bars to look through.

It's dark in the garden, the high fences beyond cast shadows across the ground. There's only a little grey light from above, and for a moment I can't take in what I see. Then there's a flash of light across from me. Two tiny green circles.

The lune turns his head and the reflection from its eyes goes away. Another one comes up to him, and they sniff each others' faces, noses touching, parting, touching, like a lover's kiss.

There's a strange vividness to the scene below me. My eyes take in the darkness, expand, adjust, and the silver-haired lunes before me almost glow. Five of them, maybe six. Two stand and touch noses, others lie under

233

a tree on the far side. As I watch, one of them lifts his head, ruffed neck flexible as a swan's, and rises to his feet. He swings long-legged across the garden, raises his head and inhales.

A sound comes out of his throat, a low-pitched whine, neither plaintive nor painful. It sounds cautious. He looks around, and one of the standing lunes comes over from the corner. The two of them stand, facing forward.

They can't see me. Surely they can't see me.

The second lune makes a noise, a choking bark, and they all stand. It's a big garden, the size of a small field, and when they run towards me, I have plenty of time to clutch the bars and watch how they move together like a shoal of fish.

First one then another lifts their heads and intones. They wail against each other like a choir, each howls and draws breath and howls again, with no moment of silence, nothing but pure, eerie sound. Their voices ring together, modal, cold. Loten.

One of them comes up to the fence, then bares his teeth. His face creases and snarls, a mask of savagery. I see the weight of his teeth, the length of his glistening pink gums.

He looks up.

I let go of the bars, flatten myself down and bruise my back and chest as I roll over the hard metal frame on the roof. Pushing myself off, I fall, hang alone in the air for a weightless, sickening instant and then land hard on my feet on the stone pavement. My knees fold under the impact, I land in a crouch, slapping my palms down, jolting my head. Then I'm up, wrestling with the door and back inside the van.

'What's going on?' Nate speaks, and hearing words, a voice using actual words, is almost more than I can take in. 'Lola? What was that about?'

And I've no idea what to say.

# 17

My report is still not done when Hugo calls me in to tell him how things went. He sits behind his desk, upright in his chair. He's not a catcher; well into middle age, he's more likely to do coordination, shelter management, central message boards, the higher end stuff. His solid face shows more lines than usual, there's a pallid tinge around his eyes, but that's all the fatigue he shows. He's alert and weary at once, like a soldier.

'So, what can you tell me this month?' he says. There's an air of resignation in the room. The short-straw party happens soon. We both know that after this month, I may be sent elsewhere.

I draw breath, let it go without speaking, draw breath again. 'It was pretty quiet last night. Quieter than it's been for months. We just had one collar.'

'You and Nathan Jensen?'

'Yes. Bride Reilly suggested I take him, since my own trainee was off sick. Though if it's all the same to you, sir, I don't think Nate and I work together that well. He wouldn't be my first choice if I'm sent on another catch.'

'Hm.' Hugo meets this with a neutral face. 'So what were the events of the night?'

I swallow. 'Just one collar. A man named Peter Seadon. Not a big offender.'

'And may I ask, was this collar done – in a manner that would not call your methods into question?' There's no suggestion of criticism or confidence in his tone. Hugo must be one of the only men in the world who can remind me of my faults without suggesting insult.

'We tranked him.' His eyebrows move just a fraction. 'Sub-Kendalling, perhaps, but he was a runner. We'd never have caught up with him, and he was heading for the woods. He was big and strong, healthy-looking. There was very little medical risk in it.'

'I see.' Hugo rests his hands together and leans back. 'And was your trainee involved in this?'

Can I be trusted to look after a kid who's relying on me. That's what he's asking, that's what the committee will want to know. 'I left Nate in the vehicle. He followed me in it and helped me to load this Seadon once he was doped, but no, I tranked him on my own. It was a one-man job.'

'Which you performed.'

'Yes. Seadon was going fast, I had to make an instant decision. It was all too rapid to make a good practice ground. Nate could learn by watching, but I hadn't seen him in action enough to be sure he was ready to do the job. I thought it safer if I did.'

Hugo looks at me for a long moment. I stop myself speaking to fill the quiet. 'Hm,' he says at last. 'Well, that may be to your credit. It seems you took the appropriate action. For which we must be thankful.'

I say nothing, plait my hands in my lap. Hugo told me about the strawing a month ago. He seldom repeats himself.

'Was there anything else of note on the patrol?'

This is it. 'There – there was an incident later on in the night, but it wasn't an offence. Just a security breach in someone's house, I think.'

'You think?' There's nothing in his tone to suggest a threat.

'Yes. Truthfully, Hugo, I don't want to drag someone through the courts if it was just a broken window or something.'

'Sympathy?' There's mild disbelief in his face. I try for my professional voice and ignore the disbelief at the idea of me sympathising with someone.

'A waste of our time and resources. It was a bit of a curious one, but –' This is close to the edge. If I lie to my boss, if I'm caught lying to him, I'll still be mopping floors when I'm seventy. 'To be honest, I'd like to request a little slack on this one. It struck me as odd, but I couldn't really put my finger on why. It might be a hunch, or – well, I've been under some pressure lately.' Hugo's face barely changes, only his eyebrows settle a little. 'I don't want to end up spending resources on something that's just me getting worked up because I'm – sleep deprived. It might make more sense if I can have a think, check it out on my own time, and come back if need be.'

He doesn't take his eyes off my face. 'What was this – curious thing?'

I hold my knees together. I don't know why I shouldn't be calm. 'A few people in a garden. Most likely a family that broke through a window that's being fixed this afternoon. That's why I don't want to waste anyone's time but my own on it.'

'Well. Lola –' He leans forward. I stop my arms

coming up to cover me. 'You've always been a depend-
able worker. I know a lot has happened to you recently.
I wouldn't like to see you compromising your work
because the pressure has got to you.' He sighs.
'Investigate this event if you like. I can put in a request
for you to be spared full moon duties for a couple of
months. That should give your real trainee time to get
back to his job.'

'Thank you.' This is a serious gift. If I'm under
threat of strawing, the last thing I can afford to do is
ask for favours. With Hugo asking for them for me,
I'll be safe.

'All I can suggest is that you be cautious. You've
been a reliable operative, Lola. I'd like to keep it that
way.'

So I can write my report and make no mention of
the detour. I haven't lied to Hugo. I can work unobserved
on this, and not have to come up with a reason why.
Say what you like about understaffing, I tell myself as
I leave Hugo's office and pick my way through the
rushing crowds, but it does get you some slack if you
want to work alone.


I'm quiet when I go round to Paul's in the evening,
hoping to relax. I wear my gloves on the way in to the
building, in case any of his neighbours see me. He's never
asked me to do it, but people get curious if a non is
dating a lyco, even in DORLA. Lycos, from the little
experience I've had of it, are worse. He'd say it was none
of their business, but I don't feel like going through the
effort of telling them that. I wear my gloves and spare
him the trouble. I wouldn't do it for anyone else.

I'm really looking forward to seeing him. When he lets me in, though, he's pale and looks at me slanted. 'Hey.' His voice is husky, tired.

I follow him through to his living room. 'Are you okay?'

He touches my waist briefly, and then lies down on the sofa. 'Migraine. I get them sometimes. I can feel this one coming on.'

I sit down beside him, turn his head towards me. 'Are you all right?'

He half-smiles, unhappy. 'Not really. Right now I've just got buzzing lights all over the place, but in about half an hour my head's going to feel like it's being hit with a hammer.'

'How – how often do you get them?' I touch his head, trying to block the hammer blows. 'Is it a moon night thing?'

'No. I just get them sometimes. I've been a bit stressed. Work.' His eyes close. Against his bloodless skin, his eyebrows stand out black, as if drawn on with charcoal.

'Well, well what do I do?'

He squints up at me. 'Nothing. It'll pass.'

'Nothing, hell.' I sit down on the floor, so my head's level with his. I can't have Paul's head hurting. 'Want me to speak to some medic friends of mine? I can get you real doctors' supplies stolen from the stores. We could get you some morphine . . .'

'No, thanks.' His hand flops onto mine, rests there, limp. 'I don't much like medication.'

'But your head's going to hurt.' Paul can't get sick. I have to stop him getting sick.

'I'll be okay.' He's too sick to even open his eyes and look at me.

My voice comes out very small. 'Should I go away?'

'No . . . I don't know.' Oh God, now I'm confusing him. I'm making it worse.

'I'll do whatever you want.'

'Could you – could you –' He opens one eye, shades it. 'God, I hate the flashing bits.'

'Me too . . .' I don't know what to say.

'Could you just – give me a hand into the bedroom and then stay here? I mean, in another room, not making any noise?'

'Okay . . .' I'm sitting back on my heels, nodding my head like a kid.

'Fun date . . .' He covers his eyes, bites his lip.

'Come on, don't be silly.' My voice has become high-pitched, quavering. 'Let's get into the bedroom.'

I help him up, lead him to his bed, close the windows, draw the curtains, pulling them tight to shut out any glimmer of light that might come in and scald him. I take off his shoes, arrange the covers, close the door behind me and put cushions against it so no light can creep in under it. I take off my own shoes, put them down by the door. Then I think he might trip on them coming out, so I move them across the room by the bookshelf, where they look untidy, so I move them again, leaving them by the front door. If someone else came in, the shoes might be crushed by the opening door, so I move them back just a little, just ahead of where the door would be if it opened.

The boards make tiny creaks as I stalk back on tiptoe. I wave my hands, trying to shush them, but every step makes a sound. The kitchen has a solid floor, so I stand there, look around. I'm hungry, but I know the fridge door creaks as it opens. There's food on the sideboard.

241

Cereals, a crunch with every bite like gravel in my mouth. Apples, the noise of cracking chalk. A packet of plain biscuits, if I ate them there'd be a sound like breaking plastic. Why can't they sell food that doesn't hurt him?

There's a banana. Maybe I can have a banana. I peel it fast, the outside coming off with a sound like tearing cloth, and take it into the living room. I stand balanced in front of the bookshelf, trying to find something I want, making no stir as my eyes go over the shelves. Paul is the one who reads. I don't know how to pick something.

I pick one book because it's got a long title. Another I take because there's a picture of a paper doll on the cover. I pick a third because I've read it before, it'll be something to do with my eyes if I don't like the others. I want to fold paper, make something, a crane or a frog, but I don't know if he'll hear the sound of it creasing.

Three books and a peeled banana. I sit myself on the sofa, my island, where I'll stay and keep quiet and not venture off until Paul's head is better. I curl up, pressing my knees into my chest until I'm tiny. The banana is starchy and soft as I bite into it, and the pages make almost no noise turning.


It's hours later when I hear him speak. Time has gone dead, minutes have lasted longer than I could count, the second hand on my watch has lingered at every stop. It's gone so quiet the room beyond my little patch on the sofa seems two-dimensional, painted onto the great body of silence around me.

Paul's voice calls from the bedroom, unsteady, hoarse, but I hear it. 'Lola?' It has the fragility that comes from hours without speech. 'Are you still there?'

'Yes.' I sound strange in my own ears, almost like a cry. 'Yes, I'm here.'

'Would you come in here?'

I pad through, shoeless, walking on the balls of my feet. Paul's lying just where I left him. Even in the dark, I can see how wan he looks.

I sit on the bed and rest my hand on his chest. 'How's your head?'

He takes hold of my hand. 'Better. Still pretty horrible, but better. Are you all bored out there?'

'Only boring people get bored.' It's something he's said to me. I couldn't answer the question. 'Would you like a glass of water or something?'

'Yes, please.'

I soft-foot through the flat, fill a glass, return. He drinks it with his head propped on his hand, then lies down again, setting his head on the pillow as if a sudden impact might dent it.

I'd like to lie down with him, but the migraine's taken up all the space in the bed. 'Are – are you hungry?'

He makes a pained face.

'Okay, no.'

'I'm sorry to flake out on you like this.'

'Oh, that's right,' I say, my voice as close to gentle as I can bring it. 'You get blinding headaches so you don't have to take me out. If I had a penny for every man who'd tried that one . . .'

'It's nice of you to stick around.'

This was where I wanted to be. If he didn't send me away when his head hurt, if it made him feel better to have me in the next room, it means he wants me around. I don't know how to explain this to him. As I move lower to bring my head level with his, I think how it's been this way from the start. He's always assumed things are okay that I wouldn't have risked suggesting. They don't even seem to bother him.

'I didn't want you dying when my back was turned,' I say. It's the closest I can get to telling him I love him.

I stay the night. I lie very still beside him, waiting till I'm sure he's asleep before I let myself drift off.

I don't know when the mists clear, but somehow I've come to earth and this is what I see. The sky above me is bronzen with light, a gold beacon burning and casting everything into perfect, gilded beauty. It isn't the sun. It's a cold night, I can feel the wind in my eyes, but nothing can touch me. Under my coat of thick grey hair, tinted silver by the blazing moon, no chill can penetrate and I'm warm. As darts whistle past me, I know I'm running, my feet are shod with hard, tough skin and the ground is dewy between my toes, but I'm safe, nothing will cut my feet, and I'm not tired. I run, the ground slips under me faster than I knew it could, and there's nothing but the rhythm of my feet beneath me and the light, the smell of fresh clean earth, damp leaves, wood smoke, cold, pure air.

'Are you okay?' I open my eyes. Paul's face is a shadow above me, his hand on my shoulder.

'What?' I've fallen back into my body with a shock, my arms and legs in the bed are not where I thought they'd be.

'You were whimpering in your sleep.'

'Whimpering.' I touch my face, my fingers cautious.

'Yes, you were making funny noises. Not the usual piano music. I thought you might be having a nightmare.'

'I was dreaming.' I take hold of his arm. I'm not sleepy any more. 'Paul, what's it like to lune?'

He rubs his face. 'I thought we'd done that one.'

'You said atavistic. I can hardly spell atavistic. I want to know.' I try to grin. 'If you tell me something, I'll make up some convincing stories of everything pornographic I did in the creches.' His forehead wrinkles and he looks at me, steady blue eyes, and I look down. 'Bad joke. I just – I don't know. You seemed okay with it. People do it. And I can't ask my sister, she'd just clam up and get all tense that I'm dwelling on our differences.'

'Will you introduce me to her some time?' He tugs a lock of my hair, rolls me on top of him.

I let him. 'She doesn't know I'm seeing you.'

He lets go, half sits up, lies down again before he dislodges me. 'What? Why not?'

'I –' I hold on to him. 'Becca doesn't get my life. She'd like to be able to pin it down. If I told her about you, I'd have to – to have a formula. I'd have to give her a definition, and then come back and act it out.'

His chest raises me like a wave as he sighs. 'That doesn't make any sense.'

'Anyway, her husband left her pregnant with what could have been his son. He went to another country. He wouldn't even come back for a blood test.'

'That's pretty sorry.'

'I don't think she wants to hear about men right now.'

'So I can't meet her?'

'I don't know. Maybe.'

'Lola?' Paul picks up my head so I have to look at him. 'Just how many people have you told about us?'

'I – A couple.'

'Who?'

'My best friend, Bride?' I say this with a slight plea in my voice like a homework excuse.

'That would be the woman on the phone? Who you had to tell because she heard me answer the phone in the middle of the night.'

'My friend Ally.'

'Who's she?'

'He. He's – he's just someone at work.'

'Who else?'

I squirm my head free and sit up, hugging my knees. 'That's kind of it.'

'Er – Lola?' Paul's almost scowling, but his voice is restrained. 'That's not very many.'

'Well, have you told everyone?'

'Yes!'

'Oh.'

'Lola, is this a relationship or an affair?' The question blindsides me. I drop my head to see his hands fidgeting on the covers.

'What do you mean?' I almost whisper.

'I mean, why the secrecy?' He looks at me, and for a moment his face is tense, still. Then it creases up, and his head tilts on one side. 'Are you keeping quiet to make me more easily disposable?'

'God, no.' I want to put my arms around him, but he's mad at me and I can't. I take hold of his knee and hold tight. 'It's not a secret, you're not a secret. I just – it's been going so well. I – God, Paul, you're the best thing that's happened to me in years, maybe ever.' This isn't me talking, I don't talk this way, but I make myself carry on. 'I didn't want to say anything because I didn't want to jinx it. That's all it was. I didn't know any of this was going to happen, and when it started, I just – I didn't want to admit to myself how much I hoped you'd stick around. I didn't want to admit how disappointed I'd be if you didn't. That's all it was. I wanted to keep you.'

Paul looks at me. His hands on the blankets loosen.

I push my hair out of my face, tell myself that my hand can't be shaking. 'And that's the speech,' I say. 'Honest-to-God, cut out my heart and show it to you truth. Don't go looking for another one.'

'Oh.' I hear Paul let out a breath, and then he reaches over and hugs me to him. My back is stretched in this position, but I don't ever want to move. 'That's all right then, isn't it.' We both laugh a little, and I crawl closer, hold on.

'I wish you wouldn't worry,' he says. 'I'm not going anywhere.'

'Did you think this was an affair?' With my face buried in his neck, he can't see me, I can ask him things.

'No. I hoped not.'

'Not even when I asked you home right away?'

'Well, I wasn't going to say no.' He laughs, his fingers trace the outlines of my spine.

'My mother would have told me you wouldn't respect me.'

'Glad you didn't take her advice.' He shifts position without letting go. 'Honestly? At the time I thought, well, this ended up in bed sooner than I expected, but I wasn't going to object. I'd kept thinking about you ever since we met. When we got to go out, I thought I'd have to spend weeks trying to seduce you.' He rocks my head to and fro. 'You saved me a lot of cold showers.'

'I read in the papers that cold showers were supposed to stimulate the hormones.' This is easy; nothing can come of me saying this.

'Yeah, maybe that's true.'

I tighten my grip. 'You've got to appreciate me saying nice things,' I say into his shoulder. 'I don't do it very often.'

'When you do, you do it properly.' Paul strokes my neck, inhales the smell of my hair. 'I'm going to write that lot down and frame it.'

'Don't you dare. My reputation would never recover.'

We sit for a while without speaking.

'Can I ask you something?' I say.

'What?'

'I was dreaming about luning.'

He disengages his head from my shoulder and looks at me, smoothing the hair back from my face.

'I dreamed I was this guy we collared last night. He was running away from us. Not running away. Just running, and we were behind him. I tranquillised him. But in the dream, the darts never hit me.'

'Was that good or bad?'

'I don't know.' I close my eyes as we lie down. 'What about my dream?'

He sighs. 'It's – it's hard to talk about. It's hard to describe not having words.'

'Is it cold? I dreamed I was warm. Too much hair for the cold to get in.'

'Oh.' He laughs. 'No, it can be cold. Cold gets in between the hairs.' His fingers creep through my own hair, touch my scalp. 'It can get right up against your skin. But you feel everything. It's harder to think of cold as bad. It's just another thing you're feeling.'

'Is it nice to run? Like in a dream, when you don't get tired.'

'You don't expect to. I mean, there's never a moment when you say, hey, look at me go! It doesn't work like that.'

'Sounds like you remember some of it,' I say. 'Most people don't.'

'You remember bits of it if you think about it when you wake up,' he says, toying with my fingers. 'But don't quote me on that, I don't want to end up messing with legal precedents.'

'I dreamed I was looking at the moon. I was following it like a moth. It looked golden.'

He laughs. 'No, it's not golden. You don't exactly see in colour. Not in the same way.'

'Black and white?'

'No. Not like a black and white movie. You don't look and see it's different. I mean, when you look at the world now, you see what you expect to see, these are the colours that exist. And the same when you're luning, only the colour range is different. It isn't exactly colours, not the ones you see, but you understand what you're seeing. As far as you understand anything in that state.'

'Oh.' My voice trails away, sinks. 'And following the moon?'

249

'No, you don't do that either.' His hand cups the back of my head, his palm wider than my neck. 'Everything else is before you. Why would you follow the moon?'

I close my eyes, bury my face against his chest. So I was mistaken. Everything I dreamed was wrong.


Five days later, Nate is dead.

# 18

This is what happened.

Even a boy wouldn't walk through the parks alone after dark, not after he's hunted in them. He was cutting past one of them, walking around the perimeter, heading for whatever he does when he's home. They think someone followed him from inside the park. Sanctus Park, where the trees grow all around the edges and you can hide. It was along Nate's nightly route.

They think someone knew he'd be there.

Nate walked a long way before he died. A hundred, two hundred yards, not knowing he was being followed. He didn't know this was the end of his life. If nobody warned him, he couldn't have known that he should have loved those last hundred yards, that they weren't just an obstacle to getting to where he planned, that the sounds of his feet on the pavement and the wind in the branches were all he was ever going to have.

Some people take out handkerchiefs as we sit gathered in the lobby, someone from above standing up to make the sad announcement. Bride's beside me, and I don't look at her. I stare into my tea, milkless, sugarless, the colour of old leather. I don't cry. Perhaps there's somebody here who knows whether Nate would have loved the street where a bullet hit him in the head and spilled all his ability to love across the unswept cobbles, but I don't know who to ask.

'Are you okay?' There's a hand on my shoulder, Ally's. I twitch, brush it away. 'He worked with you, didn't he?'

I stare up at Ally. 'I hardly knew him.' My lips are cold as I speak.


The announcer only gives us a minute to take in the news before calling on people to report. Names are read out. Bride Reilly. Gus Greenham. Lola Galley.

When I go inside and meet the people there, I see Hugo is among them. Others I know by sight, or by name.

Alice Townsend. High on the committees, wears heavy, sharp-framed glasses that prove she's a handsome woman and can get away with wearing them, chignon hair, posture, thirty years in Personnel. We still call it that. There was a time when some optimists thought we should keep up with the times and change the name of Personnel to Human Resources. It didn't happen. None of us could face the remarks of prisoners about whether we're really human. Ms Townsend was one of the people who declared there was no point changing.

Amit Aggarwal. High in security. I've heard it said that there's little that happens in the cells that he doesn't know about. Fifty years old, and he never forgets a name, a face, an event. Often he's present where it's not strictly his concern, at the invitation of his superiors. They know they can ask him years later what happened, and he'll know. He's slight, skinny, he doesn't have a cop's face. There's something strung-together like a mannequin about him, like you could pick him up easily. No one would speak harshly to him, even if you didn't know he'd remember it for the next twenty years; just the way he looks somehow stops you. He looks fragile, unless you remember who he is.

William Jones. I look at him. William Jones is at the top, so high he doesn't even have a department. He meets government ministers. He interprets policy. He's a sign something terrible is going to happen, because why would he bother speaking to a legal adviser who'll never make her mark and earns her living defending derelicts and junkies? He sits there, beside my boss, his clasped hands resting on the table top. Doubtless he was a handsome man in his youth, and even now, despite the scar that runs across his forehead, his is a striking face, regular features lit with a spark of intelligence, a quizzical twist about the eyes that's always there. It must come from when he was young, because I haven't seen him make jokes. Something about him suggests a light that's gone out. His eyes on me are utterly serious.

'Hello, Lola,' says Hugo.

'Here I am.' My voice is hoarse, it doesn't stand up to things. I clear my throat. 'What's all this about?'

Ms Townsend leans forward. 'I know you will have heard about Nathan Jensen's death. You were at the meeting, weren't you?'

'Yes. Yes, I was.'

'We feel we should warn you . . .' Ms Townsend sighs, leans forward. Her tone is not unkind. 'You should consider the possibility that you're at risk yourself.'

'At risk.' There's nothing I can do with my face.

253

'We think it's likely that Nathan's death is connected with the Seligmann case.'

'Nate.' I can't feel my hands. 'Nobody called him Nathan.'

'Nate.' Ms Townsend glances at the others.

'Is that what you're telling everyone? Everyone you called in? That's why, isn't it? You think he'll come after people who interrogated him.' My words run together too fast, but I can't slow them down.

'It seems likely.' It's William Jones who's speaking. He speaks gently, but there's an underlying note of professionalism in his tone, as if he were speaking to a member of the public. As if he's spoken that way so much he can't stop the habit.

I swallow. 'Is – I heard a rumour Nate was training to guard military lock-ups. There's no chance this is some military conspiracy, is there?'

Alice Townsend's look of pity seals my mouth shut. 'It's true he expressed an interest, but he was too early on in his training to have got to that stage yet. I'm sorry, Ms Galley. It's Darryl Seligmann you need to be worried about.'

'Oh.' She's very, very sure.

William Jones leans forward. 'Seligmann refused to cooperate with any psychiatric examinations, and there's very little we know about him, but he bore all the marks of a man who would keep a grudge. Is there anything you can tell us, based on your experience of questioning him?'

'I only did it once.' This won't save me.

'It was you who captured him.' Amit Aggarwal speaks from the corner of the room without raising his voice.

'Oh, yes,' I hear myself say. 'I've no doubt I'll stick in his mind.' The words make me laugh, and I grab hold of my sleeves, drag breath into my lungs, stop myself. Holding onto my arms, I can feel I'm rocking a little. I can't do this here. 'In – in the interrogation, he was hostile. He said funny things.'

'What did he say?' Hugo leans forward. He's outranked by everyone here, but I'm his.

'He called us soulless.' It's the only thing I can remember, the only word I can hold on to. I sit before four powerful people and my legs are numb and I can't remember how to cry, and it's how I feel. Soulless.

'Soulless?' Jones leans forward. 'That's curious.'

'It's new to me,' Aggarwal says softly.

'Is that all?' Hugo's face is expressionless as ever, and it's a hiatus in this empty white room.

'I – I don't remember. He threw some words around, said some things, you – you hit like a girl . . . I don't know. I don't know.'

'All right.' Ms Townsend raises her hand. 'We don't have to do this now. Tell me, Ms Galley – Lola – what do you think you'll do?'

'Do?' There's chalk dust on my eyelids, I can't see straight.

'Well, we're talking to the people who've had contact with him. For the moment, we're considering him dangerous.' She speaks calmly, she's the woman from Personnel, breaking this to me is her job. Her voice and her face won't mesh in my mind, the images are coming from different places. 'Now, most of the people who interrogated him don't feel themselves to be in too much danger.'

'Why?' My voice is pitched like a child's. I shouldn't

have come in today. I should have stayed at home. I should be sick, I want a migraine like Paul's, something to hold on to.

Jones looks at me; there's awareness in his face, with a faded overlay of sadness. 'He was blindfolded.'

'Blindfolded.' They blindfolded him before they interrogated him. They must have known in advance, they must have gone down to his cell already resolved to do things to him he'd never forgive.

'There are few faces he'll recognise. I'm afraid yours is one of them.'

'Bride. What's Bride doing?' Bride will have a joke, a saying, a way of making this ordinary.

Ms Townsend speaks again. 'Bride Reilly has requested a temporary transfer to another city. We've agreed.'

'Transfer? She can't transfer. Her husband's sick, he's not supposed to have any excitement. He can't just move house, he's sick.'

'Lola.' Hugo's voice stops my words as they fall from my mouth, tumble and scatter on the floor like pebbles.

'On a positive note, Lola,' Ms Townsend continues with a businesslike sigh, her voice still at a soft pitch, 'you'll be pleased to hear that because of what's happened, we've discussed the case of you and Sean Martin a few days earlier than expected, and decided that you should not be disciplined. We thought you'd like to know that before you make any decisions about what to do.'

'But you were going to straw me. I was supposed to be strawed.' The meeting was three days from now. In two days I was going to prepare myself, wash my hair, get some speeches ready in my defence. They can't just be making a decision now, when I'm not even wearing my good suit.

'Your record is good and it's kept on being good after that event. And I think we can all agree that the circumstances were – well, worse than you could expect. It's good news, Lola.' She keeps saying my name. 'I hope you're pleased.'

'Pleased.'

'But, now you have to decide what to do.' She shuffles some papers. The others watch me. I want Hugo to speak to me, but he's just looking at me, and I have to shake out of myself the urge to reach for his hand. 'Most people have taken temporary transfers. Do you think that's something you'd like to do?'

'Transfers.' I can't go away. I don't know anyone in another city. Becca lives here, Leo, Paul. Who could I talk to? 'I – I don't think I could afford a move, to rent somewhere else, I mean, I don't have much money saved or anything, I – I don't know . . .' They can't mean I'm not safe here. I'm never safe here. Never, and things happen, I lose blood and pieces of flesh and – How would I move?

'Well, you just take some time to think about it. We could deal with accommodation somehow if that's a problem. The alternative is staying. You can carry on working here; I won't say we don't need the staff. If that's what you decide, I'd suggest certain precautions, maybe staying with a friend or family rather than living at your own address.'

'My address.'

'Yes, it would be quite easy to trace you. Somewhere else might be safer.'

So I can't go home. My hideout is discovered. I'm

257

locked out of my kitchen and I'll have to eat somewhere else, my little blue bedroom is forbidden me and how am I going to sleep in another bed? The pillows will be the wrong thickness, the sheets won't be the texture I know. I can't sleep.

'You'll need to give us a contact number, but don't tell us the address. You should be as discreet as possible. Assuming this works for you – do you have family you can go to?'

'My sister.' My voice isn't certain, it's stunned. Would Becca even take me in?

'Though if you wish to be extra cautious, someone less easy to trace. A friend, perhaps? Do you have a boyfriend?'

No one knows about Paul. When I'm with him, no one knows where I am. Can I really go to him and expect him to take on a commitment, a fugitive, risk his life and have to see me every minute he's at home?

'I'm sorry,' I say. 'I can't do this.'

'It's all right,' Hugo says. His tone is as flat as ever, but he leans forward a little, putting his bulky shoulders between her and me. 'I think we've finished here. And you don't need to decide now.'

There's quiet as the others look at him, and then Jones puts down the papers he was holding. 'All right,' he says. 'That should be enough.'

I rise before they tell me to go, stumble and hit my hip on the chair as I stand. They sit in their seats, balanced in them, held up. My limbs half-remember how to walk, it feels queer and wrong but I move forward. I don't look over my shoulder as I go out of the door.

\*

When Becca lets me in, she has Leo on her hip. He's holding his head up now, eyes round as marbles, the brown irises huge in his face. He makes a noise of pleasure to see me and flaps his arm, and something in me breaks.

'Look, it's Auntie May,' Becca says, and hands him over to me. I take hold of him, wrap my arms around his small body, hold his head against mine. He's warm and smooth in my arms, scented with powder, but still he's too little to hide behind.

'Come in, May, I was just making some tea,' Becca says, wiping her hands on her trousers. This doesn't make sense, Becca never wiped her hands on her trousers or her eyes on her sleeve, she scolded me for doing it. Where's my sister?

'You seem – okay,' I say, my hand around Leo's head for support. Fine hairs cling to my palm, and his scalp is soft and hot. My fingers stray over the empty patch on his skull, the great gulf where nothing but a layer of skin covers his brain, and I lift him up, hold him steady.

Becca sighs, not sadly but calm, as if she'd just woken from a deep sleep. 'I feel fine. Lionel hasn't called, before you ask. Nothing's happened. We've just had a nice day, Leo and I. We went out to the park for a walk, it's a beautiful day for the time of year.'

'You took him for a walk?'

'Yes.' She pours tea.

'Which park?'

'Well, Queens, it's nearest.'

'I – I took him to different ones.'

'Well, I'm not as energetic as you.' Becca sits cross-legged on the sofa and smiles. Her feet are bare.

'I could have taken him out.'

'Well, you haven't been taking him out these last couple of weeks, May.' She cocks her head at me, admonishing.

'I – things have happened.' She's taking him to the parks. What am I going to do?

'Oh, Mum came to visit the other day,' Becca says, picking up some of Leo's clothes from beside the sofa and folding them.

'Why are you folding those?' I say. I sound confused. 'They're so small already.'

'Hmp.' Becca nods at me with a critical grin. 'Well, you were never the one for domestic tasks.'

'I can be domestic.' I can. If she'd seen me cleaning my plates, painting my walls, sweeping my floor, she'd know I'm not the scruffy little kid she grew up alongside. Once I had my own place, I learned what it meant, and I got old enough to do chores. I help Paul keep his flat tidy. She doesn't know it, but if I'm in the house, I help. I'm not a burden.

'Anyway, Leo and Mum are hitting it off, I think. He was so good. He didn't cry once.'

'Oh.'

'She asked about you.' Becca looks at me, her face a mixture of caution and censure. She knows this is risking an argument.

I put a cushion under my head and lean back. 'She asked about me?'

'Yes, she wanted to know how you were.'

'What did you say?'

Becca shrugs, brushes her hair back. 'I said you were fine. That I'd been seeing quite a lot of you, that you'd been giving me a lot of help with Leo.'

260

'I – I have been helping.' I've been round here a lot. Becca's had a lot of sleep because of me, a lot of fresh fruit from the shops, a lot of free hours. I have been useful. I look at my sister, resting back on the sofa, her face calmer than I've seen it in months, and Leo bats his hands against me, showing off his arms, enjoying himself. The room smells of talcum powder, and I'm starting to understand how tired I am. The word *tomorrow* drifts into my mind, and I can't handle it. All I can think now is that I'm comfortable on this sofa, how much effort it would be to stand up and leave.

'May, are you all right? You look a little grey.'

'Grey.' Our mother used to call me peaky. You have to eat your greens, May, you look far too peaky. Don't wear that, the colour makes you look peaky. Peaks pushed through me, angles came out in my face like mountain tops above clouds. Becca called me spiky; sharp-edged things inside me forcing their way out into the light.

'May –' Becca brushes her hair off her forehead, the old gesture that's come back since the baby, and leans forward. 'Is something wrong?'

'What?'

'You're just sitting and staring and repeating everything I say. Is there something bothering you?'

Leo struggles in my arms, leans back against me. He wants space. When he learns to walk, there'll be no stopping him; he'll run right out into the world without a backward look. 'I don't feel very well,' I say.

'Are you coming down with something?'

'No.' I blink. There's a blue haze, and I can't wake my voice up. 'No. Someone's died.'

261

'Died?' I see Becca sit up on the couch, come to attention. Concerned, puzzled. Not threatened, nothing after her. Her face, frowning, is still pretty, and the word in her pleasant accent has no meaning. A story in the paper. Nothing real.

'A boy I worked with. Someone shot him.' Leo pants against me, and I lay him down on a little mat in front of the sofa. I don't know how to handle him.

'Who?' She knows it means something to me. She's trying to be involved.

'No one's been caught. But we think we know who did it. We don't know where to find him.'

Becca's hand covers her mouth. The nails are unmanicured, but the fingers taper, shapely and long.

All at once the weight of my head is too much for me, and I lie down. Becca's image floats horizontal, and I can't get my eyes to right it. 'They think he might be after me.'

'I – I don't understand, May. What's happening?'

I shut my eyes. 'I don't know.'

'May, wake up!' I open them, shade them with my hand. Becca's not sitting cross-legged any more, she's on her feet, and she's taken Leo in her arms. 'You have to tell me everything that's happening.'

My voice comes out like a wail. 'You won't like it.'

'I don't care.' In her tone I hear years of discipline, protecting Leo from harm, pulling him away from the kerb. 'Tell me what you're talking about.'

If I close my eyes, it can be as if I was telling a dream. 'I arrested a prowler. A man who was out on purpose. He almost killed my partner. I interrogated him. He's crazy, I think. He's got a grudge against us. Someone who interrogated him with me was shot last night. They think it might be this man, and he might be after me, too.'

'Why?' The question is hushed, and I don't look at her.

I can't even shrug. 'He seemed the type.'

'May. May, open your eyes.'

'I'm tired, Becca.'

'May, look at me, this is serious.'

'I'm so tired.'

'May, we have to talk about this.'

'There's nothing to say. Maybe we'll catch him before he kills me.' My body is solid, tangible. There's no way I can conceive not being alive, not ever feeling anything again. Even in this dull confusion, I can't understand it.

I open my eyes a crack, and Becca is sitting opposite me. Leo is in her arms, restless, he wants to be put down so he can kick his legs, but she isn't letting him go. The poise of her upright spine is almost military. 'There is something to talk about, May,' she says. 'What about Leo?'

'Leo?' I look at her properly, but I can't lift my head. My skull is full of lead, dull base metal weighing me down. 'Leo wants to lie on the mat. You should let him go.'

'May, if there's someone after you – what if they follow you?'

'They followed Nate. Forensics said they followed him two hundred yards along the road.'

'Oh, my God.' She hoists Leo and stands. 'May, I'm sorry to do this, but you have to leave.'

'Leave?' I say the word, and as I say it my ears start to ring. 'I just got here.'

263

'May, you said there was a man following you, a crazy man. What if he comes here? Leo's here, May. How can you take chances with his life?'

'I'm risking Leo's life.' I'm doing this. She holds Leo as a block between us, there's discomfort in her tone. She doesn't want this. She wants the discomfort away, and me with it.

'I am sorry, May, really I am. If you knew how I hate doing this –'

'Doing what?' I sit up. My head sings. 'Cutting me off? Sending me away?'

'This isn't about you, really . . .'

'I see that.'

'Oh, May, don't take it like that. Please?'

'Don't take it like that.' My words are flat in my own ears. 'How am I taking it?'

Becca stiffens, raises herself to be tall. 'I am sorry to do this. If it wasn't a question of Leo, I wouldn't have to, but I can't take any risks with his life. If you love him, you'll understand that.'

'Since when did you become the arbitrator of love, Becca?'

'He's my son.'

'I've been good to you, Becca. I've helped you every day. I've shopped for you, I've looked after Leo. I have helped you.'

'You've helped Leo, at least.' She looks away the moment she says this.

'What does that mean?'

'You haven't spent much time with me, have you? You've come, picked him up and left.'

'You said you wanted to sleep.'

She shakes her head. 'Let's not do this.'

'And I've been here the past few weeks.'

'You hardly have a thing to say to me, May. I'm sure Leo doesn't press your many buttons.'

'That's what this is about? I thought you were wild with concern for your son.'

'I am. Oh, May, let's not do this.'

'No. You say things, you – sandbag me with these things, and then you say "Let's not do this" and expect it all to go away? I always knew you were one for the last word, but this is – you're not this stupid, Becca, you never were.'

'Stop it!' Leo starts to cry. Both of us react, Becca turns her head and I start to my feet. She looks away from him at me. Our eyes meet, and the single second it takes stretches out for a long time before I sit down. 'I'll – put him down in the other room,' she mutters.

'Are you just going to let him cry?'

'He's *my son*! It's not up to you. You handle your children your way, and let me handle mine.'

'I don't have children.' My voice is dead. I stare straight ahead and my face doesn't move at all.

'And whose fault is that? Mine?' I say nothing. Leo sobs between us. 'Oh, May, I'm sorry. This isn't – May, I'm just – scared for Leo.'

I draw in a shuddering breath. 'I know.' This is my sister. I can't be hating my sister.

'No, May. I mean – be honest. If you were in my position, wouldn't you be saying the same?'

'Yes.' Truth falls out of my mouth, plummets to the ground. 'Yes, I would.'

'I'm sorry for what I said.' The schoolgirl phrasing stabs me in two places at once. The shelter of it, the life protected from the world that swallowed me up.

But there's the familiarity too, my sister who always talks this way, even when her own life is falling apart. 'Really. I'm so sorry. I wish you hadn't taken it like this. But it's not your fault. I wish I could have put it to you better. But – it's just . . .' She sits down on the sofa, strokes the head of her crying son. They're far away from me. 'Leo's everything I have, May. If anything happened to him, I'd die.' She looks down. 'I'm telling you the truth now, so I hope you're listening. I don't want to have to go through saying all this again. I've heard nothing from Lionel, nothing. He's still abroad. I sent messages to let him know when Leo was born. I got Leo's blood group tested on my own and sent him the results. I even – named him for his father. But I haven't heard a thing. And it isn't because he's too hurt to speak to me. I know that now. He was upset at the time. Now he's – it's just easier for him not to have to come and sort this out. He doesn't care too much, May. He just doesn't care enough. But if Leo's all I have out of that marriage, I can't be sorry.' She ducks her head, rests it on Leo's. 'Don't expect me to say this again. Leo's everything I have left out of six years of doing everything I could to make a marriage work. He's all I have left. I can't take any chances with him. If anything happened to him, it would be the end of me. I'm sorry to do this to you, May, really, I'm so sorry. I hope they catch the man soon, so you can come back. Leo loves you.' She squeezes her eyes shut. For a moment, I think it might happen, but she doesn't say she loves me. 'You're good with him. You've been a great help to me, more than anyone, and I am grateful. But please, for me, just do this?'

For me.

She didn't speak for Leo. She asked me to do it for her.

'Of course I don't want to put him at risk,' I say. My voice breaks, but I won't, I won't cry. 'I – I didn't even think about it when I came today . . .'

She could say, of course you didn't, it would take a mother to think these things. She doesn't. Instead, what she says is, 'That's not your fault. You live in danger all the time. You must get used to it in some ways.'

I shake my head, my eyes closed. There are no teardrops to fly from my eyelids as I shake. 'Not like this.'

Becca swallows, 'What are you going to do?'

'I – I don't know. I can't go home.'

'Do you think he's watching your flat?' The concern is back, she speaks softer.

'He could be. I can't risk it.'

'Where will you stay?'

It's a weapon, and I hesitate a moment before throwing it. 'I've been seeing someone for a few weeks. Maybe I can stay with him.'

'Oh.' It's very quiet. 'What's he like?'

'He's nice.' I stare at my hands. 'He treats me well. He's a social worker, very respectable.' Social worker, not DORLA. I spare her the wondering if he's like me or like her. 'But I don't know if he will. I only met him after Leo was born. He might not be willing.' If this ends things with Paul, I'll stay in my flat and wait for Seligmann to come and get me. Even as I think this, I know it's not true. I'll keep going. I always do.

'What's his name?'

'Paul Kelsey. He lives in north Sanctus.'

I look at her, and she tries to smile. 'It's a nice area.'

'Yes.' Yes. Yes, if you don't have to catch in the park, I suppose it is.

She sits on the sofa and holds her son.

'I guess I should go now.'

She doesn't stop me as I rise. As I reach the door, she says, 'You will keep phoning me, won't you?'

I turn, lean my back against the door. 'Do you want me to?'

Her face creases. 'Of course I want you to.'

'All right. I'll call you.' I turn around.

'May?'

'What?'

She makes a helpless gesture as I turn back. 'Should you – give me your boyfriend's number? So I know where to call you?'

'I might not be there.' I should smile at her, give her a hug. Instead, I stand against the door. It's the most I can give her. 'I'll let you know where I'm staying when I call.'

Twenty-eight years lie on the floor between us.

I don't know which of us it is that's turned her back on them as I once again face the door and go through it.


'You can't just go in there, he's on the phone,' the man tells me.

'I need to speak to him.'

'Can I help you at all?' He has a narrow face, his Adam's apple stands out like a kink, as if his neck had been broken in half and set wrong. His hair is thin, but he stands in front of me as calm as if he was twice my size. There's no harshness in his tone.

'No, I need to speak to Paul Kelsey.' I step back. The dizziness that's been swirling around me all day rises, and I haven't any fight left. 'It's all right, I can wait.'

'You might have to wait a while.' He gestures me to a chair. 'Can I get you a cup of coffee, tea, water?'

My throat closes. There's no room inside me for water. 'No thank you.'

I stare at the wall. Every now and again Simon, the man who stopped me in the hallway, comes back and checks on me, offers me magazines and biscuits. After half an hour, I take a magazine to free myself of his restless hospitality, and push the pages to and fro, half-dazzled by the shiny images. Sleek-limbed women in shimmering dresses, page after page of adverts. Articles on cleaning your skin, maximising your assets. It's been a long time since I've held one of these expensive magazines. I try to imagine, if I were beautiful, whether things would be better. I can't make it fit. Faces break so easily.

I've lost an hour of my life looking at glossy photographs of people I don't know when I finally hear a voice. 'Lola, hi! I never thought I'd see you reading a fashion mag.'

'It's not mine.' Paul stands before me, and for a second it's as if I've never seen him before.

'What are you doing here?' He sits on the chair next to me.

Simon comes back. He's relaxed, greets Paul as if they've known each other a long time. 'Hi, Paul. This lady said she wanted to speak to you?' It's his responsibility I'm here, he's checking it out.

'It's okay, she's my girlfriend.'

'Oh, this is Lola.' He smiles, he thinks he knows me. 'Nice to meet you at last.'

'At last.' I shake the hand he holds out, I remember how to do that. 'I mean, nice to meet you too.'

'Sorry to keep you waiting on the visitor's chair, you should have said.'

'It's okay.'

'Do you want to come into my office?' Paul stands, gestures. I let him escort me into another room. Books on the walls, a box of tissues on the desk, files. He closes the door behind us. 'Not that it's not nice to see you,' he says, 'but what's up?'

'I –' I sit down. I have to get this buzzing out of my head. 'Why didn't you think I'd read a fashion magazine? Do I look untidy?'

'Oh God, wrong thing to say. You look great. I just haven't seen you reading one before. Can I get out of this without offending you somehow?'

'No. It's okay. I don't like them.'

'What's up?' He seats himself. 'Coffee?'

'I don't want anything to drink!'

'Okay, okay, just being nice.'

'Paul, can I stay with you?' I have tried to think of ways of leading up to it, of ways to say it. I can't think of any.

'What, you mean tonight?'

'No. I mean for a while.' Time, turn back. I don't want to have to ask this.

He frowns. 'I guess.' He doesn't sound as if it's a big deal. 'What's going on, is your window leaking again?'

'No. Something's happened. You – you shouldn't say yes. You should ask me about it and find out what it involves.'

'Well, I kind of just did . . . Hey, are you okay? You seem a bit strained.'

Having to tell it again is hard work, it's dragging stones uphill. I go through it again, the death, the man after me. I name no names, I keep it short. He only needs to know the bare minimum, because he's either going to say yes or he's not, whatever I say, and I cannot drag the details up one more time.

'They said I shouldn't be living in my flat,' I finish. 'But if I stay with you, it's a risk you should think about.'

'No.' There's no way telling what kind of no that is. 'No, that's okay. You should stay.'

'What?' I squint at him, raise my hand to rub my eyes and let it droop again before it reaches them. 'Aren't you going to say no? I'm bad luck right now.'

'You shouldn't go home.' He comes and sits beside me.

'Aren't you scared?'

He shrugs. 'It's not me anyone's after. And I've dealt with crazy people before, I'm not too worried.'

'You should be.'

'I'm more worried about you.' His face takes on a confessional look, there's a tentativeness in the way he reaches for my hand that's unfamiliar, it isn't Paul's touch. I have to pull back the reflex to push this strange hand away, tell myself that it's Paul and he's going to let me stay with him. 'If there's someone after you, I'd be happier knowing where you were.'

It doesn't make sense. It's a thing to say, it's polite and kind but it doesn't make sense, I can't understand why he's taking this risk. I don't argue. I should, for his sake, I shouldn't be endangering him, but I'm too tired. I let him guide me out of the building.

He asks whether I need to pick up some stuff, and he's right, I hadn't thought of that. We go through my flat block, into my flat, the key turns in my lock with a small click and I know I won't hear that sound again.

I tug things out of drawers, stuff a suitcase without folding, not knowing much of what I take. Paul is hyper, he moves from room to room remembering I need a toothbrush, a hairbrush, things that aren't in my cupboards. After a while I wander into the bedroom and make him follow me, I reach out for him, kiss, pull him down with me. I lean and push against him, trying to rub some life into my flesh. He's far away from me, further than he's ever been when we were like this, and I feel very little, but still I'm grateful. When I was younger, we used to talk about 'christening' rooms. Even numb and confused as I am, there's some distant sense of relief that I have someone with whom to give my room its last rites.

Later, we go to his place. I've been here enough that there's some familiarity as I walk up to his door. It isn't coming home, but it's a respite of sorts. He clears a drawer and tells me it's okay, it was time he tidied anyway, and doesn't press when I ask to leave the unpacking for a little while.

In my handbag, there's a gun. I walked into Weapons, mentioned that I knew Ally Gregory, went from place to place with no air of wrongdoing. I told Paul months ago that if you look like you should be there, no one will stop you. I went into a storeroom, lifted a gun off the wall and put it in my bag, took a box of bullets to go with it. Another time, it would have frightened me to do this, and there was fear in me somewhere, but all I could feel of it was a prickling heat on my arms. Nearer my hands than my heart. I took a gun, ammunition, and moved, quiet as a ghost, back to where I wanted to be. It wasn't even difficult.

# 19

I wake in the middle of the night and find that the mist has cleared, leaving everything outlined in frost. Sounds are etched against the air, objects are stark and so sharply real it almost cuts me to look at them. What I see is corners, doors, places I can't see round. I can't see under the bed, I can't see what's behind the door, and outside this room there are city streets with corners everywhere I look. There are so many hiding places in the world, and someone who wants to kill me might be in any one of them.

Seligmann. He was stronger than me even when he was tied down. Now he's loose and he has a gun. And there were more of him. There were three of them that attacked Marty and me. Three. Maybe others. Faces I wouldn't recognise.

Ripples go through me. This isn't nerves, this is fear. On moon nights I've patrolled, I've tracked through the forests, black-barked trees with snaking branches like an army around me. That was in the night time. For a moment, I looked away, and now it's come to this, the whole world has become forest.

I lie awake a long time.

*

Officially no one knows where Bride's been sent, but this is DORLA, and it only takes me ten minutes of asking people to find out. There weren't many choices, anyway. If she's taken a work transfer, it won't be to the country: outside the cities, lunes go for the livestock, and guarding it is a specialised job. I hear nons have a better time of it in some parts of the country; after all, it's time-honoured. Out in the country, they say the farmers see the use of us. In some parts. In others, locals hunch their backs and put their heads together and don't speak to nons at all. Cities are full of country nons who couldn't take it any more and begged for years to get a transfer. There are areas of the countryside where DORLA members are sent as a punishment. But Bride won't be there, she wouldn't know how to play shepherd. She's a city girl.

There are two different rumours, one that she's gone north, the other south, both to cities within a hundred miles of us. I phone both and simply ask to speak to Bride Reilly. The second call finds her.

'Hello, love.' Her voice is resigned, not unfriendly.

'Bride.' I sit in my tiny office behind my locked door, and stare ahead of me. Plastic Venetian blinds over my window, grey with age, and grime in the strings where my dusting can't reach. I don't know what to say to her.

'So.' Her voice is too bright. 'Where are you calling from, pet?'

I rub my mouth. 'From my office. From home.'

'You're still there?' The cheerfulness goes out of her; she sounds wary. 'I – thought you'd have taken a transfer.'

'Like you?' I turn my head at the sound of a clatter

275

outside, stand up to look out of the window. Someone's dropped a bottle. I sit back in my chair, trying not to notice how breakable my knees feel.

'Well, yes – I'd have thought it was the best thing for all of us. Some bad lune out there gunning for us . . .' It isn't confident, it's subdued. She's done me no wrong, I know that, but I'm alone here. She's done something different. She left without telling me. It's only because Alice Townsend told me that I even knew she was leaving. Bride pulled up stumps and went without a word, left me to look around and find the world suddenly without her. The worst of it is, I can see her point. I can feel how hard it is, the struggle to remember other people, the impulse to elbow and scratch and grab for what I can.

'It's okay, Bride.' My throat is sore, and I don't know if it is okay, but I can't talk like this. I can't afford to let a conflict rise. Better to patch up a friendship than let it drop. 'You probably did the right thing.'

There's a pause. She hesitates before asking, but she's known me a long time. 'How come you stayed, Lolie?'

I rub my mouth. 'I don't know.'

'That's not much of a reason, love. Not that I'm nagging, but wouldn't you rather get out of this bastard's way?'

'I can't. I – I let him scare me before, and I don't want to run.'

She doesn't answer. I'm trying not to resent her running without a word, and she knows it, knows she can't push this.

I don't tell her I've screwed up too many times. That Seligmann almost killed Marty and tore all the hope out of him before he was even twenty years old, and I didn't prevent it. That I was the one who brought Nate down to Seligmann's cell on the first day. That I wouldn't even go near Seligmann after it happened, that others went in and drew his fire and all I did was let them, so long as it meant I didn't have to think about him. I always despised people who martyr themselves, I don't know why I'm doing it now.

'I'm sorry I didn't tell you I was leaving,' Bride says. 'I should have done, I know . . .'

'How's Jim?' I cut across her. I don't want to listen to this.

'He's fine.' Her voice is very quiet. 'I drove us up, we found somewhere to stay, we're settled in now.'

'How's the new place?'

'It's all right. Not a palace, but we can afford it. It could be worse.'

It could be here. 'And you're working okay?'

'Oh yes, I'm settling in fine here.'

Settling in. 'Bride,' I say, my voice tightening. 'How long do you think you'll be away?'

There's a long silence before she answers. 'Well, we're renting on a short-term basis. We can renew the contract every two months. And all the jobs I'm getting are quite short-term. I'm not worried about it, really.'

Bride is away in a strange city. She doesn't know how long before it'll be safe to return. If it's months, she – settling in. I shake my head. Surely she'll be coming back.

'Hey, hey.' Bride comes in with a strained giggle. 'What about that young fellow who answered your phone at midnight? What's going on there?'

I close my eyes, let go of the thought that this call would be easier if I was making it from Paul's flat. He's been so good to me. I've been eating proper breakfasts every morning because of him. When I wake up shaking in the night, I have something to hold on to. Even if he's sleeping, it's better. Just the warmth of his skin, the solidity of him lying curled on his side make the fears seem like themselves, like fears of what may happen, not like living creatures already upon me digging their claws into my back. 'Well,' I say. There's no way I can say all that to anyone. 'It's fine. He's still around.' If it hadn't been for Paul, would I have fled to another city?

'There's a thing,' she says. She's happier talking about this. 'You're a desperate liar keeping him a secret from me, you know. I shouldn't forgive you for that. So what's he like, this young man of yours? Is he handsome? Do tell me he's handsome.'

'Yeah, he is.'

'Wonderful!' she crows. There's a shrill note of relief in her tone. 'So, details – big, small, dark, fair . . . come on, Lolie, don't be mean.'

I'm not in the mood, I can't play. 'He's tall, black hair, blue eyes . . . Listen, Bride, I should probably be working.'

'Oh.' She goes quiet like a slapped child. Even in my sore and stiffened state, there's a pang at the sound. 'Look, I'm sorry, Bride. I'm just a little tense right now, and I do have a lot to get through . . .'

'Of course.' I've never before heard Bride sound submissive.

We both sit and say nothing. Neither of us hangs up.

'I'm sorry I didn't tell you I was going,' Bride says.

'It's okay.'

'I wouldn't stay if I were you.'

'I'll be okay.' I say it quietly, and add nothing to it, and she knows we aren't going to talk about it.

'I'll light a candle for you.' I say nothing. 'Tell you what,' she says with a nervous laugh, 'I'll light one for you if you light one for me.'

'You can be the good Catholic girl,' I say. 'I haven't been to church for years.'

'I would,' she says.

I sit and hold the handset for a moment. Stained glass, blue against the dull grey sky, incense. Thinking of the candles, a flicker goes through me and I crave them, the pure ivory wax and the soft, orange glow of the flames. But I know I won't do it. There are too many death-bed conversions in the world. I can't plea-bargain with God.

'Tell you what,' I say. 'When you go to light one for me, light one for yourself as well, and I'll pay for it. I'll buy you a drink when you get back.'

'Yeah.' Her voice quivers. 'Yeah, you do that, love.'

In that instant, I can't take it. 'I have to hang up now,' I say. 'I'd better go.'

'Do you want to give me your number?' She speaks quickly, as if she thinks I'll hang up before she can ask.

I sit still, resting my head against the receiver.

Bride doesn't say anything.

'I'd better not,' I say.

'Okay, I'll not give you mine then.' She's talking quickly. 'Better both ways, eh, Lo?'

'You can call me at work.'

'Yeah, you too. Well, I mean call me again . . .'

'Yeah.' I can't say anything else. 'Bye, Bride.'

Her goodbye sounds from the handset as I lay it down, tinny and small and a long way away.

*

I sit in the canteen, nursing a cup of coffee. The vending machine spatters and gasps every time you work it, and my paper mug of liquid is not appealing; it's coffee-flavoured water and I can taste the water and the flavour separately as I sip. Still, it's hot. The drink burns through the card, keeping my fingers awake.

I've caught myself developing habits that I struggle to restrain when I notice them. There are moments when I catch myself thinking that if I can keep from being afraid I'll be safe. There are moments when I catch myself thinking that if I relax for a second, that will be the second the attack comes. Mostly, there are moments when I catch myself thinking that I should be able to find some state of mind that will get me through this, that if I can just be right in myself, then the blow won't fall. My mind tugs this way and that like a sackful of mice, and I know I have to stop doing it.

Entangled in my thoughts, I don't notice Ally approach until he taps me on the shoulder. I flinch away, half-stand, spilling hot coffee over my wrist. I stand up, shake my arm, cursing and hissing.

'You okay?' Ally reaches out as if to touch the burn, then pulls his hand away.

'Just a scald,' I say through my teeth. 'Too painful to be serious, you haven't burned any nerves out. Warn me when you're coming up.'

'I tried, you were just staring into space.'

'Are you going to just stand there? Get me something cold, will you?' I glare at him, my hand covering the burned spot.

Ally looks at me a second, then goes off and approaches the drinks dispenser and returns with a can of Coke. 'Here.' He passes it over to me. It isn't chilled as it should be, none of our machines are in perfect order, but it's cooler than tap water.

'You'd better drink this afterwards, I hate Coke,' I say, pressing the metal to my forearm. The burn still stings underneath, but the cold smooth surface numbs it a little.

'How's things?' Ally says. His hands drum together in his lap, a sound that irritates me. His heels tap on the ground as well. He's restless as ever, but his movements are awkward, out of sync with each other. I suppose he's worried.

'Not great,' I say, keeping my face turned towards my damaged wrist. 'But then they wouldn't be. I'll live.'

'Have you heard anything?'

'Nothing. Not since I was told what happened. I keep waiting for the phone call that says, hey, it was all a mistake. Think it's going to come soon?' I try to grin at him.

Ally frowns. 'You aren't staying at your own place, are you?'

'No, but I'm not saying where I am staying. No offence.' I don't want him to know.

'Whatever.' He turns his head away from me as he says this, cranes his neck to look at the clock, tapping his fingers on the back of the seat.

'You in a hurry?'

'No.' He sighs, and turns back to me. 'Listen, Lo, can we go somewhere private?'

'What?' I stiffen. 'I'm not in the mood for games, Ally.'

'No, I – I want to talk to you.'

'Talk to me here.'

'Can't we go to your office or something?' Ally takes

a lock of his hair and winds it round his finger; he pulls hard enough to hurt.

'Talk to me here, Ally. I'm not in the mood for cloak and dagger.'

He glances around, taps his hand against his jaw.

'No one's going to listen,' I say. 'Come on, what's so secret?'

Ally chews his lip, then leans forward. I shift back in my seat a bit. I don't want confidences. 'I heard something, okay?' He speaks quietly. From a distance, he might be telling me anything. 'Someone I know in Forensics was talking to me, he wanted my advice on bullet making.'

'Bullets?' The word comes out too softly, and I struggle to find my proper voice. 'What, has he got a grudge against someone?'

'Listen to me, Lo.' Ally looks over his shoulder.

'You're acting suspicious,' I say. 'Everyone's going to eavesdrop.'

Ally takes hold of my arm above the burn and shakes it. I say 'Hey!', but he shakes for just a second more before letting me go. He has to reach right across the couch to do it. 'Lo, this is – look, just listen to me, okay? He was talking about the bullet Nate was shot with.'

I take my wrist away from him and tend it in my other hand. 'What about the bullet Nate was shot with, Ally?' I don't sound like myself.

Ally's hands tug at each other, and he looks down at them. 'They dug the bullet out of his head,' he says. 'It was silver.'

'What are you talking about?' All my skittishness has frozen.

Ally stares down at the floor. Even through the rags of hair hanging around it, I can see his face contort. He takes a deep breath, and doesn't look at me. 'You remember after Johnny was killed? There were rumours going around that there was something odd about the bullet he was killed with. I just found out what was odd about it, Lo. It was silver.'

'Johnny?' I hear myself speak, like a child asking for someone in the dark.

'Yeah, Johnny. Johnny and Nate. That's what I heard, that they were both killed with silver bullets. This guy from Forensics, he wanted to do a comparison of the bullets.'

My face is cold, disconnected from the rest of me, disembodied. 'He thinks someone from DORLA killed them?'

'No.' Ally looks up at me. 'No, that's not it. He was asking about how well we guard our stores. And whether someone could make bullets on their own, home-made ones. I don't know, I'm not Forensics and I didn't see them. I'm just . . . He . . .' Ally rubs his face. His shoulders are hunched as he looks up. 'I just thought you might want to know about it.'

# 20

Silver bullets.

When I was nine, I saw bullets being made. We were taken to a factory where machines whirred and flashed past and bullets piled up in great containers, not burnished as we'd expected silver to be, but dull. They could have been steel or lead. We tried putting our hands into them like lucky dips, but the metal was heavy and resistant, we couldn't push through it. It was a standard trip to be taken on, every non school takes its pupils on tours of the factories where lycos spend their time manufacturing for us. Usually, the children are bored; the irony of lycos working to supply us only occurs to the grown-ups. An unpopular job. 'I work in metal processing' is a phrase I've heard more than once. Still, the money's good because it has to be, they're better paid than steeplejacks or slaughtermen, and the factories are always humming. The graffiti on the walls and the rocks thrown at the chicken-wire covered windows don't stop the machines.

Mostly I was disappointed. I wanted the bullets to be shiny.

When you melt metal down, it holds together, heavy and lithe. I've seen them pour it. I think of the pain of boiling water on my skin, and when I imagine molten metal I can only imagine how it would feel to the touch. Thinking of pain of that calibre is impossible, like trying to invent a new colour. Like trying to imagine things in Paul's description of lune monochromatic vision. Or perhaps it would burn out all your nerves before you could feel it. Perhaps. It's hard to believe that. No one gets used to the heat of hellfire. I don't understand how anyone could melt down silver to make a bullet without fear of the heat overcoming them.

The human skull isn't very thick. I used to think of human flesh as tough, because of an experiment I did when I was a child. I tried to bite my tongue. There was discomfort that rose smoothly to pain as my teeth pressed down, and the flesh thickened under them, became dense, fibrous, hard to get through. I wasn't going to put it to the test, of course, not all the way, but I seemed to have discovered something. Under pressure, my tongue was tough meat; biting through it wouldn't be easy.

It was only years later I understood that it wasn't the resilience of my tongue stopping me. It was the pain.

I thought the skull was a fortress. Curved like the sky, smooth and beautiful, a stone-walled bastion for the butter-soft brain that carries so much inside it. But really, it isn't so strong. A hammer will break through, without even needing much strength of arm. A chisel, a rolling pin, a lead pipe. A little fall will put a crack in it. Just the distance between eye-level and the ground. It doesn't need a bullet. Five or six feet will do the trick.

Johnny is rotting in the ground. The charge has gone from his body. With nothing to hold it upright, his flesh went slack, and now the microbes have him. Somehow they knew. His life left him and with it went all protection, and somehow the worms knew that it was their time, that they could open their mouths and bite.

Johnny will be pulp and curds now. Tiny creatures will have breached his surface. No violence in the grave, only hunger. Even that hunger will not be violent. Just insensate, relentless. Little spores will send thread-thin tendrils down through Johnny's arms and face, and nothing will stop them taking root. Soon, he will be honeycombed all through. Perhaps some of the skin is still left, but it wouldn't be smooth to the touch. It will break under the impact of a fingertip, yield and sink into the teeming marsh beneath.

And Nate. They won't let us go to the funeral. Just the family, we were all told. Only his own flesh and blood. But I know they mean to cremate him, and I've seen cremations before. A fine coffin of polished wood and gleaming bronze handles, a crest of flowers on top. Dignity, arrangement. Hair coiling in on itself, half-settled blood boiling within the flesh. The body won't long withstand the flames.

You wouldn't know it from the coffin. But then I look again inside my mind, and I see something else. A fallen tree, hewn and scraped and slashed into place. How much damage the wood took to become that handsome casket. And the lilies and orchids on the top are dying already, their spines broken when some diligent florist clipped them from the ground. More than one dead thing goes into the fire. Only the handles are truly free, the nerveless tranquil metal. It comes out of the mines to be fixed onto a wooden box, and scalds no living flesh when it melts.

There's no reason, not a technical one anyway, why you'd make a bullet out of silver if you were hunting in the daylight. It's too soft. There's the question of the alloy, as well. We use a special combination, enough silver to trigger the allergy, enough hard metal mixed in to give them some stopping power. Silver isn't a practical weapon.

It can only be a symbol. I can think of no other reason in the world why someone would put together an expensive, inefficient set of bullets and shoot two of my people.

It's beyond insult. It's beyond attack, beyond curses sprayed on our office buildings every night and fucking skins and bareback and night after night with teeth at your throat. It's beyond being beaten up in bars and getting followed home and wearing gloves in summer.

Another part of me can't take it in. I have a chilled, fragile urge to laugh, because there's an awful comedy to this. It's so perfect. Of course. They lay down rules that set us to guarding them from each other every month. We bleed and die and have to treat them with tender caution because if we hurt them the least little bit when they try to kill us, then the next morning they'll rise from their beds and sue. For this, they call us names and pay us nothing and let it be known that they despise us. Liberals hate our methods, reactionaries hate our kind, children laugh and the old shake their heads at the state of the world that has us in it. And finally someone takes silver, the one defence we have, the only thing in this life that hurts them more than it hurts us. They didn't need to. A lead bullet would have done just as well. There was no need to use our only weapon, to flaunt and mock with the killing, to shoot at us as if we were . . . what was Seligmann's word?

Soulless. Ghouls that walk among the living, shut out of the bright world and foraging on the edges. Be good, or the barebacks will get you. And perhaps it's true, perhaps Seligmann thought himself in hell, perhaps he was afraid of us. I stood back and watched Nate beat him until he couldn't sit up. And now I'm not even sorry. I should have let Nate kill him when we had the chance. Even as I think that, I know I wouldn't have done it, not faced with a real flesh-and-blood man whose life was so far beyond me that I wouldn't have dared snuff it out, but I'm not sorry for hurting him. There's no pity in me left. Maybe that makes me what he called us, soulless, the spooks, the bogeymen. It's not what I'd have chosen to be.

Someone thought they would make a grand gesture, find the best, most beautiful insult, so perfect you could mistake it for justice if you half-closed your eyes. They found silver and melted it down and followed people I knew down the road to hit them in the back of the head with this final, artistic affront. Someone put thought and effort into this. They cared enough.

It's an impossible desecration, beyond belief. But now that it's happened, I can't push it away from me, I can't fault it. A silver bullet. Of course. What else? It's the final wrong anyone could do us, the last twist, the perfect consummation.

# 21

Paul is already home when I get back. He rests on the sofa, his feet bare, a book held above his face – something about ancient Roman portraits with pictures in it. His soles are dusty, flat, the skin on them dark as hoofs.

'Good day?' he says, sitting up and laying his book open-faced across the arm of the sofa.

'No.' I speak staccato, close off the word before it starts to shake.

'Bad day?'

'Yeah.'

Paul sets up a cushion for me, arranges it and waits for me to join him. I walk to the sofa and sit, upright, straight-limbed, without expression. 'What happened?' he says, touching my hair.

I pull my head away. 'I don't want to talk about it.'

'Are you worrying about Marty?' His face is sympathetic, and I feel an ugly thump in my chest. I haven't thought about Marty once since Seligmann escaped.

'No. I said I didn't want to . . .' It's too much trouble to finish the sentence.

'Oh.' Paul puts his hands blamelessly in his lap. 'Well, would you like to talk about something else?'

'I don't know.' The words make no sense. I stare at the painting that hangs on his wall, a home-made thing, the canvas tacked roughly to the frame, the work of some friend of his. Bright fresh colours smeared into patterns, the paints not fully mixed so that different colours swirl together. The beauty of the materials. Adult finger-painting.

'Oh. See, that's a problem. I'm going to have to not be curious about your bad day, which means we've got to talk about something else, or we'll just spend the evening carefully not talking about your bad day. Very awkward.' He nods at me, not really serious.

'Stop,' I say. I raise my hands, parallel, touch my temples. The painting will never hang in a gallery, but there's some eye for proportion in it, the colours are nice. I don't want colour. I want the world white and soundless, cool, air around me. If I get sick, perhaps I can lie on a wheeled bed in a tiled operating theatre with a clean echo and people around me in thin safe masks, and I won't have to move or speak.

'Hey. Hey, are you okay?' Paul shifts on the cushion, looks into my face.

'No,' I say, trying hard to make my voice normal. 'No, not really. I – People were talking a lot at work about the boy who died, and it was – I'm upset, I guess.' I try to lighten up, but my laugh sounds bitter. 'Not that I ever liked him.'

Paul puts an arm around me. I flinch, stop myself from pulling back. He rests his arm a moment on my tense shoulders, then takes it away.

'I've been thinking all day,' I say. 'I've had enough thinking.'

'Do you want to go out?' Paul sits up, crosses his

legs. 'We could go to a movie. You wouldn't have to think or talk about anything at all for two hours straight.' I twitch, stiffen my hands. That would be my reason for going to the cinema. It unsettles me that Paul can put his finger on it, drag it out into the light so casually.

'Or we could go to a meeting or something. I've got an old school friend whose boyfriend writes the most god-awful conceptual poetry and gives readings every other week, we could go to that. Last time I went he read out a sonnet that included a five-minute silence in between each quatrain and gurning every other rhyme. It was oddly compelling after a while. How about it? Maybe some *schadenfreude* would pick you up.'

'I don't want to go out.' He can't just pick me over, toss my faults from hand to hand like jokes. 'I get enough looking over my shoulder in the day without adding the cover of night to any stalkers, thanks.'

'Oh. Sorry.' He strokes my hand. The tolerance burns my skin. 'Well, okay, we'll stay in then.' He rises, goes over to the window and pulls the curtains closed. Crossing to the cupboard where he keeps his drinks, a battered pine construction with old postcards of land-scape paintings and a few cocktail recipes tacked to it, he crouches down and pours me out a glass of whisky. I didn't ask for it, and it hasn't been my habit to drink when I got home. Not while I've been living with him. He hands it to me, and I look at it without speaking for a moment. Then I raise the glass, knock back the whisky and set it down on the table with a hard clatter.

'Another?' He stands beside me. Something about him is poised, alert, as if he were standing on the balls of his feet.

'No thank you.' I stare at the empty glass. A little film of whisky runs down its inside and settles on the bottom.

Paul sighs, rubs his head. His hands open and close. Then he shakes them and comes round the back of the sofa, touches my shoulders, starts to massage them. His thumbs easily find the knots. By now he knows where my tense places are, on my back.

I wriggle in his grip. Once I've started, the pressure of his hands feels more and more and more irritating against my twisting shoulders, and I wrench myself away to find my hands have become fists. 'Stop it!' I say.

'What?' He stands away, his hands raised as if innocent.

'Just – stop it. Stop treating me like an invalid.'

'I'm not.' He backs away.

'I – I don't want it. I've seen you give me drinks, I've seen you rub my shoulders, propose trips. I know the repertoire. Stop trying to fix me.'

'I was trying to cheer you up.' He walks around the sofa to face me.

'Don't try to do things with me.' I don't know what I'm saying. Only that my hands are clenched and my shoulder blades are folded tight, there are straps around me, binding me.

'I'm trying to be nice, Lola.' He sounds almost as if he's giving me warning.

'Nice doesn't cut it. Nice isn't helping. This isn't a nice time.'

Paul shakes himself. When he speaks, I'm startled at the pitch of his voice. 'Well, God damn it, Lola, what do you want? I live here. I'm doing my best and you're knocking back everything I try. And you're not trying

293

at all. You're just sitting there, it's no good. I can't just ignore you sitting there like a death's head. I *live here*.'

I freeze. 'I know this is your place, Paul. I can't go back to mine.'

'I know.' Paul puts his head between his hands and presses. 'I know that. Just – please try to be nice while you're here, eh?'

'You sound like my mother,' I say. 'While you're under my roof, you do as you're told.' Though it was Becca she said this to, not me. My stay under her roof was always considered more transitory.

'Lola, for God's sake! *Please* don't take things out on me.'

'Why not?' The words are out of my mouth before I know I'm going to speak. What I felt when I talked to Bride rises in me again, the passion to live, to rend whatever stands in my way. My fingers claw in my lap, I look at Paul. I want to touch him, caress, drive some passion into the air around us, but also to hurt him. I remember how his hair feels, the fine, tough strands, and my hands tug at the cloth of my jacket. I've seen how pleasure changes his face, traces itself around his eyes and mouth, but how would he look, how would he sound, if I hurt him?

'Because –' He's pacing now, raising and dropping and raising his hands, caged. 'Because it's fucked up, that's why. I've been nothing but nice to you, Lola. It doesn't mean you can turn on me because you've had a bad day. You've got a problem, deal with it. Don't fire on the nearest safe target like a coward.'

'You think I'm a coward?' I laugh, the sound echoes, hard-edged and acrid like a dropped coin. 'There speaks the respectable man. You go out one night with a trank gun and the moon up and see how liberal you feel.'

'That's nothing to do with me!'

'No,' I say quietly. 'You're right. It isn't. Try it some time, and then call me a coward.'

'I *can't.*' His voice is as quiet as mine, and just as harsh. 'But that's not to do with me either. Don't try to justify attacking me by flashing the DORLA card.'

Flashing the DORLA card. He's seen me do that, he's seen me get past people by flashing the card. He remembers.

'Then don't call me names,' I say.

'What has the one got to do with the other?' The phrase is scholarly, educated, and I slam my fist against a cushion. 'And leave the fucking cushion alone.'

'Why, do you feel sorry for it? Go on, take the cushion's side against me.'

He looks at me, and his face collapses in laughter. 'For God's sake. This is getting ridiculous.'

I knock away the hand he reaches out to me.

'Lola, stop it. Why are you being such a bitch?' The word is sharp-pointed and savage, but his tone is more questioning than anything else.

'I told you not to call me names.'

'Oh for God's *sake*!' He flings away from me again. 'Lola, I'm prepared to be nice about anything if you'll work with me, but this is just fucking ridiculous. I've had enough, you can just sit there and simmer.'

Simmer. I'm a pot that will burn his hand if he touches it. 'Of course. You only sympathise with those doe-eyed enough to beg for it. I forgot you were sentimental.'

'Here.' He takes a knife off the sideboard, a small one for cutting fruit, and tosses it over to me. 'You

295

want to sit there playing knife-thrower, use a proper weapon.'

'Oh, wonderful, now you're giving me props. Get me to act out your little scenario rather than deal with me. You're such a fucking child.'

Paul slams his hand into the wall. I flinch at the sound, shrink back into myself. Then he turns around, and I'm angry with him for making me shiver. 'If you're going to hit the wall, I think I'm entitled to hit the cushion,' I say. 'And wake the neighbours up while you're at it, I'm sure they'll appreciate it.'

'Lola.' His voice is slow, precise, fierce. 'Leaving aside the fact that it's seven o'clock, I have to tell you that I've had absolutely all I'm going to take of this. I don't want you picking fights with me, I don't want you throwing out barbs about everything I do or say. You're not the only one who's had a bad day.'

'Oh, you've had a bad day.' My voice is hard.

'Yes, I've had a bad day.' He flexes his fingers, looks at the door. 'Whatever you say about your job, I'm sure it's true, but, but no one likes dealing with social workers either, and I'm trying to do my best too. You're not the only one outnumbered, you're not the only one fighting uphill. I do a hard job, Lola. And I haven't laid it on you. I know you're going through something really bad. But I'm – for God's sake, I'm taking a risk even having you here.' The blood stops in my veins at the words. 'And you're not the only one who's, who's got a life to deal with.'

He's put our lives in separate categories. 'You can't blame me for not reading your mind.'

'I don't want you reading my mind. All I'm asking

is that you think about the possibility that you might not be the only person who can get upset.'

'You didn't have to risk yourself,' I say. I'm beyond emotion; I feel what he's said as a physical pain in my chest. 'I told you when I asked you, you didn't have to take me in.'

'I wanted to, God damn it. Christ, Lola, you think I don't know what it's like for you, you spend all your life thinking "no one understands me", and it's just not true. I know what you're up against. I wanted you to stop fighting the world for a bit. I thought if you stayed here you'd know not everything was against you. But if you're going to carry the fight in here, then – then you're still staying here,' he starts to look confused, frustrated with his words, 'but you're not going to fight with me. It's just – it's just bloody ungrateful, that's all.'

I sit. I stare. Everything he's said has been in the past tense. 'If you invited me here to prove a point,' I say, my voice unsteady, 'you might have tried telling me. If you wanted to turn me into an object lesson, you should have let me know. You think I should be grateful? If you can dare stand there and tell me that you wanted me so you could prove something, if you wanted a woman you could fix, then I'm sorry I trusted you.'

'Jesus,' Paul says. He's gazing at me as if I was a news bulletin of an atrocity, a self-inflicted wound. 'You really don't like men very much, do you?'

'I don't have a problem with men,' I say. 'I have a problem with lycos.'

We look at each other. What we've said hangs tattered on the walls around us, closing us in, it's everywhere we look.

Paul speaks quietly. 'That's the worst thing I've ever heard you say.'

I swallow, say nothing.

'You actually think it's all right to say things like that.'

I can't speak. My teeth ache and I have to press them together to keep the pain out.

'Lola, if I said something like that to you, you'd kill me.'

Could he say that to me? All I can see is that he knows he might. If Paul calls me a bareback, I'll die. I make myself meet his eyes. 'People say – something like that – to me all the time. It won't kill you to hear it the other way around.'

He opens his mouth as if to shout, then shuts it fast. In the second that takes, I've heard so many answers – that I've no right to pass on abuse, that he's never done anything to deserve it, that insults are my lot in life and no fault of his. Instead, he gestures as if pushing aside a heavy branch, and speaks in a tense, quiet voice. 'If you feel that way, Lola, then why are you seeing me?'

I can't tell him I love him.

'Come on, Lola, you always have an answer for everything. If you feel so badly about lycos, then why are you sleeping with one? Why not stick to people like yourself?'

People like me.

If he thinks this is self-hatred, that I wouldn't want someone like myself, he's wrong. I know he's wrong. I wouldn't want someone like myself, but that's not because I'm a bareback, it's because I'm me. But why would he say that, if he doesn't believe, deep down, that I should know myself for a freak?

'I just met you, that's all,' I say. 'You were interested. Bareback girls are sluts, didn't you know?'

He covers his forehead. 'You're not a stupid woman, Lola. Why do you come out with such stupid things?'

I open my mouth to say, Well, I guess I didn't have the advantages of a lyco education, but I stop. Paul has always somehow made me ashamed of cheap remarks, and even now, sitting shaking on his sofa, his warm untidy sitting room as empty and cold around me as an Arctic wasteland, I can't say it.

'See,' he says, soft as snow, 'when you say those things, you really are the way people see you.'

'Who sees me?' My throat is closing up, a wire inside pulling tighter and tighter.

'Nobody,' he says. 'But if you want people to treat you like a person, if you hate it so much when people point and call you names, why the hell do you play the bareback card so often?'

Bareback. The word, in his voice, cuts a red, wet piece out of my heart.

I curl up, wrap myself around a cushion, turn my head away from him and burrow into the sofa. My voice is barely audible. 'You said you didn't use that word.'

'Why not? You say it yourself.'

'It's different.'

'Of course, everything's different for you. Lola, you really need to get over yourself.'

He says it, the adolescent phrase, the simple, snap-out-of-it solution. Get over myself. Not the world, not life, not silver bullets in the back of men's heads. Myself, as if I was a wall I could scale, as if I was a grief to recover from.

I lay my cheek on the cushion, turn away from him. 'Leave me alone.'

'I'm not the one who started this, Lola.'

'Leave me alone.'

'What, have you had enough fighting? Guess you wouldn't be so tired of it if you'd been doing all the shouting. It's hard to take, isn't it?'

'Leave me alone, leave me alone, leave me *alone*!' Something black and scalding floods me, and I turn and hurl the cushion at him. It flings itself out of my hand, spins in the air. He catches it, stands with it in his grip, and this maddens me. I throw another, then another, pull and wrench at the sofa, dislodging all its comforts, laying waste.

He stands, the cushion in his hands, looking at me. He doesn't say a word. I curl up, press my face into the last cushion left, cover my head with my arms, wrapping up as small as I can go.

Finally I hear a sound. He tosses the cushion down, picks up his keys and heads for the door. 'I'm going out,' he says.

There's nothing I can say.

I hear the door open, and then he speaks. 'I've got my mobile with me, call me if anything happens.' He sounds no less angry than before. 'And don't forget to lock up after I'm gone.'

Then the door slams, and he's gone. It's a long time before I can move.


He's gone for an hour. In this time, I raise my head and look about me. There are cushions all over the room. I want to lie down, but I can't, my tiny island that I've

300

left on the sofa is too small, it confines me. It's long, weary work to stand up, fetch the cushions one by one, replace them one by one.

The sofa is reassembled, but it doesn't look right. Something about the angle of the cushions is wrong, it's become different, as if a new piece of furniture had replaced the old when I wasn't looking. But since there's no one here to see, I can get back on it. It'll do to lie down on.

The feeling of shame is like a bridle, it checks me every time I turn my head. Too much of what he's said is just. Still, I think Becca has betrayed me, still I think Paul shouted at me, but they both of them said things that I can't shake off. My sister and Paul tangle in my head, I fight both of them at once, hear again what they said to me. What I want to say to them now is that I know I'm not a good woman. I never was. Most of the time, I'm not even a pleasant woman. But if they'd had my life, if they'd had everything that happened to me happen to them, would they have been any better than I am?

The trouble is, I don't think Paul would consider that an excuse.

I lie very still. It's too empty in here. I wish I hadn't quarrelled with Paul. He's gone, and I may have driven him away for good. That thought is worse than anything, it cuts so deep that I don't even have the strength to watch the door, search the corner for assassins. All I can do is hold a cushion, pull it to me as hard as I can.

He said he'd keep his mobile with him, he said to lock the door. Those were things about my safety. The more I think about what he said, the more the bridle tugs. Because the overwhelming thing is that he fights fair. He didn't say I was a bitch, he said I was being a bitch. He didn't say I was a coward, that I was stupid. He said that was how I was acting. It's such a big difference. He didn't call me a bareback. He said it was a word I used. I called him a lyco, I said I didn't like lycos, but he never called me a bareback.

I hold tight to the cushion, because this is no good. I really am in love. The thought is not a happy one, it brings no warm flushes or songs about Paris in the springtime. There aren't many roses in my view. It's a cold, tight absence in my chest, flowing cool through my veins, making me need him, need to get close enough for him to warm me up. The timing is bad, the prognosis worse, but for all my doubts and fears and grudges against the world, I can't stop shaking and holding the cushion and wishing for him to come home.


When he does return, the sound shakes me, as the door comes open with a sudden bang. Paul enters the room with a startled look on his face, as if he was expecting more resistance.

'Didn't you double-lock the door?' he says. There's a slight awkwardness to his voice, a little resignation, a little frustration. 'Come on, Lola, you know you have to be careful.'

'I'm sorry.' I sit up on the sofa, balanced back on my heels. I can't look at him. My eyes are closed, keeping down tears. I sit still as a sacrifice and let him see me.

He sighs. 'You know you should be more careful.' I take the reprimand. He isn't free of the argument yet,

302

not completely, but this reproach is better than some things. It's not an attack.

'I'm sorry.'

I hear the sound of his keys being set down on the table. 'Listen, I got a paper,' he says. It's an attempt at peace. 'Do you want to read it?'

He's been out, he's been somewhere where he needed a newspaper to read because I drove him out of his own flat. I sit vertical on the sofa, ready to topple. 'I'm sorry,' I say, because what other words are there?

The sound of something soft being laid down as he puts his paper on the table, and then he's round by the sofa, his hand rests on my head. The gesture is like a teacher patting a boy he's fond of, and I lift my hands, both of them, to catch hold of him, keep this concession pressing down on me. 'I'm sorry.'

He sighs again. 'It's okay,' he says. 'I know you're under a lot, I shouldn't have yelled. Just – try to be a little nice, okay?'

'Okay.' My voice is quiet. He's earned the last word.

His fingers wriggle a little under my clasp, tapping on my scalp. 'I don't know what to say now,' he says. There's an echo of rueful humour in his words that I lean my tired soul against.

'That's okay,' I say. 'Just – we needn't say anything.'

He takes his hand off my head, leaving me with a bereft moment before he comes and sits down beside me. I lie down, let my upright spine give up its guarded equilibrium and slump with my head in his lap. He pats it. His touch is light, almost absent, although I know he's paying attention. It isn't passion, it isn't ease. I don't even know if it's forgiveness. But I lie in his lap, let him pet me as if I were a child. Not his child, there isn't that much intensity in his hands on my hair. It doesn't matter. I'll take whatever's going. Anything that will let me lie down. I've been balanced too long.

# 22

Centuries ago, before we discovered anti-allergens, there was only one way to treat a silver wound: whisky and a saw and make your peace with God before I begin, my boy. As long as the silver stays in the wound, the allergy keeps going: white cells rush in and attack the inflamed flesh, the body fights itself. Tissue dies and dies, and you have to cut it away before the necrosis spreads. It used to be a punishment for prisoners of war, to cut open their flesh and stitch a silver ball inside, then wait for moonrise. The guards would lock themselves away in their compound, or chain themselves up if they were on the move, and lock up prisoners together. Sometimes they'd take bets on what would be left in the morning. That got condemned as an atrocity by the middle of the twentieth century, but by then some research-minded army doctors had learned something useful from experimenting with the survivors. There are several good serums now. Inject some and the necrosis can be stopped, as long as you've removed the source.

Seligmann's friend, the man I shot, will have had to rely on traditional methods. There have been no hospital reports of a man with silver necrosis in the arm: he didn't go in for treatment. But pliers or scalpel or woodwork saw, they must have got the bullet out, because no bodies have been found with a rotted-off arm, no severed limbs found floating in the river.

I shot him near the joint. Not easy to fix. He'd need someone who could steal hospital equipment. An orderly, a nurse, a doctor, even a cleaner from the city hospital, St Veronica's. That's the place to look.

A little hacking gets me in, and it's there I find something unusual. There's no record of instruments going missing, but used scalpels and forceps get incinerated when they're discarded; someone would only need to grab a used sharps bag. Missing drugs, though, are another matter. The stores are watched, and thanks to this we've struck gold. The day after that night, the Day One that found Seligmann in our custody and this friend of his hobbled and suffering the torments of silver because of what I did to him, a little jar of pharmaceuticals went missing.

Lydia was at the hospital, and she knows medicine better than anyone else in DORLA that I know, so I approach her and show her the notes.

'It was a jar of Oromorph,' I say. 'You familiar with that?'

She shrugs a little as she thinks about how to answer, and I realise it's not the right question. Lydia studies, studies, reads every trade magazine, spends her wages on new textbooks. No one will ever call her Doctor, probably no one will ever come to her with more than a bite wound or a silver bullet lodged in their flesh or a tranquilliser overdose, yet still, for some reason, she carries on, trying to feel like a doctor in herself.

'I mean, is it a good choice? What kind of person would choose it?'

Lydia shrugs, folds her hands. 'It was taken off a patient's bedside table in the orthopaedics ward. The patient was sleeping, he asked where his pills were when he woke up. Someone damn alert, I think.'

A bedside. 'Probably not someone with access to the store cupboards, then? I mean, to take such a risk?'

Lydia shrugs again, and as she does, I can think of answers to my own question, none of which are cheering. It sounds like a risky way, but, like taking a discarded sharps box off a trolley, it's an opportunity seized. Someone with regular access to the store cupboard would be the first suspect if something went missing from it. And this was Day One. A and E would have been full of people, all the injured people we brought in from the shelters, patched up as well as we could manage and healed up a little in the ricking process, but still, Day One is worse than a Saturday night. Everyone in the hospital would be tired themselves from the night's luning, stressed, a little overwhelmed at the new influx. People would get careless. A good day to steal something.

'It's a good place to do it,' Lydia says. 'They label the pills with the patients' names rather than with what they do. If you were looking for a painkiller in any old ward, you'd likely find you'd picked up an antibiotic or a diuretic.' She grins, and both of us laugh a little at the idea. It's not funny, not really, a man with a rotted limb fed a diuretic, conscious all the way through as they pulled a bullet out of him, but we need to laugh about something. 'Orthopaedics, I mean,' she says when we stop. 'You're looking for a painkiller, you have to choose from a range of unlabelled bottles – unless you want to take the time to look at a patient's chart, which is gonna slow you down – then orthopaedics is the place to go. You pick up a bottle in there, it's a good chance it'll be a painkiller of some kind.'

She really does know a lot. She really would have made a good doctor.

'So we want someone who knows about medication?'

Lydia shrugs a third time. It's a frustrating thing to see, a smart person helpless in the face of too many variables. 'Someone with some knowledge of the hospital, anyway.'

'Tell me about Oromorph,' I say.

'Well . . .' She touches her forehead, pats her hair. The braids are tight and flawless, they aren't coming down. 'They were pills. Oromorph's an opiate, it's a pretty common painkiller.'

'What does it do?'

'It's analgesic, dulls pain. Quite powerful. It's a narcotic.'

'Wouldn't a local anaesthetic make more sense, if you were going to take a bullet out of someone?'

'Harder to administer, though. You need to know where to inject.'

And harder to steal, too, on the spur of the moment. You'd need a syringe, for one thing, and even a half-sane man wouldn't use someone else's syringe, surely –

'So we're looking for someone who wouldn't know how to administer a local?'

'Maybe.'

Or someone who just couldn't get hold of any. The more I think about this, the more the anaesthetic seems like a chance snatched up, less essential to the plan. You can take a bullet out of a man without drugs, if you've got someone strong to hold him down.

I exhale, press my hands to my head. 'So we want someone with some nous who's prepared to take a risk, who doesn't plan in detail, who stole some Oromorph because it was better than nothing.'

'I suppose. Listen, I have to get going.' Lydia stands, walks out of the lounge where we've been sitting. On the way, she throws in the bin the paper cup that held the coffee I bought her. I have the feeling that's about all she can tell me, but it's better than nothing.


My mind is running well, the gears mesh smoothly and I'm having good ideas. I'm still making notes on the pad when the telephone rings.

'Hello?'

'Hello, this is a call for Miss Lola Galley regarding an enquiry she made.'

'I'm Lola Galley.' It's a young, female voice, sing-song, automatic.

'Hello, Miss Galley. You made an enquiry last month regarding a telephone call that was made to an unknown number.'

I sit up. This is the call Ellaway made from the shelter, that first day. He made a call from his mobile, to someone, we don't know who. A tall, dark-haired man came and picked him up. This could be a piece in the sequence, what happened that morning. 'Yes. Yes, that's right. You've found out where he called?'

'That's right, Miss Galley, do you have a pen?'

I take down the number. I take down the address. I thank the little switchboard girl, replace the receiver without looking at it, and sit, pen in hand, reading what I've written. For a moment, there's just a nagging sensation, a sense of something tugging inside my head. Then I look it up, and it's there for me to see.

It's an address I recognise. Just east of Five Wounds park, it's a house, a red brick house with a fenced-in garden. I've been there before. With Nate waiting, I climbed onto the roof of our van and stared over the fence, and saw half a dozen people luning in the open air.

'What was that about?' Nate said, and I didn't know what to tell him. He died with the question unanswered.

Ellaway called the house where people were running loose in the open air. They howled at the sky, and I saw them. I watched them in the cold, bright moonlight.

'I'm here to request official support on an investigation I'd like to make,' I say.

Hugo's eyebrows move ever so slightly. 'An investigation? Is this in regard to one of your own cases?'

'Yes, it is.' I'm not going off my route on this one, this isn't whim or error. This is what I saw with my own eyes. 'Some evidence has come to light concerning my client, Richard Ellaway, which I consider to be suspicious. I believe it needs to be investigated, and I'll need official support.'

Hugo sits in his chair and regards me. His face is neutral, and I take this as encouragement. He hasn't stopped me.

'You know, I'm sure, that Ellaway's called his own lawyer into this, Adnan Franklin.' This needs to be explained. It's not my fault, and it's an important factor. 'Mr Franklin is a famously successful lawyer, and he's very concerned with protecting his client's rights. If I'm to look into these circumstances, I'll need DORLA behind me, or Franklin's liable to interfere. Or at least, he may. If I have to defend my position against him, I'll need more than my personal opinion to justify myself.'

'I see.' Hugo sits forward, the chair creaks under his weight. 'And your opinion is what?'

There's something steadying about Hugo's inscrutability. I look up at him, and he's massive, a foot taller than me, broad as a door-frame; he could probably pick me up in one hand. It doesn't have to matter. This is the size I am, and I'm sitting up straight with something to say.

'I think I mentioned,' I begin, 'that the last dogcatch I went on, I noticed an incident that I wanted to look into. Nate Jensen was with me. At the time, I merely thought it was – unusual. What I saw was a group of lunes, all together in the open air.' Hugo's eyes flick towards me. 'I don't mean prowlers, not in the usual sense. They were all on private property, inside a garden. It had a high wall, I had to climb onto the roof of the van to see over it. A lune could jump it, but still, it was clearly put there for privacy. About ten feet high, with metal bars at the top. And inside, there was . . . well, it was a pack. That's the best way I can describe it. Perhaps half a dozen lunes, it was too dark to count them properly, all seeming – very harmonious.'

'A family group?' Hugo's hands lie heavy on the table, he's quite still, but his eyes are intent.

'I don't think so. There were no children, at least. They were all adults. And I walked back there a little later; there was no sign of a window having been broken or a door damaged.' This is true. A swift, hurried stroll I took, telling no one where I'd gone. The house was still there, handsome and intact. 'There was no way that was accidental.'

'Hmn.' Hugo drums his fingers on the tabletop, once. 'Would you say that was illegal activity?'

'Technically? Probably yes. A lawyer could make a case defending them, perhaps, because they were on private property, with a wall keeping them in. But like I said, no lune would have a problem jumping it if they wanted to. And just because they weren't making any attempts to when I saw them, it doesn't mean they haven't at other times. A lyco lawyer would say it was a grey area, but I say yes, it was criminal. It would rest on whether the garden was completely secure, and I say it wasn't.'

Hugo lets this sit for a moment, then gives me a little nod. 'Go on.'

I sit back against the chair, make myself relax, and change the subject. 'When Dick Ellaway was arrested, he claimed that he'd been trying to get to a shelter when he started furring up. Rather a thin story. And I got someone to look at his car. He claimed it broke down just before curfew, but the garage that has it had a responsible owner who didn't fix it, so we got a chance to look at it, and the engine looks like it may have been tampered with. And Ellaway left it in this out-of-the-way garage and didn't mention it to me, like he was hoping I wouldn't think to check it out. I didn't trust his story, so I spoke to the person who'd been on shelter duty the night he was brought in. Alan Gregory. Now, there was an under-age girl there who took up most of the attendants' atten-tion, so Ellaway wasn't monitored that closely, but he made a call on his mobile. Later, someone came and picked him up, but Ally couldn't describe him very well. But he made a call, and I had the phone company inves-tigate the number he'd called. And it just turned out, I just heard today, that the number he called was the house where I saw the pack.'

Hugo regards me. His face is as still as a mountain.

'I want to investigate this,' I say. 'When a client gives an implausible excuse for being out, and makes calls to a house where I've seen people lune in non-secure confines, I think it's altogether time to question his story.'

'I understand you're defending him?' says Hugo with a bland trace of irony.

'If I'm defending him, I want the real story. And times aren't good right now. I'd say it's time to be careful of any suggestion of prowling in groups.'

I say this without bitterness. It's a fact. That I manage to say it plain and straight is a small triumph that I hold cupped in my palm, keep quietly to myself.

Hugo sits up. 'I agree with you,' he says. 'Under the circumstances, we should treat this as highly suspicious. What do you need to take this further?'

The triumph glows, swells, filling my hands. 'Official approval, mostly,' I say, keeping my voice level. 'A partner to go and question this Ms Sanderson with, but I can organise that myself.'

'Ms Sanderson?'

'Yes, that's the name of the house-owner. I looked her up. Sarah Sanderson, she's a theatre producer. A successful one, I'd think, if she can afford a house in Five Wounds so near the park. I checked her record. One arrest when she was eighteen, but she was never charged for it. It seems she was trapped in an office building whose security system had gone haywire and locked everyone in; it was only when the city power got shut down at night that the doors opened.'

'I remember that night,' Hugo says, quietly. He looks at me. 'A couple of years before your time, I think,

314

Lola. You would have been – well, about sixteen, I suppose.'

Sixteen. Another night in a creche. I close my eyes a moment, and look back at Hugo. 'A well-known night?'

'Oh, yes.' His tone is almost expressionless. 'Everyone who was operating in the city then remembers it.'

'Did everyone in the building get arrested?' I say.

'More or less.' Hugo studies his hands. 'Though certain areas were overrun, it wasn't possible to arrest them all.'

'It sounds like a disaster,' I say. The word *overrun* brings images to my mind that I don't want to think about.

'It was.' Hugo sighs. 'Mass tranquillisation, packed cells, major property damage . . . and the days afterwards. We had to arrange negotiations with the city council and a government inquiry, in the end. A complete amnesty for all those caught in the building, in exchange for an amnesty for all methods used by all DORLA agents making the arrests. The hospital was awarded a national commendation, and the company responsible for the security system was sued by – I don't know, maybe a thousand people, enough to ruin them anyway. I don't suppose you would have been told too much about it. It was decided not to dwell on it in front of new recruits. It was considered too discouraging.'

'Discouraging?' I almost laugh, the word said with no sense of bathos, no derision, but I collect myself. 'So, our Ms Sanderson was in that. Interesting.'

'Yes,' Hugo says. 'As I remember it, the mood the morning after it happened was . . . quite stricken. I understand that most who were involved in it became rather reclusive, at least for a while.'

The image of it, packed cages, dozens ricking together, is a terrible one. Stricken. I don't want even to imagine the sound of that much weeping. 'Most of them,' I say. 'But I wonder if Ms Sanderson found she had bit of a taste for it.'

In ten years I've seen dozens of people caught out in the moonlight. Accident, carelessness. Always, I've been bitter, outraged, blind angry at the thought that people could be careless with something so dangerous. But the word *prowler* conjures up something different. Not the average citizen, milky with absent-mindedness, sated with their rights, satisfied as babies in the knowledge that the world is theirs.

I've been imagining it in Ellaway, the man who damages his own car and waits for the moon to rise. I saw it in Seligmann. Prowler is a word that makes all of us close our fists and set our mouths, turn our heads aside. Prowler is in every scar that traces a cage over my body, every frightened glance over my shoulder, every locked door and gloved hand and every piece missing from my flesh. When I cradled Leo in my arms, I stroked his soap-soft skin, sang him songs and promised him fishies, I told him that this was a good world. I told him that there were treats and games, and that I loved him, that I wanted him happy, that no one could hurt him. But even when I did it, even with his loose, downy head pressed against my shoulder, I knew that I was telling him stories. There's never been a time when the world was not at war, there's never been a day that went by when some man did not kill another, when some people didn't starve because others didn't care enough to feed them, there's never been a day when the world was one I could give to him. I tell myself that even the average citizen wants the world safe and kindly, that no one really wants the prisons full and the soldiers busy and the world full of cutthroats. But as long as there are prowlers, I know this can never be so.

It's a cancer inside you, a hunger that doesn't go away. The prowler makes his decision, and his decision is this: I will not be kept out of the moonlight. If I meet someone there, I'll fight, I'll kill, I'll rip open living flesh. I have seen barebacks on the streets, scarred faces and too few fingers, people on crutches, people in wheelchairs, people with dead eyes, people with missing eyes, people with missing friends. I know this, and still, I will not be kept out of the moonlight.

It may be different inside their own minds, the images may be different, the words. But this is what it comes down to. And I wonder more about it still, because haven't I myself beaten a man bloody? We all of us have our own impulse to prowl. A prowler is the insects in your mind, the whispering demons that make your own little wishes gigantic and imperative, worth hurting for. Every thief, every killer, every father with a leather belt and assassin with a loaded gun. This is why I can't give him the world. A prowler, silver-grey and white-toothed and beautiful, is the simplest, purest image of this. The evil of the world, down on all its four feet.


Ally doesn't much want to leave his test range, but I stand there until he gives up and comes with me. We go in one of the patrol vans. On the way, I explain.

317

Ally listens in silence, trying to fix the catch on his seat belt. I tell him that I think Sarah Sanderson is a prowler and may give me some information about the Ellaway case. The only comment he makes is when we drive up to her house itself.

'They were luning in there?' he says, pointing to the garden wall.

'Mm-hm.' I put the brakes on.

Ally shakes his head. 'That'd never keep a lune in.'


And when Sarah Sanderson opens her door, I lose every thought I've had before now, because I recognise her. Months ago now, but I know this woman. Floaty clothes, good skin, dancer's posture. She opens the door, and her eyes flicker over me before she says, 'Can I help you?' in a vibrant voice that's only a little tense.

'Good afternoon, Miss Sanderson,' I say. 'We've met before, if you remember.' I wait to see how she'll answer, but she says nothing, looks at me, holding on to the door. 'I came to your friend Lewis Albin's house some months ago, to make some enquiries about my client, Dick Ellaway. You remember, don't you?'

She frowns, a delicate wrinkle on the bridge of her nose. 'Yes,' she says, her voice soft. 'You're a DORLA agent, aren't you, Miss – Galley, was it?'

'That's right.' If she'd pretended to misremember my name, I would have known she was acting, and I think she knows that. She's a smart woman. 'May I come in, Miss Sanderson?'

'Is it necessary?' She rests her cheek against the door.

'I'm afraid so. There are some serious matters we need to discuss.'

'Oh . . .' She bites her lip, looks inside, then takes her hand off the door. 'All right, then.'

Ally and I walk into her house. There's embroidered cloth pinned to the walls, theatrical posters, a long strip of indigo silk wound round the banister that leads upstairs. She leads us through a doorway where shadow-puppets are tacked around the frame.

The room isn't empty. Lewis Albin sits on a sofa, straight-backed amid a tangle of cushions. Another woman rises to her feet as we come in, a woman with glossy black curls pulled back into a neat bun, square cheekbones and precisely defined lips, black-framed glasses on a half-sensuous face.

'What's going on, Sarah?' Albin says.

Sarah raises her hands. 'Miss Galley here says she wants to ask some questions about Dick Ellaway.'

'Sit down,' he says, more to Sarah and the other woman than to me. 'And you are, sir?'

'Alan Gregory,' Ally says, showing his card and retreating to lean against the wall.

'How can we help you?' Albin keeps his eyes on me.

'I'm here investigating serious evidence in the Ellaway case,' I say, not looking away. 'I have some questions I need to ask Miss Sanderson.'

Sarah glances at the other two, and I turn to her before she can say anything. 'Miss Sanderson, you are aware of the laws governing curfew and confinement on full-moon nights?'

'Of course.' She takes a cushion into her lap, picks at the seams.

'Then you're aware of the penalties for violating them?'

'Yes.'

319

'Miss Sanderson, last moon night I and another agent witnessed a serious violation of those laws on your property.'

'A violation?' Albin says.

'Mr Albin, I was addressing Miss Sanderson. Miss Sanderson, you are aware that half a dozen adult lunes in your back garden on a moon night does not comply with the laws of confinement?'

'Wait, wait,' Albin says. He doesn't sound too disturbed; his tone is quite courteous. 'Ms Galley, the laws you're talking about lay down safe confinement in a private place. Surely the garden isn't a major violation if it's secure?'

I look at him. The scar on his face is pale and thick. The dark-haired woman beside him is holding her knees, tense, and there's a scar on her hand. Lycos don't have scars like that, not many of them. Groups of lycos don't all have scars, it's us who all have cuts and slashes, because we're the ones who have to deal with lunes. The scar on Albin's face is very much like mine.

A light flares behind my eyes, then another.

'Mr Albin, were you involved in this incident?'

Albin shrugs. 'Yes.'

'Lewis –' The woman beside him speaks, quick and low.

'It's all right, Carla, there's not a lot we can do about it if there's a witness. Nothing very terrible is going to happen.'

'So you were involved in this too?' I say to Carla. She looks down.

'May I ask your name?'

'Carla Stein.' It's muttered, nervous.

'I'm going to have to ask you all to come with me,'

I say. I should feel powerful, or angry. I don't. Carla's anxiety, Sarah's silence, they're getting to me: I'm the one causing this unease, and somehow I'm sharing in it.

'Why?' Albin says. He doesn't move from the sofa.

I put my hands in my pockets. 'Your friend Dick Ellaway, my client, was found illegally out on a moon night. A bad lune, Mr Albin. He took the hand off the man who tried to catch him. And the next morning, he made a call from the shelter, to this address. And we already know he's been calling you, you told me so yourself.

'Now let me explain a scenario to you. Half a dozen people decide they don't want to spend the moon night indoors. There's a garden out back of this house, with a good wall, and that's where they go. They think it'll be safe, because the wall is solid and can't be broken through, but what they haven't realised is that it'll be quite easy to jump over it. Once the moon has risen, you can make leaps you wouldn't believe. And someone in the group sets out to do just that.

'I believe you tried to stop him, Mr Albin. The witness at the shelter said he had scars on his back, and then there's that mark on your face. All of that goes with one luning man trying to stop another from doing what he wanted to do. I don't think you like him that much, or at least, not any more. Certainly you didn't know him as well as you thought you did. You wouldn't see it, I suppose, but there's nothing that stops a bad lune, nothing at all, trust me.

'And he got out, and then a catcher tried to stop him. Well, you know how that turned out.

'And then there's the little story he told me about his car breaking down. It didn't break down: it was broken. I'd thought he damaged it himself before the moon night began, but I was wrong. Wasn't I? You see, I thought he was acting alone. There was no way he could have got back to his car in time to tamper with the engine the next morning. But if he called this house, let everyone know what had happened to him, it would be the easiest thing in the world for one of you to slip out and do a little tampering for him. Just to make sure nothing bad would happen to him after he mauled someone.

'Your wall is higher than it needs to be which makes me think you've done this before, maybe even make a habit of it. I think the likeliest situation is that you and your friends do this often, and because all of you are used to keeping within the garden, it didn't occur to you that someone would try to break out. I think that Dick Ellaway was a new introduction to the group, someone you met through business and found you had some ideas in common with. He's successful, he's a professional man, he doesn't look like a killer, not in the daylight. It didn't occur to you he might not be willing to stay inside your little garden. But it should have. You must have known it was possible. And you must have known that anyone who got out would be capable of doing things that would destroy people. The man your friend ran into had a wife and three children, Mr Albin. Do you know how much you bleed when someone tears off your hand?'


Ally and I arrest the three of them, take them out to the van. It's not designed for daytime arrests, and Carla looks close to tears when we lock her into the lune cage, flinching as the door clangs shut, but we have to make the best of what equipment we have.

Criminal negligence, violating curfew, and conspiracy to pervert the course of justice. We drive them back, lock them in the cells. Albin asks to make a phone call, and I shut the door on him without a word.

# 24

'You can't do this,' Ellaway says.

'Watch me.' Ally pushes him so he falls face-down on the desk. There are things on the table top, pens and a calculator, and he makes a sound of pain as he lands. Ally's hand presses hard against the back of his neck as I fix the cuffs around his wrists.

'What are you doing?' It's a young woman who speaks, one of the crowd around the door; short, Asian and stocky, she's wearing a green suit. She looks very smart. I flash my DORLA card at her, and she takes a step back.

'Call security,' Ellaway says into the desk.

'Mr Ellaway, you're under arrest. Security aren't going to stop us,' I tell him.

'You can't arrest me, you've already charged me, God damn it!'

'Yes,' I say, 'but we've got some other charges to add to the list.'

Ally jerks him to his feet and pushes him towards the door. Ellaway's colleagues look at each other, but when we hustle him through the crowd parts. Later on they'll tell each other how shocked they were, and that'll be their contribution. That's all the help Ellaway's getting from them.

'Conspiracy to pervert the course of justice, mainly,' I add, just for the record. 'We've had to reassess you.'

Ellaway makes a lunge at me, but Ally has hold of him, and Ally has been wrestling lunes since he was eighteen. It isn't even a contest.

'Don't bother,' I say. Pausing in the doorway, I turn to the woman in the stylish green suit. 'You might want to explain to his boss where he's been taken. He's been charged with attempted murder already, as you may know.' I don't raise my voice over the sound of Ellaway's struggles. It's easier to ruin a man than I thought. 'Some further charges have come up, so we're having to re-arrest him.'

'Call my fucking lawyer,' Ellaway says.

'I wouldn't bother,' I say without looking at him. 'Albin's already confessed.'

'His name is Adnan Franklin, he works at Franklin and Wilson in south Kings . . .'

This is his survival instinct, I suppose, the list of people to call in for his protection. Franklin isn't going to like this, and I'll have to go ten rounds with him, but in the end, what can he do to me? I have the weight of DORLA behind me. He can damage my reputation amongst his wealthy clients but I live off pro bono anyway; he can threaten to sue me but he'd have to take on the whole department, and unless he sends in the army he isn't getting Ellaway away from us. There's not much he can take away from me. Unlike Ellaway. Ellaway has a lot to lose. And there's nothing in the world that'll make me let him go this time.

*

Several people in the entrance foyer turn to stare as Ally and I drag Ellaway through, but we don't pause to explain. He doesn't stop struggling until we get him all the way down to the cells. He's way past escaping now, and he must know that. He still yanks against Ally's grip, making it difficult, showing us he's not subdued. As we get down to the cells, their bleak fluorescent light and bare brick walls and barred cages, he spits at my feet.

I hit him, once. He staggers back, and Ally loosens his hold enough that Ellaway knocks his head against the wall before regaining his feet.

'Don't do that again,' I say. It's a cold and facile victory, I know, but I don't care enough to stop myself.

'Where do you want him?' Ally says.

I shrug. 'Put him with the others.'

'What others?' Ellaway's voice is jolted as Ally lays hold of him again.

'You giving them the chance to sit together and make up a story?' Ally asks.

I shake my head. We can bug the cells, and there's no need to say that in front of Ellaway. 'Like I said,' I say for Ellaway's benefit, 'they've already confessed.'

'Confessed to what? What are you talking about?' We harry him down a flight of stairs. Ellaway tries to look down at them, and Ally grabs his hair, pulling his head up so there's nothing guiding him down the steps but us.

'You'll see,' I say.

The corridor we have the others on is narrow and windowless, with six cells in a row. Even with the lights on, it feels dark. Ellaway is marched down it, his head still held forward, and I see the prisoners stand up as we enter. There's a bruise on Albin's face, I see, and one hand is limp at his side; all of them hang back a little from the front of the cells.

'What's going on? How come you're arresting him again?' Carla's voice rises high and scared.

'Hello, Dick,' Albin says over her, and she covers her mouth and turns away.

Ally releases Ellaway's head. Ellaway looks over the three prisoners. 'Oh, Christ,' he says.

'What did they arrest you for?' There's no echo down here, the cramped walls deaden sound. Even so, Albin's quiet voice carries.

'It's all bullshit, they've already charged me . . .' Ally cuts Ellaway off in mid-sentence.

I unlock the gate to the nearest empty cell. 'Conspiracy to pervert the course of justice,' I tell Albin. My voice is neutral. 'Tampering with evidence is a bigger charge than violating curfew.'

'Can they do that?' Carla says.

'I wouldn't waste your time wondering.' She flinches as I speak, and goes to the bars that separate Albin's cell from hers.

He goes to meet her, reaches through and gives her a brief pat on the shoulder. 'Can we have some blankets?' he asks me. 'We've only got straw down here.'

I ignore him, open the door, and Ally pushes Ellaway through. He's up to the front of the cell as I turn the key in the lock.

'I wouldn't grip the bars if I were you,' Albin says, raising his hand. There's a stark purple bar across the knuckles. 'They have rules about it.'

'What the fuck?' says Ellaway.

'They're charging us with violating curfew,' Albin tells him. His damaged hand brushes against the scar on his cheek. 'The night you mauled an op. And with tampering with evidence to cover it up.'

'That's enough,' I say. An op? Short for operative, I suppose, but it's not a word I've heard before.

'I want to see my lawyer,' Ellaway says.

'I'm sure you do,' I say.

Turning my back, I open a panel on the wall that controls monitoring of the cells. While I'm punching in my identification number, my authorisation level – I have the go-ahead from my superiors for any process I care to request – and my specification – that all activity in the cells is to be recorded – Ellaway says several more things about wanting his lawyer. Finally, Sarah, who's been leaning against the wall shading her eyes, looks up at him. 'Give it a rest,' she says.

'We have to get out of here.'

'You're not helping.'

'You're making my head hurt,' Carla says, not looking at anyone.

'Sarah's right,' Albin puts in. 'They're not going to let us see any lawyers. I guess the answer to my request for a phone call is still no, Ms Galley?'

I don't reply. 'Want to set up an interrogation?' Ally says. He's taken the keys to the cells and is passing them from hand to hand.

'I'll submit a report and we'll go from there,' I tell him.

'Can we at least have a DORLA lawyer to advise us?' Albin says.

'Later.' I close the panel.

'We'll be happy to confess.'

328

'What the fuck are you talking about?' Ellaway hisses.

I turn and look at them. If they confess, then Ellaway's finished. He's responsible for everything he did that night, because he was out illegally, and nothing Franklin can do will save him. The best he can hope for is a reduction from attempted murder to GBH. Ellaway's looking at Albin, and Albin's looking at me.

'Who picked Ellaway up from the shelter the morning after it happened?' I ask Albin.

He doesn't hesitate. 'I did.'

'Ally, is this the man you saw?'

Ally frowns. 'No. I don't think so. He was skinnier, darker hair.'

'You want to answer that question again?' I ask Albin.

'I told you. I did. My hair looks darker the first day after a moon night.' Albin keeps looking at me.

'And you've gained weight since it happened.' I say. 'Okay. You have a think about answering that question, and I'll have a think about getting you a lawyer.'

'I'm telling you the truth.'

'There are four of you in here,' I say. 'I saw at least five, maybe more, that night in your garden. You think about what you want to tell us, and I'll think about you.'

'Ms Galley!' Albin says, but I'm already walking away.


I don't have to buy my own coffee for the next few days. Word has gone round, and I'm known as the woman who brought in the people who mauled Johnny, tracked down some regular, organised prowlers. People stop me in the corridors to ask details and congratulate me.

No one I speak to has run into something quite like this before. People sometimes lock up together – lovers or families with small children share the same room; if someone visits a close friend on a moon night they might share the same lock-up for convenience, same as they might share a double bed – but outdoors, breaking curfew in a pack, that's news. None of us like the idea. Free-ranging, people are starting to call it, a name picked up from listening in on their conversations in the cells: Albin said something to the effect that we couldn't hold them forever, because a little free-ranging was not a major offence. It's the closest he's come to saying anything incriminating. When Ellaway starts to shout, they silence him. Mostly, the two women wonder how long we can keep them and what we're going to do, and Albin tries to reassure them. Otherwise, they talk about books and music, Sarah's latest production, some antiques that Albin has been trading. It's an education to listen to them, but it doesn't give me many clues.

After several days of art and culture, I give up listening to the bugs, and look into their records.

These are professional people. None of them have money on the scale that Ellaway does, but they're all successful, well thought of, and well-off. Albin has a degree in art history and another one in architecture; he's connected with several museums in a freelance capacity; he's written two books, one scholarly and one popular. I find a copy of the popular one at the

330

local library, a lively how-to-value-your-own-heirlooms guidebook with colourful pictures. The library sticks a piece of headed paper into the front of each book to stamp the date of each withdrawal; in the front of Albin's book, there are four, perhaps five of these papers stuck on top of each other. Plenty of people have been reading it. His scholarly book is called *No Other Gods*, and it's on the influence of totemic art on colonial and post-colonial imagery, God help me. A quick scan of other books on the subject shows *No Other Gods* crops up in quite a few of his colleagues' bibliographies. I try to read it, but I never went to university and haven't the patience to keep up with his academic style. Neither DORLA nor the police has ever arrested him for anything.


'We've got to wait this out,' he told the others in the cells. 'They won't leave us down here forever.'

'That's what you think,' Ellaway muttered. None of them could see the cameras.

'And for God's sake, Dick, keep your head and don't make things worse.'

'You think they can be worse?'

'Yes, I do. So don't antagonise them.'

'You didn't antagonise them,' Sarah said. 'Look what they did to you.'

'I'll be fine, won't I, Carla?'

'Well, they didn't break any bones,' Carla said. She got quieter and quieter each hour we kept her down there. 'The swelling will go down if you don't move it.'

331

'All we can do is wait,' he said. 'In the end, they'll get to us.'

Nobody sounded comforted by this, but they didn't contradict him.


Sarah Sanderson, now she *has* been arrested. The night Hugo told me about, when she was eighteen and the city overran with lunes, doesn't have many official records. I go down into the basement and look at the arrest files. It's cheerless work. Every shelter lists its inhabitants, plus write-ups, notes, details. For that night, the records are scribbled and sparse.

> Satchiko Immamura, age 28. Notes: brought in tranked at 8.45.
> Joseph Nolan, age 65. Notes: brought in 8.45.
> Sarah Sanderson, age 18. Notes: 8.45.
> Dharminder Kang, age 37. Notes: 8.45.
> Alice Goldberg, age 30. Notes: 8.45.
> Antoinne Washington, age 37. Notes: 8.45.

It goes on for pages. It's hard to imagine so many bodies crammed into so few cells. There's nothing in the records to show how eighteen-year-old Sarah handled being crowded into a cage with strangers and left with them all night. It doesn't even show if she was tranquillised or not, and no one's going to remember.

There isn't much else I can find about Sarah, except that she works on innovative shows that either meet with spectacular success or absolute failure, that she's a founder member of a theatre group I haven't heard of, and that her name gets written on the programmes in medium-sized print.


'They could keep us here forever, you know,' she said on the morning of the second day.

'They won't,' Albin said.

Sarah rubbed her hands in her lap and didn't look at him. 'Nobody knows where we are.'

'They'll notice we've gone.'

'If anyone asks where we are, the ops won't tell them we're here.'

'Don't prophesy doom.'

Carla sat huddled in a corner and said nothing.

'This is doom,' Sarah said. 'I don't need to prophesy when we're already at their mercy.'


When I look into Carla's records, everything stops.

As the days pass, she sits quietly in the cells. Albin and Sarah chat, and she puts in a word now and then; when Ellaway raises his voice she asks him to stop; when Albin paces his cell in an attempt to get some exercise she leans against the bars and watches him; she kneels in her corner, heaping up the straw in an effort to make a comfortable pallet, her head ducked over the task; she avoids people's eyes when they bring down food.

This is what I find on her. She grew up in the country and came to the city to study medicine. Since then, she's been working at St Veronica's hospital in paediatrics. Her name is down on a contract as Sarah's tenant; they've been living together for four years. She was arrested once, three years ago, luning in Five Wounds, and it was reckoned to be an accident.

And two years ago, she was brought before the Medical Council. They handed down a six-month suspension, but didn't strike her off. Everyone wrote in references about what an excellent doctor she is.

A bottle of Oromorph went missing from the store cupboards. Everyone was surprised when they traced it back to her.

## 25

'Your sister called,' Paul says.

I stop in the doorway, pull off my gloves. 'My sister?'

'Yeah, Becca.' He's leaning against the opposite wall, his hands pressed flat against it. 'She called about an hour ago.'

'You've been home that long?' I hang up my coat, go over to give him a kiss. 'How come she had your number, anyway?'

'I guess she looked me up, I'm in the phone book. She knew my name, anyway. She wanted to know how you were.'

'Well, I guess you told her.' I sit down on the sofa, take off my shoes and try to squeeze some warmth into my feet. My head is full of bottles of Oromorph, and I don't want to talk about my family.

'Yeah, I said you were fine. She's nice, your sister. You should introduce us.'

'You forget,' I say, 'I'm not allowed anywhere near her as long as there's a target on my head.'

'Did you get home okay?' He sits beside me and takes my cold feet in his hands.

I stop. I walked all the way to the bus stop without looking around me, I sat on the bus and didn't make a head count of the passengers. No, I sat on a seat and looked without seeing out of the window at the rain and thought about the four people we have down in the cells who mauled Johnny and who steal Oromorph, the three people who attacked Marty when they were luning, the people who shot Johnny and Nate with silver bullets. The ones we have, and the ones still out there. I thought about our free-rangers down in the cages, about what would happen to them tonight, and I knew I wouldn't stop any of it.

And all the time there were others of them out there, and I didn't look around me. I shiver, and the back of my head, still unbroken by a bullet, tingles.

'I – I did. Jesus.'

'What?'

'I wasn't even thinking about it. I just came home and didn't look anywhere.'

'Well, that's good, isn't it?' Paul pulls off one of my socks and interlaces his fingers with my toes.

'No.'

'You reckon someone's still after you?'

'Yes,' I say, 'I reckon someone's still after me.'

He sighs. 'Hasn't anyone caught anyone yet?'

I shrug. He doesn't get to hear of bruised citizens sleeping on straw in the dark at the bottom of my building. He doesn't get to look into my dark places. 'Haven't you cleared the city of child abuse yet?'

'No,' he sighs. 'God.' I lie down, rest my feet against his chest. He covers them with his hands. 'Anyway, I had a nice chat with Becca.'

I look up at him with suspicion. 'What did you talk about?'

'She told . . .' Paul stops as the telephone rings, and looks over his shoulder, his hands still on my feet.

'Shall I get it?'

'No.' He glances back at me, gives me a mock-frown. 'You're supposed to be in hiding.'

He crosses the room to answer it, and I sit back up on the sofa, pulling off my jacket for something to do. When I think of my own flat, it gives me a nostalgic wrench that I can't handle, so I try not to think of it. And staying here is good. As Paul leaves the sofa, there's a sense of loss, and I realise how close together we've been living. Having him on the other side of the room feels like a long way away.

'Hello?' He looks up at me, sitting lonely on the sofa, and holds the receiver a little way from his mouth. 'Hang on a minute, Lola, I'll be back in a moment.'

I lean back, watch him.

'Yes,' he says. 'Yeah. No, I haven't.' There's a pause, during which I smooth the fabric on one of his cushions. 'Well look, we can go over it tomorrow. Okay, bye.'

'Who was that?'

'Work.' He rubs his head. 'But I'm not going back in. They can just wait till tomorrow.'

'Are you too busy to work tonight?' I say as he rejoins me.

'Might be.' He grins. 'Anyway, I've had enough work for one day. Where were we?'

'You were going to tell me what my sister's been saying about me.'

'She hasn't been saying anything about you!' Paul gives me an amused look. 'Why, is there something to tell?'

337

I shrug. 'No. Just that last time we spoke she forbade me her house.'

'Well, she was worried about her kid, you can't blame her for that.'

'I'll do what I want,' I mutter, trying to sound only half-serious. Little children grow so fast, and Leo will have changed so much since I've seen him.

'She said you'd been a big help with him, by the way.'

'With Leo?' I look up.

'Yeah. She said you'd been taking him for walks every day, playing with him . . . I didn't know you'd been around him that much.'

I sigh. 'I'm not going broody, if that's what you're wondering, so don't start dropping tactful hints.'

'Now that's unfair, I've never dropped tactful hints,' Paul says, folding his arms. 'It's bad manners, accusing your lover of things your previous lovers have done.'

'Fair enough.' It's a reasonable point.

'No, she said you and him get along great.'

I brush my hair off my face. 'It's easy to get along with someone portable.'

He laughs.

'No,' I say. 'I just – Leo's my friend. He doesn't criticise me. And he's a great little boy, I mean, he'll be a nice kid when he grows up. I mean, the poor little guy, the world's so big for him. He needs someone on his side.'

'Do you miss him?'

I look down. 'Yeah.'

'Well, Becca could visit us here, you know.'

'I don't know.'

'Why not?'

'I don't know if she wants to see me.'

338

'Oh, come on, you tell a woman with a tiny baby that some sniper may be after you, of course she's going to be worried about you coming to her place. You can't take that personally.'

'This relationship must be going very well if you're starting to criticise how I get on with my family,' I say. 'Mind you, if you start trying to make me call my mother, you really are in trouble.'

'I was only inviting your sister over,' he says. 'Or are you too worried about people after you?'

'Whoever's shooting my friends, I don't think it's Becca.' I pinch the bridge of my nose, trying to keep the comedy image of Becca firing a gun blotting out the phrase 'shooting my friends'.

Paul sits in silence for a moment. 'Don't they have any information at all?' he says in the end.

I look at him. 'Are you tired of me being here?'

'No . . .' he says, and the telephone cuts him off in mid-syllable. He sighs, stands up. 'That's not it at all, I'm concerned for your life rather than trying to get you out of my flat – hello?' He frowns. 'Can I help you?' There's a pause, and then he looks up. 'It's for you.'

I stand, cross the room to the phone on my half-shod feet. Paul puts an arm around my waist as I take the receiver, and I lean against him. 'Lola Galley.'

'Lola, hi, it's me.' It's Ally.

I stiffen a little in Paul's arms. 'What is it?'

'Who was that? Is that the guy you're seeing?'

'That's top secret for my own security, remember? Mind your own business.'

'Who is it?' Paul says quietly, and I shake my head, rest against him.

'Why are you calling?' It comes out a little abrupt,

but Ally's voice sounds wrong inside Paul's flat, I shouldn't be hearing it.

'Got something I thought you should know.'

'Can't it wait till tomorrow?'

'I thought you might like to know in advance, that's all.' I can hear the rattle of his fingers tapping against the phone. 'Someone threw a Molotov cocktail at the building half an hour ago.'

'What?' I stand up, disentangle my hand from Paul's and push my hair out of my face.

'Yeah. Didn't catch anyone, it was late and you know no one walks in front of our building if they can help it.'

'What, you mean the office building?' Paul touches my shoulder as I say this.

'Well, yeah, what did you think?'

'What happened?'

'Well, it didn't catch. And it didn't go through a window, either, I mean, that's why we've got all that chicken wire. But the front of the building is pretty well scorched. I didn't think you'd like to come in tomorrow morning and see it without a warning, that's all.' He says the last part rapidly, as if defending himself.

'What floor?'

'I don't know, Lola, throwing height. What did you think?'

'Not the cell level, then.'

'No, higher.'

'And what's the reaction down there?'

'Well, they haven't told us anything yet.' He says this without passion, and I don't ask anything else.

'Well look,' I say, 'thanks for telling me.'

'That's okay. I just thought you'd like to know.'

'Yeah, thanks.'

'At least you won't get a shock tomorrow, that's the main thing. And there's no real damage done. Not to us, anyway. But I reckon there's going to be some clamping down done soon.'

'Okay. Look, I'll see you tomorrow.'

'Okay. Burned building and all. Hey, at least it's covered some of the graffiti.'

'Okay, bye, Ally.' I hang up and lean back against Paul.

'Who was that?' he says.

'Ally.' I pull him back towards the sofa, drape my legs across his lap.

'Who's Ally, your other lover? Your boss? Your ex?'

'Well, kind of,' I say.

'What, your ex?'

'Not really. We were very young at the time.' I tuck my head into the hollow of his neck and hope he'll leave the subject there.

'Why do I get the feeling,' says Paul, 'that if I ask you anything else about this guy I'll get an "I don't want to talk about it"?'

'Because you're very very perceptive?'

'Hmp. You're not still seeing him?' He says this more as a statement than a question.

'No. We just work together.'

'Do you like me better?'

'Much.'

'Okay,' he says. 'Oh, and how did he get this number?'

'I had to give my boss a contact number. Just the number, not the address. Tomorrow I'll tell him not to give it out.'

'Right, well, that'll do.'

Paul kisses my nape, and I stretch my neck out. He brushes my hair aside, and I see it tumble around my face in a dark curtain. When I sigh, he tilts my face towards him and I uncurl my legs and shift across the sofa to sit over him. His scalp is warm against my fingertips as we kiss, and when his arms come around me I close my eyes and press nearer to him, needing this, needing a moment outside time.

The telephone rings again. 'I don't believe this,' Paul mutters, and I take some comfort from the fact that he's as upset at the interruption as I am.

'We could just ignore it,' I suggest, but he's already stood up.

'Hello? I'm sorry? No, I've told you before.' He gives me a look of wide-eyed despair. 'No, I'm sorry, but I'm not . . .'

Someone threw a Molotov cocktail at the DORLA building. A half-full bottle, a crash of glass, a spreading ball of flame. Liquid goes so far, a spilt cup covers the floor, a single teardrop spreads as wide as a penny. Half a litre of alcohol is enough to burn a lot of people.

'I've had enough of this,' Paul says, hanging up. 'We're going out for a walk.'

'Who was that?'

He shrugs. 'Double glazing. Come on, get your coat. It's stopped raining, and if the phone rings one more time, I'm gonna have to pull it out of the wall, and then I won't be able to use it when I calm down.'

'Someone's after me,' I say. 'And, and . . .' I almost tell him about the Molotov cocktail. Almost.

Paul sits down. 'You'll be safe,' he says. 'No one's going to get you. You'll be with me.'

'Not that I don't appreciate it,' I say, 'but if someone

fires a bullet at me, I don't know how much help your escort will be.'

'No one's going to shoot at you when there's a witness,' he says.

'Not unless they feel like shooting the witness too.'

Paul takes me under the arms and sets me on my feet. 'You can't hide in here forever, you'll wind up a crazy old woman throwing knives at cracks in the floorboards. We're going for a walk, and no one is going to shoot you, and you'll see how much better you feel about everything.'

It seems so easy to agree with him; one walk doesn't feel like a fatal idea. But isn't that the kind of thinking that makes you careless and gets you killed? I don't even know. I've never been in a siege before.

'Come on. Half an hour of fresh air. We'll go to the park, it's lovely at night.'

'The park's lovely at night?' Paul lives north of Sanctus. Woods all over it, clumps and patches of trees. Marty's blood soaking into the ground.

'Have you never been? When the lights are lit, it's pretty. Come on. Nothing's going to happen. We'll be safe, really.'

He thinks he can look after me, and he may even be right, but in secret, I take my gun anyway.


It isn't night-time yet, not really. It's only the winter that makes everything so dark. As we reach Spiritus Sanctus, the gates are wide open, and the path that stretches in front of us is lined either side with lamps, tall, ornate pillars decorated with ironwork around their bases and bowed, glowing heads. There are people walking down it, their shadows long and vertiginous, some holding hands, some walking with their hands in their pockets, even joggers.

A patter of claws sounds behind me, and I drop Paul's hand and whirl around, my hand going for my pocket. For a moment there's nothing, I can't see anything, and then I realise I'm looking too high. Lune height, and this is not a moon night, people are just out for a walk and the sheepdog running along the path is not my responsibility to catch. It goes by me in a rush, and after years of training I still can't stop myself flinching as it passes.

'What's the matter?' Paul asks.

I shrug. 'Oh, I just – don't like dogs.'

'You don't like dogs?' He sounds as if this was a puzzling thing to say.

'No, I don't like dogs. I bloody hate dogs. They're stupid animals.'

He puts an arm around my shoulders. 'Some of them are clever, you know.'

'I – I mean it's stupid that they exist. They've . . . Dogs are all pedigrees nowadays, or mongrels that are cross-breeds from different pedigrees, no one knows what a real dog would have looked like before we started breeding them this way and that. They're – freakish, they're, I don't know, wild animals boiled down into pets that are too stupid to do anything except love whoever happens to be their owner more than they deserve. It's . . . They're like dancing bears, like someone had bred a chimp to walk on its hind legs because it'd be cuter that way.'

'Hm,' Paul says. 'You'd prefer them wild?'

'No. God no. Then we'd have wild animals all around

344

us.' I scan to and fro, we're not too near the trees and no one near us is looking our way, I can't see any shooters. It's just too many nights out in the cold that makes me feel that the forest is around us every day.

'So this isn't because you had a bad dog experience?' Paul says, unafraid of dogs and dark woodlands and strangers.

'Well, yeah, I've had those too.' I say it to make him laugh, but he doesn't, he just hugs me with one arm and keeps walking. I don't mention what those are, training for dogcatches, collaring used-up greyhounds and family pets turned savage.

'Is it me,' Paul says, 'or were you reaching for an imaginary gun when you heard that dog?'

'It could be either of us.'

'Is that how you work on moon nights?'

'Yeah. Action girl. The new, sexy me. Chicks with guns. Like the image? Moon-night clothes, heavily wrapped up in protective gear. Impenetrable. Kind of a wetsuit look.'

'I knew a guy in college who had a wetsuit fetish.'

'That's weird.'

'I think he liked the rubber-clad yet sporty connotations.'

'That's still weird.' Though there are internet sites dedicated to moon-night gear, sleazy shops that sell reproductions of it – or, I suspect, worn-out gear that some sly entrepreneur sells out of the back door when it fails its durability test and is set to be destroyed. Every now and again, someone sends an e-mail circular drawing our attention to such sites, and every time, I don't look. I don't want to know. Paul's arm, muffled by his coat, is solid, definite. I reach across him and tuck my hand into his sleeve, rest my gloved hand inside it, and the movement of his wrist is warm and responsive and all I need, and I bless him for not being fascinated with wetsuits or rubber-clad sportswomen. With so much threat in my life, so many injuries and harsh, physical damage, it's better to be with a man who just likes flesh, who thinks it's there for good uses and not bad.

'Do you want to go through the woods?' We're at the end of the path. A cluster of trees is ahead of us. Without the sound of an engine in my ears, without a dirty window between me and them, they're oddly vivid, like images through a magnifying glass. I listen for the silence of them, but all I can hear is the sound of footsteps on the path, voices in conversation, the whisper of the traffic on the streets all around us: the non-noise of a city in action. There's something wrong about this view of dark trees, as if I'm missing something. This doesn't feel like my life.

'I don't know,' I say. Anyone could be in those trees. I spent a long time learning that.

'You scared?' His hand cups my head.

'Sort of,' I say. The feel of another person beside me is something I've got used to, it's been a long time since I let anyone touch me. All the time before Paul, there was space around my body, not blank space but resilient, elastic, crackling with static, keeping me inside it. It feels so much better to be defused. His hand on my head is a consolation I did nothing to deserve, and I owe him something for that. 'I – I'm not used to the idea,' I attempt. 'Apart from the fact that I'm possibly being stalked, I mean. I don't go through woods at night unless I have to, unless I'm in a van with a partner

346

and cages and weapons.' For just a moment, his arm stiffens around my neck, and I press on. 'The thing is, for me this is seeing something familiar from a different angle. Dark woods give me the spooks, I've lost a lot of skin in places like this. I'd – sort of like to see if I could walk through it now, when it's different, but it's not so much because I want to. More like I'm daring myself.'

The look on his face is a little nonplussed, but he doesn't make sarcastic remarks and he doesn't nod with false understanding. We go into the woods. The leaves underfoot are curved and brittle with frost, they crush underfoot with a soft, rustling sound. I keep reaching out to touch the branches, the bark, textured wood pressing its shape through my woollen gloves. It's dark here, darker than I'm used to. With no floodlights from a van casting a dull yellow glow, colours are subtle. Lichen shades eggshell blue against the trees, ivy leaves hang white-veined from their stalks. My heart beats inside me and my cheeks are flushed with tension and I keep hold of Paul's hand. It's damp underfoot, the smell of rain is in the air and my gloves are wet where I've touched the trees.

'Look,' says Paul, and I see that there's a clearing ahead. There's a rough bench, a fallen trunk with its top hewn flat enough to sit on, and on either side there are flowerbeds planted with rose bushes. Most of them are bare, the stalks pruned down with only a pale circlet of wood at the stump showing where the flowers grew, green stems and arched, maroon thorns, but there are a few blooms left, deep, blown roses. From a distance, I think they're white, but closer up I see they're a pale lavender, a fine, fragile colour, somehow old-fashioned.

'Here.' Paul takes hold of a stem and tilts it towards me. 'Put the flower against your mouth.'

'What? Why?' There are smart remarks I could make, but I don't, I smile as I ask him.

'They taste good after a rainfall. They're full of water. Here.' I lean forward, over the thorns and the frosted ground, and lay a soft, cool petal against my lip. Paul shakes the blossom just a little, and rainwater runs into my mouth. The taste is startling, sweet like nectar and at the same time fragrant with the flower's perfume. I close my lips around it, and the sensation possesses me, scenting my mouth, hazing my eyes. Blinded, I lean back against a tree, my mind on nothing but the taste of roses.

Paul's in front of me, his lips against mine, tasting of the same scent. I kiss him without opening my eyes, pulling him close, the chill air brushing my cheeks and his mouth the only warm place in the world.

'We're supposed to be watching,' I whisper.

'It's okay . . .'

'Someone could shoot me.'

Paul wraps himself around me, his arms holding me against the tree, his back between me and the outside. 'The bullet won't get to you,' he says. 'Not while I'm in the way.'

My heart beats fast, and I no longer know why. I open my mouth and let him in.

# 26

Once, when I was twenty-four, a group of teenagers started up a little campaign against DORLA. They sent boxes with mousetraps inside, envelopes with razor blades inside the flaps to slice the fingers of anyone opening them. A letter bomb arrived but didn't explode; a computer virus was sent that shut us down for two days. Death threats were posted to the home addresses of some of our higher officials. We begged the government for metal detectors or X-ray machines, but had to make do with appointing people to put on rubber gloves and open all incoming letters. It was a godsend of sorts for some of us – those missing a hand or foot, with permanent limps or missing eyes. People who'd been invalided onto the restricted pay scheme suddenly found themselves doing active duty, being paid as if they mattered. All our mail arrived late and opened, and some letter-openers got their fingers cracked in mousetraps or their faces splashed with bleach.

It lasted about two months before we caught them. And when we did, we interned them, about twenty people in all, we locked them in the cells for six months before we let them speak to their lawyers. We set up searches, made arrests. We arrested people who knew the prisoners for failing to report them. We arrested members of their families for providing them with financial support. We arrested people who'd expressed admiration for their cause. We arrested everyone who'd ever made a prank phone call to our offices. The public railed against us. People wrote us hate letters, shrill with disgust, and we arrested them.

Within a few months more, it died down. There's only so long most people can stay angry about a cause. By the end of the year, we were back to dealing with the usual round of hate mail and abusive phone calls, but there were no more razor blades in our letters.

None of us were killed in that campaign.

Silver bullets have taken out two of our people. I don't think there's a man or woman born head first who doesn't want to see the killers burn.


With this investigation, every day becomes Day One. Phone lines are choked, people dash down corridors, people return from the water cooler to find their inboxes overflowing. There are taps on the phones of all our free-range prisoners. Their houses, unoccupied now for days, are under constant surveillance. Pictures of Darryl Seligmann have been sent to the police; people are interviewed who knew him at his last place of residence, and the one before. Colleagues of the people we've imprisoned are being watched. Attacks on the building step up; another Molotov cocktail is thrown, things are pushed through the letter box. We bring in whoever we can, vandals get sentences handed down fast.

This is a legalistic hunt. Seligmann has already committed a crime, he was already a wanted man, so we go after him. No one knows where he is. Lyco after lyco gives us 'kept to himself' and 'unpopular' and 'I didn't really know much about him' until there are paper stacks inches high, and still we can't find him. We look for him openly, we co-opt the police and scrape money together from somewhere for a reward and sound the alarms. But the others, Albin and Sarah and Carla, are invisible. No one but us knows where they are. We don't speak to their colleagues, we just send people to follow them. We watch from the outside, and as far as the lyco world knows, the three of them have just vanished. We're waiting. Sooner or later, someone has to make a mistake, and when they do, we'll have them.

It's been four years since I saw a purge. I want to see this one.


The lights are bright down in the cells. One of the tubes is broken, it strobes on and off so fast it buzzes. It'll be a while before it gets replaced. I have a trolley of food for them; on the smooth, sterile floor of the detention area, the wheels murmur. I hear Albin's voice say 'Hey,' and the sound of people scuffling to their feet.

I draw parallel with them. Ellaway looks the worst. There are bruises on his face now, around his neck, one eye is swollen shut, and he cradles what looks like a broken finger in his one undamaged hand. He's staying here for a while, then. There's no way DORLA will release someone looking like that. He squats in the back of his cell, and looks at me with black, glinting eyes.

Albin looks bad too, his face blotched and cut, his nose knocked out of true. Carla has a bruise on her forehead, black and glossy as poppy petals around a corrugated scab in the very centre. It's the sort of wound you make shoving someone's head against a wall. Sarah's face is unmarked, but she holds her neck at a bad angle. It gives an almost quizzical tilt to her head. There's a nerve you can pinch in the neck; if you do it right, you can produce vomiting, blackouts, the symptoms of a migraine, serious effects. It looks like someone didn't do it quite right.

I stand with a trolley full of food for these people, and don't say anything.

'Ms Galley,' Albin says. 'Have you come to – to advise us?'

'I brought your dinner,' I say, and pull out the first food tray.

'Will you be our lawyer?' Albin says.

I turn, a tray of food in my hands. 'What?'

He comes up to the bars. His hands are clasped in each other, and he stands a little distance away from me. 'They won't let us call outside, and they won't let us talk to anyone. They won't assign us anyone in here.' He touches his battered face. 'You're the only person we know.'

'You don't know me.' I look away from him, send the food through. 'You don't want me.'

Ellaway makes a hissing sound in his corner.

'Please, Ms Galley. We need someone. Look at us.'

I look, and look away, and keep on handing out the food.

'Please, we need someone on our side.'

I back away, stand against the opposite wall. 'I'm not on your side.' There's a bright, harsh echo in here, and I speak softly, keep my voice beneath it. 'Those people you killed were friends of mine.'

'We didn't kill anyone.'

'You'll get a lawyer when they assign you one,' I say. The wall is cold against my shoulders. 'They'll assign you one when you've got something to tell them.'

'We've told you everything. We've confessed. I don't know what else you want us to say.'

'There are two men dead. One of them had three children. One of them was nineteen years old.'

'It wasn't us.'

'Why would you do that?' I close my eyes. I should hand out the food and go, but I keep talking. If Seligmann were here, he'd be throwing out a new curse every time I spoke. Something about Albin's bland denial keeps me talking to him. 'Why would you go to the trouble of forging bullets and shooting two men?'

'We didn't. Ms Galley –'

'Give me something better than that and I'll be your lawyer,' I say. My eyes are drifting behind closed lids. 'I just don't understand why you hate us so much. You'd think you'd get tired after a while.'

'We don't hate you.' It's Carla's voice, and I open my eyes. She doesn't speak softly. She cries it out like a child.

'We didn't, anyway,' Sarah mutters. 'You're not the one who can't move her head.'

'You're wasting your fucking time,' Ellaway says. Something stiffens inside me at the sound of his voice. 'She's not going to help us. She's going to let us rot here, unless she gets fed up with your bullshit and decides to get a leather belt.'

'Is that what happened to your face?' There's no softness in my voice.

'Fuck you,' he says, and turns his back to the wall.

'You should mind your manners,' I say. 'Really. Why else do you think you look the way you do?'

'Fuck you.'

'Don't you people get bored listening to him?' I ask. 'Why don't you drop him in it? We could move him to another block.'

'Dick, give it a rest,' Albin says. 'Won't you help us, Ms Galley? Just ignore Dick, you can't pay any attention to what he says.'

'She's already my lawyer.' Ellaway raises his voice. 'I don't see her helping me out.'

'Dick.' Ellaway turns around. 'I'm trying to beg for help here. You have any better ideas, let's hear them, and if you haven't, then keep quiet and keep out of the way.'

The two of them glare at each other, Ellaway crouched with straw around him, his suit stained and ripped at the collar, Albin on his feet looking down. There's a pause, one of those silences that stretches out second by second and makes people cover their ears, waiting for it to crack.

I press my hands together. 'I'm not going to help you,' I say. 'I can't.'

'Please. We need someone.'

'Yes,' I say. 'And till you start telling us things, no one's going to be assigned. And no one's going to listen to anyone but an assigned lawyer. I can't help you. You're beyond help.'

Albin looks at me. 'Do you like any of this?' he says.

'What?'

'Look at us. Look where we are. Do you like working in an office above cells full of straw with us in them?'

He raises his hand; the bruise I saw last time I was here is indigo across his knuckles.

'You think you can make me want to help you?' There's no feeling in my voice.

'Most people work in offices with a mailroom downstairs.' He looks around him at the concrete floor scattered with anaemic, frayed-looking straw, the white walls smudged with black fingerprints and small, brown traces of blood. 'Not this.'

'We have a mailroom too.'

'Please. No one knows we're here. You have to help us.'

'I've told you,' I say. 'I can't.'

I look at them, these people who killed Johnny, who shot Nate, and I wait for the hatred to rise. The memory of Seligmann's skin rasping my palm as I slapped him tingles in my hand. If I wanted to, I could go inside any of these cells, lock the door behind me, add some bruises of my own. Upstairs, with the images of Johnny and Nate clear in my mind, I would have said I could do it. Now I'm down here, where it's white and echoes fragment our voices on the tiles, I can't recapture the feeling.

'It's out of my hands,' I say. 'Lawyers can't appoint themselves. You won't be given a lawyer until you confess.'

'We've confessed to everything we've done!'

'All right, I won't argue with you. I'll just say that we hear that a lot. And really, for your own sake, you should believe what I'm telling you, because it's the truth. I don't blame you for not wanting to confess. It may go hard with you if you do. But you will be better off in the end. And that's the best advice I can give you.'

'Won't you even hear our side of it?'

'Frankly,' I say, wheeling the trolley around, 'I don't want to. I don't think I'm going to like anything you've got to say, and I've got enough problems as it is.'

'You know you could help us if you wanted to.'

'When did I say I wanted to?' I don't know why this man is acting like I owe him.

'Lola, please come back.'

I stop the trolley and turn around. 'Don't ever call me by my first name again, Albin. Ever.' He looks at me out of blackened eyes, and I turn away.

'I'm sorry,' he says, and people scuffle in the straw around him. 'I really didn't mean to offend you, but please come back and talk to us, no one else will even talk to us . . .'

'You're making a mistake,' I say. 'What the hell made you think I'd care about saving you?'

'I don't know, maybe you're a nice person?' There's a thin note of desperation in his voice.

I push the trolley forward. 'I'm a nice bareback, Albin. Think about the difference.'

'Does there have to be one?' He's raising his voice, trying to keep me here.

'I wouldn't have thought so,' I say. 'Once upon a time.' The trolley whispers under my feet. 'But apparently, there does.'


Upstairs, part of me wants to go back down and keep talking with them, try to understand. But prowlers don't help you, they don't care if your mind is beating itself like a fly against a window: they aren't going to open the window and let me out.

There's a message on my answerphone from Sue

356

Marcos, saying that someone I called in her building has been round and brought them some food. Her voice is more tired than pleased, but I e-mail the neighbour anyway, to say thank you, and that I'd avoid sausages as Julio is tired of Debbie cooking them.

I'm just finishing up when another call comes in. It's Adnan Franklin, wanting to know what's happened to his client.

'Why?' I ask him. 'Is there a problem?'

I can hear Franklin sigh down the telephone. 'Yes, Ms Galley, there's a problem. He's missed an appointment, I can't get an answer at his home number, and his secretary tells me that he was taken from his place of work by a man and a woman a few days ago.'

I turn in my chair to look out of the window. The pane is grimy, and beyond it, I can see the sunset, a mackerel sky with cold fronds of cloud streaked across it. 'I don't know anything about that, Mr Franklin.'

'The secretary described the woman, and it sounded like you.'

'How did she describe her?'

'Ms Galley, my client seems to have been arrested.'

'I only want to know how the secretary described her. I'm not unusual looking. And if all you have to go on is a small, pale woman with dark hair, or something of the kind, then I'm sure you're too good a lawyer to leap to conclusions.'

'Is our client in DORLA custody?'

The sun is hidden behind the clouds. They shine very white over the city. 'I don't know.'

'How could you not know?'

'As far as I know,' I say, 'he isn't. If he's missing and no one's told me he's here, then he's probably not. But

357

if he is and I haven't been told, then it'll be a secret, and I won't know anything about it.'

'I find that hard to believe.'

'I can't help that.'

'Ms Galley, please tell me. Is Mr Ellaway in your custody?'

I look out at the dusk. There's a break in the sky, high up, and the moon is already visible, a faint opal crescent. 'Not to my knowledge,' I tell Franklin. 'I'm sorry I can't help you, really I am, but I just don't know where he is.' A wind rustles through the trees as I speak, but the clouds stand still in the sky, translucent and narrow and shining bright enough to dazzle you.

# 27

When Hugo calls me into his office, he does something I've never seen before: he takes his phone off the hook. 'Lola, sit down.' There are creases under his eyes, the flesh under them loosened as if someone had been pulling it about.

'Hugo. What can I do for you?' I sit in the chair facing him. It's a wide, sturdy thing, big enough to accommodate a man his size. The back of it rises around me, giving me the feeling of leaning against a wall.

Hugo steeples his thick fingers for a moment and studies me. 'I have to ask you,' he says, speaking slowly as if each word was heavy, 'whether you've had any contact with our free-ranger detainees.'

Am I in trouble for speaking to them? 'I – took the food trolley down to them once. Why?'

'When you were down there,' Hugo unlocks his fingers and lays his hands on the desk, 'did you have much conversation with them?'

'Mostly with Lewis Albin. He wanted me to plead their cause.'

'Mm.' Hugo inclines his head. 'And what did you say?'

Everything that happens down there is recorded.

I'm not sure why he's pretending he doesn't already know. 'That they'd get a lawyer when they were assigned one.'

He sits up. 'It may be that you get assigned to them,' he says. The change of tone surprises me a little. 'Richard Ellaway is your client already, and it's likely they'll all be tried together. Would that be acceptable to you?'

I look down at my hands, trying to think of what to say. This is a high-profile case. Never mind the city, everyone in the country is going to hear of this. People will take sides. Nons will want to see the free-rangers swing. Lycos will be divided, caste loyalty will war with the knowledge that they're killers. And I'm going to lose this case. I can't get them off, and I don't want to. It may show me as a good lawyer with a doomed cause, a poor lawyer who isn't trying to win, a show-trial accessory in DORLA's latest purge. This is a long way from defending moon-loitering alcoholics.

'I – go where I'm sent,' I say. 'You know my experience, it's your call if you think I'm up to it. If I'm assigned, I'll do it.'

Hugo regards me for a moment longer.

'Is it likely that they'll get assigned a legal adviser soon?' I say to fill the silence.

'Not immediately,' he says. 'Although if you wanted to start acting as one unofficially, I'm sure you'd be allowed a certain amount of leeway.'

'Why?' Hugo is not the man I normally ask such questions. I've known him a long time, and over those years I've got used to his expressionless face, his neutral comments. Asking him about my position with other people is an uncertain business.

'Well,' he sits back, 'it seems you already know them. You've had contact with them a couple of times, at least, which is more than most people here. And you arrested them yourself. It gives you a certain prestige. Besides, they did ask for you; it's possible they'll be more communicative with you than with a stranger. Albin has asked several people if you'll represent them.'

'Why would he?' I really want to know.

Hugo's heavy face remains impassive. 'I think he likes you.'

I look past him, out of the window at the grey, rain-smeared sky. I have no response to that.

'In any case,' Hugo says, 'we've arrested another one.'

'What?' I sit up in the huge chair. 'When?'

'This morning.'

'How – how?' This is startling news, this is crucial.

'He's been leaving messages on the answerphones of three of them, Albin, Sanderson and Stein. This morning, he went round to knock on Albin's door, then Sanderson's. He was quite agitated by the second house, banging on the door and shouting up at the windows. That's where the surveillance team arrested him.'

I'm leaning forward, ravenous for information. 'Is there evidence that he's a free-ranger himself – I mean, not just a family friend wondering where they'd got to?'

'Oh, they recognised him down in the cells,' Hugo says. 'No discussion of the murders, of course, but the free-ranging, they talked about that straight away. He's one of them, no doubt about it.'

'Jesus.'

'In any case, they've been asking to see you again,' he tells me. 'They're becoming quite a nuisance. It would be a favour to all of us if you'd go down and see them.'

'Of – of course,' I say. 'I'll go now.' I stand up, ready to head downstairs.

'Lola,' Hugo says.

'Yes?' It isn't courtesy to just run out.

'You'll have to use your own discretion in this. But any information you can give us is valuable, whether you represent them or not.'

'Okay,' I say, barely listening. He nods at me, and I gather myself up and go.


It's quiet on the stairs. My shoes are low-heeled and rubber-soled, I gave up high heels when Seligmann got loose and took out this old pair, scuffed and cheap and easy to run in, and they make almost no sound as I walk down the steps. There's a tube flashing overhead, and the steps are concrete, dingy. The change in light stings my eyes as I go through the door into the white-tiled corridor, and I stop for a moment, blinking, shielding my face.

'Is that you, Ms Galley?' Albin's voice sounds from the end of the row. 'Please come in.'

There's a dark-haired man in the cell beside Carla's, standing with his hands pressed against the partition. I don't make much noise as I walk but he turns at my step and comes up to the bars, reaches through them with a bruised hand, saying, 'Lola, thank God, you've got to help us.'

362

I stand frozen on my feet, just beyond his extended hand.

'Lola, angel, I'm so glad to see you, they're accusing us of murder, these agents arrested me and they said I'd killed someone called Nate Jensen, do you know who that is?'

There are bruises on his face, one of his lips has a little cut, just at the edge where it splits over the canine if you punch the cheek. My heart beats, echoing through my chest.

'Lola, for God's sake, say something.'

'She isn't going to help us, Paul,' says Sarah. 'I told you, it's not going to happen.'

'Lola, please.'

My mouth fills with ice and I can't speak.

'Lola, what's happening? Is there some place we can talk alone?' Paul's hand comes back through the bars, holds on to them with a light grip. I've seen his hand curved that way around my wrist. 'Listen, I – I guess this is a shock to you, I mean – I know I should have told you about – oh God –' He turns around in the cell, a full circle. Pacing the bars. 'Lola, I'll beg if you want me to, but you've got to believe me, I never heard of Nate Jensen before today. Please, don't just – don't give me that face, just – please, say something.'

My legs shake. I take a step back to keep from falling.

The other prisoners are at the back of their cages, far away from us, watching.

'Lola,' Paul says as I turn around. 'Lola!' I keep a grip on the bundle of papers in my arms, one foot follows another and I hardly sway at all, my eyes filled with white. It isn't until I get out into the stairwell that

I start to run. I stagger up it for a few paces before I slip and fall, a step digs into my shin, and I sit wordless. It's cold and filthy here, I can't stay here, but there's nowhere else left in the world I can go.

# 28

It doesn't take very long before everyone knows. This is DORLA, after all.

No one speaks to me very much. Hugo asks me where I'll stay now, and I can think of nothing to say. I can't go home. I can't go back to Paul's place. Sitting penned in my chair, I think this, and even to think his name twists a blade inside me. Bride's gone away. Becca won't take me.

My eyes are crusted and ache as if I'd spent too long in the light. I look at Hugo out of them. 'I don't know,' I say. The voice isn't mine, and I can't feel my limbs. 'Maybe I could fuck Ally Gregory for somewhere to sleep.'

Saying this is the end of me. Hugo's face barely changes, it just – settles, goes still like sand settling underwater. I didn't know I was going to say it, and once I've said it, all the doors open and everything comes rushing in. I can't keep my memories separate any more. The look Hugo gives me is one I've seen before, one I've given people myself. It's the way people look at twitchers. My body lies limp in his chair, and gives up. My eye jumps, and my hands start to shake. I look down at them through the haze, watch them jump and crawl in my lap like dying frogs, and I can't make them stop. What I feel, above everything else, above the memories and the pain and the din inside me, is a sense of sick inevitability, like a fallen sinner who finds, when the last day comes, that she was right all along. She always knew she'd end up in hell.

The first night I'm given an empty cell to sleep in, one of the longer-stay places that has a sink and a mattress. I have blankets, more of them than the prisoners have, and I'm wrapped in my coat, and still I shiver as drafts blow through the bars. The bars bang against me when I turn over, they loom above my head when I open my eyes. My vision is striped with them, in the half-dark they waver and shift, focus and unfocus, and when I cover my eyes the image of the bars still swims in front of them.

Within half an hour, the whisper goes from cage to cage. There's a DORLA agent sleeping in the cells, there's a bareback down here. When I first hear the hisses, I think it's my imagination, that I'm hearing the sound of the bars. Then I start to make out the words.

*Hey skin . . . Skin girl . . .*

I can handle this. I've had this all my life. I turn over and pull the blankets over my ears, but still I hear it.

*You're gonna die down here . . .*

They can't reach me. They can't touch me here in this cage.

*Let us see your soft pretty hands, skin . . . Who's the bareback whore . . .*

Something touches me on the arm, and I fly up, my body vibrating like a plucked string, scrabbling at the

366

place I was touched. Looking around me, wild in the dark, I can see that the cells around me are empty. I look down. A cigarette packet. A lucky shot. I pick it up, open it to see if someone hated me enough to throw their cigarettes away, but it's packed full of dirty tissues. I close the packet, don't look at what they're soiled with.

*We can get to you, skin . . . I'll be first, skin . . . You'll scream for it . . .*

They see me as I drag my mattress to the middle of the floor, as far away as possible. I know they can see me.

*You won't get away . . . Frigid bitch, let's see you lie down . . .*

Names I've heard before. Bareback girls are sluts. Bareback women are frigid. Bareback flesh needs a good workout because they never fur up, they like it rough. Bareback children fuck their brothers and sisters. This is what they say, this and other things. The whispers scuttle from cell to cell like rats. They tell me what they're going to do to me. They tell me what I am.

I bang on the door, try to sound the alarm, but that happens a lot down here. Nobody comes.

The memory of Paul's skin possesses me moment to moment, and I can't predict when it will come. When I look in the bathroom mirror, though, I don't think he'd recognise my face. There are no smiles now, no concessions, my eyes don't close. It's a face that I recognise, the hollow sockets, the damaged teeth, all the ugliness that I spent a lifetime trying to hide, that I knew in the end I would never escape.

I take blankets, fold one into a pillow, layer others into a mattress, push my desk back, lock my office door. This is where I sleep now. Chairs tower over me. In the middle of the night I dream of Paul and wake up longing for him. The pillow I've folded is hard, rigid fabric, an uncomfortable place to smother my sobs, and my hands grasp the institutional blankets and remain empty. I could sculpt him from clay, the line of his neck, the soft veins along his arms, his waist, his jaw, alone in this dark room I could make a statue of him and it would be right, anyone would see it and know, yes, that's him.

It can't even be called weakness, it hurts so much. Things don't annoy me any more, nothing hurts my feelings. I look at the world through the same red shadow, and the pain comes and goes according to its own tides, and the world seems barely real.

That isn't so, though. It's the reality of this that hurts most. I can't make it stop. It isn't an argument to be conjured out of existence by an apology, it isn't a state of wounded feelings that can be cajoled away. My lover is down in the cells with his fellow killers. There's a lock on the door. I struggle with it, fight it, cry to the world to change. It doesn't happen. It can't.

One day I walk out of the office, through the streets. People jostle me. I don't step out of their way. I walk and walk, find I've got as far as St Veronica's and turn to go inside. I sit in the Accident and Emergency department for two hours, watch the crooked limbs, the choking children, the man who staggers in clutching his chest. A nurse passes me and stops, asks if I've checked in at reception.

I look up at her, and I can't feel my face. 'No,' I say, 'I'm not sick.' As I stand up, I brush my hand against her arm, feel the smooth non-texture of her uniform. The sensation of the fabric stays in my memory for hours.

Nobody sends work my way. My hands shake, my skin prickles. Everything about me is raw, as if I'd lain with a lover made of sandpaper. I can't stop thinking about skin cells. Once after Paul left my flat, I lay down on the bed, pressed my cheek against the pillow, thinking what I'd learned in forensic classes when I was thirteen, that a little dust from your skin remains on what you touch. I loved the thought, that Paul was still on my pillow. Now I can't tell if there are any skin cells of his left on me. I don't stop taking showers, telling myself that if I can keep my hair clean it means I can survive, but there must be a vestige of him somewhere around my office, from the days when I still lived in his flat and he'd kiss me goodbye and send me to work with traces of him still on my face and clothes. If my coat brushed against something, if I touched a shelf with the same fingers that touched him, there must be something of him left. I neither scrub the office nor refuse to dust it; I go on as I have always done, not trying to keep or purge whatever remnants of Paul may be scattered. To do that would mean knowing which I preferred to do. Instead, I live inside my own, scraped, scarred skin; I drag from place to place trailing blood like a snail, and people start to step aside when I pass them in the corridor, they start to avoid my eyes.

I can't stop dreaming of Paul at nights, and I wake up crying because even in dreams, I can't find an answer that will make any of this go away.

# 29

Ally comes to see me. I'm resting my head on my desk, my eyes beating from another sleepless night. I turn at the sound of his knock, a rapid percussion against my door. It's only when I see it's him that I straighten up. 'Ally.' I rub one hand against my eye. 'Come in.'

He twines his fingers, steps lightly, more tentative than before. 'Jesus, Lola,' he says. 'Are you okay?'

'I guess I look bad,' I say.

'Well, I've seen you look better.'

I don't ask when. 'What do you want?'

He lays his hand on the back of a chair, drums his fingers against it. 'Can I sit down?'

'Yeah.' My hair clings to my face, static. It itches. The idea of shaving my head passes through my mind. I know I won't do it, but I know, too, that the idea doesn't bother me as it once might have.

'I – just . . .' Ally taps his feet, shifts in the chair. 'I thought I'd let you know – you still have the Ellaway case, don't you?'

'I suppose.' It's a strain on him, on everyone, me being like this. I know that. I know it, but I can't care enough to stop.

'Well, the man who – you remember I told you he

made a call from the shelter, the first night we picked him up?' I remember. It seems a very long time ago. 'And a dark-haired man came to collect him? Well, I went down to the cells and I ID'd him, it was, your, it . . .'

'You can say his name, Ally.' There's a silence, broken only by his tapping hands. 'I won't die of it.'

Ally inhales. 'Well, it was Paul Kelsey. That's the guy who came to collect him. That's all.'

My mouth floods and I swallow. 'I figured,' I say.

'Yeah. Yeah, I guess it's not a big surprise.' Ally looks at his hands, I look at mine.

'That's it, then.' My hands shudder on the desk, a little vibration like an aftershock.

'Yeah.' Ally tugs at a lock of his hair. It's still hanging down to his shoulders, tattered. He hasn't cut it since he lost the bet and I handed him the scissors.

'Thanks for telling me.' He doesn't want to go, Ally, he's still sitting there. I don't know how to help him.

'Yeah – well – listen, Lola, is it true you're sleeping in the cells?'

I don't think about why he asks. 'I was. I didn't get much sleep. Too many cellmates calling me names.' It's a simple phrase, a playground phrase. It suffices. 'I'm sleeping up in my office now.'

Ally frowns, rubs his hands on his thighs. 'Well, listen, that's no good. If you – you could stay at my place, if you needed somewhere to stay.'

One of my hands flicks open as a spasm passes through it. 'Have you been talking to Hugo?' I say.

'Hugo? What? Why?' He looks up at me dark-eyed as I stand. He sounds sincere.

'Never mind.' I walk around the desk, sit on it, next to him. 'I'm a target, Ally.'

He shrugs.

'Do you want to die?' I'm light-headed, dizzy.

'I'm not going to die. Do you want to stay? You can if you want.'

He looks at me, angular, restless.

'I've been thinking too much lately,' I say. 'I can't stop remembering things.'

He leans back a little, trying to get the measure of me. And it's true what I've said. Memories have hailed down around me, and I can't get away from any of them. I want to push Ally, slap him, I want to scream.

I reach out and pick up one of his dancing hands.

'What are you talking about, Lo?' he says. He's smiling at me; his face is tense. His hand tries to get out of my grip, the other hand knocks against the chair.

I close my shaking fist around him hard enough to still his movements. 'Oh, Ally, for once in your life, sit still.' And I lean forward and kiss him, grip his ragged hair to pull his head back. His whole body stiffens, his mouth is tense against mine, but he kisses back, there's a moment when his mouth opens and his lips move, tasting of chewing gum, a moment of desire or reflex in which we're kissing, his unshaven face rasping against mine and cutting into my skin before he pulls his head back with a jerk and tries to look at me.

I open my fist, strands of hair stick to it and I lift my hand away. His eyes are wide, staring up into my still face.

'No,' I say. 'I don't think I do want to stay with you.'

It's a black and bitter ascendancy. As Ally stands, backs out of the office, I stand and watch him, wanting the taste of chewing gum out of my mouth, my lips scored with his. It's impossible to believe that next time I see Ally, things won't be as they always were, he won't be casual and active and boyish, that he'll remember this. It doesn't feel real that this happened.

I get a memo, telling me that the prisoners have once again asked to see me. I look at it for several minutes together before I tear it up, halves, quarters, fragments, until the letters are too scattered to mean anything, throw them into the bin and lay a piece of paper on top of them, to hide them from sight.

I've never been an interrogator, not really. Seligmann was the closest I got. I'm not considered damaged enough, not marked in ways you can see. Interrogators are men, usually, men with missing feet, ruined faces, mauled genitals. The worst, the unusables, the ones who'll never be the same again. They mop floors and work nights, and some of them, that's all they do, but others work the prisoners, details get passed to them that the rest of us don't know. We learn a little about interrogation skills in school, and it's men like those who teach us. They can never face down a lune again, but a lyco, that's different. The game levels. The interrogators may be missing a kilo of flesh, but it doesn't slow them down. They don't mark the prisoners, not too badly, nothing that won't heal. They learned a long time ago that however much flesh you take from another man, it'll never replace your own.

*

If you feel badly about lycos, why are you sleeping with one? That's what he said. He knew I'd find out.

He was right. Why would I let some brief passion come between me and my life, between everything the world has been to me and my reason? I should have known. Yet even now, I'm thinking about it, going down to help out these people who killed two of my kind, and for what? Blue eyes, long-fingered hands, a voice?

None of those are as small and unpersuasive as they should be.

He knew all the time. He went out into the parks with me, he took me for a walk, he said he wasn't afraid, that no bullets would get to me. I should have known then. No man takes risks like that.

Why did he have me in his flat? To study, to watch, to betray? Or did he like me a little, enough to want to keep me out of harm's way for a while?

And now we're living together again. Him downstairs in his cell, me upstairs in mine. It wasn't how I hoped it would turn out, but it's a new intimacy, of a sort. I could try to save him. I could go down to the cells myself, take my love out of him with a steel cable. Pull him apart, see where the secret was that made me want him so badly. I could let him lie to me again, I could plead, I can hardly be lower than I am, I could cry and abase myself. The choices freeze me, I'm caught in their glare.

There are times when I think it would have been easier if he'd just shot me like the others.


Sometimes I ignore the phone, sometimes it's less trouble to pick it up. When it rings this time, I look at it for a few moments. It rings again, then again, the sound loud and wearying in my small office.

'Hello.' I've given up saying my name when I answer it. Everyone knows about me now.

'May?'

I thought I was beyond surprise, but this doubtful voice makes me sit up in my chair. 'Becca? Is that you?'

'Yes, it's me.' She hesitates, the pause grows.

She won't let me see her. We haven't spoken since that day. This is the first thing I remember, but the thought doesn't last long. I remember, all at once, a lot of scraped elbows and tangled hair that she fixed for me, a lot of fights that she was ready to apologise for before I was. I'd kick and throw things, she'd just shout. Becca's never raised a hand against anyone in her life. Becca took a lot of name-calling in her day, a lot of comments on me, and she didn't like any of them; and just now, she's the only person in my world who doesn't know all that's happened to me.

'Becca, I'm sorry we parted so badly last time,' I say in a rush, forestalling her sounds of hesitation. 'I shouldn't have spoken the way I did, and I'm really sorry about it.' My throat hurts as I say this, a sharp pain like a plaster coming away from damaged skin.

'Oh.' She sounds floored. 'Oh, that's all right, that is – I should have made allowances. Of course you were – you do see why I said it, don't you?'

A month ago I would have thought she was trying to prove she was right all along, make me the bad one. Her voice quavers a little at the end of the sentence, I can see her, standing up straight, good posture, her shoes clean, trying to do the sensible thing. It's strange how easily I can see what I couldn't see before, that she wants to be reassured. 'Of course I do.' My voice is a little hoarse. She's so alone, Becca, she doesn't have anything but Leo left. 'I wouldn't want to endanger you, you know that. I love you. I was just upset.'

I actually told her I love her. I close my eyes to listen as she says, 'I know. But you see why I said it, don't you?'

She still thinks I'm mad at her. 'Of course I do.'

'I – oh, I was just wondering how you were.' There's a stammer to her voice, the strain of sounding casual makes it go high-pitched.

I take a shaky breath. 'Well, not so good, as a matter of fact. Some things have gone wrong . . .'

'What's happened?'

I don't know how I can repeat it all, put it into words for her. I'd have to listen to myself. 'Well, you remember I told you . . .'

'Oh, wait a moment.' There's the sound of crying in the background, then her footsteps. She's gone to pick up Leo. He must have grown since I last saw him.

There's a long pause, sounds of mothering.

When she comes back, the sound is muffled, as if the phone is tucked under her chin, and I can hear little squeaks, almost clear. She's holding him. That's his voice. If I sit very still, I can hear him breathing.

'I'm sorry about that,' Becca says, 'he just woke up, you're still there, aren't you? I hope you don't mind, only . . .'

'It's okay,' I hear myself say. 'Of course you had to pick him up.'

'Is something the matter, May?'

It's just the sound of my voice. The thought that she'd reckon something had to be wrong for me to be tolerant of her would have made me angry with her before. Now it just makes me almost smile. 'Yeah. I was staying with my boyfriend, the one I told you about. Now it turns out he knows the people we arrested, the ones who killed my colleagues. He's – in with them.'

'What?' Leo chirrups down the line, and Becca's voice is hushed.

I sigh. 'Yeah. Turns out he was gunning for me all along.'

'Oh, May.' There's no reproach in her tone. She doesn't like that it turned out this way for me. There's a silence. When she does speak, she cuts right to the chase. 'Were you in love with him?'

I look down at my shaking hand. 'Yeah. Yeah, I was.'

'I'm sorry.'

'It can't be helped,' I say. 'That's kind of the worst thing, though.'

'Yes. Yes it is.'

This has happened to Becca, hasn't it? She knows how it is to lose a man, be left empty-handed and hulled out? 'Are you okay?' I ask. Though it's all right if she isn't, I don't need her to be the strong one. We're neither of us going anywhere.

'I'm all right. A little tired. I don't get out much. I've spoken to a lawyer, he says he can track Lionel down.'

'Would it change things?' Paul didn't leave me pregnant, at least. I'm too careful for that. I wonder, a little, what difference it would have made.

It would have been a lively child.

Becca sighs. 'No. I wouldn't take him back. It'd be better for Leo, though, he'll want to know him when he grows up.'

'You'll tell him, then?' He could spend his whole life not knowing. It won't make him feel good, hearing the whole story.

'He might understand.' She half-laughs, but her tone is serious. 'Anyway, you've seen moon nights yourself, you can help me explain.'

I blink, clear my throat. 'Yeah. Yeah, I'll do that.' Auntie May can explain it, darling. Ask her. He won't grow up saying 'What's wrong with Auntie May?' after all.

'Where are you staying, then?' Becca says, and I wipe my eyes with the back of my hand.

'At work.'

'At work? You aren't at his place any more?'

'No. I haven't been back since he was arrested.'

'Well, if it's empty, you may as well make use of it, surely? It sounds like he owes you that much, and he's hardly going to stop you if he's in prison.'

This time I laugh. Decorous Becca. She's tougher than I thought. 'I'm worried it may be watched,' I explain. 'There's more of them out there.'

'Oh.'

'So I probably shouldn't come and see you, either.'

'Oh.'

'Could you – I mean, I know journeys are a problem with a small baby, but could you – you don't think you could come and see me here, do you?' It isn't easy to ask, but I'm so tired. I have very few memories of wanting my mother when I was hurt, but I need to see Becca.

378

'Of course I could,' Becca says. 'When shall I come in?'

I bite my lip, steady my voice. 'Well, any time, really. I'm pretty much here permanently.'


Becca was the pretty one, that official position one sister always holds. Taller than me though not tall, blessed with full, rounded lips and cherry-blossom skin. Even when we were children, her socks didn't slide down, her calves shaped themselves like buds and held the fabric in place. Unlike me, fidgety and awkward, chewing my straight bobbed locks where Becca brushed her curls aside with a graceful hand. Becca would try to comb my hair and pull my jumpers straight, but nothing lasted. Her arrangements went crooked on me.

Lionel and she were both management consultants once. I shook his hand when she introduced him, I said nothing in Becca's presence, ever, that let her know what I thought of the job. Twenty-somethings paid three times more than my superiors, hired to give advice to their elders because they had a degree in something.

I don't even think about what happened to me when I was twenty-two. Becca was there, sometimes; she visited me in hospital a couple of times. Perhaps she even wanted to say something, to help. But I lay still in bed, staring at the ceiling, all my focus on keeping my eye from twitching, I didn't talk to her. And that was the year she married Lionel. At the wedding, I sat in the church on a hard wooden pew. Becca had mentioned, cautious and doubtful, that maybe I'd like to be a maid of honour, a bridesmaid, something. I told her I was sick, and she sighed and hung up the phone. So I sat and watched her flanked by her golden-skinned friends, and Lionel shook my hand briefly at the reception.

Within eighteen months, Becca was no longer a high flyer. She gave up her job, decided she'd rather sit in a library, catalogue shelves and stamp books, wipe the dust off her hands with a clean white handkerchief. They invited me over, Becca and Lionel, Mr and Mrs Keir, and Becca mentioned it – mentioned it, rather than broke the news – over dinner. She said that she couldn't handle the stress. Lionel put his hand on her wrist as she held the ladle and said, 'Not everyone's cut out for that life.'

He hadn't taken off his suit for dinner. Not even his tie. I looked at him, sitting straight backed, his elbows taking up half of the table, patting his pretty little wife.

After that, I took to wearing short sleeves when I met him. With lycos, I usually cover up. When I played squash with Johnny, we wore shorts and T-shirts, we saw each others' scars. Lionel saw it. I flaunted my disfigured flesh, I let him see my skinny limbs, I scraped my hair into clips to exaggerate my peaky features and said nothing to him as I sat with my healed wounds gnarled on my skin and faced him.

Becca thought he'd stand by her when she fell pregnant after that night in the shelter. I don't know why she ever thought that.

Becca was beautiful. Becca honestly did mean well. It didn't save her.

She comes to see me the same evening. I think of telling reception to expect a Mrs Becca Keir to come by – a woman with a buggy isn't a common sight here – but

380

it turns out she gets shown up all right. She announces herself as Becca Galley.

Her eyes take in my office, the badly folded blankets humped in the corner, the bin full of old sandwich packets, a toothbrush on the desk, the oppressive mess of someone living in a confined space. She doesn't comment. She parks the pram in a corner and comes over to kiss me on the cheek.

'You look pale,' she says, and lays her hand against my face.

I leave it there. 'I haven't been getting much daylight.'

It's still hectic outside the office, though it's dark, past sunset on a winter's day. I go over to the door and close it.

'It's a little stuffy in here,' Becca says. 'Do you mind if I open the window for a moment? Just to air it, it's cold outside.'

'Sure.' Maybe it'll make the room better. I go over to the pram, where my nephew lies. He isn't sleeping. He lies on his back, gripping one foot in his hand, gazing up at the paper whirligigs that hang over him. I made those. They're still there.

'Hey, boy.' I put my hand on his chest, feel it rise and fall, fast and light as a rabbit's.

Becca closes the curtains and turns around. 'You really do look pale,' she says.

'I – I'm not feeling too good, that's all.'

She passes me, lays a hand on my shoulder. 'You'll feel better,' she says. 'It does get better.'

I want to explain that it isn't just losing a lover, it's my colleagues lying dead and a cellblock full of successful citizens who still want to kill us and a breach of faith with the world. I don't. I always laid too much on her.

She hands me Leo. He lies against me, heavier than I remembered, a wisp of dark hair growing on his head. He looks a little like his mother. As I hold him, he arches his back, whimpers at the feel of this new woman, this half-forgotten stranger. Becca sits down and watches me with him, and when he starts to cry for her, she doesn't take him back. She sits quiet, and I rest Leo's face against mine, and the two of us cry together.

After a while, she stands up and puts an arm around my shoulder. It's an old embrace, only half-intimate, dating back to when we were children, but she's still taller than me. I rest my head against her shoulder, and she doesn't move away.

# 30

Once I asked Paul what it felt like, furring up. He made a face, rubbed his head, thought about it. Every time I asked him questions like that, he'd tell me that there aren't words to describe the state because when you're in it words don't apply. 'The closest I can get is, imagine trying to do the splits with every muscle in your body at once.' That's what he said. 'Only they're trying to do it on their own, without any help from you.' Muscles hurt when they're stretched, he said, and I told him I knew that, DORLA makes you do workouts and physical tests if you do catching duty, and I knew how sharp the nerves go when you pull against them. Only you're not pulling against them, he said, they're pulling you.

I kept meaning to give up asking him questions like that, but I couldn't stop. He must have felt, then, that he was right to despise us. That even we felt our deficiency.

Now it's moon night again.

No one's going to send me out. If I had a home to go to, they might send me there. Instead I have blankets, an office room with a lock on the door. They aren't even putting me on the switchboards. Hugo said it had been decided I could do with a rest.

Nobody notices as I head downstairs.

The camera is unmanned. It's a cramped room, packed in behind two-way mirrors; wires line the floor and press through my shoes, and there's two chairs, both hard plastic and stackable as if they came from a school-room. The sound comes from each cell separately, every cage is miked, and a bank of switches and cables domin-ates the space. You can adjust what you hear without affecting the recording, if you plug in a set of head-phones. Classes on bugging were never my favourites, they were for the kids who would have been recording engineers or musicians, but I remember enough, I can operate this equipment.

Right now, I can hear all the voices together.

'. . . and then they offer us aspirin, can you believe that?' It's Sarah's voice. Her mouth is puffy. All of them are marked. They'll heal up when they rick, they'll be fine by morning. It's usual to offer prisoners aspirin on moon nights; it doesn't make much difference to the pain of furring up, but we aren't qualified to prescribe anything stronger.

'You should have taken it,' says Ellaway. 'You're all crazy.'

'Shut up.' It's Paul's voice, half-whispered and emphatic. One side of his face is stained purple, his eye is swollen. It gives him a tipped, off-balance look. My hands twitch as he speaks.

'It's the law, I think,' Albin says. 'Does anyone know what time it is?'

'I think it's about five minutes.' Sarah kicks at the straw.

'Maybe she sent the aspirin down.' Paul sits crouched against the back wall. He looks at no one as he says this.

'For fuck's sake, we've been over this –'

'Enough.' Albin's voice cuts across Sarah, and everyone goes still. 'Sarah, stop bitching, we're in this together. Paul, stop whimpering, this is not about your love life. Now, if anyone else has anything they want to add, let's hear it now.'

Nobody looks at him. They all duck their heads and go quiet.

'Right,' he says. 'We'd better assume sunset's happening now.'

Ellaway makes an angry gesture and retreats to the back of his cell. The others look around, start checking how much straw they have.

I flick switches, turn dials, slot a plug into place to listen in to Paul's cell, and put on a set of headphones. They're large, soft, they cup the sides of my head like hands.

Most people fidget before moonrise, tense up. Nobody likes imminent pain. Paul, though, seems relaxed, or at least, matter-of-fact. He sweeps the straw across his floor, makes a heap of it. I cover my mouth as he starts to unbutton his shirt, and he pulls it over his head with only a few buttons open. He always did that. I'd undo it, open it out and push it back over his shoulders, running my hands down his arms, but if left to himself, he'd strip it off like a T-shirt. His back, turned to me, is marbled with bruises. I watch the shift and weave of his shoulder blades under his smooth, battered skin, flexing like wings.

He drops the shirt over the straw. Someone says

something to him, and he turns. 'Well, this stuff scratches like hell,' he says.

It's Sarah speaking. I watch her mouth move, soundless. Probably she's pointing out that if he rips up his shirt, he won't get another one, and she's right, he won't. He shrugs, picks up the shirt and tosses it onto a shelf above his head. One hand runs through his hair and he rubs his scalp. It's a habit I recognise, something he often did when his clothes came off and air hit his skin. The other hand undoes his belt, and he kicks off his shoes.

This is nothing I haven't seen before. I just thought it was mine. The others are peeling their clothes off with equal composure; they don't stare at each other or avoid looking. This is familiar to them. I can't take my eyes off him, but they barely notice. He's theirs.

I listen in to his cell, the sound of him breathing, the soft crackle as his bare feet tread on the straw.

The moon will rise in a couple of minutes.

Paul shakes his head, swings his arms around a couple of times like an athlete and then lies down. He inhales, sighs, inhales again. He doesn't fidget. Instead, he lays his hands over his chest, not crossed but side by side. His head shifts a little on the straw, but it's a hard floor, he's never going to get comfortable.

A voice sounds over the intercom. I jump at the sound, Paul just opens his eyes and turns his head, then closes them again. 'Attention please: moonrise begins in one minute.'

Paul's hands rise and fall on his chest as he breathes in, breathes out, relaxing. A strand of straw clings to his arm at the elbow. He doesn't brush it off. He lies there, quiet as a man waiting to fall asleep.

The process takes hold of him a few seconds later, and he stiffens and breathes a little faster. His eyes shut tighter, his forehead wrinkles. It looks like the face of a man trying to keep discomfort under control, but when a muscle tightens in his jaw, as if he clenched it, it doesn't stay still but flexes tighter and tighter, pulling his face into line. The changes come on gradually in the first minute, but then they quicken.

He arches his back, his legs press against the ground. A spasm passes through him, jolting him against the floor, but he reaches back with his head, breathes hard, and the shuddering stops, his legs still and stretch out. His stifled moan rises over the grating click as his knees flex and unhinge, bending backwards. The arms go slower, the bones in his shoulders grind like an arthritic joint, trying to find a position.

I take hold of the headphones with my shaking hands, clutching the soft pads closer to my head, and Paul twists on the floor half-formed, like a misshapen child that should never have been born, like a man crippled from hours on a rack. Already his face is going, dark hairs are twining out of his skin, trembling like flowers turning in the sun, but his voice as he gasps and murmurs is still my Paul's.

Then another spasm takes him, shaking his arms into place at the front of his chest, and this time he can't control it. He opens his mouth and there's a high, shivering whine, inhuman, not animal, almost instrumental like a choirboy's treble, and as he drags air into his lungs his chest rises and rises again, the muscles on his stomach shift and flatten themselves as if he was lifting a heavy weight, and he topples onto his side. I can see the tail form, his coccyx rise and stretch, and for a moment it's almost sexual, memories tumble inside me, but then his mouth stretches out, and there are his teeth, pushing out through his gums like a cat's claws, too white against the flushed, darkening gums.

His legs kick against the ground, and I know he's lost. He could handle the pain at first, he could bear it, but his mind is changing inside him and his reason is going. He's forgetting how to endure. There are more cries, and I don't recognise them, the voice is wrong. He can't talk himself into calmness, he can't talk at all any more, his tongue has stretched and flattened and he couldn't speak to me if I asked.

As he rolls over, feet on the ground, the contractions slow. Here and there a muscle twitches, he raises one foot off the ground, then the other, but it's over, he's all right now and it's over. He looks around the cell, stretches himself.

Then he runs at the bars. He slams into them, scrabbles to keep his balance, turns around and studies them. One foot reaches through, but he can't follow it, he's caged.

At this moment, some people start to tear at the walls, bite themselves, panic. I wait, watch, one hand against my mouth, but Paul doesn't do it, he circles the cell, goes round at a rapid trot, as if gauging the distance.

I turn up the other microphones. They can't speak now, they can't say things I can't stand hearing. There's a yell from one of the other cells, a crash. Ellaway is throwing himself against the walls. Paul turns, crouches, his teeth are bared and there's a low, rasping snarl coming from his throat, but then Albin shouts out and he turns away, goes quiet. Instead, he paces up to the corner of his cell and sits down near Sarah. She reaches her head through the bars and they touch, nose to nose.

He's touching her, that sharp-edged woman, the woman who told him I wouldn't help, the woman who insisted so much against me. We've been over this, she said. Now he's sitting beside her and they smell each other's faces, moving their heads like a dance.

Albin barks and she rises to her feet, goes over to him. Paul gets up again and starts to circle his cage.

Ellaway is still worrying the bars, howling. Bad lune. The noise he's making seems to intimidate Carla, who huddles in the corner of her cage furthest away from him, whimpering to Albin, who goes over to her, touches his face to hers. It's a trouble to him, Albin, caged between Sarah and Carla, that he can't be near more than one person at a time.

Paul's out there. Once we lay in bed together, and he said he thought lunes were beautiful. I study him, the dark, glossy hair, the swinging limbs as he paces, his swift, sure gait. I don't know any more. He was always beautiful.

I open the door and step out into the cellblock. All heads turn as it closes behind me. The smell in the room is sharp, ammoniac, the smell of luning.

My legs aren't quite steady, my hands twitch, and I'm slow and graceless as I approach the end cell. I hear my own voice, faltering, lost.

'Paul?'

He turns. There isn't even a pause. He runs straight at the bars, mouth open, teeth vivid and huge in his mouth, and he flings himself at me. The cage door shakes as he crashes against it.

389

My hands cover my face, as if fingers could keep his claws out.

Paul backs away, studies me. His eyes are grey, black-rimmed, his neck is poised like a cobra's. He looks at me, this creature he can't reach, with a steady, predator's gaze.

When you love someone, you tell yourself that they're not like other people, that they're too special for that. But Paul paces the bars like any other caged lune. Why be surprised? This white-toothed fast-paced lune that hurled himself at me jaws open is Paul just as much as the one who talked his way into my life. There's nothing in his cell that wasn't in my bed.

It's a long time before sunrise. The announcement comes, and I hear over the tannoy. They hear it in the cells, too, they look up at the sound of her voice, but it doesn't register much with them. No one understands language when they're in that state. They're tiring by this time. Carla sits in the corner of her cell, as close to Albin as possible, Albin is cleaning himself, and Paul – Paul is still pacing. It's a slower walk, to and fro in front of the bars, swinging his head as he turns. It isn't until Albin yells to him that he stops, turns, sits down on the straw. Ellaway is still tearing at the walls. The others turn at the sound of Albin's voice and settle, but Ellaway doesn't calm down. He's been like this all night, furious at his cage, snarling at Paul if he gets too near, relentless. He's going to start hurting in a minute.

Paul looks around him. He raises his head and howls, and the others join, there's a moment when a chord rings through the echoing cells, but then it stops. Sunrise.

Paul turns in the straw, he rolls over and over, he kicks at the air and wails. The sounds cut me bone-deep. My hands tighten over my padded ears, I can hear my sharp inhalations, and Paul thrashes and cries. I knew this would happen, I knew it's happened last month and every month before that, I knew that he was down in the cells with people knocking bruises into his flesh, hitting him hard enough to draw blood. When I was away from him, I knew all that, and I could stand it. If I didn't have to listen to him cry, I could go on bearing it. But as he stretches out, as his limbs rise and his muscles drag themselves into place, I hear him, and the lupine howl deepens, grows ragged, until it's a man's voice that's moaning.

Then there's a break in it, he drags in air, I hear him panting for breath. His body is still contracting, hair sloughs off and the skin beneath is flushed scarlet like a newborn's or a fever case, but he's trying to recall himself, he's still half-luning but he's rising by the moment, and with every second that goes by he understands better what's happening to him.

He falls back onto the straw with a groan, his arms and legs still stiff and frozen into place. If he leaves them for a few minutes, they'll loosen, he'll be able to unfold them. He doesn't wait, though. His face convulses as he bends one arm at the elbow, then the other. He closes his fingers one at a time, biting his lip as the stretched and abused muscles resist. It doesn't stop him; he starts to work his face, too, clenching and unclenching his eyes, opening his mouth wide, pulling his lips over his teeth. It should look ugly, lying on the floor grimacing, but it doesn't. It's almost graceful, like a child. As the red fades from his skin, I see I was right. The bruises have healed up as he ricked back. He's pristine again.

The straw crackles as he pushes himself into a sitting position, rubs his hands over his face, gives a sigh like a tired runner. After a moment he shakes himself, covers his arms, and I realise how cold it is down here. No one heats the cells, and it's winter. Paul grabs one of the bars and pulls himself to his feet, reaches up onto a shelf to take his clothes down. He shakes them, examines them and holds them to his face. They're dirty. As he dresses, I see the others are also getting to their feet, shivering in the morning air. This is the coldest time of day.

Carla walks to the edge of her cell, reaches through. Albin touches her hand, a brief greeting like a kiss of peace given during Mass. Then he crosses to the other side, touches Sarah's hand, and Sarah crosses to Paul to touch him. I stand up, but he doesn't see me behind the mirror. Letting go of her hand, he glances over his shoulder to where Ellaway is sitting against the wall, head in his hands as if hungover. Paul shrugs. I see dislike on his face before he turns away, sits back down without passing the greeting along.

'What's to remember?' he says. He's a little hoarse, but it's the right voice now, I recognise it. 'Still, not much else to do.'

'Wait for them to come round and have another little chat with us,' says Sarah. She sits down as Paul has, cross-legged against the wall.

'They won't,' Paul says. 'Not for today, at least. I don't think so. They'll have been up all night. Lola was always in pieces on the first day, I doubt she could have hit a cushion.'

He said was.

'Did I dream it,' says Albin, 'or does anyone else

have the feeling Paul's girlfriend was down here last night?'

I stiffen as Carla shrugs, Sarah pulls a face.

'Maybe,' Paul says. 'I don't – maybe she was.' It's almost a sigh. He closes his eyes, and they all follow suit. They just sit, cross-legged, for ten minutes, silent, absorbed. They're so contained. I almost bang on the glass to disturb them.

Ellaway sits out, scowling. After ten minutes, he breaks in, saying, 'For God's sake, what are you all playing at?'

'Remembering.' Paul opens his eyes and gives Ellaway a look. His voice is sharp. 'You remember better if you do this just after sunrise. Remember? We taught you. Oh wait, you didn't stick around to try it.'

'Paul.' Albin speaks, and Paul looks round. 'It's too early for this.'

'I'm sorry.' Paul doesn't sound very sorry. 'Just – stop him talking. I don't want to listen to him talk.'

'Please don't,' Carla says. Her voice is almost inaudible. 'Let's not have bad feelings so soon after.'

'Fine.' Paul drops his hands into his lap. 'Sorry, Carlie.'

'Do you think they'll leave us alone today?' Carla says.

He looks at his hands. 'I don't know. Maybe.'

'Do you suppose when they were hunting they –'

'Anyway,' Albin interrupts, giving her a serious look. He doesn't finish the sentence.

They sit in silence.

*

393

I retreat to my office, smooth the blankets over the floor. It's a hard surface to sleep on, but I'm better provided than anyone else in this building. Carla was right to wonder; it's possible that there are others of them out there. Tonight's catchers may have collared more of their friends.

It's a long time before I fall asleep.


There are dozens of reports, scores. Underage children trapped in alleyways. Junkies trying to devour the bark off trees. Regular loiterers caught for the fifth, sixth, tenth time, out in their favourite places, howling at the moon. That's the thing about lunes. Lycos are cautious, they can link one thing to another and avoid stupid decisions, but lunes don't remember what they've learned, not all of it, not all of them. In the daytime, they'd know better than to reoffend in the same spot over and over, but when night comes, they forget fine details like that. They go back to their old haunts.

So when I find a report of a man collared who was running on three legs, I'm not really surprised to see it was in Spiritus Sanctus that they caught him. The report hasn't put the facts together yet, but the details are all there. It was even in the same section of the woods where Marty got torn up.

This man was in a bad way. The best part of his right front leg was useless. Nobody could get near enough to investigate. He was crazy with it. In the morning they found a big scar on his arm, on what was left of it. The necrosis was rampant. Already most of his fingers were beyond help. He cursed and raved at the shelter workers, spat and kicked at the nurse who tried to examine him. That's why they kept him in; they thought they'd better hospitalise him for his own good.

I pick up the telephone and call the shelter.

'Hello?' My spirit sinks a little as I recognise Nick's voice. This would have been easier with someone I didn't know.

'Nick, this is Lola Galley speaking.'

'Hello, Lola.' Even this early in the morning, there's a little warmth in his voice. I guess he likes me.

'Listen, I've been reading a report of a lune you had in your shelter last night, a – David Harper?'

'Bad lune.' There's hours of fatigue in his voice.

'Is he still there?'

'No. Ambulance came for him half an hour ago.'

Half an hour. There's still time. 'Okay, listen, Nick, this is important. It's very urgent that you get in touch with the hospital. Call the police as well, and we'd better send over some DORLA guards too, seeing what happened when we trusted hospital security with Seligmann.'

'Slow down, Lo,' he says. 'What do I tell the police?'

'He's a major suspect in the Marcos and Jensen case. At the very least, we can probably charge him with attempted murder. Sean Martin and I can witness that. We need to arrest him before he leaves the hospital.'

'Free-ranger?' he asks. The story must be all over the country by now.

'Yeah. Yeah, I think so.'

Nick's good. He doesn't waste time with questions, he gets straight off the line and starts making arrangements. I make other calls. It only takes ten minutes to find the man.

Necrotic arm, a wound that wouldn't heal when he ricked. Only silver does that. This man was in Spiritus Sanctus. There was a deep, rotten wound in his right front leg. I think he got it from a silver bullet. I think Marty put it there.

# 31

'I've got a proposition to make.' I say this before any of them can say a word. All of them but Ellaway have risen to their feet as I come in, and they stand back a little. Their eyes are on Paul.

He looks at me. Already there are fresh bruises around his eyes. 'Lola,' he says. I don't move. He grips one of the bars, searching for words. 'I've been asking to see you.'

I've never seen him look like this, this pinched, desperate expression. It's how all our prisoners look after a while, it's how we look on moon nights. I thought that Paul was free of it. 'You look bad,' I say.

He tilts his head. 'You look a little peaky yourself.'

I tense at the word. My mother always called me peaky. 'I haven't been sleeping that much,' I say. 'It happens when you find out you've been used.'

'What? Lola, I wasn't using you . . .' His voice is hasty, I raise my hand to cut him off.

'Anyway, I've got a proposition for you. A change in the terms of your captivity. And I'd advise you here and now to take it; I had to do a lot of fast talking to get my boss to agree.'

'Are you going to help us?' Albin says.

'That's not my priority.' I press my hands together for a moment, then make them lie still at my sides. 'We've arrested another man. We have good evidence that he's one of you. Now, he isn't admitting to anything.' He's cursing his captors and cursing the doctors worse for letting them stand guard. They say that he pulled the drip right out of his arm. That was before the doctors decided there was no saving it and amputated above the elbow. 'We want you to identify him as part of your conspiracy. If you do that, then DORLA will assign you a lawyer. You'll be represented as a group. Some of your rights will be restored. You'll be provided with blankets and mattresses. If you don't identify him, we'll simply throw him into the mix and keep waiting for confessions, yours and his.'

'A DORLA lawyer or an outside one?' Albin asks, as Sarah says, 'You're holding out for confession because you don't have evidence, aren't you?', and Paul says, 'Would it be you?'

'A DORLA lawyer. Possibly me. That decision will be taken after you've identified him.'

'If we don't confess, you can't convict us. There isn't any evidence.'

'We can wait a while for your confessions, Miss Sanderson.'

'Supposing we plead guilty to a lesser charge?' says Albin. 'We'll all admit to moon loitering. We really didn't hurt anyone.'

I look at him. 'Did you ever meet Johnny Marcos?'

'That's Ellaway's fault,' Paul says. 'You can fry him, go right ahead.'

'Paul!'

'That's all right, Mr Albin, I'm listening to everyone's opinions,' I say. Ellaway mutters in a corner. Paul gives him a look that would split a log. I swallow. That's Ellaway's fault, he said. That's all he has to say about it. 'You can plead guilty to those if you like. Only I had the impression that you confessed to those charges pretty much as soon as I arrested you. It's not much of a bargaining chip.'

'It's the truth. Please be our lawyer, Ms Galley. I swear, you can make a really good case for us.'

Ellaway comes up to the bars. 'Don't tell her fucking anything, Lewis. You can't do this.'

'I wouldn't bother, Mr Ellaway. We've got all we want to know about your mauling Johnny.' I mean to say Johnny Marcos, but the name gets mangled in my mouth. 'That's attempted murder at the least. You're going down whatever happens.'

'Well, that's one good thing to come out of this.'

'Paul.' Albin's voice is soft.

'Paul, nothing, Lew.' Distantly I recognise the name. The first night we met he told me about a friend who tried to get him to eat bananas. Lou. Lew. He made me laugh, at the time. 'You think we'd be in this if it wasn't for that man?' Paul turns to look at me. 'You never told me you were defending him, Lola.'

My face won't move. 'But you knew anyway.'

'You didn't tell me anything about him. If you'd told me what you thought, I could have told you what happened.'

I try to take a deep breath, but I can't, my chest has stiffened and I can't get any air in. 'I don't – You're a murder suspect, Paul. I told you someone shot my colleague. I told you I couldn't go home, and you – I can't even go home now, you know. Were you planning to kill me all along?'

Paul's hands come off the bars and he draws them back into his cell. 'You were living with me, Lola. We were never more than five feet apart. If I'd wanted you dead I could have snapped your neck then and there and had done with it.'

He used to hold my face between his hands. We'd make love sitting up and he'd cradle me, take the weight of it, my head fitting into his palms. Did he think of it then? Or has he thought of it since, lying here in his straw? One good wrench. That's all it would have taken.

'Nicely put, Casanova,' says Albin.

'Jesus, Paul,' Sarah says from her heap of straw. There's a hysterical note to her voice, her eyes don't focus on me. 'How did you get her into bed in the first place?'

I turn to leave.

'Wait – Lola!' Paul shakes the door of his cage. 'Don't go, I'm sorry, I didn't mean that the way it sounded – wait, come back!'

I turn, my pulse beating in my ears. I'm angry with them now, I've shown them my pale face and broken heart and let Paul humiliate me in front of them all. But I know fear when I hear it. Sarah calls after me too, and I see, quite suddenly, what I am to them. A link, a hope, a fragile, touchy, brittle link that they're wheedling with desperate care, playing for their lives with glass cards.

'I'll bring him in,' I tell them. 'You should identify him. It'll get you all some legal counsel, him included. He'll be down later in the day.'

*

400

They're surprised that we bring Harper back in a group, two guards besides me, which makes me wonder about them – anyone who can hate us enough to shoot silver bullets at us and yet expect a dangerous prisoner to be escorted to the cells by a lone woman less than five-and-a-half feet tall must have a skewed view of the world. It's an almost mythical view of us. The absolute enemy, a force of evil, yet with no actual police techniques to make things happen. Though I suppose if you only ever see us through luning eyes, you might get some simplistic ideas.

Harper struggles hard between his two escorts, both of them interrogators with wounds that don't show. I walk ahead, not touching him. When we bring him down to the free-rangers' cellblock, he stops struggling, stares around him, glaring at the prisoners.

'Jesus, what happened to his arm?' says Paul. The bandages are still fresh. It hangs by his side like a wing on a plucked chicken.

Does he think we did that? 'Silver wound that he didn't get properly treated. He'd be fine if he'd gone to a hospital.'

Harper struggles behind me. Apart from damning us all to the flames, he hasn't spoken a word since we arrested him.

'So.' I look at the prisoners, who are glancing one to another, restless. 'Are you going to identify him for me?'

They stand in silence. Paul bites his fingers.

'You remember the terms. This is your only chance to take them up. I won't be able to make the offer more than once.'

'No,' says Albin. His voice is heavy.

401

'Yeah. Yeah, he's one of us,' Sarah cuts in, a little shrill.

'He isn't, Ms Galley. I wish I could ID him, but I've really never seen him before.'

'Come on, Lew, they've got him now. They'll give him a lawyer, won't they? He is one of us, Miss Galley. Lewis is just trying to cover up.'

'We can't make a case if we have to include a stranger, Sarah.' Albin's voice is cold, somehow hushing everything in the room.

'Paul.' I step forward a little, lower my voice.

He looks at me. 'Please get me out of here, Lola. I can't take much more of this.' His voice is as low as mine. I flinch at the sound of my easy-going Paul pleading.

'Do you know this man, Paul?' My voice shakes with strain.

Paul looks at Albin, at Sarah, at Harper standing mute behind me with a guard's shock prod held against his chest. For a moment, Paul covers his face, and it's quiet, there are no sounds. Then he lowers his hands and shakes his head. 'No,' he says. 'No, I don't know him.'

I could have made the offer stand. They would have talked to me. All the things I could have given them are out of reach now, days without interrogation and legal counsel and blankets slip out of my grasp. My head hangs down under its own weight.

'I'm sorry,' I say. 'I can't – give you anything, then.'

'He is one of us, Miss Galley! Don't listen to them, don't listen to them!' Sarah's voice rises and rises, the echoes shatter around her, screaming off the walls.

'He looks familiar,' Carla mutters.

I turn. 'Familiar?' Is she trying to compromise – has the incarceration rocked her brain so badly she thinks she might reach a halfway point? Did he go out with them once a long time ago? 'What do you mean?'

She's hunched in a ball in the corner of her cell, her arms wrapped around her knees. It's the same position she's been in ever since we locked her up. Her fingers cover her mouth as she speaks. 'I – I don't know. I just think he looks familiar. Maybe I know his face.'

'Carla?' Albin walks up to the bars that divide their cells, but I interrupt him.

'Thank you, Mr Albin, please don't talk to the suspect.'

'Suspect?' His voice is soft with anger as he turns on me.

'Dr Stein, if this is just a man you ride on the same bus to work with, that's not going to help you very much. Can you tell me what you're talking about?'

Her shoulders rise to cover her as she shrugs, like a bird fluffing its feathers against the wind. She lays her head on her knees, her arms around it, and goes quiet.

There's a long pause.

'Mr Ellaway? Do you have anything to contribute?'

Ellaway glowers at me through the bars. 'Yeah. I know him. We all do.'

'Do you? Tell me his name, please.'

He glares, his face almost hot with fury.

I sigh. 'So the majority view is that you don't know him? Guys, take him to Block C, please.' Harper is dragged out. I hear him try to break out of their grip as they push him through the door, but weeks of silver poisoning have taken their toll. He's a sick man now.

I turn to look at the prisoners left behind.

'Please be our counsel,' says Albin. 'We really didn't know that guy.'

'Yes we did, yes we did,' Sarah whispers. She's collapsed in a corner, and she's weeping. I've heard tears like that before, after interrogations, exhausted, confused tears. She's losing herself.

I spread my hands. 'You have to give me something,' I say. 'I can't just take you on. You have to give me something I can use.'

'We can tell you all about the night John Marcos was mauled,' says Albin. 'You were right about it, you know. I tried to stop him, but he got over the wall. It was the first time he'd been with us, you see. This thing, it just started out with Paul and Sarah and me, we'd meet people from time to time and start including them. Dick was interested, we thought he might work out. Usually – usually I can make them back down. I – I didn't think he'd turn out the way he did.'

'How did you start out?' I say. All of a sudden, our voices are calm, reasonable.

'It was the three of us. Paul and I, we're cousins, more or less, four times removed or something but we knew each other when we were kids, we'd been in the same lock-up room sometimes when we were little. And Sarah and I went out with each other when we were about fifteen. We knew each other pretty well. We started out just sharing a lock-up room.' I wrinkle my nose. Three mixed friends together is a bit peculiar, if not scandalous. Most people wouldn't do it. 'But we figured – Paul got us into remembering. You can, you know, better than most people bother to, if you do some mental exercises, sort of meditations, straight after. And after we were eighteen, things changed. Sarah got locked outside one

404

night, with a lot of other people – it was an accident, nobody's fault.' He looks at me, forestalling accusations.

'I know.'

'How do you know?'

'I've seen your records. That night is famous.'

Albin sighs, glances at Sarah. 'Well, it was an accident. But Sarah remembered, you see, she remembered quite a lot of it. And she was outside, with other people, she said it was quite different. And we figured, after a while, that we'd be okay if we were outdoors. And it was different, it was so completely different. It was – *right*, you know? You shouldn't be indoors when you're like that. The walls, the heat – We're meant to be outside. And it's a great life experience you're missing, locking yourself in a little room.'

'A life experience,' I say. That's what it means to them. Not blood soaking into the ground, scars in flesh that can't rick and heal, damage that never goes away.

'Paul, you should be telling her this,' Albin says. It isn't until he says it that I realise it's true. These are the things Paul never told me.

'I –' Paul looks at me, grips his hands together. 'I thought you'd hate this.'

'Yeah?' My voice is flat.

'The way you talk about lunes, I didn't think you'd get any of this. And there's no reason why you should. I mean, I don't know what it's like from your view, and there's no way you could see it from mine.'

'Thanks for reminding me.' My voice is almost a whisper, but it's still too loud, loud enough to be heard.

'Lola?'

'And while we're talking about life experiences, I don't suppose you've ever had the primal danger experience.

405

Having your hand ripped off, that's an experience you'll never forget.'

Ellaway sits in his corner, his back to us.

'I didn't do that,' Paul says. His voice is hoarse, pleading.

I look at his battered face. 'All the time you've been down here, I haven't raised a hand to you. I don't suppose it excuses me in your eyes.'

'I love you,' says Paul. 'I wish you'd believe me.'

'It's the Stockholm syndrome,' I say. 'You have to love me in here, I'm your best hope of salvation. Once you get out, you'll start thinking it over, and you won't need me any more, and then you'll start hating me for everything I've done.'

He doesn't say anything.

'You might be right,' says Albin. 'I hope you're not. It's a shame. If you'd been a lyco, I might have asked you to join us.'

'I'm not a lyco,' I say. 'There's no part of me that's lyco.'

'We really didn't kill anyone.'

'I know Johnny's wife,' I say. 'He has three children. They're falling apart.'

'We didn't kill him. I've been trying to find out about him since Dick – There wasn't anything in the papers about him losing his hand.'

'It happens too often. And the shooting, that didn't make it either. But barebacks die young. I don't suppose it mattered too much to an editor that he died of a bullet rather than a bite.'

I'm standing here talking to them. I should hate them, they may be lying to me, twisting my mind around their hands like twine. It's strangely restful, though. If I said

406

these things to a non, it would just be griping. And most lycos would shrug it off. I guess I have my captive audience now.

'I'm sorry about the man,' Albin says. 'I wanted to give some money to his family, only I couldn't do it without getting caught. Guess I could do it now, if I ever get out.'

I could say you can't buy off people, but what would be the point? Sue Marcos needs money. 'Do it direct,' I say. 'Don't go through DORLA. It would just get soaked up somewhere. Tell her you spoke to me.'

'Do you believe us?' Albin asks. 'I mean, that we didn't kill anyone?'

The hush rings in my ears, and I'm tired. I take a deep breath. 'I don't know,' I say. 'If it turns out that you're lying now and you did, then you're the worst man alive. But right now, I don't see it.'

All of them turn in their cells. The straw rustles like trees in a storm.

'Why did you think we did?' Paul says. 'No one gave us any evidence. They just dragged us all off and started kicking the hell out of us and asking the same questions. What was it? Were we just getting tarred with the same brush because you knew we'd done one thing?'

'I've heard enough they're-all-the-same comments to last me a lifetime,' I say, angry. 'Barebacks are this, barebacks are that. You don't think I'd start doing it myself?'

Paul shrugs. 'You might. People tend to pass along whatever happens to them.'

'The man we arrested was wounded by a silver bullet and didn't go to hospital. Someone stole some Oromorph that day to dope him while they pulled the bullet out. And you, Dr Stein, you had a prior for stealing

Oromorph. It looked like you were in the habit of self-treatment.'

I didn't mean to say all that. It came out in a rush. Paul has no business thinking I'd . . .

'I took Oromorph once,' Carla says into her knees. 'I thought it might make furring up easier, that we'd be calmer afterwards.'

'It didn't work,' Albin adds. 'We just got stupid. But she only did it the once.'

'If one of us had a silver wound, I'd never just treat it with painkillers,' Carla mutters. 'Look what happened to that poor man you showed us. I worked hard in medical school. I know what happens if you neglect wounds like that. I worked hard.'

It's then that I start to almost believe them.

# 32

'Ally,' I say, 'have you got a minute?'

He's testing catching poles. There's a machine you put the loops onto, with weights you can add and take off like in a gym; they have to be able to stand double the strain a lune is likely to put on them. Ally is holding one of the weights, and when he sees me his hands sag, as if it had grown suddenly heavier. 'What do you want?' He lays it down on the floor. 'I'm not in the mood for this.'

'I'm not going to do anything.' I hitch myself up onto a table and sit there, hands at my sides. 'I want to talk to you.'

'I don't especially want to talk to you, Lola.'

'Are you mad at me?'

'I don't like being messed around.'

I shrug. 'Nobody does. Are you going to listen to me or not?'

Ally stares at me. The look is what Becca would describe as 'as if he'd never seen me before', but that's not quite right. It isn't my face that's unfamiliar to him. 'I can't believe you, Lola. You just wander in like nothing's wrong and expect me to drop everything?'

Part of me cowers, but there's no way round this but

a bold face. 'More or less. It wasn't about you, you know. You shouldn't take it personally. I've treated other people worse than you.'

'Christ.'

'I need someone to help me out, and you're my best bet.'

'I've heard that once too many times.' Ally opens his mouth to say more, and I clench my hands behind my back, but he stops there. There's a lot he wants to accuse me of, I know, and there's a lot he wants to ask me. I don't think he's going to. He doesn't know how. We met when we were too young. Even when I was fourteen and resolved to fight him off, I'd just scratch and kick. I wouldn't even say no. We never talked about what we did.

'It's about the prowlers we're after.' I keep my eyes on him as I say this. His gaze flicks away from mine, then back, then away again. 'I'm not sure the official line is right.'

'You came up with the official line.' He adds a weight to the machine. The loop of the catching pole snaps and the weight crashes down, making us both flinch. 'Damn.' He rubs his fists together.

'Some of it, yes I did. But now I'm not sure it's right. I still think Seligmann killed Nate and Johnny. And I still think Harper was with him. He reminds me of Seligmann, this new one. The way he's acting down in the cells. I went to have a look at him; he spits at us and won't talk to us. Doesn't that seem odd, I mean, different from how all the free-rangers are acting?'

Ally takes the damaged pole in his hands, holds it close to him. 'You want to let him out, let him out. Slip him a file when no one's looking, leave the door

410

unlocked, elope with him. Don't ask me to help you out.' There's a glare on his face, a wildness. He must want to say this very badly.

I take a careful breath. This has to sound calm. 'That's not what this is about, Ally. It's not personal. I've been thinking about the evidence. The only real evidence we've got that ties them to Harper and Seligmann is that one of them once stole a bottle of Oromorph. The more I think about it, the more shaky that sounds, because it's not a proper treatment. She's a doctor. This guy lost an arm. I don't see how she could have allowed it to happen. I saw the doctor's report of his condition, it was a botched job.'

'You like her, huh?' Ally's still hugging the pole. 'Think she's a good doctor?'

'Yeah, I think she probably is. They didn't strike her off for stealing drugs the one time they caught her. If she'd been useless, they would have. I – I think we've all got it wrong. These people are convenient. I mean, they moon loiter every month, and if you ask them about it, they'll preach to you. Looks like they've got a whole philosophy going, or at least a whole lifestyle. I mean, what could we possibly hate more? They think we're cripples, I think. Albin almost looks like he feels sorry for me, sometimes. And we're looking for people who prowl, and who think we're the enemy, and this lot come along, and it sort of fits. But I don't think we've got enough evidence for it, not really. I think we all just – thought that someone out there was gunning for us, and these people were the type.'

'They are,' Ally says. His hands are tense around the catcher. 'I know you've been down there. Think they're that sweet and friendly to everyone? You just don't want

411

to think it. They're your kind of people, that's why you can't handle the idea.'

'What?' I don't know what he means, and still the accusation is frightening.

'Of course they are. I've seen your sister, I remember what kind of accent you came to the creches with. You're a lawyer, for fuck's sake. You want this lot to like you. You reckon they're the kind of people you should have been. What, you think if you'd come out foot-first, you'd give a damn about any of us? You'd have gone to college with those people, you'd have been out there with them on moon nights. I've seen you staring out the window, all that stargazing. I reckon given the chance you'd love the moon. Too bad for you you came out crippled.'

I sit, my hands holding the table edge, mute.

'Don't look surprised, princess,' Ally says. 'You were fucking one of them, weren't you? Why wouldn't you like them? Too bad for you they're in jail now. You just don't want to think that they did it because it'd spoil your little dream, that maybe they might accept you, that there's still a part of you that could be like they are, like you reckon you should have been. Shame. You used to think with your head.'

I slide slowly off the table, land on my feet. 'I'm sorry you feel slighted, Ally. I'm sorry you reckon you're not good enough for me. I'm sorry I still give a damn about my sister and don't hide her from you in case she touches a nerve. And that you think this is about caste. You know what? Maybe you're right. Maybe I do think I should have been more like them. But you know, I reckon if I had been, I wouldn't have ever taken a silver gun and shot two men down.'

412

'You did take a gun,' Ally says. 'I know one went missing from the store room.'

'And if I did, who do you think I was planning to shoot?'

'I didn't tell anyone. I've got some loyalty, even if you haven't.'

'I'm sorry, Ally,' I say. 'I don't feel that loyal to you.'

He shivers. 'Why doesn't that surprise me?'

'Maybe because you tried to fuck me when I was a kid.' It's out now, and I was the one who said it. I'm shaking, inside my chest everything is red and jolted, but my twitching eye has stopped and my face is still. 'Perhaps. But I came to you because I need help with this, I want to send down the right people. I say there's three of them, Seligmann and Harper and one other. There's going to be other free-rangers out there, one or two, because I saw more of them in the garden that night, and if we waste our time trying to get them, someone may end up deciding that we've got them all, and whoever was with Seligmann and Harper will get missed. That's what I don't want to happen, Ally. And if someone doesn't help me, then it might. I can't make arrests by myself, Ally, look at me. I couldn't bring in one man, never mind two.'

'Oh, I'm sure you could manage,' he says. His jaw is clenched.

'Are you going to help me?'

'You don't need help. You don't have any ideas. What are you going to do, wander round the city and knock on every door? There's no one to arrest.'

'I think there is.' I put my hands in my pockets, curl them up. This is my piece of news. I thought I wanted

413

to tell it to someone receptive, but mostly I just want this over with. 'I went over Harper's record. And his files. I've done a lot of research today. And you know what I found? He's got a brother. Steven Harper. Minor record, a little shoplifting when he was a kid. He tried to train as a nurse, but he dropped out of the course before finishing. And you know where he works now? He's a cleaner in St Veronica's.'

'What are you talking about?' Ally shakes his head, dodging.

'I'm talking about Oromorph, is what I'm talking about. Someone stole some Oromorph from St Veronica's to patch up David Harper when Marty shot him. Dug out the bullet, gave him some painkillers, made a real fuck-up amateur job of it. It was an un-labelled bottle. Steven Harper took it off a bedside table in the orthopaedics ward. He cleaned everywhere in the hospital, he knew it was a good place to get painkillers, though he didn't know enough to stop the gangrene. He could have walked through any ward in the hospital, lingered wherever he liked, and if he was pushing a mop, who was going to stop him? He could have even picked up the stuff off someone's table if he made out he was dusting it. I showed David Harper to Dr Stein. She said she didn't know him, but he looked familiar. She doesn't know him. What she saw was a family resemblance. It's Steven Harper we're looking for, that's our third man. He might even know where Seligmann is. And I need someone to help me arrest him. Are you coming or not?'

'I was a kid too, you know,' Ally says. He holds his hands still at his side.

'I don't want to talk about it.' I turn my back.

'You mean you can dish it out but can't take it.' His eyes are narrow as he stares at me.

'I don't think you want to talk about it either.' I look back at the wall.

'No?'

'And you're probably right, I can dish it out but can't take it. You can say a lot of bad things about me, and I'll probably have to agree with you.'

'You had to bring it up, didn't you?'

'Yeah, well, you had to do it in the first place.' There's a dent in the wall, brown plaster showing through the paint. 'You weren't the only one. I wasn't the only one. That's the best that can be said about it.'

'We were kids.'

'Yes. Too young.'

'I've still got a scar on my arm where you bit me once.'

I remember the taste of blood in my mouth, salty and tainted. 'First of many. Nothing compared to what lunes took out of you.'

'Lola,' he says. It's a sigh, hoarse and weary.

'That isn't even my name,' I say. 'No one called me that at home. That's a creche word. And don't pretend a bite on the arm puts me in your camp. Do you want me to remind you what you did to me?'

If he said yes, I couldn't do it, couldn't say the words. I stare at the wall and remember how easy it was to say the same words to Paul. I could always tell him things. The first day we spent together, we were so pleased and excited, both of us wanted to run out and tell someone how good it had been, but we couldn't leave the room, so we told each other. I'd never even been with a lyco before Paul. It was different, it was nothing like the creches, nothing like men who learned about girls locked up on moon nights. I didn't tell him that, it was the only thing I didn't tell him. At the time, I felt I had to keep a loyal silence, I didn't want to insult Ally. Pushing the memory away is like running against the wind, it leaves me limp.

'I didn't know how to think about it at the time,' I say. 'I still don't. But it shouldn't have happened, Ally. Not all the boys in the creches did it. Some of them didn't. You did. And if you didn't know any better, then that's your fault too. I didn't want to start learning it that way.'

'Holding out for someone special?' There's bitterness in his voice. He's trying for sarcasm, but it falls short. There's genuine disillusion there. We must have had illusions once, to lose them like this. How did we come by them, all we malformed sidelined children? Though I can't feel free of illusions, even now.

'No,' I say. The anger has fallen away. It was too hot, too heavy, I couldn't keep hold of it. 'But some consent might have been nice. It . . . to know it was worth something, even just fun or curiosity. Not just something to do because you're locked in all night. Something that made me feel like a normal teenager, not a bareback freak. It would have been nice.'

'You are a bareback, Lola,' Ally says.

'You think I hate us, don't you?' I don't look at him, my head's too heavy to lift. Instead, I slide down the wall, sit with my knees under my chin. 'You think I hate being trapped in a bareback body and I hate all the others for being like me.'

He says nothing.

'I don't, you know,' I say. 'No more than the rest of

416

us do.' I don't hate barebacks, not really. Just sometimes, the walls press in on me, and I think about forgetting it all, about having something else to worry about, having different worries in different years instead of always the same unrelenting round of prejudice and poverty and wondering whether I'll be hurt come next month. Not these same people, with the same problems, the same worn-out solidarity that gets us all through the same day. Sometimes I get thirsty for a little starlight.

I see now, clear and cold, that I haven't forgiven Ally. His inexpert fingers finding no pleasant secrets in my scanty, half-formed flesh are a violation and an affront that I may never get over. We've spent too many years pretending for it not to be dangerous now. And we've both spent all of our years pretending we never look at lycos and wish for a little time on the other side of the bars.

Stupidly, my eyes are stinging and my throat aches. I thought I'd done enough crying. 'We should go and arrest this man,' I say. My voice doesn't work well, and there's a wave of misery that I should show this weakness. I always got by with Ally by being a substitute boy, as much as I could. He knew I could kick and bite, but I never wanted him to see me cry.

'For Christ's sake, don't.' Ally takes a pace back from me. 'I can't take it. You've done everything else, just don't start crying as well.'

He thinks crying is blackmail. He's one of those. Or maybe he just can't be in the room with a crying woman he isn't allowed to comfort. 'I'm not crying.' I wipe my palm against my eye.

'Yeah, right, of course you're not.'

I rest my head on my knees, say nothing.

417

'You really think he did it?'

'This Harper brother?' I press my hands over my eyelids. 'Yeah, I think he did. I think I'm right this time.'

'Does Hugo know you're doing this?'

'He won't be surprised. I thought we ought to get a head start, in case he runs when he finds his brother's gone.'

'Okay.' Ally drums against the wall for a second, then takes a cautious step up to me. 'Come on, let's go.'

He holds his hand out to help me up. I look at it for a moment, but I don't take it. I push against the wall and get to my feet by myself.

# 33

Ally has a car, an old vehicle with dents around the doors. For someone who loves good design as he does, the car must be a trial to him, a thing of little style and less beauty that he can just about afford. Its engine runs well; I can imagine him huddled under the bonnet in his free time, taking apart and putting together the few worn-out wires and cogs that he owns. We hesitate in the car park, pause by the doors. I keep looking at him. Then he digs into his pocket and throws the keys to me without a word.

We don't speak as I drive to the hospital.

I park the car and keep the keys in my coat pocket, and we go in together. We don't speak to the receptionist. I turn down a corridor and Ally follows. It's quiet in here, the air is still and somehow without temperature. Time seems to get soaked up by it. The linoleum is old, curled up at the edges, and it shines. I wonder how many hours of a man's life cleaning a single corridor takes up.

Ally and I don't speak. He looks through windows on one side, I look on the other. We pass a couple of people cleaning, a slight black woman with her hair in a net, a Mediterranean-looking woman, stocky and middle-aged.

419

I could stop and ask them if they've seen Steven, but they work with him, they'll care if he disappears.

It's Ally who finds what we're looking for, a tall white man pushing a trolley with bottles of detergent and bags of waste. Ally sees him through a window, and calls to me with a quiet, 'Hey.' He moves aside as I go to look through.

I hadn't expected him to look so young. Fair hair, stocky, bent over his mop. I can see the side of his face, bent towards the floor, and I know it's him. The features, the square forehead and wide jaw and rounded, narrow nose, they're familiar. I can see why Carla thought for a moment that she recognised his brother's face. He doesn't look like David, though, not really. He's big, Steven, muscular in a way that looks almost misplaced, an accident of build rather than the product of deliberate exercise. He doesn't move like a big man, he doesn't have Hugo's deliberation, there's no sense of strut or grace or power. Steven's big like a teenager, loaded down with a body he isn't sure how to use. I keep expecting him to bump into himself.

We wait for him to come into the corridor. He pushes the trolley ahead of him, and doesn't really look at us, starts to steer round.

'Steven Harper?' I say.

'Yeah?' He stops the cart but keeps his hand on it. The disposal bags swing.

'Come with us, please.'

He frowns. There's a mild belligerence in his face, as if he was accustomed to orders he didn't like, but no real fear.

'You're under arrest. Come with us, please.' I take the DORLA card out of my pocket.

He studies it for several seconds before he turns and starts to run.

Ally catches him up, pushes him against the wall. Though Ally's fit, he's also rangy and Steven's bulk must outweigh him by stones, and a struggle in these silent corridors is wrong, it's like shouting in church, besides which, the outcome isn't clear. So I take a shortcut. It's only Ally who will see, and he knows the worst of me already.

It's a few quiet paces to come up behind Steven and touch my gun to the back of his neck.

'Hold still,' I say. My voice is calm, I don't feel anything but a quiet necessity. A year ago I might have made some crack, that the wards were overcrowded and I didn't want to add to them, that I was curious to test the doctors' skill, I might have made a joke about shooting him. 'Hold still,' is all I need to say. If he threatens us too much, I really might kill him.

Ally looks at the gun for a long moment before shoving Steven away from him and twisting his arms into the handcuffs.

'I'm going to put the gun in my pocket,' I say. 'If you try to run again, I'm going to take it out.' The click of the safety catch is the loudest thing in the lulled, soundless corridor.


We push him through the lobby of the DORLA building, and no one stops us. He isn't struggling. He keeps looking at me, his eyes on my hands, his big shoulders humped against us. His eyes are dull. We take the stairs down to the prisoners' block, and he looks at his feet and descends with ponderous care.

There's a murmur of conversation as we push open the door, which stops at the clang.

'Who have you got now?' Albin says. He stands away from the bars. His focus isn't on Steven, but on Ally.

'Dr Stein, I'd like your attention, please.' Carla sits huddled in her corner, her head wrapped in her arms.

Paul stands up, approaches. He opens his mouth as if to speak to me, but then closes it again with a look of helplessness. I suppose he wanted me to greet him.

'Do any of you recognise this man?' I don't turn my head, I keep watching them as I ask.

'Not this again,' Albin says. He doesn't speak with contempt; he sounds doleful.

'I'm not saying anything,' Steven says behind me.

I hear him flinch as Ally does something to him. 'I wasn't talking to you,' I say as calmly as I can. It shouldn't be bothering me, the thought of them seeing me harry someone.

There's a general shaking of heads, while Carla stays huddled, looking at him. She's chewing her lower lip, white teeth biting into soft pink flesh; her skin is very pale under the lights.

'I know her,' Steven says. 'That's Dr Stein, she works at the hospital, I know who she is.' He says it fast, with something like aggression, as if he thinks identifying Carla will put him in our favour.

'Ally, don't,' I say without looking round. There's no call to hurt him.

'I don't know him very well.' Carla looks across to Albin's cage. 'He's a cleaner at St Veronica's, that's all. Why are you arresting him?'

'Ally?' Paul says to me.

422

'What?' I'm irritated, pulled off course. There's so much to get through before this can be over.

'That's Ally.' Paul indicates Ally without looking at him. 'Is he the one who called the flat, the one you don't want to talk about?'

I struggle for a moment before I remember. Yes, Paul's heard his name, the day Ally called to warn me about the Molotov cocktail someone threw at us. We'll have to ask the Harpers about that; there was a wave of vandal attacks after we started the purge, but that one came before it. It won't surprise me at all if they had something to do with it. Paul heard me say Ally's name, he asked me about him. I hear Ally shift behind me, look at Paul in front of me. There's no way I can turn.

'That's the one.' I say it as drily as I can. I mustn't sound shaken. Paul will see guilt, secrets. Ally will think I'm trying to push him out of my life, that I don't want to mention him to my friends. And they'd have reason to. They would have reasons.

Paul studies him. My breath quickens, and I have a sudden impulse to step between them, block Paul out.

'Well,' my voice rings too high in the space, 'I reckon we'll put him in Block D, Ally. Not with any of his associates.' This is important, Ally, it's worth thinking about, we've got a hold over him if he doesn't find out his brother's here, and that's useful information, you want this investigation to come out right, please think about what I'm saying . . .

'Don't bother introducing us, I know who that is,' Ally says. I turn and see him standing there, behind his prisoner, and he's standing still.

'Shall we take him to D, then?'

Nobody moves.

'Do you still not want to talk about it, Lola?' says Paul. 'It seems like we're running out of secrets.'

Please, Paul, keep quiet, remember where you are. You don't know all my secrets. This one, I know now, I could have told him. If we'd been alone together, if we could have touched each other, I could have told him what happened between Ally and me, I could have tried to explain it. But with Ally standing right here, Paul must know I can't talk about it. Telling Ally I hate the memories he pushed into my head is one thing. Saying it to another man in his presence is another. After everything that's happened, all the good and the bad, I can't do that to him.

'I don't think so,' I say. 'We're not out of secrets yet.'

'Glad you remember where your priorities lie, princess.' Ally doesn't look at me as he says it, he doesn't take his eyes off Paul.

I turn to him, whisper as quietly as I can. 'Speaking of priorities, Ally, can we please take the prisoner to Block D and stop hanging around here?'

'Princess?' Paul says. 'What happened to angel?'

Dear God. 'Paul, for your own sake, I think you should stop it.' I try not to sound too much like I'm begging.

He looks at me. How can his eyes on my face still make my heart shiver? 'It's all right, Lola, I wasn't really talking to you.'

'This isn't a pub, for God's sake.' I give up my careful phrasing. No one else is bothering. 'Don't keep starting something. You're going to get your head kicked in. And Ally, if I find that you've done it, I'm going to be very upset.'

'Warning me off him?' Ally says. 'Sweet.'

'Ally, can we talk about this somewhere else?'

'Lola doesn't think you did it,' Ally says to Paul. They stare at each other. If this was a moon night, they'd be circling. No, they wouldn't. Ally wouldn't.

'She's right,' Paul says.

'Why do you think she thinks that?'

Paul shrugs without relaxing his stance. 'I don't know. Maybe she's brighter than you.'

'You think?'

'If you're just looking for the nearest lyco to lock up and reckon any of us will do, yeah, I think she probably is.'

Ally nods. 'See, I reckon she's stupid. I reckon she made it easy for you to con her. But then, she's easy anyway. God knows, she's easily had. But I guess you know that as well as I do?'

'Ally.' My hands are shaking so hard I can't control them. They move to my gun of their own will. 'Take the prisoner to Block D straight away, or God help me.' Steven Harper watches us with a withdrawn glare, taking it in. God damn Ally to hell for doing this to me, but damn Paul too for being stupid and starting it, and damn myself because I should have seen this coming. Not that my damning anyone will make much odds. In this white prison, I can't see God forgiving any of us.

'We have a prisoner to deal with, Ally,' I say. 'And since he killed two of us, I think you might try getting mad at him.'

'I didn't kill anyone,' says Steven. 'I didn't kill any of you, I don't know what you're talking about.'

My hand settles in my pocket. I hoped this wouldn't happen, I was still foolish enough to want Paul to see me the way he thought I was. It isn't possible any more. My

425

hand closes around the gun, and I let go of the last piece of me that hoped for better things.

'Harper, turn around.' I aim the gun at his wide, solid chest, and he takes a step back. 'Out through the door and up the stairs. Ally, would you open the door for him? I don't think he can work the lock in those cuffs.'

I don't look at anyone as I escort them both into the corridor. I keep my eyes focused on the dull, dark metal, like a proper agent of the law, like a woman with no one watching, like a woman on her own.


We lock him up in a cell by himself, no one to talk to, no one to tell him things. As we pass into the corridor, I grab Ally by the arm. He turns, towers over me. I let go, hold my fist against my stomach.

'If you ever do that again, I swear, Ally, I will kill you. You think this is about loyalty? What about the dead men, are you loyal to them?' I'm hissing at him, my voice echoless along the stairwell. 'You want to call me names, do it to my face, don't do it in front of the prisoners, don't fuck up this arrest and this case because I've worked my guts out to get this right and if you fuck it up now I'll kill you.'

'I fuck it up? I wasn't the one who started all this, princess. Kill your man downstairs if you want to keep the peace.'

'Don't you dare start saying he started it. If you start pointing fingers like a kid, I'll kill you.'

'You didn't mind fingers when you were a kid.' His hand comes around my head, digging into my scalp, dragging me back. I struggle against him, staggering a little to keep my feet, and I don't answer, I don't have

426

anything to say that can take any of this away. He pulls my head down and his arm is behind me, forcing me forwards. His face is twisted around the eyes, his lips are tight. Nausea rises in my chest. I struggle to keep breathing, one breath, another, if I can breathe calmly then this will stop, and I pull against his grip. He despises me for what I let him do to me, I know that now. I can't blame him. I despise him for it too, and myself, and if he despised what he did, how could he feel anything but anger for the person who didn't stop him? We struggle on the landing, tussle like two kids fighting for space, but his arms are too strong and I can smell the gunpowder on his sleeve and I can't get out of this.

I bring my knee up. It's a familiar move, simple. I stare at him, feeling once again the adolescent wonder to find it's so easy to stop a man twice your size in his tracks. It isn't a hard blow, just a knock that makes him drop my head and stagger back a few paces, hunched over. 'Been there, done that,' I say. All I can do now is hurt him. I turn and run down the stairs, don't look at him. Even now, the habits of childhood are too strong for us and he lets me go without a curse because he can't find the words to say what I am.

# 34

That night, I think of Steven. That big, imprisoned young man, trapped in his clumsy body. When he furred up, his size would make him formidable.

People look at my hands and change seats on the bus. No one likes the body I'm trapped in, either. I've evolved, I've picked up weapons to get me through the gauntlet, resentment, spite, a sharp tongue. But then, I didn't have alternatives.

I make a decision.

Steven is asleep on a pile of straw. I knock the gun against the bars to wake him, tell him to get up. He demands to know where I'm taking him, and I aim the gun and march him downstairs without a word.

When I push him through the door to the free-rangers' block, I find most of them asleep. They wake suddenly at the sound of the door closing, sit up, all of them on guard. It's bright down here, the lights never go off.

Albin blinks at me. 'What are you doing?'

I open the cell at the end, and send Steven inside. 'I'm giving you a chance to save yourselves,' I say. Paul pulls himself to his feet, and I look at him for a moment. I can't turn away from him. I have to close my eyes to break the connection before I can go back out.

I listen in, I watch. It isn't a secret that I'm watching the prisoners, it can't be, because there I am, my head clamped between earphones, waiting. And it's known that I moved Steven Harper from Block D into his present company. Nobody says anything about it. Possibly I'm contagious, possibly they're embarrassed, there are lots of reasons why people would wish to avoid me nowadays, but I start to wonder if the real reason is that they're stumped. Nothing out of any of the captives, and Seligmann, the prize, the one that got away, is out in the ether, tantalisingly there but invisible. There have been other arrests, mine are not the only ones. People whose hate mail we've been ignoring for years, people we knew sprayed curses on the walls of our building, people with records for moon loitering. Jerry, my client and Paul's, the wino who brought us into contact, is locked up, awaiting trial, him and dozens like him. No bail, no release before trial, no outside contact, it's an across-the-board decree from the highest in our ranks. There have been a lot of distraught friends and family in our lobby, demanding to know whether we have this person or that in our confines; a few of them got put in the cells too, the aggressive ones, the ones who provoked attendants into deciding to take the fight out of them. It's very stupid to annoy a DORLA agent in such times.

And still, nothing. No confessions, no good evidence, no end in sight. And somewhere on the sidelines there's me, doing unaccountable things. I brought in the free-rangers, after all.


A day passes with not much exchange. Paul lies on his back in the straw, his hand over his eyes. He doesn't say anything, and it becomes clear, after a while, that he's suffering from a migraine. Everyone stops their desultory conversation about the food they've been given – which Steven was putting the odd comment into – and tries to stay still; they pass him some of their straw, which he doesn't seem to have the energy to arrange; Carla makes him drape Albin's jacket over his eyes, to shut out the light. I watch this for half an hour, biting my thumbnail, pulled this way and that. In the end, I get up, go to a store cupboard, go into their cellblock, stepping as softly as I can.

They look at me without a word.

'This is the best we can do,' I say. 'First-aid kit. There's a couple of painkilling things in there, I don't know how they'd work.' I push it through the bars of Carla's cell. 'I've counted what's in there. If I find there's more missing than should be . . .' I need a threat, but I can't threaten to send in interrogators, to with-hold food, to play white noise to keep them awake at nights. I could, but I can't bear to. 'Then I'll report myself to my boss for letting you misuse government-issue drugs, and they'll pull me out of here and you'll lose your last link.' I speak as quietly as I can. Paul lifts the edge of the jacket off his eyes, freezes for a moment as the light gets in and then lays it down again.

Carla looks at me, her face uncertain.

'Thank you.' It's Albin speaking, his voice surprised but not without courtesy.

With a sudden wrench, Paul sits up. His face convulses as he does, he puts his hands on either side of his head as if to hold it together. 'I just want you to know,' he says, hoarse, 'that the last migraine I had, the one I had when you were there, that was after we knew someone had seen us in the garden. We didn't know it was you.' His head is sinking down, his hands clench in his hair, but his eyes, a little crossed, stay on me. 'The others thought I should stop seeing you. They thought I was endangering us. But I wouldn't. That's where that migraine came from, because they wanted me to leave you. And I wouldn't.'

His face is white against the tiles, and he sags down again, covering his eyes. He lies still.

'Well,' I say. My voice shakes a little. 'Now I know.'

I turn around and leave without saying anything else.


'Does anyone know you're here?' Albin asks Steven.

'No.' He doesn't move his head as he talks.

'Did they charge you with anything?'

He frowns at Albin. 'Charge me? They just pulled me in here.'

Paul lies with Albin's jacket folded under his head. His eyes are half open, his tentative fingers are rubbing at his temples in precise, masseur's circles.

'That's pretty bad for you,' Albin says. He sits leaning against the wall, his neat legs trailing across the straw, one hand resting in his lap. It's an informal posture for him, asymmetrical. He looks at Steven with amiable concern. 'Hard to know what to tell them.'

431

'What'd they do to your face?' Steven hunches. He isn't facing Albin, he looks sideways to talk, his eyes on the scar Ellaway put onto Albin's face months ago.

Albin shrugs. 'Like I said, it's hard to know what to tell them.'

Steven frowns, rubs his fists together. He drops the conversation.


I don't watch when the interrogators go down. I take off the headphones and walk quietly back to my office.

Ally isn't among them.

That doesn't make it any better.


Afterwards, there's a kind of lull. They sit in their cages, separate, each concerned with their own bruises. I didn't watch, I couldn't, but now I stare, wide-eyed, trying to see the remnants of every blow. It doesn't look too bad, I tell myself, there's no permanent damage done. Hard questioning, with the occasional slap to remind them that they're helpless. Steven's nose is bleeding, he keeps touching it with the back of his hand, always surprised to find new blood there.

'Put your head back,' Carla says. 'Pinch the bridge of your nose.'

He looks at her, creases his face and then does as she says.

'No, the bridge. Higher up. No, not like that, like this, look.'

Steven studies her.

Carla sighs. 'No, further back.'

He cranes his head, his hand blocking his field of vision. Carla shakes her head, points, looking as if she's trying not to call him stupid.

I'm seeing what Steven sees. There really isn't a difference between how she does it and how he does.

Carla points one more time, then lowers her hand as if tired, gives him a brief, dead-eyed smile that wouldn't convince Leo.

It's the smile that does it, and her posture. Something in the way she lays her hands in her lap. I see suddenly, and with a slight sense of shock, that she's doing it on purpose.


The nights should be getting shorter, we're past the solstice, but on my pad of blankets, each night seems longer than the last.


'You know, you were talking in your sleep,' Albin tells Steven.

'Yeah?' Steven rubs his head, looks at Albin's worn, imperturbable face.

'Yeah, you were.' Paul is standing up, leaning against the bars, stretching one leg out behind him.

'What was I saying?'

There's a definite pause before Albin shrugs. 'Oh, nothing really.'

He doesn't say it convincingly.

I play the tapes over. Steven's a sound sleeper, he hasn't said a word.

*

433

'Do you think we might get out again if there's another power cut?' Albin asks Sarah.

She looks at him, dark-eyed. 'Yeah. And maybe it'll rain keys as well.'

'You got out in a power cut?' Steven says. He leans forward.

Albin shrugs. 'It was a while ago.' I have to hand it to him, he can sound nonchalant in a prison cell. 'Nothing major.'

Steven glances around. There's nothing for him to see. 'I reckon that's why they've got me here,' he says.

I raise my hands to the headphones, look at the switch-board, the camera, anything that might not be recording this. The green light is on, but I want to break the camera open to see if it's working.

'What, you got out in a power cut?' Albin looks only mildly interested.

'No, I mean, loitering. Being outside, yeah?'

'Well, yeah.' Albin shrugs again, unimpressed. 'That's mostly what they lock people up for.'

'Yeah, but I mean, I was really – out, you know?'

'Everyone who's out is out, kiddo.' Sarah glares at him. She's been huddled in a corner for the last hour, her eyes are still wet. Her voice is too high. 'You think it's something special?'

Steven glares back at her, turns to Albin. 'How much have you been out?'

'Oh, I don't know. Can't really remember when we started.'

'You been doing it for years, then?'

'How come you work in a hospital?' Albin says.

'What?'

'How come you work in a hospital?'

434

Steven rubs his hands together. 'I don't know. Tried to train as a nurse, once.'

'Oh, I wouldn't do that.' Carla's voice is soft, musical. The edge to it is narrow as a scalpel.

'What? Why not?'

Carla shrugs, smiles. She tries to toss her hair out of her eyes, manages quite well despite her sprained neck. 'Well, you wouldn't be very good at it, would you?'

Steven sits back, stares at her, too startled even to scowl.

'Well, I saw the floors after you'd cleaned them,' Carla sighs, as if he'd asked. 'And the way you crashed around the beds, disturbing the patients, it wasn't very good. I don't think you had what it took.'

'What the – what the fuck do you know about it?' Steven manages. This pretty, well-spoken woman has decided to insult him for no reason. I'd be upset too.

Carla shrugs, gesticulates, her hand waving through the air like a dancer's. His back turned to Steven, Albin leans forward, watching. Carla smiles, her white little teeth glittering, her eyes crossed like a cat's, her head at a dizzy angle. I can see her hand, tangling straw behind her back, but Steven just sees a smiling mask, and the wheeling, drunken pitch of her voice could be mistaken for carelessness. 'Come along. You don't think no one saw you take them, do you?'

'What the – what are –' Steven gets to his feet, goes up to the edge of his cell, but there are bars and then space, Paul's cell is between them, and he can't loom over her so far away. Paul sits cross-legged underneath them, one fist resting against the other.

'I didn't say anything,' Carla says. 'I felt sorry for you. I didn't think you'd get another job if people caught

435

you stealing drugs. I don't know though, I think I should have told. Now I've got to know you a little. I think I should tell them, when I get out.'

'I'd talk to a lawyer when you get out.' Paul doesn't move, doesn't look up when he speaks. 'See if you can justify it to him. If you ever get out. You'll never get a lawyer in here. You could be here for years.'

'Why did you take them?' Albin picks up the rhythm, it goes from one to another like a game of catch. 'Couldn't you handle the furring up?'

'You should be able to, you should handle it.' Sarah's rocking in a corner, talking more to herself than to Steven. 'You think it's worth it, running around outside, you think you're worth it? You don't get any of it, you're not worth it, you're just too stupid to think of anything else.' The others look at her as she starts to cry. 'You could have left people out of it, you could have just kept to yourself and not dragged people down with you but we're all in here and we'll never get out and you're going to die down here, you're going to be here for the rest of your life and they'll kill you in the end and throw you out of the window . . .' Her voice rises and rises; she faces him in a crouch, her hands clawing her knees, and she stares at him like he was a locked door. She should be in a hospital. She's come loose. 'You wait here long enough and you'll see if it's worth it,' she cries, and then she wraps her arms around herself and starts chanting in a whisper. 'You wait for them and they'll cut you with a silver knife and leave you to rot on the floor, they'll cut your eyelids off and wait for you to go blind, they'll break your fingers and give you a key you can't turn in the lock . . .'

As Steven stares at her, it happens, so quickly I don't

436

see till it's too late. Paul's hand comes through the partition, grabs Steven's leg and yanks it from under him so he falls. He falls forwards, his face knocks against the steel bars and he falls backwards, his head cracks the floor as he lands. Paul's face is still the same, it's intent and pale but there's nothing alien in the features as he says, 'You could end up like your brother.'

And just like that, they stop. Sarah huddles into herself and weeps silently, and the others turn their faces to the wall, lie down as if to sleep, and they don't say another word.

# 35

There's a bar looping out from the wall, and that's where they chain him. Two guards bring him up from below, cuff one of his hands to the wall and leave him standing there. His hand is tethered too low down and he has to stoop, bent over to one side.

'You needn't stay.' I sit on the only chair. There's a desk in front of me, not a solid wooden block with drawers and status, just four legs and a Formica surface like something out of a schoolroom. It doesn't hide any of me.

'We're just down the hall if you need anything,' one of them says.

'That won't be necessary.'

He gives me a suspicious look, wondering whether to be amused. Chain her ex-boyfriend to the wall and lock the door behind her. There's another fillip my reputation can do without.

'This won't be an interrogation,' I say, and I succeed in sounding sharp. 'You can escort him back when I call you, but until then, you needn't waste your time unless you have nothing better to do. Do you have anything better to do?' I don't sound defensive, I sound biting. I hear in my voice that I outrank them both.

'Yes, Miss Galley,' he says. He isn't happy, but he's not obliging me unhappily, he's obeying me unhappily. There's a difference.

They go out and close the door. It's only when I hear it click that I look at Paul.

He looks tired. Pulled down by his chained hand, he's clumsy and off-balance, as if he'd been knocked into that position. His gaze flickers over me, watchful. An inmate's look.

'Well.' I sit still in my chair. 'You're quite an interrogator.'

Metal clinks against metal as he tries to stand straighter. 'Will you take these off?'

'I don't have the keys.'

'You could get them.' His eyes are bloodshot, the blue I loved so much enmeshed in red filaments.

'Someone else would have to stay in the room. I'm not rated to handle prisoners solo. I want to talk to you.'

Paul jerks his arm. Metal digs into his wrist. 'Have you got me where you want me now?'

'No.'

'Why not? I can't run now, you always know where I'll be. I can't even stand up straight unless you let me. Doesn't that make you feel better?'

'No.'

'I wasn't going anywhere, you know. You could have trusted me.'

'I did.'

'Yeah, up until the moment they arrested me for knocking on a friend's door.'

'I've just seen you and your friends work over a man you've got nothing against. You don't know anything

439

about him except that I think he's guilty of something. And you knocked him to the ground. I heard what you were saying to him, and there are words for that. It's called psychological torture. Or bullying, if you want to speak social-worker. So don't tell me that when push comes to shove you won't fight for yourself tooth and nail like everyone else.'

'I never did. You always say you expect people to fight it out, then act betrayed when they do. I never said anything. If he did it and I didn't, I'm not going down for him.' He's right. It's normal to fight for your life and rip apart anything that gets in your way. It's only trees that live off air and sunlight; we have to kill every time we want to eat. Animal or vegetable, we live off each others' flesh. I think this every day. I ought to be used to it by now.

I don't move. 'I guess I thought you were a nicer person than me.'

'Well, I'm not.' He covers his cuffed wrist with his free hand, his arm covering him.

'I can't get you released, not yet.' Because he was wondering, he was worried that he might be destroying his chances, that if he said the right thing I might let him go. I should put him out of that misery, at least.

'You could if you wanted.'

'We can help each other.'

Paul leans his head back, stares at the ceiling. 'Fuck you,' he says. 'Thanks a lot.'

It hurts, badly, but it isn't the end, he still cares enough to curse me. 'You've got the makings of an interrogator, you know, Paul. You're good at knowing how people work. You're just used to using it to be nice. But we need information out of that man, or more of us are going to die, and I think you might be able to get it.'

He shakes his head a little, mutters something.

'If he confesses, you go free. They can't hold you any more.'

'You can't.' He stares at me. 'You'd really keep me here to do your dirty work for you, wouldn't you?'

My hands twitch, and I press them between my knees. 'I would.' It's raining outside. Water clatters against the window. 'I'm not asking you to do anything I wouldn't do myself.'

'Then you're a bitch.'

The word from Paul is a slap, but I can't be weak. 'If you like. I've spoken to my boss. He agreed with me, after I showed him the tape. They're not going to interrogate you again.'

'What?' Paul's head comes up with a jolt.

'I've called off the dogs. No more question sessions, no more beatings. And I was able to do that because of what you did to Harper. My boss agreed with me. He thinks you should be left alone. If you keep trying to get things out of him.'

Paul blinks. I hear him inhale and his breath is shaky. He's too smart not to know what this is, an exchange, a sell-your-soul deal. Take on the job of the torturers, do it to others and they'll leave you alone. Be a devil instead of a damned soul. But I've just told him no one's going to beat him any more, that he can sleep at nights knowing no one will come in and wake him and bang his head against the wall. After everything he's been through, he's going to be left alone.

He turns his head away. He doesn't want me to see

441

tears in his eyes. It's a measure of how much I've lost him.

I wanted something normal. It's out of my reach now, and all I can get is something crooked and dark, and finite. Once he's out of here, he won't accept these terms any more. What I make him do to get him out will drive him away from me as soon as he steps out the door. I should give him up now, get used to being without him.

I cross the room, lay my hand against his face to turn it towards me. 'Hey – hey,' I whisper. His skin is pitted and fragile from too long without sunlight. He leans back against the wall, raises a hand to push me away, and I catch it, hold on.

'Stop it.' His eyes are closed, he won't look at me, but we're pressed together and he doesn't struggle. He's had too many moments of sleep on bare tiles and hard-fisted interrogators and cold, floodlit nights, he's too weakened to turn away comfort.

'It's okay.' I stroke my thumb across his face, wiping away the tear.

'What have you done?' he says into my hair.

'I'm sorry.' My eyes close, I lean against him, he's gaunt and filthy and familiar. Our clasped hands fall to our sides and hang there, a pendulum pulling us down.

I raise my mouth to his, and he flinches. 'No.' His head turns aside. 'Not that easy.'

'How easy do you want it to be?' We're so close, less than an inch away from a kiss.

He untangles his hand from mine and takes my shoulder, holds me away. 'I don't want to kiss you.'

'Don't you?' His hand is warm through my shirt. He could always hold back when I couldn't. It was one of

442

many advantages he had over me. The handcuffs chink against the bar.

He pushes me back further. 'Not like this.'

I open my mouth to say, you didn't used to be conservative, but I stop myself. This isn't a game. I'm asking him to destroy a man, and if he doesn't want to seal the bargain with a kiss, we'll have to find some other way. I turn around, walk quietly to my desk, sit down.

'If you want to get anything out of this man, you'll have to know what you're looking for.' My voice has calmed. 'If I give you the information, it'll help you, you and the others.'

Paul leans against the wall, trying to get his breath. I'm steadier than him. 'You can't bring them up here,' he says. It sounds almost like a plea.

'No, you'll have to pass it on to them. He'll be there too, but you can get round it. I've seen his records, he didn't get much schooling when he was a kid. If you tell the others in, I don't know, French, German, some other language, he won't be able to understand you.' I don't say it would match perfectly well with the way they've been treating him. 'You do speak some other language, don't you?'

He doesn't look at me. 'Spanish. A little Albanian and Turkish, too, but the others don't speak those. Or Croatian. I know some Croatian, Lewis knows some Russian, I might be able to get something across.'

'I'm sure Spanish will do.'

'Yeah.' He stands awkwardly, his manacled hand holding him down.

'Okay.' The sound of my voice makes him shift a little, but there's no good position he can stand in. 'Cheer

443

up,' I say. 'You're gonna get to hear all the stuff I never told you.'

He doesn't respond, and I lay my hands on the table. There's a slight tremor in them, a seasickness.

'You were arrested for the murder of Nate Jensen, weren't you?'

'Whoever that is.' It seems to cost him some effort to put it so mildly.

'It's complicated. This man, Steven Harper, he's a prowler. You know what a prowler is?'

He nods. His long back is hunched against the wall.

'Oh, for God's sake,' I mutter. 'I'll be right back.' I leave the room, leave the prisoner unguarded long enough to get another chair. He's turned away from the door when I return. 'Here.' I set the chair down beside the bar. It's only once I've done it that I notice I've taken hold of his shoulder and steered him down into it. His arm hangs out to the side, dangling from its cuff, but he sits better, upright. His eyes close for a moment, and I realise it's the first time since his arrest he's had a chair to sit on. The thought gets to me, and I turn and seat myself back at the desk before I weaken.

'This man, Steven Harper. He's one of three. There's him, and his brother, and there's a third man called Darryl Seligmann who's still out there. We –' I stop, rub my forehead. This isn't a procedure briefing, I can't tell it like this. 'Do you remember the night we met?'

Paul looks at me, doesn't answer.

'You remember I was drinking because something had happened. What happened was that me and my trainee, Marty, the boy in the hospital, got set on by a pack of three prowlers. Marty shot one of them in the leg before they ripped his throat open. I tranquillised

444

one and the other two got away. David Harper, the one Marty shot, he got away, and the third one, I think that was Steven, the one in your cells.'

'You think that?' Paul's voice is flat.

'I think so.'

'So the man who lost his arm, that was because your boy shot him.'

'And because he wouldn't go to a hospital.' I don't look away. If I apologise, everything's lost. 'The one we caught was Seligmann. We interrogated him, but all we got was threats and curses. Don't shrug. There was something – wrong about that man.'

'You interrogated him.' Paul looks at his dangling arm.

'Yes. The night we first went out, there was a bruise on my hand you noticed. I got it hitting him.'

Paul lowers his head, shuts his eyes tight.

'You didn't have a problem with it at the time. You asked me, I told you how I got it. You still went to bed with me the same night.'

'I wanted you.' He doesn't say it with spite, he doesn't emphasise the past tense. It's just resigned.

I take a breath. 'Would you feel the same way now? Now you've been through an interrogation, and a woman you wanted told you what I did, would you still sleep with her?'

He doesn't look at me, he looks into space, trying to find an answer.

I wait it out.

'Yes,' he says.

I look down a moment. We go after what we want and push aside whatever's in our way. 'It was my first and last serious interrogation. I was terrible at it, I was

445

more scared of him than he was of me. Later on, he injured himself so that we had to take him to hospital.'

Paul almost laughs. 'He injured himself.' He mouths the words, hardly speaks them.

'Believe me, if we'd injured him it wouldn't have been an injury that meant taking him out of the building.'

He looks at me and I flatten my hands on the table. 'Do I know you at all?' he says.

I stop myself from rubbing my eyes. 'You probably know me better than anyone.'

There's almost a look of wonder on his face. 'I'm glad I'm not you.'

There are too many answers to that, and all of them stray from the point. 'He went to hospital, and they didn't guard him properly, and he just got up and walked out of there. And not long after that, the boy I interrogated him with, the boy who did a much more thorough job than me, was shot in the head when he was walking home. That's who Nate Jensen was.'

He keeps looking at me.

'Two months before that, another man was killed in the same way. Johnny Marcos, the man your friend Ellaway mauled.'

'He's not my friend,' Paul says. 'I bloody hate him.'

We have to keep moving forward. If we stop, we won't start again. 'They were both shot with silver bullets.'

'Why?' Paul frowns. He isn't looking away now, he's paying attention.

'I don't know. Symbolism, maybe. Seligmann really hates DORLA. Now, you were arrested partly because of Ellaway and partly because of the Oromorph, but there were only three on that night. We have two. Seligmann's

446

missing, and we need to find him before someone else gets hurt. Steven probably knows where he is.'

'That's what you want me to find out? Where this Seligmann is?'

I look back at him. 'You're going to do it, aren't you?'

There's only a second's pause, but in that time we both know what's happened. Later, perhaps, when we're free, we'll blame each other, we'll throw accusations or say them silently. But neither of us can claim innocence, ever again.


Down in the cells, the guards lock him in. They check him over, his friends, looking to see what was done to him, and there's nothing to see, no bruises or cuts, he's still wearing the same worn clothes, and no one speaks till the guards leave. They've become very quiet in the presence of DORLA workers, playing invisible by going still, like birds hiding from a hawk overhead.

The door closes and leaves them alone, and they start moving again, press towards him as best they can. There's a tangle of 'What happened?' and 'Are you all right?' and 'What's going on?'; as they hear their voices clash, they all subside at once. Paul sits against the wall, looking straight ahead.

'Who did you see?' Albin asks.

Paul doesn't turn his head. 'Lola.'

'Did she say anything about representing us?'

He starts to speak, then gives it up as if tired. A few seconds pass as he stares into space before he finally speaks. 'Nada.' He says it slowly.

Albin frowns. Steven is hunched in a corner, his arms

folded across his chest. He watches, his face blank with wariness.

Paul looks down, looks back up again. He hasn't glanced at the others once since he came back down. His eyes crease at the corners and he chews his lip.

I thought he'd tell them, I'd expected conversation in a language I couldn't follow. It would have riled Steven, made him aggressive or brought his defences up, he'd have known he was being plotted against. I was expecting a scene.

Paul rests his head against the wall, gazing at nothing. Then he starts to sing. The others shift and look at each other for explanations for a couple of bars, and then they go still. It isn't a tune he sings, it's sentences that run on from note to note, rhythmical and simple. I listened to enough of his music to know what he's doing: it's an improvised recitative. He doesn't have an operatic voice, and it rings glassy off the walls. There's nothing lupine about it, none of the soft, carrying wail you hear on moon nights, but something about it makes my skin prickle, makes hackles rise on my neck as much as they ever did in response to a lune's call.

# 36

I've been lying. If I ever said 'they' about the Inquisitors, I was lying. The word I needed was 'we'. Because we were part of it, my people, my whole kind was part of it, down to the last man. We change our names, we change our methods, but this is my history. Four hundred years ago, I would have been a hooded Inquisitor, and I can think of nothing at all that excuses me now.

It's quiet in the church. I wanted it to smell of incense, but that's the smell of Mass, and there's nothing here but someone sweeping, a couple of people looking at the ceiling, a middle-aged woman on her knees in the Lady chapel. My soft running shoes squeak against the tiles. I've never found a church where I could walk soundlessly. The Aegidan shrine is where I remembered it, just a little place set into the wall, small enough to fit perhaps three people at a time. I stand in front of the icon. An ageing man, a hind held in his arms. God sent a hind to nourish him with its milk, that's how poor Giles was. His face is smooth, tranquil, a soft beard trails down his chest, his eyes don't look out of the picture but off into the distance.

My hands clench and unclench, and I shift my feet. I hadn't thought about what to do when I got here, and now I'm standing before the shrine, mostly what I feel is a sense of discomfort, as of a badly faked performance.

It would be comfortable to sit down, but there are no chairs nearby. I hesitate at the opening for a moment, then step inside and kneel down. There are cushions provided, an act of kindness, and I kneel on one, hands together, looking at the painting. It's a familiar pose, from a long time ago, and though I'm out of practice and feel uncertain at taking up such a posture, faith doesn't go away, not altogether. I'm afraid God will strike me down for trespassing in his house when I don't properly believe. It's faith of a sort.

Is this what you would have wanted, I say. Giles was a mortal man once, a hermit who lived in the woods, he had a cave for meditation and such was his devotion that what he wanted most was to be left alone to pray. A hunting party shot him by accident, and the king visited him as the arrow wound healed, but Giles wanted to be left alone. A sage, a miracle worker, later on an abbot of a monastery the king built because he admired Giles so. A true holy man.

The thought of the real Giles strengthens me somehow. I've always believed in an angry God, but perhaps the gentle Giles, if I'd met him, might have had a kind word for me. It's better, it has to be, that there are good people in the world. I wish I was one of them.

Is this what you would have wanted? I don't think it can be so. A renunciate who wanted to be away from the world with his prayers couldn't have felt much enthusiasm at the thought of a vast network of cripples taking criminals and ordinary citizens by the heels, of prisons and interrogations and acres and acres of paperwork obscuring what we do. All the forests you loved cut down for us to tell lies on.

Do you love us, Giles? We could have prayed to another saint, a saint of guards or justice, but we have you, saint of cripples. Because of our disability. The answer that my mind makes is that he must. Saints love mankind. Not because we're good, but because they are, because saints love sinners with a boundless compassion. That's what a saint is. It's an apologist answer, the kind of answer I found glib when the nuns said such things, but it feels true as well. My mind finds the answer without thinking, reflexively, and I can't think of an alternative.

Then what are we to do? Because what I know about Aegidans, I didn't learn from the nuns. The *Summis Desidrantes Affectibus*, the Witch Bull of 1484, was a decree by the Pope, Innocent VIII, declaring the existence of witches. Thousands died because of that Bull. We don't believe in witches any more.

It was faith that made us. We were a holy order, once. We found witches, and we fought for God's law on earth, and we tortured people to death. We're still the same race, the same people now, that were able to accept such a proposition. And we tried to save people, too, we didn't want killers laying waste around us, and that was real, unarguable, even to an atheist, and it's still around us. How can we be so corrupt, and still try to fight the wickedness of the world?

What am I to do, Giles? Am I dragging souls down

451

with me? When I put Steven in with the others, I had a sense of what they'd do, do for me and spare me having to do to him myself. By all laws, that's damnable. We have to catch Seligmann before he kills anyone else, but I don't believe that excuses tormenting another man to do it. Steven certainly won't forgive us. I'm making people commit sins they wouldn't otherwise have committed. I've read of martyrs who wouldn't plead guilty or not guilty at their trials, who stopped the trials from going on by their silence, knowing what the penalty was: pressing. They let themselves be crushed to death with weights, sometimes for days at a time, rather than involve a jury in the sin of their execution. That's holiness, that's what God intended us to be. What am I to do, Giles? There are too many people caught in this tangle I've created, and every direction takes us nearer the pit, and I can't see any way out. Look at them, the prisoners, ready to drag the answer out of Steven. Look at Seligmann, wherever he is, willing to hunt down God's children on moon night. Help me, Giles. We're all lost. We may yet have another Inquisition, but there's no second Crucifixion promised to redeem us from our sins. We have to choose, and I can't find a choice.

Do you love me, Giles, I say. The saint gazes out of the painting, holding the deer to his breast.

# 37

They talk.

They talk about being outside, they talk of planning free-range nights and avoiding being caught, making a little war between themselves and DORLA. There are war stories they swap, furring up with injuries, fights with other groups, escaping catchers; the stories don't sound true to me, because they're too simple, they make life sound easy, but Steven listens to them. He listens, and sometimes he opens his mouth as if he wanted to join in. They don't let him, they keep talking right over him, spinning tales about their dangerous lives.

They talk about the hospital, about things that happen there, all the violent cases Carla has handled, the addicts who wander in trying to steal the drugs, about how much easier it is to steal things if you're higher up the ranks.

They wake Steven up during the night when he was sleeping quietly and ask him, 'What did you say?'


We did a lot of things to people in the old days. We studied it, how to get around religious precedent, figuring out ways to get confessions without violating the laws of God. Inquisitors laboured under the rule that you couldn't torture anyone more than once. We solved that: any cessation of torture was a 'suspension', and if you torture him again, it's just continuing the first, the only session. You weren't allowed to shed blood: we found things to do that didn't. There were always threats, too, and they worked. Enough people confessed on the rack before anyone started turning the wheel. It wasn't even cowardice. They knew what the rack did, how it pulled each bone slowly from its socket, so that every other torment, hanging and dropping and crushing, was considered a lenient preliminary, and they knew they'd be torn to pieces unless they confessed.

I read about that when I was sixteen, young enough to take fright at such stories. It was in a book written for lycos; it wasn't about us, the Aegidans only got a chapter. The author said that torture was a form of oppression that oppressed not just the victim but the general populace as well: if you know what can be done to you, you always go in fear. It's true, it's fair, people are afraid of us. But we're afraid of them, too.

I don't know what they're planning. I don't know what Paul said to them.

I wish I spoke Spanish.


When we couldn't use torture – the laws of some lands forbade it altogether – we found other ways round it. Walking was a common one. You take hold of a person and march him up and down, up and down, up and down, up and down, hour after hour after day. You do it in shifts, round the clock, no sleep, no rest. It sounds gentler than the rack, but it works. Very few people withstood it. It wasn't dramatic, but I imagined it with a sixteen-year-old's intensity, still young enough to take everything personally, and when I thought about it, it was horrific. The body isn't meant to do certain things. If you force it, it fights them. I found that out years ago. The pain isn't the worst of it, the worst is the damage, the *wrongness* of what's happening to you, and every drop and fibre of you screams, no, no, not this, until there's nothing else in the world. Days walking, *days*. The flesh on my feet ached at the very thought.

Sarah looks white, bleached. Dark patches are growing around Carla's eyes. They sleep when they can; they wake each other up. Always, Steven is awake. They tell him he's talking in his sleep, they shout at him to stop it. When he's awake, they talk to him pleasantly: Carla, skin peeling around her mouth, chats about the hospital as if she were on a tea-break, and when he sleeps, they reach through the bars and tug at him, shouting at him to stop talking.

After two days, he starts to mutter as soon as his eyes close.

The easiest, the best of all our tricks and tortures was the *tormentum insomniae*. We just kept the suspect awake until he confessed. Symptoms of sleep deprivation include: disorientation, nausea, memory loss, slurred speech, dizziness, hallucinations. That's the medical list. It doesn't mention the emotions, though you can list those too: confusion, helplessness, panic. You can't describe it, can't imagine it if you haven't seen it done, and even then, it's hard to take in, how much cruelty there is in such a simple action. The truth is, after a terrifyingly short period of time, without sleep your very soul starts to disintegrate.

Witch-burners used it, and so did we. It was the peg on which the whole bloodbath turned. The clean, easy method that led innocent men and women to confess a pact with Satan. The Inquisitors discovered it, but we used it too, often enough, because that's what we were, back then, specialists, yes, but still witch-burners. We just found witches in one particular field. Even if they hadn't killed anyone, back then, we pressed hard for evidence of commerce with the devil. I think, I'm certain, we really believed it might be so. We'd seen lunes, after all, and if the devil wanted to talk to a man, moon night was the time. Much easier than to believe he'd deal with a daylight, speaking, soft-skinned human being. We certainly refused to consider that maybe, amidst all the fetters and racks and textbooks of interrogation, he was whispering in our ears all along.

He must have been, though. It was never about luning. How else could it be, when five ordinary people – a little wealthier than most, a little better educated and better spoken, but normal children of God, born healthy and raised in civilisation – can, by themselves, with no guidance or prompting, discover and use the mainstay of the Inquisition?


They let Steven catch a few minutes' sleep. All of them sit with their backs against the wall, covering their eyes. Paul's head hangs down between his knees, his legs are folded up and he slumps like a dropped puppet. They don't say anything to each other.

Steven turns his head, mumbles something. Paul looks up, lets a hand fall off his knee. He reaches out for Steven, and as he does, Albin says, 'Wait.'

Paul looks at him, expressionless.

Albin's voice is dry, hoarse. 'See what he says.'

And Steven speaks.

At first, it isn't words. He speaks in phrases, sentences, there's pause and emphasis as though he was talking sense, but it's just sounds, the syllables are right but they don't link up; it's like listening to a foreign language.

Paul blinks, his eyes close, his eyes open, and he reaches for Steven again. As he does, Steven turns a little and says, 'Darryl, where've you been?'

Paul's hand stops.

'Why won't he help? He's a doctor.'

'No, no, not a work-related dream after all this time,' Sarah whispers, hands to her eyes like a child.

'Parkinson should know I'm here.' He sounds like he's arguing.

If it wasn't for the creches I'd think he was faking, the calm, reasonable voice, hardly slurred, almost like he was talking awake, but I heard a lot of sleep-talk for eighteen years, and that's how it sounds.

Then I think – *Parkinson?*

Carla sits up. 'Parkinson? Did you hear that? Wake him up, wake him up.'

'Who's Parkinson?' Paul mumbles, reaching through the bars to shake Steven, and I think, Parkinson? The doctor at St Veronica's? The one that delivered Leo? The one I talked to – the one who was in the hospital the night – the night Seligmann . . . escaped.

457

Walking out of the hospital under the eye of security would have been next to impossible. I thought at the time they must have turned a blind eye because he was one of them and they didn't care for DORLA. It wouldn't have happened that way. DORLA or not, no security man worth his salt would let a charged criminal with a bitten wrist walk off. If someone in the hospital distracted them, if someone with authority created a window . . .

'Why didn't you say anything?' Carla is smiling, her voice is almost friendly. She's been keeping a man awake for almost four days. Whatever her motives, that smile is one of the bravest things I've ever seen.

Steven thrashes, kicks at Paul's hand, yelling to be let alone.

'No, no, listen, I'm trying to help you. Look, I can't get out of here yet, but I reckon I could get word to someone, only I didn't know who to ask. But if you know Dr Parkinson, well, I do too, a little, and he knows lots of people, I bet he could help if I got word to him.'

Parkinson was there. And he was visible, he talked to me, he got a good look at the team. Was he on the right floor for his department? I don't remember, but maybe it was more than chance that I met him. It's a big place, St Veronica's, a big place and a busy one. The odds of just bumping into someone are not high. If he heard someone from DORLA was coming, though, and made a point of being out in the major thoroughfares, keeping an eye on things, that would make it possible. A man brought in from DORLA with a bitten wrist wouldn't be his department, but doctors and nurses and patients talk. It would be all around the hospital within minutes. Parkinson would have known Seligmann was there. I struggle to explain further, but that's it, my brain blurs, I need sleep, I'll never get through this without some more sleep.

'Just leave me alone,' Steven says, his voice drunk with fatigue.

'Don't you know Parkinson? I'm sure I could get word to him,' Carla says, cracked lips stretched into a smile.

Steven stares at her, and he can't make her out, he's sick and confused and tired to death. 'He – prolly know I'm – he wouldn't –' He pushes at the air, as if shoving away a ghost, and collapses back into the straw.

'Won't you let me help you?' Carla's eyes are glazed like a doll's.

All right, I say, it's enough. I've got a name, it makes no sense he'd be involved but I've got a name, you can leave him alone. I say this in my head, desperate, I mean it so hard there's a moment of surprise that she keeps talking to him before I realise she didn't hear me.

I pull myself to my feet, swaying. I've had more sleep than them, and even so, I'm tired enough to sit down and cry. I don't, though. I press my hand to my throat, and walk out, up the narrow stairs, my hand still resting there. It's a minute before I recognise the gesture: an old one, from when I first started to work here. There used to be a pendant there, a medal of St Giles I was given at school. It got taken off and thrown away when I was twenty-two, but all of a sudden, I want it back.

I make it all the way up the stairs, into the Containment department. Nobody's much surprised when I go in and give orders.

Steven is separated from the others, put in a cell by himself, monitored. The rest of them go upstairs to A Block, are given mattresses, blankets, pillows. I don't wait around to watch it happen. I will not take the credit for that gift.

# 38

There's only one way to do this.

What I want is to talk to this doctor. No, what I really want is to go back to church and pray for forgiveness, spend days on my knees and beg the saints to intercede for my ruined soul. That's what I'd like to do, but as long as I have unfinished business, then nothing's going to help my soul very much. Any sensible saint would tell me to sort out my good works first and save the introspection for a better moment.

I need to talk to him, and I can't think of any other way.

I don't want to do this.

The idea, my only idea, takes hold of me early on, and it shakes me so badly I get stupid; all other ideas clot in my brain. I spend a day looking out of my window, walking up and down, a tight, sick knot under my ribs, and every time I think of it the knot twists, and fat white grubs squirm in my throat. I know I can do it if I have to, and that's worse, though what I'm feeling, for once, isn't really about guilt. My conscience hurts at the idea, but I've done terrible things before now, and this one won't hurt anyone but me. Me and my daughter up in Heaven.

If she's in Heaven, she's beyond my reach, I can't hurt her.

I don't want to do this.

The first thing to do is ask Hugo to help me get the free-rangers released. I tell him the story, tell him what I need.

'The story won't work from inside DORLA,' I say. My hands are folded, my face is still. I meet his eyes, gaze to expressionless gaze. He was right all along. If you stay dead on the surface, you don't get pitied, you don't get pried into, nobody presumes on you with their judgements. A blank face gives you privacy.

'Everyone will know that they were here.' His voice is as calm as mine, and for the first time I understand it, this quiet, neutral gentleness of his. 'They won't be able to explain it away, such a long absence.'

'They won't have to. We met in here, there's no need to hide that. If they're back in the world, it doesn't look like duress. If they're in here, it does.'

He looks at me without aggression. 'What do you hope to achieve by this?'

I don't make a speech. 'I don't know. I'd like to try it.'

'And you're certain these individuals – they won't be released unconditionally, you understand, they'll be charged with loitering and bailed – you're certain that they have no involvement in the killings?' He says the word 'killings' with no inflection, and neither of us flinches.

'Yes,' I say, 'I'm sure.'

*

I'd like it if they could just be released without cere-
mony, without my having to see them. It isn't possible.
I commandeer an interview room and call up the only
ones I need, Carla and Paul. Though really I just need
Carla. At the thought of what I'm going to do, my
mouth turns sticky and the knot tightens inside my chest,
but it'll have to be done, I must get used to telling this
story.

They look better. They've been tidied up, given clean
clothes, though just the grey tracksuits we keep to hand
out on Day One mornings to the lycos who wake up
naked, and they look unfamiliar. They look a little
shrunken, but better than they did.

Paul sits in his chair. He looks at me and says nothing.

Carla breathes lightly, holds herself together. 'We were
told our release was conditional, we had to do something for you.'

I keep the face I learned from Hugo. 'That's not quite
right. You'll be released in any case, but there's a course
of action I need to take that may go a long way towards
proving your innocence. If you help me with it, you'll
be helping yourselves.'

They are both innocent, and it's not much of an
inducement, but neither of them says anything. They've
been in the cells long enough to learn not to make
provocative remarks.

'Obviously you could argue your innocence in court,
but the best thing for you is if the real culprit is caught.
I – we have a suspect, and you can help me gain access
to him.'

'Parkinson?' says Carla. 'Why suspect him?'

'Do you know him?' I ask.

'Professionally. We work in the same hospital, that's

all.' She stops talking, waits for me to answer her question.

'I think there had to be someone in the hospital who helped our suspect to escape.'

She doesn't ask why I think it's Parkinson.

I keep my face still. 'I need you to refer me to him as a patient.'

'Why?'

'I can't arrest him without evidence. I'd like to be around him a little.'

Paul hasn't taken his eyes off my face.

Carla looks down at her hands. 'He does gynaecology and obstetrics. Why would I refer you?'

'You say we got talking while you were here, I asked you about something outside your area.'

'What?'

I draw a quiet breath. The air is cool in my throat. 'I told you I was having trouble conceiving and I was worried about it.' Paul flinches; his face jerks with a convulsive half-laugh.

'You'd see a fertility specialist about that, it's not his field.' Carla's lips barely move.

'Tell him I was worried about my past. You say I had a miscarriage a few years ago, and was worried it might have caused permanent damage.'

'He'd check your records, they'd show it wasn't true.'

I don't look away from her worn, chapped face. 'It is true. The records would show it.' I see Paul flicker in the corner of my vision. I don't move my head.

Carla's face pinches at the eyes for a moment, then she folds her hands. 'How long ago?'

'Six years.' I don't have to do the maths.

'When you were how old?' The look on her face is familiar – the impersonal autopilot professionalism that takes over when you've had too little rest and too many surprises.

'Twenty-two.' Paul keeps looking at me. I should be able to read his face, but it's still, mute. 'After it happened they checked my family records, and there's a history of miscarriage.' When we were young, we didn't know our mother miscarried twice before we were born. It only came out after what happened to me. Becca felt sorry for her when she heard the news; after she told me that, we stopped speaking for months. She said she could be sorry for two people, but I didn't believe her, not then. I'm sorry, now, about Becca, but only about Becca. There were lots of things I didn't forgive my mother for. Not warning me is the one I can't let go.

Carla's hands twist. 'I – I don't know if I can give him enough reasons.'

'He treated my sister, that's a start. You know more about medicine than I do. Make something up.'

'Was it Ally?'

Paul's voice is hoarse, quiet. It takes a moment to recognise it. 'What?'

He doesn't answer.

'You mean was Ally the father?' My throat is pressing tighter and tighter, it's difficult to swallow. 'No. He – we trained together, we trained on dogs. His name was Robert. He's gone to another city now.'

There are lines around Paul's eyes. When I first knew him, when things were good, they were just little traces, tiny tracks in his skin, but now they're deep, sharp. 'Were you planning an abortion?'

I stretch my hands, stare at them, keep myself still. 'No. I wasn't. I was going to keep her.'

'Her?'

My fingers bend back as I stretch them out. Little patches of white bloom at the tips of the nails. 'They did an ultrasound. She was a girl.' No one says anything. 'I was going to call her Ann.'

He stares at me, creasing his face against the light from my window. 'Why would you have kept a baby?'

'She was mine.' I can't explain it, not here, not any more, I don't know what to say. Of course he'd suppose I was planning an abortion. That's what he'd think of me. I thought of it myself, I sat down and looked at the blue strip and read my bank statement and looked around my tiny flat, and knew what would make sense. I hadn't counted on feeling anything. But I had scars running up and down my limbs, and I knew what it was like to be torn at. I thought of a suction pump, tearing at my skin, dragging me mangled out into the light, pulpy with blood, and I knew I couldn't do that to her. And I had a leaflet, a green-printed pamphlet from the chemist's, talking about giving up smoking and taking exercise and eating balanced meals. What I understood then was that she needed me healthy. Whatever happened to me happened to her. Ann was the only person in the world, ever, who was utterly on my side. 'Let's say I went bitter after the miscarriage,' I say aloud. 'Let's say it turned me sour.'

'Did you?' he says.

'I asked you about luning and you couldn't explain it,' I say. 'Don't ask me to explain this. Let's say this is the thing I can't explain.' I worried about luning, I asked him questions he didn't dare answer. Now he knows:

466

he's not the only one with an ugly secret. It's a gift, of sorts, it's the best I can give him.

'Were you going to get married?'

I shake my head. 'No, no. I told him I was pregnant, and I told him to leave. I didn't want him around.' He just looks at me, wordless. I close my eyes for a moment, screen myself behind the lids. 'It was a long time ago. I told him to leave because we'd been going out for some time but he hadn't been a very good boyfriend. All right? He was fond of making clear what I couldn't expect from him. Big on boundaries. There are lots of boys like that around. I could take it when it was just me because I thought I was in love with him, but I couldn't deal with that and a baby as well. I was better off on my own. I don't think I would have –' I stop, the words hitch in my throat. What I was going to say was, I would have left him sooner if the sex was better. I would have been better able to think straight. As it was, he kept me compliant with little more than sheer, desperate frustration. We don't discuss this, but bareback men are not good lovers. Any man whose first experiences are furtive scuffles in a locked creche, never knowing when the girl may change her mind and put a knee in his groin, is liable to have difficulties. I was too young. I was still trying to stick with my own kind, then. It was before Paul, before I really understood what I was missing. If it hadn't been for Ann, Robert might still be in the same city.

Paul stares into his lap, shakes his head. He's bewildered, lost for things to say.

Carla sits up straighter. 'Can you tell me the circumstances of the miscarriage?'

My jaw aches, my teeth are too hot. I must get used

to telling this story. 'I got knocked over on a moon night.'

'You went out?' she says.

'I hadn't told many people. It was the fourth month. I didn't know there was a tendency to miscarry in my family.' She stares at me, and I press my hands down on the table. 'I hadn't talked to any older women about it, and I was twenty-two. I was broke; catchers get bonuses. I thought I could just operate the van. But someone came at us unexpectedly. I got mauled. This lune got me down and worried at me, dug a piece out of my hip.' The scar is still there, a deep hollow in the flesh. Paul asked me about it once, and I wouldn't discuss it. 'It wouldn't have been fatal. I just lost a certain amount of blood. They patched me up at the shelter, told me to go to A and E next day if I wanted it checked. I didn't start bleeding till early the next morning.'

My throat closes. I can't say any more.


I remember lying in the hospital, staring at the ceiling, the plaster rose around the light fitting. That was when I started the twitch. My eyelid jerked and crawled like a hooked worm. I stood up and stared in the mirror till it stopped. When the nurse came in she almost dropped her tray at the sight of me on my feet. I almost remember the pain.

Becca sat by me for a while, but I wouldn't talk to anyone.

The doctors told me to come in for after-care check-ups. I didn't go. I haven't been to a gynaecologist in six years.

Most days I can look at six-year-olds and feel okay. I'd like to say some of this to Paul, but I can't talk. Carla agrees to refer me. It's unlikely, she says, that Parkinson will insist on seeing my husband or partner; he'd refer me on after a single appointment. She says this without either of us looking at Paul or asking him anything.

# 39

Carla calls me a couple of days later and tells me she's got me a private appointment with Parkinson. His fees are considerable, but I can get DORLA to pay them. She says she told him various medical details, that I shouldn't explain much when I go. I just turn up, talk about conception, don't try to justify myself. She's done all the work. Her voice is neutral, she doesn't betray herself. I wish we could have been friends.

I don't hear from the others. They go out back into the world, probably start piecing their lives back together, see doctors, psychiatrists, friends. Someone. Paul doesn't say goodbye.

In the days before the appointment, I find a new church. It's large, Gothic, airy. Blue and red glass shines in its lead-framed windows. There are pamphlets, flower arrangements, charity boxes, dark wooden pews. I sit and look at the beautiful windows; I stand before the black metal racks and light pale ivory candles and drop my coin in the box. Sometimes I pray.

There's a shop at one corner, selling mostly postcards, crucifixes. When I was younger I used to wonder about such shops, money-changers in the temple, but I suppose the church needs maintenance. I turn the rack of crucifixes and find, at the back, some little medals of St Giles, round and inexpensive, nine-carat gold or pewter. I buy one, a small pewter disk, and hang it around my neck. It dangles below my collarbone, almost weightless. My reasons are mostly pagan, I'm sure; to give me courage, to bring me luck, to ward off the evil eye, perhaps. I don't think about it too hard. This cheap, undecorative jewel around my neck makes me feel a little better.

I'm there so long that the priest approaches and asks if he can help me: a man with thick white hair and bright blue eyes in a pink face, tall and bulky but light on his feet. He tells me his name is Father Dominic. It sounds an ominous name to me, but I suppose not everyone thinks of the Inquisition when they think of the Dominicans. He seats himself beside me, heavy and kindly on the bench, and I tell him I'm partially lapsed and haven't been to Mass for years, and he doesn't seem to mind. He asks me if I'd like Confession, and I think about it for a while.

'I don't think I'm ready yet,' I say in the end. 'I might be ready a little later on. I don't know.'

'What will happen later on?' He says this amiably.

I interlock my hands. 'There are some things I have to do. Reparations.'

He studies me for a moment. The whites of his eyes are yellowing a little, but the centres are clear blue. 'I often think,' he says, 'it's unfortunate the way we divide ourselves. People from your walk of life come here quite often.' He gestures towards St Giles, pale and steady in his shrine. Then he smiles, showing square, slightly stained teeth. 'Though not always to Confession. They always seem more burdened than the rest of our congregation.'

For a moment tears rise in me and I fight them down. I can't afford them. A line of music comes into my head, Purcell. Paul played it to me one night. 'Art thou forlorn of God and com'st to me? What can I tell thee then but misery?' What do I expect this nice priest to tell me? Though I long for salvation more with every day that goes by. 'It's curious,' I say eventually. 'Most people who lose their faith say it's because bad things happen. You know, how could there be a God if such terrible things happen in the world. I seem to go the other way. The worse things get, the more faith I feel.'

'That sounds like a good thing to me,' he says. No solution to the problem, but he's trying to help.

'Either that, or I only talk to God when I want something.'

'We're most of us like that, at times,' he says, and I think, when I want something, perhaps, but what I want is a better soul and a better world to keep it in.

I close my hand around the medal. Father Dominic says I'm welcome back any time, and then he goes off to talk to the choir conductor. I buy some more candles and set the wicks alight, and wait out the time until my appointment looking at the wavering, dazzling shoal of flames.


Parkinson has a private clinic, away from the hospital. The stairs have green carpets, there's an old-fashioned lift with bronze doors and wire mesh around the shaft. I make no sound as I walk across the floor.

The receptionist, middle-aged with brown, undyed hair, shows me into a waiting-room. There's a chandelier hanging from the ceiling, and, unable to concentrate on the magazines laid out, I stare at it, focusing and unfocusing my eyes. Little spheres of colour appear, refracted from the crystals as my vision blurs.

It's a long wait. I don't look at the other women. I stare at the ceiling, my hands limp and dormant in my lap. My heart pounds in my chest, the veins in my neck pulse, but I don't feel any emotions, nothing but the beating of my heart.

Finally Parkinson appears at the door, says, 'Ms Galley?' My hand rises to my throat as I stand, and the medal is there. I pad across the floor, into his cream-walled examination room, and prepare myself.


I'm stripped, exposed, there's nothing between me and the world. I stand behind the screen and pull on the gown, open at the side, short sleeves, high, confining neck. The last time I wore one of these, I was at the hospital, they put a needle in my arm and I woke up wearing a gown. It had flowers on it, shaped like those stickers old people put in bath tubs to stop themselves slipping. This one is pale blue, plain, a better class of invalid wear. The chain presses against my neck as I tie the gown shut, and I pull the pendant out to stop it pinching.

Parkinson asks me about my past. He's good at it, he doesn't lower his voice or look flustered, he's matter-of-fact and polite, as if he were asking about my feet. I tell him how old I was when I first had a period, I tell him if it hurt, I tell him what contraception I've used in my life, I tell him about my lovers and my body and my daughter. I watch him move and listen to him talk, and give him everything I ever was. I trade on what I have.

He tells me he's going to do a full examination, just to check. He says, raise your arm, lean this way, lie down, legs apart, relax.

For days I've been thinking this man could have released a killer back onto the streets.

Be a man, that's what they used to say. A way of steeling yourself, living up to the best part of yourself, proving that you had the qualities that God intended you to have. Courage, endurance, will. No crying, no excuses. It was a powerful thing to say.

I lie down and set my legs, and be a woman.


I'm afraid of being sick, my throat is hot and my stomach feels displaced, and I'm scared of crying, because I remember too much of the night I lost Ann, but then I say, no, let it happen, be at the nadir if you have to. I close my fingers around the necklace, and stare at the ceiling, plaster roses around the light, and ask St Giles to help me.

Parkinson sees me lying silent. 'How's your nephew?' he says.

I swallow. 'He's all right. He's growing well.'

He nods, whether at the thought of Leo growing or at some new discovery in his examination I can't tell.

'My sister's been relieved ever since he was born safely,' I say. 'There's a tendency to miscarriage.' My voice drags down at the last syllable, and I lose the rest of what I was going to say, but he nods again.

'I've had a look at your records,' he says. 'Though I'm not sure that need be a cause for concern. The evidence that miscarriage runs in families isn't conclusive. And in your case, a traumatic miscarriage is quite possibly a one-off event.' He's reassuring, confident.

Traumatic miscarriage. I turn my head aside. 'Not unlike the chance of having non children,' I say. 'You know, no matter how many pamphlets she read saying it didn't run in families, my sister worried up to the end.'

'Ah, yes.' He glances up at my face, sees my fingers still clutched around my medal. 'Now anmorphism, that was considered hereditary for a long time. The Middle Ages had a great many theories on the subject.' Anmorphism, the medical term for my disability. Doctors aren't allowed to say bareback.

'Really?' All I know about the Middle Ages is the Inquisition.

'Oh, yes. They even conducted experiments.'

I don't know if I want to hear this. The only experiments I've heard of were done in prisoner-of-war camps, captive civilian women in labour. The experiments they did, head-first deliveries, feet-first, should never be talked about by anyone.

'Relax, please.'

I try to relax.

'Midwives claimed to specialise in reversing the position of the baby in utero, turning them around, you know. They were quite in demand, women who claimed they could prevent the birth of anmorphic babies.'

I've heard of midwives in the seventeenth, eighteenth, nineteenth centuries who specialised in disposing of anmorphic babies. If the head emerges first, place a bucket beneath the woman and it drowns before it's all the way out: legally not murder, if it isn't fully born. Or a quick scissor blade through the soft part of the head. Post-partum abortions.

475

'That wouldn't work though, would it?' I say. My feet are so cold.

'Apparently it did, occasionally. Very hit and miss, though.' He presses down, and I put my teeth together. 'It's a more complicated business than that, of course; chemical changes, oxygen supply to the brain. It's a subtle degree of brain damage that causes anmorphism. Far beyond medieval technology.'

There's a silence. He doesn't look at me, not at my face, his hands keep moving. 'I thought it was impossible to affect births one way or the other at all,' I say.

He still keeps examining. 'Not to modern technology, no. We understand the process a great deal better, nowadays.'

I open my mouth to say, 'Really?' What I say is, 'Isn't there a law about it though?', and it's not what I meant to say, it was the wrong thing.

He shrugs. This is uncomfortable for me. 'An old one.'

'Yes,' I say. I don't know, I'm guessing, I keep on guessing. 'I suppose incompetent midwives kept causing deaths in childbirth by doing it wrong.'

'Indeed.' He nods when I say the word incompetent.

'Though I suppose nowadays the risks are far fewer.'

'Oh, of course.' He smiles without looking up. 'There have been so many technological advances in the past few hundred years, it's quite astonishing.'

'Curious,' I say. The thought of Ann stabs me for a second, and then the moment passes. I keep my voice light. 'If it were possible to prevent anmorphic deliveries, I would have thought we'd have heard about it. You'd think there'd be great demand for it.'

He withdraws his hand, reaches for an instrument.

476

I hear a metal click, it sounds like a speculum, but I won't look, I stare at the ceiling. 'Oh, there would be,' he says. 'Not very practical, long-term, though. Imagine the chaos if anmorphic individuals suddenly stopped being born.'

I imagine it. DORLA would die off in a generation. Ageing catchers against younger and younger lunes, until a new society took over.

'How long have you been trying to conceive, Ms Galley?'

'N-nine months,' I say, hasty and breathless. I hadn't thought about it, the answer comes out shakily.

'Well, I wouldn't worry too much if I were you.' He sounds almost like a grandfather. 'It's quite normal for couples to take up to a year or even two years to conceive.'

'A year?' It doesn't seem right. It was so easy to conceive by accident.

'Oh, yes. It's a common mistake. And you seem to be in good shape. I wouldn't be surprised if you found yourself pregnant any day.'

'So I might be having a baby soon?' My voice quavers, it's pathetic, I can't bear being this way.

'It could be. In a moment I'm just going to give you a quick X-ray, just to be doubly sure.' He turns the speculum a little. I flinch before I can catch myself.

'It's too bad you can't really prevent anmorphic babies,' I say, trying to cover, reaching for a subject. 'My sister would have been so relieved to know about it.'

'Well,' he says. His voice is quiet. 'It isn't such a disability, after all. We could prevent it, but I wouldn't consider it ethical. Prejudiced, really.'

It isn't such a disability. I lie still and let him touch me, and listen to him say those words.

'It can be difficult for anmorphic parents, though.' He speaks quieter still. 'They can often feel isolated in an entirely lycanthropic family. And of course, anmorphic children often benefit from having an anmorphic parent.'

I think, against all my principles, against all my defences, I would have wanted Ann to be a lyco. It would have been better for her, it would have been good for me. She could have been my hope of reconciliation. Maybe I would have liked lycos better if I had mothered one.

'It isn't altogether conventional,' he says, 'but those cases, now, they're the ones in which a physician feels more inclined to – intervene.'

Cases in which a physician feels inclined to intervene. Cases in which a physician feels inclined to intervene. I play the words over in my head, trying to pull them apart like mesh, looking for what he just said. Cases in which a physician feels inclined to intervene.

I think he just offered me a bareback baby.

'Really?' I say. He isn't looking at my face. I stare hard at the ceiling, and keep hold of the medal. The thought runs through my head – the medal, he's seen me clutching it all the time. He must think I pray to St Giles, make him my saint, make a point of being a bareback. He must think I'd want a bareback baby.

Something comes together in my head.

It may be that the saint just helped me, it may be that I've just witnessed divine intervention. Because what he's offered me is as illegal as hell.

'Quietly, of course,' he's saying, 'and for a consideration. Obviously, there has to be discretion . . .'

He's asking me not to talk about it, he's talking about a secret business set-up. He puts me on my feet, takes me over to an X-ray machine.

Soon, it will sink in. I'll understand what's happened. All I can feel now is wild, empty. I have to go somewhere quiet and think about this. But the only thing in my mind now is the medal, that he saw me holding it and he told me something. Divine intervention, bringing me to the verge of understanding everything that's happened. I stand before a screen and wait for the click of the X-ray, wait for the light to go through me.

# 40

'Sue,' I say, 'it's Lola Galley.'

There's a brief silence. 'Hello, Lola.' Her voice is limp, without inflection.

'Listen, I wanted to ask you something.' She doesn't respond. 'How's the baby?'

'Nearly due.' She knows that isn't what I wanted to ask.

'Listen, could you tell me the name of your doctor?'

'My GP?'

'No, your gynaecologist, the one you're seeing for the baby.'

'Dr Marshall,' she says.

There's a pain deep in the pit of my stomach, I'm holding myself tense. 'Dr Marshall? Is he your regular doctor?'

'I saw him when I had Julio,' she says. She sounds tired.

'Oh.' Maybe I'm wrong. Maybe I've got some sort of brain fever, I'm dreaming up solutions. Marshall. It's such a respectable name.

Then something nags at my mind, it's a moment of puzzlement before I put my finger on what's bothering me. 'Didn't DORLA fix you up with a doctor?' I mean, after Johnny died. DORLA sometimes looks after widows, for a while.

'I'd just made a change,' she says. This conversation is tiresome for her. 'I didn't want to change again.'

'A change?'

'After Johnny lost his hand.' She says it flat, without a tremor. 'They found me a doctor then, but then I went back to my old one.'

'How come?'

'I don't know, Johnny thought it was a good idea.' I'm pulling her through bad memories, she doesn't want to be talking about this.

'Who were you with before?'

'A Dr Parkinson,' she says. The name doesn't mean much to her; he's just the man she went to see, there's no pause or drama in the way she says it.

There's an acrid taste in my mouth. I uncross my legs, cross them again. 'You saw him at the start?'

'Yeah.' There's a shrug in her voice, this isn't interesting to her, but she can't face making me leave her alone.

'Did he – what do you think of him? I mean, how come you changed?'

'He seemed okay.' There are spaces in between her answers. I can hear the voices of her children in the background. 'Why? Are you looking for a gynaecologist?'

She isn't lying, I think. She doesn't sound like she's lying. He didn't make her the offer he made me. 'No, I – Sue, I'm sorry about this. Did Johnny ever say anything about him?'

'Just that he thought we should go back to Dr Marshall.' I notice the 'we', even talking about her

481

own body she says 'we'. It must have been a good marriage.

'Didn't you talk it over?'

I've pushed it too far. 'He'd just lost his hand.' There's an edge to her voice, a rising note. 'He'd seen a lot of doctors. He wanted me to go to a different one, that was fine with me. They put you in stirrups, you can't see one from another anyway.'

It's almost hope, what I hear in that last sentence. Though she's telling me to go to hell, there's a trace of her old vitality, it's a crude and offhand remark almost like a joke. She used to be funny, when Johnny was with her.

'I'm sorry.'

She doesn't say anything. Her children talk in the background, but I can't make out what they're saying.


After the examination, I walked out with my coat wrapped around me, my head ducked against the still air. Soon I can go home, I told myself, this will be over soon and then I can go home. I went back into the church. Father Dominic wasn't there. Other people were wandering to and fro, so I headed straight for the Aegidan shrine and knelt down, to make sure I'd be left alone. I was shaking, I was sick, I stared at the picture of the saint but I couldn't find a word to say to him. Some candles were burning before it, but there weren't enough candles in the world to light for my Ann. The church was quiet but I didn't hear it, sounds raged in my ears, and I felt blazing, wicked, unforgivable. Take your pain to God, the nuns would have said. I felt a kind of desperation, a need for there to be some force for goodness, something absolute, something right, and that I longed harder and harder for faith the worse the world became.

*I am angry*, I told the saint. I couldn't think of any other words. I said it over and over again, until there was nothing in me but those words, *I am angry, I am angry, I am angry.*


Creches. Separate schools. Moon nights, nights we think about more than the people they affect ever need to. Scars, teeth at your throat, blood soaking into the grass. DORLA, day after day until you're too old to work, trapped in a grey building with people like you on the inside and words spray-painted on the outside. Bareback. Fucking skins. Every insult and wound and violation the world can throw at you, from the day you're born wrong till the day you die used-up and battered beyond repair.

That elegant, highly trained man put his hands in me and offered to force on my child the same life sentence that fell on me.


Supposing he made the same offer to Johnny, I ask St Giles. What would Johnny have done then?

Johnny had lyco children and he loved them. Their lives were better than his, or they were while he was alive taking care of them. He wouldn't have wanted his baby imprisoned in bareback flesh.

Would Johnny have exposed him? Threatened to? If it came out, Parkinson would be struck off, I'm sure of that, maybe even imprisoned. Nobody's allowed to damage babies at birth, and that's what he offered. I take a breath, kneel back on my ankles, grip my hands together. It would look like prayer at a distance. The saint rests easy in his portrait, cradling a deer in his arms, calm and tender.

Make me calm, God, I say. Make me calm, so I can think about this. I came back to the church to think, after I called Sue. The DORLA building closed around me till I could barely breathe, but here, I can stand it. Make me calm, God.

Johnny didn't expose him. Parkinson is still working away, so Johnny can't have exposed him. But maybe he threatened to. It could be he needed money, after he lost his hand and got demoted and had to feed his children on a cripple's pay; it could be he wanted money for silence. Guilt plucks at my insides as I think that, accusing a dead man. But maybe he was driven to it. Maybe not: Johnny played inside the rules. If he did, he would have been worried, miserable, wondering what to do. Where should he go, who should he tell?

I remember the last time I saw him. It seemed like he wanted to tell me something. I wish hard enough to hurt that he'd told me, but it's no good wishing now.

Parkinson is mutilating babies. This I know. Parkinson was involved in Seligmann escaping, that I believe. Why would he do that?

They can't have been friends; I can't imagine Parkinson as a prowler, not that kind of prowler. And Seligmann hates barebacks, Parkinson's creating them; they can't be on the same side.

I feel my mind tangle like a drawerful of string, and I say again, make me calm, God. Supposing Seligmann and Parkinson didn't know each other well, that

Parkinson helped him escape not because they were friends, but because it benefited him somehow. It seems likelier. How would Parkinson benefit?

'Excuse me, miss.' A voice comes from behind me and I startle, rise up on my knees. It's a moment before I remember that 'Excuse me, miss' is not the beginnings of a threat.

A man in faded jeans stands behind me. 'We need to do some work in here.' He indicates the shrine, the wax-crusted candle stand, the bank of flowers underneath the icon, the lilies shrivelled at the edges, dripping petals and fragments down onto the floor below. 'Would you mind moving for about half an hour? I'm sorry.'

'That's all right,' I say quickly, not thinking about it, and stand up, look around me for somewhere else to go. There's another alcove on the other side of the church, a painting of the Virgin in it, a great swirl of blue cloth around a pale, tear-eyed, expressionless face. I head for it, wondering whether this was some kind of sign.

Kneeling before the Virgin, I take another deep breath, trying to clear my mind. I play over another piece of music Paul made me listen to, Pergolesi, I think: *stabat mater dolorosa, iuxta crucem lacrimosa, dum pendebat filius.* The mother of sorrows stands beside the cross of tears where her son hangs. I repeat the words in my head, steadying myself with the repetition, the precise Latinate vowels. *Stabat mater dolorosa.*

The tearful eyes distract me. The perfect holy mother, weeping for the world.

I close my eyes. How did Parkinson benefit? What happened, what was the result of letting Seligmann go?

We went looking for him all over creation, we arrested

485

innocent people and charged them with murder, the murders that Seligmann committed. Would Parkinson want a man he was helping to –

There's an assumption I've been making all along. It comes on me from nowhere, stands before me, quiet and certain. I said, the murders that Seligmann committed. Why should I assume he committed both of them?

Because he escaped, because Nate died, because they both died from silver bullets. Who makes silver bullets? I can't see Parkinson bothering to make one himself. Seligmann might, but it would be an awkward business. Who makes silver bullets?

We do.

Supposing Johnny went to meet Parkinson, to talk or accuse or threaten. He would have been wary, Johnny, he would have been meeting a man with power and an unknown will, a man with a terrible secret. Supposing he was nervous, that he didn't feel safe. It's a feeling I've been living with cheek to cheek for months. What did I do when I felt so afraid?

I took a gun from the stores. It's still in my bag; I've been carrying it so long I'd almost forgotten about it. I took a gun. It wasn't even difficult. It wasn't difficult for me, it wouldn't have been difficult for Johnny. There would have been two silver bullets in it. And if he put it down, or if Parkinson took it away from him, there would have been no need to forge silver bullets. They would have been right there. No symbolism, no insult. They were in the weapon in his hand.

And once he'd killed Johnny, he would have been stuck with it. A government-issue, controlled-supply silver gun, which, for all he knew, Johnny might have checked out like a library book with a serial number and a promise to return it tomorrow. If anyone found him with it, that was the end. But how to get rid of it?

Parkinson is intelligent. He's educated. Years of training to use his mind would send it into overdrive when he tried to plan, make him see the dangers and pitfalls of everything he did. But then, suddenly, into his hospital comes a man with injuries, a man with a grudge against DORLA, and a man who needed help to escape. A man who might dispose of the gun for him, if Parkinson distracted Security for him. A perfect chance. Divine intervention.

Only Seligmann had a grudge, and a gun, and suddenly he was free to do as he wished. A silver gun. The man I saw, the man I injured, could never have resisted the temptation.

Parkinson let Seligmann go, and Seligmann killed Nate. A silver bullet. We decided that Seligmann killed Johnny too. It gave us the perfect suspect. The perfect scapegoat, too, because we were never, ever going to give Seligmann a fair trial. We would have railroaded him to hell if we could have managed it.

The scent of fresh lilies drifts across the church, heady and beautiful. There are still flowers in the world.

This is my theory: Parkinson killed Johnny with a gun Johnny took from the stores. To take our minds off Johnny, he let Seligmann go and, whether to dispose of or to use, he gave Seligmann that gun, and Seligmann shot Nate. He didn't help David, he let his arm rot untreated, but he gave Seligmann a gun.

I haven't the first fragment of evidence.

There's only one possibility left: that Parkinson is hiding Seligmann, that he's in too deep to let him get caught. If he is, I can find him, and then we'll know. If he just let him go, then the murders will not be solved, not by any means I can think of. But if that happens, I'm still bringing Parkinson down. I'll go to Hugo, I'll go to the police, the medical council, the newspapers, I'll chain myself to his door if I have to, but I'm going to bring him down. I feel the fury rise in me again, and I know I can do all of this, I can and I will.

Opening my eyes, I look again at the Virgin. Despite the tears, her face is peaceful, uplifted, sanctified. I want justice, I tell her, not vengeance, I want justice. I know, though, that I'm wrought through with rage, that I'm murderous with fury, that I am not sanctified. I want goodness, I want the glory of God, but I'm angry enough to kill. Find room in your heart for a sinner, I say, and weep for my sins along with the rest. I'll fly to your forgiveness, I want to be forgiven, but first I have to fight.

# 41

Information is easy to get, if you want it badly enough. It takes an hour staring into the white screen of my computer, and that's all. The basic hacking skills we learn as part of our unofficial training. I search for a while, I slip in through a few back doors, and I find the answer.

Parkinson is a wealthy man. He's wealthier than you'd expect even the best consultant doctor to be, if he was working within the system. His wealth is stored in many places. Some of it is realised in property.

He has a house in Benedict by the river, where he lives. It's lovely, that part of the city. He has another house between Queens and Sanctus, rented to a family; a house north of Five Wounds, divided into flats. It's all rented. There's only one place in his name I can't find a tenant for, a small basement flat. It's between Abbots and Five Wounds. It's near St Veronica's. Possibly he keeps it as a pied-à-terre, somewhere to spend a night if he works late at the hospital. A man running away from St Veronica's wouldn't have to run far.

It's near where the Marcos family live.

That isn't evidence, it isn't relevant to anything. I don't know why it should make me so angry.

I sit by a window watching the sky, and I wait for the night. I don't feel vulnerable. I feel taut, perfected. I am vibrant with fury. The sun goes down, sinking to the bottom of the white sky, and then the light fades, and I know I'm ready.

There's no full moon.

The streets are oddly distinct. Buildings rise around me, so solid I almost feel their shapes at the back of my eyes. My trainers press and tense around my feet as I walk, the tap of the lace against the right shoe counters the rhythm of my steps. The grey paving stones in the yellow light dip and rise, uneven, as if I were walking over broken pack-ice, the Arctic sea under my feet, but the ground is stable and still, it meets me squarely as I pace it. Every brick in every building is different, and I look around me at this unnaturally real world.

I say his name in my mind, Seligmann, Seligmann.

Sooner than I expect, I'm in the right street.

The house has black iron stairs leading down to the basement flat. The building towers above, three storeys, massive and weighty with a solemn green front door. There's railings and a gate blocking the steps: a little push reveals that it's locked. My bag makes no sound as I set it down on the other side, and then I wrap my coat around myself and climb over. The stair doesn't creak as I descend; the wire mesh presses through my soles and I can see down, a great looming distance between me and the ground.

A wooden door, glossy black, the numbers on it in old, half-tarnished bronze. A curtained window, dim light coming through it. No flickering: no one's watching television. Not too bright: the room isn't occupied, the light's coming from a back room. A sense of freedom surrounds me, of being still uncommitted, able to walk away from this, as I try the window.

It's a sash window, and it gives a fraction before sticking. I peer through the glass in the half-light, and see a lock not fully in place. The wood is old, venerable. I reach into my bag, take out the chisel I bought today. The plastic handle is cool in the night air. Ally taught me how to do this, I remember without emotion, and I dig in through the wood.

It's strenuous, but I don't make much noise. There's a hissing sound overhead as I work, wind through the branches of the trees lining the street. Rowans, I think they are, clumps of red berries still hang from their wintery twigs. They're supposed to be lucky trees; if you plant one at your door evil spirits can't pass it. I must not be evil, then.

The lock gives. It was new, well-made, I could never have got past it if it had been properly in place. Seligmann hasn't been afraid for his security like I've been.

I slide up the window, slip through, land safely in a darkened room. Once inside I reach into my bag, take out my gun, put the bag back outside where I can find it if I have to run. The gun is cold, familiar, and the metal warms quickly in my fingers.

There's a sofa to get around, a rug on the floor, bookshelves. I can't read the titles in the dark. The ceiling is low enough that I could almost reach up and touch it. The wood of the doorframe is painted perfectly smooth. Light gleams on it as I pass through.

I stand in a cream-coloured, underground hallway. My gun sits warm in my hand.

Into the hush I call out, 'Hello?'

A door opens, too near to me, I take three rapid steps back. Seligmann stands in front of me, expected, recognised, impossibly real.

He says, 'What –' and then I pull the trigger.

The crash of the gun in this closed space is devastating, I flinch down like a rabbit at the sound of it, and when I look, Seligmann is on his back, blood already overrunning the soft white carpet where my bullet took him in the thigh.

I stand over him, let him see the barrel of my gun. 'I've got another bullet,' I say, and I was expecting him to answer, curse me, but he barely hears me, I barely hear myself. He curls around his wounded leg, making long, sickening sounds of pain, sobs so rough-edged I think I hear them cutting his throat as they drag out of him.

I reach into my pocket, take out a mobile and make a call. DORLA agents arrive before the ambulance.

While we're waiting for them to come, I sit down on a chair nearby. Seligmann coils himself up, his hands pressed down where my bullet smashed through his flesh. The pain absorbs him, imprisons his personality, makes him nothing more than a man in pain. There's no sound but his hoarse, ragged keening. I sit quietly in my chair, watching him, keeping him company until the people come and get us.

# 42

I tell them he mustn't be taken to St Veronica's, and they take him the long way round to another hospital. For some reason, they expect me to ride in the ambulance, so I sit beside him while green-jacketed paramedics press white bandages to his bleeding thigh and talk about drugs with long names. He won't lose his leg if they work well.

They give me a blanket. I don't know why. My coat was taken away by somebody in forensics to look at the bloodstains, which are not bad, a dry-cleaner could get them out if I took it there soon enough, they wouldn't show on the dark wool. I don't know whether they'll give it back, and I don't know how I could replace it, but I'm not cold. I want my coat back, it suddenly seems an important piece of my life, its cut and shape come into my memory with the force of a friendship. Instead, they've given me a tan-coloured blanket, and I'm not cold, but I hold it around my shoulders, to please them.


They wanted the gun, the forensics people, I had to hand that over too. I passed it over without a pang. It was never really mine.

*

At the hospital, they shine a light into my eyes and ask me questions about my name and where I live. The light is dazzling after the dark outside, it rings pain in my eyes like the tongue in a bell. 'I don't have a concussion,' I say. I think I say it several times.

Then there are police, and DORLA agents, all in the same room as the doctors. Hugo comes into the room, wrapped in a big brown coat. The fluorescent lights shine pallid on his skin. 'Hugo,' I say, and then can't think of what to say next. I look at my watch. I waited till after sunset to do this, but it's still winter, the sun sets before six. It's only a little before seven o'clock now; he must have been still at work. Surprise wraps around me, at how early it is.

The police want to ask me things. They don't get very far before Nick comes in, Johnny's old partner, police liaison. His hoarse voice sounds scratchier than ever in this sterile place, like a worn-out record, and I think of suggesting he get his chest X-rayed while he's here, then decide it would be a liberty. He takes the sergeant outside the room, and then the sergeant comes back in and takes his men and leaves. 'Are you all right, Lola?' Nick asks me.

I blink at him. 'I feel a bit strange,' I say. 'But I know what's going on. The doctors thought I had a concussion, but I don't, I didn't hit my head.'

'I think they think you might be in shock.' He sits down beside me.

'I don't think so,' I tell him carefully. 'I don't think I've got any excuses.'

He reaches into his pocket for a cigarette, then remembers he's in a hospital.

'Forensics took away the gun I had,' I say. 'And my coat. Do you think they'll give it back when they've finished with it?'

I hear the breath scrape in his throat as he inhales. 'I don't know. I'll ask.' The gentleness in his voice irritates me; he sounds like he's talking to a cripple.

'I knew what I was doing,' I say. 'I arrested Seligmann.'

'I'd have come with you if you'd asked.'

The blanket is still around my shoulders. I don't know what to tell him.

Hugo comes over to join us. 'Do you feel up to coming back to the office?' he asks me. 'I'd like to have a verbal report as soon as possible.'

I stand up, obedient. He takes me out of the hospital; Nick follows us as far as the car park and then gets into his own vehicle before I think to say goodbye to him. Hugo drives me back to the DORLA building. We don't speak on the journey. I'd like to lean my head against the window, but it strikes me that I might make a smudge, so I rest back in my seat and watch the red and white lights of cars passing us, back and forth.


Hugo sits me in a chair and turns on a tape recorder. I don't know where to begin. I slip and founder from sentence to sentence, and Hugo decides that I should just describe the arrest. I tell him I came to suspect that Seligmann was hiding in this building, I tell him I went in through the window, I tell Hugo I shot the man.

Hugo asks if Seligmann threatened me. I say no.

I don't believe this tape will be kept.

I tell him my theory, and he hears me out. He doesn't

question me. He just sits quiet, and lets my voice dig itself into the narrow recording tape.

After it's over, I go home. I go and sit on a bus and look at my fellow passengers, and I watch every stop go by until I get to the one that's only a street away from my own flat block.

My key was still in my bag, and they didn't take that away. I take it out, I fit it in the lock and turn, and I'm back in the hallway, then in the lift, then in front of my own door. I stand before it a moment, with the sense that something should happen, there should be something else that I've missed. Nothing comes to mind, so I open the door and go in.

There's a layer of dust over everything, and I see with dismay that I left a light on, that I've been wasting money and power ever since I left. Everything looks the same. There's just a slight sense of subsidence, like the cabin of a ship that's rolled sideways on a heavy wave.

# 43

'Are you feeling better?' Hugo asks me.

I sit once again in his chair. 'Yes, sir.' I don't mean to say much. I could go to jail for this.

He looks over the transcript: someone has typed up everything I told him. I wait for him to list my crimes: theft and possession of a firearm, breaking and entering, firing a bullet into an unarmed man.

'You will be pleased to hear,' he says quietly, 'that the suspect, Darryl Seligmann, has confessed to the murder of Nate Jensen.'

'He confessed?' What did we do to him? Nate beat him till blood ran from his mouth, and Seligmann did nothing but curse. He sank his teeth into his own wrist to get away from us. What have we done to him?

'Yes.' There's no expression in Hugo's voice. 'He confessed shortly before he was admitted to hospital.'

He leaves a pause after saying it, and I know what we did. A silver bullet wound, high up in the thigh. Left untreated, the best he could hope for was to lose the leg. At worst, death by gangrene. In between, a creeping necrosis that would spread down to his feet, up through his stomach and groin, ruining everything in its path. If he didn't get treatment.

'Is the confession valid?' My voice is as cool and quiet as Hugo's, and he knows I've understood.

'It is. He provided sufficient evidence and detail, all of which checks against the facts. There's no question of his guilt.'

'I see.' Hugo leaves me sitting in silence for a while, and I stay still, I don't fidget or look away.

Finally he speaks again. 'I've been reading your theory again. Your theory that it was Dr William Parkinson who was responsible for the death of John Marcos.'

He waits for me to speak up. I don't.

'I have to say, your reasoning outstrips your evidence by a considerable margin, Ms Galley.' Ms Galley. He called me by my surname. Something's going to happen to me.

I don't answer.

'You may be interested to learn that Dr Parkinson was – invited to come in for questioning, following your report.'

Invited? Not arrested, invited? 'Did he come?'

'Indeed he did.'

'What did he say?' The thought of Parkinson makes me pull my jacket around myself, press my knees together.

Hugo looks at me for a long moment. Then he looks away. 'This may be better coming from someone else,' he says.


I'm taken upstairs, into a new office, a larger one with windows on two sides. The carpet is worn, its fabric pressed flat by years of walking, and the boards on the

498

walls are pitted with use; it's a good office, by our standards, but everything in it still looks flimsy.

William Jones sits at the desk. I've met him once before, when I was warned about Seligmann's escape, when they told me I wasn't going to be strawed. He still wears the same look he had then, autopilot courtesy, like a man who's depended on his habits so long he can't get away from them. His scarred face studies me with a kind of tired compassion, and although I can't guess what he's going to say to me, I know, suddenly, that it's going to be bad.

Hugo glances at him, sits me in front of the desk and seats himself off to one side. There's a picture of a woman on the desk in a fine wooden frame; it makes the rest of the room look cheaper still.

'How are you, Ms Galley?' Jones says.

I swallow, lost for words. 'All right, thank you.' Ms Galley, not Miss. People here started using the Ms when I lost Ann. I guess Jones knows about that.

Jones looks at me. That's what I notice, that he looks. He doesn't glance down, or take a deep breath, or rearrange his hands, he doesn't do any of the things people do to take a pause before delivering upsetting news. He just looks at me, and his face is slightly, distantly sad. 'I read your report on William Parkinson,' he says. 'You're to be congratulated on your deductions. If not on your actions.'

'Did you speak to him?' I say. Somehow I feel that nothing I say in this meeting will affect what's done to me. Whatever they do, my little comments aren't going to sway it.

'I did, yes. Successfully. All things considered, it's unfortunate that you acted as you did, without prior consultation. It's going to take a little management to work things out.'

'What's going on?' I've been guessing for too long, I'm tired of groping in the dark. Jones talks like he knows what's happened, and more than anything now, I want to know.

'You must understand,' he says, 'that the procedures Parkinson has been using – they're not unheard of.'

'I didn't suppose he invented them,' I say, not sure what he means.

'No. They've been useable for a while now. Though not widely known.' He doesn't lean on words, he doesn't hesitate.

'Widely known in the medical community?' He's telling me the truth.

'No. Ethical objections. They wouldn't be accepted. It's known that experiments have been tried at various times, generally at points in history where people were more than usually disposable. Criminals, prisoners of war.' I knew this. He looks tired. There are expressive lines around his forehead and eyes, but they don't deepen or flex, he doesn't use them. 'That they were successful – well, you know the problems that would create, you said as much on the tape.'

I don't answer.

'The thing is, Ms Galley, you were right about William Parkinson. He has been using the technique he offered you. He hasn't been acting alone, though.'

I look at him. His face is still.

'You have to understand this, Ms Galley. He wasn't the only doctor using the method. And he wasn't doing it unsupervised. People knew about it. Not the medical board, but others. A few highly-placed police officials, a few government officials, and a few of us.'

The word *us* doesn't register, it's too tiny a syllable, meaningless.

'It wasn't our idea to start with, I think, but we haven't opposed it. We've been declining for too many years. Science advances, and medicine improves, and the number of birth defects falls. Cities rise, the population rises. You know yourself how understaffed we are.'

'Understaffed?' It's a word for a post office, a school.

'We have better weapons, but we aren't allowed to use them. You know that. Casualty rates are too high amongst us. We don't publicise the statistics because morale is bad enough, but I don't suppose they'll surprise you. Our retirement age is sixty, like everyone else, but about twenty-five per cent of us are invalided out by then. Injuries, heart attacks, burnout. Death in the line of duty. Higher rates of cancer, stroke, all sorts of stress-related deaths. That's why we agreed to this programme.'

'Programme.'

'An increased rate of anmorphic births. Not so dramatic as to be conspicuous, but enough to bolster us. You know yourself how much work one more pair of hands can do. The doctors are in it for less social reasons, for the most part. Scientific achievement, and the government subsidises each birth they affect.'

'Parkinson killed Johnny,' I say. It's the one true thing left to hold on to.

'Yes, he did.' Jones doesn't look away. 'It seems Marcos threatened him with exposure. And you were right about Seligmann. We have a full confession from him; he's loquacious in his way. Once he gets angry

501

enough. Parkinson did give him the gun to dispose of in exchange for hiding him. He didn't know why, but he wasn't a man to pass up an opportunity. It seems Seligmann had his own ideas about justice that Parkinson hadn't foreseen. Unfortunately. He hasn't been careful, Seligmann. Too many gestures. The programme may cease because of this, Ms Galley. A murder compromises the security too badly. Parkinson himself will not be permitted to continue, that's for certain. But you should understand, he isn't going to be arrested either.'

'You knew he was turning babies.' My voice isn't my own.

'This is going to be handled quietly, Ms Galley. It will be handled, but it will be handled quietly, and your involvement is at an end.'

'You knew? You did?'

'I knew. The thing is, you're fairly compromised yourself. Taking a gun from our stores might be a departmental matter, but breaking into a private house and shooting the occupant represents a lot of jail time. We can handle that quietly as well. We don't even need to publicise that it was you who arrested him, not outside DORLA. But you should realise what will happen to you if you try to cause trouble about this.'

'You knew he was doing this. You let it happen.' A demon kneads its claws in my throat.

Jones doesn't look down. 'If DORLA is to continue, we need help. I haven't heard any proposals to eliminate anmorphism. This seemed to be the only option.'

My hand rakes the air around my body. 'You let him turn children into – this.'

Hugo glances at Jones, and Jones sits back, waits for

me to accept it. Hugo half-reaches towards me, and I flinch, and he draws his hand back.

'You let him turn children into us.' With the eyes of two men on me, two senior men, the sense that I should hold myself together shakes me, I should find cutting words to say, I should make speeches and scald them, I should call down fires. But I can't, there's nothing to hold the pieces together, and everything comes apart. I press my hands to my mouth, trying to hold it steady, but it writhes against my palms and I hear a hoarse, ugly sob tear through me, a second, a third.

They sit and wait, they don't say anything. I draw in a breath, try to speak, and my voice collapses. With my hands at my face, I stay, hiding myself, for long minutes.

When I speak again, my voice isn't steady, it's high and tight like a child's, but the shame of silence has overcome me. 'What would you have done if I hadn't shot him?'

Jones raises his eyebrows, more in thought than surprise. 'If you had arrested Seligmann through the proper channels? Much the same as we're doing now, except we would have had to find some other means of persuading you to cooperate. Parkinson has to be protected. Or at least, what he represents does.' He looks at me. 'You mustn't shoot anyone else, Ms Galley. Not in daylight. We can't have it. I wouldn't advise it, anyway. You put yourself at a bad disadvantage. You've been handling the Seligmann case from the beginning; I would have thought you'd had a chance to see the pitfalls of making such gestures.'

I should have learned from Seligmann not to make

gestures. That's what he says. I made a gesture the way Seligmann did.

'Seligmann will be tried in our courts, and he'll be convicted for both murders. Both men died by the same gun, forensics are in our favour, and we have only his word that Parkinson ever handled it. He won't testify himself, of course. Parkinson will be handled, but not in any way you'll be told about, Ms Galley. Which only leaves us with you.' My hands are still pressed to my face. It's graceless, stupid, but I'll not lower my hands for him.

'I know you're disenchanted, Ms Galley. I'm sorry.' His voice is more weary than anything else. His hair is grey, but his brows are still dark and straight, and they don't move. 'You do understand that you will face charges if you try to overturn our processes. And since it was a lyco citizen you shot, you'll face them in a mainstream court. I'm sure you appreciate your chances. We won't intervene.' I look at Hugo, who sits, staring into his lap, as if there were a weight at the back of his head. 'We don't want to be unnecessarily harsh. John Marcos was a friend of yours, I know.' I don't answer. 'I'm sure you're concerned about his family. We've managed to secure a widow's pension for his wife.' I look up. It's paltry compensation for a murdered man, but still an uncommon award, around here. But still paltry. 'And we do appreciate your work. You put a lot of effort into this case. We're prepared to requite it. Seligmann will be tried quickly, and nothing can be done until he's safely finished with, but after that, we're granting you a pay raise.' He names a sum, a higher one than I would have guessed. I can't even react. 'This is non-negotiable. We were considering a simple bonus,

504

but this is less conspicuous. We'll give you a couple of easy cases, which you no doubt will handle as well as you usually did before all this trouble started, and the raise will be attributed to them.'

'You're bribing me?' I say it with sheer disbelief. At this moment, it feels like the maddest thing I ever heard.

'If you like,' Jones says without a flicker. 'We're giving you some reasons to keep what you know to yourself.'

'What will happen to Parkinson?'

'He'll be dealt with.'

'How, how is he going to be dealt with?'

'That,' Jones says with slow, gentle emphasis, 'is not something you will be told. I'm sorry.'

'You're sorry.'

'This is as far as it goes, Ms Galley. Marcos's widow will be taken care of, Jensen's murderer will be punished, and the process Parkinson was involved in will be, at the least, called into question. If you accept that, we'll look after you. If you don't, you will go to prison.' I look at his worn face, his extinguished eyes. 'It's the most that can be done. This isn't our world,' he says. 'Let it go.'

# 44

Nobody stops me when I leave the building. I walk, I don't look up at street signs or study the faces of people I pass. I walk with a dull, swift stride that carries me along, the streets flowing past me at such a steady speed that it seems they'd keep flowing if I stopped walking. I walk all the way to the church and go in, but I don't know which saint to talk to.

There's a graveyard surrounding the church, a little one, where the headstones tell only the dates of birth and not the conditions, and we all lie buried together.

A beam of winter sunlight stands before me, slanting in golden from outside. My hands glow under it, radiant.

The dead lie around me. The maggots are stealing away the last of their flesh.

The stickiness of birth. The jelly and whey where the soft-boned baby nestles. It must have got all over his hands.

If I tried to turn my baby within me, I'd have broken her limbs. She would have twisted and shrunk into a stone inside me, she would never have got out. We would have sunk together. How many women were pulled under the surface, all those centuries, by their dying, fractured babies?

It must have taken a lot of murders to get it right.

There will be injections now. Clean needles, scrubbed fingers. Tainting the water inside women like cooks seasoning a broth. Choking the baby in its unresisting mother for a few, measured seconds. Just long enough for a little part of its soft white brain to die.

I wonder how many adults there are in wheelchairs, in nursing homes, from days when the doctors got the timing a little wrong. What if there were only a few, only five, only ten? If they could meet, what would they say to each other?

Sunlight lies warm in my lap. It won't be long till spring.

I think about a lot of things, sitting with a lap full of light. I think about the dead, the barebacks who lost too much blood on one too many moon nights and the lyco prisoners who died in custody. I think about prison, and about hell. I think about Parkinson's soft skin and sure hands. About Ann. I think about the look on William Jones's face when he told me that it was all over. The look on Ally's face when I kicked him and ran down the stairs. The look on the face of Marty's mother, while her son lay mute in hospital with his throat torn out. And I think again about Parkinson's smooth, calm, obliging expression as he moved through his hospital.

I think about murder, about falling victim to it and about committing it. For a while I wonder whether Parkinson deserves to live. I remember the bruise on my hand when the gun kicked back and slammed a bullet

507

into Darryl Seligmann, and the way he curled round his wounded leg like a child.

Mostly, I think about getting away with things.


Back in my apartment, the tiny rooms gape around me, full of empty space. I stare ahead of me, watching the daylight fade on the walls. Despite the sounds from the other flats, above, below, around me, silence fills the flat from floor to ceiling.

I sit alone on the sofa, as if I was the only person in the world. Stupidly, I wish for Paul, I'm tired and I'd like someone to lean against, but that's gone. Probably I'll never see him again. Perhaps this is it, I think, perhaps this is the rest of my life. Knowledge I can do nothing with, my tongue stilled with a little money and my freedom, which I can use to sit alone in quiet rooms.

The people who know about Parkinson would probably all fit into my living room. I could serve them drinks. Or he could, because he knows them all, he's safe. There's nobody outside his charmed circle except me who knows what he's done. The fortunate ones can be trusted because they're part of him, they'll stay together, and I can be relied on, or can be disposed of.

The knowledge of what he's done sits beside me on the sofa, heavy and watchful.


For a day, I avoid work. I stay in bed, bury my head, sleep when I can. I don't dream.

After that, I get up. I brush my hair, wash my face and clean the water away with a towel, I tidy my clothes and put on my shoes and walk out of my door. My neighbour Mrs Kitney stops me as I go out, wide-eyed: she's heard I'm a heroine. I say, 'Good morning,' quietly.

'It must have been terrifying,' she sighs.

I incline my head, a long way away from her.

'Everyone's talking about how brave you've been, Lola,' she discloses.

'Oh.' I pull on my gloves, one finger at a time.

'Tell me, weren't you scared?' She's standing in the hallway with a piece of gossip. She must be desperate to know.

'I couldn't say.' I give her a slow, distant nod. 'Good morning, Mrs Kitney.'

I walk to the bus stop, I stand on the bus, I walk quietly into work. There will be files already on my desk, I know. New cases. Citizens who failed to make it to lock-up. Abandoned children. Homeless men who dozed off before moonrise and woke to find themselves in a different world. I shall sort through them, I shall do it by the book, put my fellow-citizens gently into one tray or another, let their lives slip in and out of my hands and tidy them back into the system. It will be simple, easy, and it won't always be wrong.

My face is pale and still as a stone saint's as I walk the corridors.

I would make it into my office, except that as I ascend, I see Paul coming the other way. His face is unbruised now, his clothes are clean, he's well. He looks like he did when we first met. I stop still, my hands press together, and I stand looking at him, making no sound, breathing in and out.

He looks up and sees me, and my calm crackles over. 'What are you doing here?' I sound hoarse, slapped.

Paul makes an awkward gesture. 'I came in to see

about Jerry Farnham. Remember? Your alcoholic client. I'm still his social worker.'

Jerry, the reason we met. 'I haven't heard anything about him. He was arrested and put in the cells last I heard.'

'I know.' He stands very still. 'Someone else took over his case. I came to see about getting him released.' He sounds almost as if that could be a problem, someone taking my case from me without my knowledge, as if I was still not past caring about it.

'I see.' I lower my head. One of us will have to walk away if this is going to end.

'Lola . . .' I don't look up. 'Can I talk to you?'

Sadness is dragging at my hands and heels like running weights. 'Let's go in my office.'

He follows me in, I sit on one side of the desk, he sits opposite me on the other. A lot of me wants to dismiss this, to say, We don't have anything to talk about, but we do. It could finish in silence and absence, but I need to talk to him, even if I don't have anything to say. I sit and fold my hands together, look down at my desk.

Paul looks to and fro, as if the right thing to say was hidden somewhere in the room, tucked between the files on my shelves. Finally he goes still again and says, 'We can't just end it like this.'

'I know.'

There's a silence. We both sit quietly, looking at each other's hands.

I thought he'd break it first, but it's me who speaks. 'Are you all right?'

He shrugs. He knows I'm talking about the cells, the deprivation, the beatings. 'I will be.'

My voice stutters a little, but it isn't nerves, the words are heavy in my mouth. 'A-are you seeing a counsellor? A lot of people do.' After we finish with them.

He turns his head aside, half-shaking it. 'Not exactly. Friend of mine at work's a counsellor, I've been spending a lot of evenings at his place.'

'I've gone home,' I say. 'I've moved back into my own flat. I'm happier in my own place.'

'I miss you,' he says. It stops me, makes me go still. He doesn't say it as a plea, there are no requests or plans in it, just a flat statement. 'You were in my apartment all the time before I got arrested.' He says 'arrested' calmly. He's brave. 'When I'm back there now I keep remembering how used I was to having you around.'

'I'm sorry,' I say. There aren't any other words.

He looks up at me, as if weighing what he says. 'Listen. If I'd told you, if you'd known before it all happened that I did this with my friends . . . I know what you think of curfew breakers. When they arrested me. If you'd known I was one of them, would you have helped me?'

I have to answer with the truth, this is a question that I'll hear all my life. It almost seems fitting to say no, to put back the old fences, get behind the bareback name and fight off the world. I think, and I imagine it, put myself into a different past. 'Yes,' I say, and I believe it's true.

He looks at me, looks away. 'Did you think I was in on killing your friend?'

I go back to that time, feel it through. 'I think – I thought you might have been.' He shifts, raises an eyebrow, and I have to explain. 'That was as bad as

511

being sure. I'd trusted you. I don't often trust people, but I trusted you.'

'Did you love me?'

'Yes.' I don't have to think for a moment before I say that. I feel soaked through with sadness, exhausted with sadness, but there's a freedom somewhere, a sense of calm. We're telling each other the truth, we can ask each other anything. A sharp-edged spring is loosening inside me. 'Did you love me?'

'Yes.'

'You said you did in the cells. Did you mean it then?'

'Yes,' he says. He says the word slowly, but there's no pause before saying it. Afterwards, though, there's a silence, we're both too tired to push forwards.

'I heard you caught the killer,' Paul says.

'Where did you hear it?'

'I – I spoke to your sister.'

I look up, but I'm beyond surprise. 'Did you call her?'

He shakes his head, turning it slowly. 'No, she called me. She called my department at work and asked around till she found me.'

Without knowing why she did it, I think of Becca and remember that I love her. 'What did she want?'

'She was worried about you.'

'Why did she call you?'

He gestures, raising his hand. 'She wanted to know what was really going on, I think. She's a nice lady, your sister. It's too bad you never introduced us.'

'You'd probably like each other,' I say. I can picture them talking, and I can see now that they'd get on.

'She said you found him by yourself, that you defended yourself when he came at you and you brought him in.'

512

'He didn't come at me.' I stop speaking, let the sentence fall. 'I just shot him.'

Paul doesn't answer.

'Do you know where I was the morning before I shot him? I was in church. I was on my knees praying to Our Lady.'

Paul looks down. 'Well.'

I tuck my chin down on my hands, clasping each other for comfort.

'Were you trying to kill him?' I look up, look at him properly, see his bright blue eyes gazing at me.

'No.' I keep looking, take a deep breath. 'No. I don't think I'm really a killer.' Whatever he says to that, I feel like I'm saying a basc-note truth about myself.

'I never thought you were.'

I want to know. 'Did you ever think that I'd hurt you, while you were down in the cells?'

'No.'

'I was trying to wound him,' I say. 'Not just because I knew he could overpower me if I tried to arrest him by myself. I was trying to wound him.'

'Still telling harsh truths,' Paul says.

There's a pause, we sit opposite each other.

'What do you want, Paul?'

He runs his lower lip through his teeth, sits back in his chair. 'I'm not over you,' he says.

'Oh.' I have absolutely no answer to that.

He shakes his head, says again, 'I'm not over you.'

It isn't I love you, it isn't I forgive you. It doesn't mean either of those things. I try to ask the question, I have to think for a while about how to put it so it isn't a request. 'Will you ever forgive me for what happened?'

He shakes his head. 'I – I don't know. I don't think much in terms of forgiveness, I guess.'

'That's not very Christian,' I say.

'You're the one who was praying, I . . . God, I don't know. I miss you. That isn't about whether I forgive you or not. I lied to you, so you didn't help me. Now – things aren't settled. I don't know.'

Things aren't settled. He doesn't know. I don't know what to say to him.

'Listen,' he says. 'Where are you in all this?'

I shake my head, open my mouth, but nothing comes out.

'If you had your wish, what would you want to happen?'

I don't know what I want now. Everything is gone. I look at him, talk normally, as if this was just a conversation. 'I wish things could be the way they were before you got arrested and everything happened.'

He looks at me to see if I mean it, then says, 'So do I.'

I keep my hands away from him, I don't reach out. 'What do you want?' I say.

'I miss how things were.'

'That's how you feel. It isn't what you want.' The look he gives me is almost wry. I guess he was used to me doing things the hard way. The blood runs through my veins cool as tap water, and I can't remember how to find things funny.

'I've done some bad things.' I speak again before he can answer me. 'Worse than you know. And I know things worse than you know as well. I'm not a real person any more.'

514

'You look real enough to me.' His expression isn't quite patient.

'Why did you come back here? After everything that happened here, how could you stand to be back in this building?'

He flexes his hands. 'I don't like black spots in my mind. I didn't want my last memories of this place to be what happened downstairs.'

That's what he says, that he wants to come back to a place where we put him through the Inquisition, because he wants better memories of it. Black spots in the mind. Brain damage at birth. 'You're a better person than me,' I say.

He shrugs. 'I'm out of their reach. They can see me but they can't do anything about it. It's sort of satisfying. No one can do anything to me now. Except maybe you.'

I sit at my desk, and I think about what he said.


I think about getting away with things.

Somewhere on the other side of this is the woman I wanted to be, the woman who would have done what I should have done, who would have known what it was. Not someone cross-hatched with scars, not someone carrying an armful of dead babies. Are there parents who accepted Parkinson's offer? People who know what he did to children?

Johnny did. When Johnny tried to protect the new children Parkinson shattered the back of his neck with a silver bullet.

Seligmann will go down for that. We give the doctor a scapegoat, we wash his sins away. Johnny is silenced.

Parkinson can tell himself that nothing ever happened, and no one will say otherwise. He can walk the streets like an innocent man.

I think about what Paul said, about wanting his last memories to be better ones.

When Becca comes to see me, she's impressed at the look of my flat. I've washed the floors, the shelves, the windows, the curtains, I've thrown away half of what I own. There were a couple of days where I couldn't sit still, couldn't even stand without pacing, and I ended up walking to a hardware shop and buying cans of paint. My living room has become paler. Becca calls the colour cream, I call it bone. It looks all right, I think. Different, anyway. I just couldn't stand being surrounded by red walls.

She sits Leo on the sofa beside me, leans him back, and he keeps upright; his spine is flat and sturdy, he's balanced. I shake his hand and tell him what a clever boy he is, and he tips forward into my lap. I hoist him up, let him gnaw at me with his sharpening gums. My free hand rests on his head, the round warm little skull sheltering his clean, unbruised brain. As he nips and scrapes my skin, I hold onto him. Parkinson delivered him. I saw it happen. I remember asking Parkinson if he would come feet first like he should, saying that Becca didn't want a bareback baby. If I hadn't been there, might Parkinson have looked at the notes, seen Becca had a bareback sister and decided she was a prime candidate for a mutilated child?

His teeth on the heel of my hand are becoming too painful, so I pull away and let him bite my fingers. His chest is barely wider than my palm, and it rises and falls against me, fast and steady. My sister's perfect son. Have I saved him?

'Becca,' I say over Leo's head, 'I need to ask you a favour. A big one.'


When Johnny went to see Parkinson, he went alone. He took a gun, and Parkinson took it off him and shattered his skull.

When I go, I go with my sister. Her thriving son rides in a pram before her, and she waits with me. She doesn't quite understand, but when I tell her I can't explain, she comes with me anyway.


The foyer carpet crushes under my feet like moss, the walls glow. There's a pretty receptionist with amber freckles and neat white teeth who smiles up at me.

'Do you have an appointment?' she asks.

'I don't,' I say. 'But I wondered if it would be possible to see Dr Parkinson. It needn't take very long.' She wrinkles her forehead. 'Could you give him a message, at least?'

'Of course.' She reaches for a pen; it's black and glossy with a gold band around it.

'Could you tell him I've been thinking about what he said?'

Her lashes flick down as she watches her hand write the message. I'll never know if she knows.

We sit in the elegant reception room for more than an hour before we're finally allowed through. I take the scarf from around my neck and dangle it above Leo's face to pass the wait, and he reaches up for it. He can grab things now, he's accurate. He catches it every time.

When Dr Parkinson finally appears in the door, Becca stands, gathers Leo up and walks in with me. I glance at her, indicate she can wait in the foyer if she wants, but she shakes her head, takes a firmer grip on her son and walks ahead of me through the door.

I study Parkinson as I come in. All the things I've noticed before, the straight back and clean hair, the skin ageing smoothly as fine suede, they're still there. His nails are pink and rather wide, the pale cuticles rise in a steep curve to cover half the area. I look him over for marks, scars, but my eyes slip up and down his face, finding nothing. He can't have passed a life with no cuts or slashes, I know. He's just a lyco. Nothing's cut him so deep that it wouldn't heal at the end of each moon night.

'How are you, Ms Galley?' he asks. There's no aggression there, not even unwillingness, which surely any straight doctor would feel if a patient turned up and demanded to see them in the middle of a working day. Jones was as good as his word, there's been nothing on the news about me arresting Seligmann, but Parkinson knows I work for DORLA. That I'm a bareback. That's all he thinks he needs to know about me.

'I'm very well, thank you. I do hope you'll forgive me turning up unannounced like this.' I'm a legal adviser in a government department, and I work hard. I'm a professional. I can do a civil voice as well as he can, if I know I need to.

'That's quite all right.' He glances over at Becca. She's sat herself down in a chair in the corner, and is sitting Leo up on her lap, pulling his shirt straight.

'You remember my sister, I'm sure,' I say. 'And Leo. You delivered him.'

Parkinson glances from me to her, just for a second. He doesn't look certain, but I sound confident about Becca's presence, and he's waiting for me to confide in him. He can't afford to protest. 'How nice to see you again,' he says.

Becca nods, and raises Leo's hand as if in greeting.

'I hope you received all the results satisfactorily,' he says to me.

He means the letters confirming that I'm still all right, that nothing has made me sterile. 'Yes, thank you.'

He's waiting for me to make the next move, but I leave a pause.

'I understand you had something you wanted to discuss,' he says in the end.

I smile. 'Yes. The truth is, I've been thinking about it, and – well, I'm interested in what you said. But there's a few things I wanted to get straight, I just wondered if I could discuss them with you first.' I sound like I'm levelling with him.

He smiles back at me and takes a seat. 'Of course. Any questions you have, I'm happy to answer.' It's a prepared sentence, one he must have said many times before.

'The thing is – well, this isn't my area. I was wondering about the legalities of it, that's the first thing.' He doesn't have to hear the warning that I'm a lawyer in that if he doesn't want to. I sit myself down opposite him and wait for him to answer.

'I wouldn't concern yourself with the legalities too much,' he says.

'I am concerned, though.' I don't sound forceful, just unconvinced.

519

'I wouldn't know about that,' he says pleasantly. 'I just follow the laws as they stand.'

'As long as they're applicable.'

'Yes, indeed. You have to exercise a little common sense when it comes to laws that are out of date.'

I smile at him. 'I think you've just told me my whole career in miniature.'

'Your career?'

'Didn't I mention it? I'm a lawyer.' There's a swift, small instant of silence. 'I specialise in curfew law and anmorphic law generally.'

'That must be interesting,' he says. His voice is too polite for a conversation this far along.

'Yes, you see, that's why I'm wondering. Most of my colleagues are involved in DORLA law somehow, and – well, if I took this course, I'm wondering about confidentiality. I'm not sure how it would be received.'

'Confidentiality goes without saying.' He sounds almost emphatic in defence of his profession. 'Cases like this are entirely personal. It's a matter of individual choice, and there's no question of revealing the patient's decision.'

'Really?'

'Of course. If you make a decision about your child's future, of course you have the right to keep it to yourself.'

'I'm not sure they'd consider it a decision I had a right to make.'

'Of course you do. No one else does.'

Becca sits quiet in the corner. Leo snuffles in her arms.

'You think it's my decision, then?'

'Of course I do.' He looks almost pleased at the

520

opportunity to expound. 'Medicine has come such a long way since the days of those laws you were worrying about, Ms Galley. We can do so many things now that would have been unimaginable even twenty, thirty years ago. Patients have every right to take advantage of the new techniques available.'

'What's the point of discovering something new if people don't get to use it?' I ask the question quietly. Behind me, I hear Becca shift Leo on her lap.

'Exactly.' A smile lights up Parkinson's face. I've said something he believes in.

'Even if it's not really ethical?'

'Excuse me?' The smile goes, he looks at me in perplexity.

'I mean, surely you don't have to do something just because you can?'

'You should give the patient all possible options, Ms Galley.' He's frowning at me now, his eyes twitch towards his watch.

'Do you, though?' I say. Becca shifts in her seat, I hear the rub of fabric against leather. She never liked arguments.

'Excuse me?'

'It just seems to me unlikely that you'd get agreement from many DORLA members. Do you think so? I'm just concerned that it's the patient's decision.'

'I'm sorry, how does this affect your condition?' Authority rises in his voice, years of taking decisions.

'I just wondered how often . . . The thing is, I just wanted to know. I know what a bareback would think of it, what most barebacks would think of it. That's why I doubt you always consult your patients, I mean, beyond a few oblique soundings-out they might not

521

recognise for what they are. I just wondered –' I almost say 'what a man like you', but I don't, I say, 'I just wondered what you reckon makes it acceptable. Injuring babies at birth. Turning them into . . .' I spread my hands wide, almost in a shrug, the thick white scar on my forearm upwards, 'well, into this.'

'Ms Galley –' He stands up.

'Johnny Marcos,' I say.

He stops. 'What did you say?'

I look blank-faced, I keep looking at him. 'You couldn't know what life is like with this disability. You're an intelligent man, though, you must be able to think about it.'

He sits back into his chair, slow, not looking away from me, not answering.

'It's really a bad life,' I say. My voice betrays me, it shakes for a moment, and I curl my fingers up tight, covering my soft palms. 'You know about the mis-carriage I had, I told you about that. That was from a lune attacking me. And the thing is, nobody was surprised. It was generally agreed that I got off easier than I might have.'

Leo whimpers in the corner, and Becca shushes him. I don't turn and look at her, but I hear her voice, tight as a stretched rope.

'We can't afford psychiatrists,' I say. 'But we suffer just about every abuse in the system, one way or another. And there aren't any compensations.'

His hands rest on the desk. The fingers are curled, as if relaxed, but tendons stand out at the knuckles, and I see he's holding them in that position, stiff like spiders.

'You've probably heard this before,' I say. 'You do remember Johnny Marcos, don't you?'

He doesn't move.

'Are you thinking about that?' I ask. 'All this time you thought I was a patient?'

'What do you want?' he says. It's the voice of a man talking to a blackmailer, a mugger.

'I want you to keep your hands where I can see them, to begin with.'

'May . . .'

I glance over my shoulder, and hear my voice going soft. 'If you want to wait in the lobby, that's okay. He's seen you, he knows you know I'm here.'

Becca looks at me, then at Parkinson, and shakes her head. Her face is pale and her arms are tight around her son, but she stays in her chair.

'It's all right,' I tell Parkinson. 'In the way you're thinking, it's all right. I'm not here to blackmail you, or arrest you. That's not my department. I'm not going to get between the mills of DORLA and you.' He thought he was safe. I can see it in his face, no one's mentioned Johnny Marcos to him before this moment. Maybe they'll come for him one day, quietly, in secret; maybe they won't. If they do, the day they do, will I get to hear about it?

He looks up at me, and I see his face draw itself tight. He looks like a younger man, steady and calm. 'I don't think you could if you wanted to.' I raise my eyebrows. 'Otherwise you wouldn't be here. What is it you want, Ms Galley?'

'I want to know why you did it.'

He looks at me, and suddenly he's older again, old enough to be my father, old enough to be beyond my reach. 'I can't say I know what you're talking about. Why did I do what?'

I smile at him, just for a moment, then I calm my face. 'I'm not asking why you killed Johnny.' He blinks, a short static twitch, as if his eyes weren't connected to the rest of his face. 'I don't suppose I could get that out of you. Maybe if I arrested you, put you down in our cells, ran an interrogation over you, but I don't think that's really my thing any more. Anyway, I can make a guess. You panicked, both of you. Johnny had a gun, he threatened you. When you spend your life hunting lunes and taking pressure from lycos all day, it's easy to feel they'd all tear your throat out given a chance. But you weren't to know that. You don't deal with us after we've grown up. Maybe you really thought he'd kill you.' He's looking at me, his eyes blue and clean, the whites bright enough to break your heart. 'Probably that's what you think now, anyway. If he hadn't known something that could ruin you, would you really have thought he was so dangerous? You could think about that, sometimes, you know, when you're waiting for a train and haven't anything else to do.'

'Is that a suggestion?' he says. 'Or just a thought you had while waiting for your own train?'

I shrug, spreading my hands, bare palms and scarred wrist open to his gaze. 'Humour me.'

He looks at me for a long second. 'What is it you want?'

'I want you to know you're going to hell,' I hear myself say.

He glances at my throat, sees the St Giles medal hanging there. Not a crucifix, something says inside my head. I'm no real Christian, just a woman making the Aegidans her own faith. A wrathful God frowns before my face for speaking so utterly beyond my rights.

It's almost reassured him, though. He didn't hear a warning against his soul, he heard a hysterical woman preaching at him.

'I'll worry about my own soul, thank you,' he says. He isn't comfortable, but he isn't really afraid of me.

'I'd like to hear your justification.'

'For my work?'

'Yes.' I nod, almost polite. 'Please.'

'My work is practised with the consent of your own order.' He looks at my pale hands. 'Has it occurred to you that one reason people with your disability experience so much discrimination is because you are so few? Most people have very little contact with you. Anmorphic people work all day for DORLA, they socialise amongst themselves, they don't meet the rest of the population very much unless they arrest them. A few thousand more members could make all the difference for you. If you want to keep the curfew system going – and personally I can't think of a better alternative.'

I sit quiet, listening to him. Becca sits behind me, rocking Leo to and fro.

'Then there's the other reason for your unpopularity, of course. You're known, infamous for your treatment of prisoners. I don't believe you can be sitting there with no blood on your hands, Ms Galley, not for a second. It seems to me that with more of you, you might be less inclined to resort to such primitive methods. I'm concerned for your victims, you know, most people are. It would be a great humanitarian advance to improve DORLA's resources. For you, as well as anyone else. Look at you. You're –' he glances down, looks at a file on his desk – 'twenty-eight years old, and already you

525

have white hairs. I don't say this to hurt your feelings, but you could pass for ten years older than you are without a question.' It's not aggressive, it's assessing, a doctor's opinion. 'I'm sure you'd appreciate more help in your life.'

I turn around, look at Leo for a moment. He doesn't want to be sitting on Becca's lap, he's decided he's old enough for the floor. He arches his back and churns his legs, wilful and determined and vitally concerned with his own wishes. 'I'd appreciate more financial resources,' I say. 'Not more children, not like this.'

'You don't like your life, I see. But I do believe that if you were more numerous, it wouldn't be so difficult for you.'

'Don't tell me this is for our benefit. You talk as if it was DORLA's suggestion. I know it wasn't. Someone came to DORLA and suggested it.'

'How would DORLA suggest it? You don't request a medical treatment if you don't know it's available. They needed to be made aware of the possibility.'

'But why would you come up with it? How? How could you do experiments to find out if it was possible?'

Parkinson sighs. 'They weren't begun ethically, certainly. Prisoner-of-war camps, for the most part, or political prisoners in countries even less civilised than our own. Experiments that tended to fail.' Fail and take the mother and child into the dark with them. I've heard those stories. 'It began as an academic exercise, really. A tremendous challenge. Think of it: no other species experiences metamorphosis at the rate we humans do, transformation from one state to another and back again. It's truly a miraculous process. Brilliant men have studied it for a lifetime and still don't know all there is to know. It's miraculous, and it's tremendously fragile. A few adverse conditions for a few minutes at the moment of birth, and it's destroyed forever. If we could just understand those conditions, we'd be so much closer to understanding our own nature. And we're doing it, we're closer now, far closer than we would have believed twenty years ago. Such a difficult process, and we're mastering it. How many medical techniques can you think of that only affect humans, that can't be tested on animals at all because there simply isn't anything comparable in the animal experience?'

'You're using research tested on humans, aren't you?'

'Discarding a valuable medical discovery for the sake of some dead sufferers who are beyond help is not an ethical practice. Ask any doctor, they'll tell you the same thing.'

'You're talking as if this – this thing you can do to children is for their own good.' It's Becca talking. Both of us turn. Parkinson's face is surprised, as if I'd brought a dog in and it had decided to voice its own opinion, and heat floods up my arms from fingertips to chest as I see my sister, her voice a little hesitant, speak my thoughts ahead of me, of her own free will declare herself against this glossy room and the articulate man within it.

He doesn't address her. He turns back to me. 'For the greater good. As for the individuals – well, they manage. You manage, I'm sure you could tell me hundreds of examples of individuals coping perfectly well with this' – he raises his hand, held stiff like an oar – 'minor disability.'

'Oh, yes,' I say. 'This is how we cope.' I reach into

my bag and pull out a sheaf of photographs. I lay them on the table before him, one after the other, like a card dealer.

The flattened silver bullet the pathologist took out of Nate's broken skull.

A crime scene photograph, an empty cell after a lune mauled a catcher. Blood pools on the ground, gels around the straw, smears up and down the tiled walls. It's an old picture. There's no one in the cell. This is how it would have looked, the night Johnny brought Ellaway to the shelter.

Paul. He stands, looking away from the camera as if ashamed. Bruises layer his chest, black and purple, cracked skin laces round his ribs. They all took pictures, the day they were released: Sarah was thinking of suing. They didn't, of course. Paul's head is averted. There's a window to his side with the sun pouring through in a cold winter blaze. His eyes are creased against the un-accustomed light.

Parkinson looks at the pictures. 'What are you trying to prove, Ms Galley? Is this supposed to disturb me? I am a doctor, I'm not unused to the sight of blood.'

I laugh, I actually laugh. 'Oh, I know you're not.' I lay out more pictures.

Nate on the slab. 'Seligmann did this,' I say. 'The man you let out onto the streets to take our eyes off you.'

Another picture. David, his arm destroyed. 'And Seligmann's friend. Who you wouldn't treat. I can't believe he didn't ask you to steal anti-allergens for him. You helped Seligmann escape and hid him so he'd get rid of the evidence for you. But you wouldn't take that risk for another man.'

528

'Do you expect me to dignify that with an answer?'

'No,' I say, 'I don't.' I lay out my last two pictures.

Johnny stands with his family. Debbie stands holding her mother's free hand, her face clean and cheerful, full of the prospect of a new baby. A little gawky, but sweet as only a child who hasn't learned her body yet can be. Julio slouches against his father, trying to look cool, and Peter stands beside him, leaning on his shoulder. Sue's pregnancy doesn't show much yet, there's just a little rounding of her stomach, but you can see it, because Johnny has looped his arms around her and is holding it, his hands cradling his unborn child. He's grinning, his jowls crease all over with the smile on his face.

The second picture comes from the mortuary. Johnny lies on a slab. His head rests at the wrong angle, the great hollow at the back of it pulling it off balance. Pieces of his face are missing.

Parkinson looks at the pictures, looks up at me.

'I don't like your theory of the greater good,' I say. 'The price is too high.'

And I reach into my bag again.

He opens his mouth again, but when he sees the gun, he closes it. His hand edges towards the telephone, and I reach out and take hold of it, put it gently back where I can see it. He feels warm, damp, his touch comes off on my skin.

'May, what are you doing?' Becca's on her feet, her arms tight around Leo.

'It's okay, Becca.'

'What are you doing?'

'This won't take a minute.' She starts towards me, but I flinch, just for a second, and she stops. 'I'm sorry about this, really I am, but this won't take a minute.'

Parkinson sits with his hands where I can see them.
'I don't think you did it out of public spirit,' I say.
'You're no hero of medicine. I think maybe you did it
for the money, and because you could. That's what I
think. Mostly, you did it because you could. Because it
didn't really touch you. That isn't so any more.'

Parkinson twitches, one hand jumps on the desk.

'Don't try to grab the gun off me. You did that once
before, remember? Not again.'

'You'll go to jail for life if you shoot.' His voice
is shaking, his face pale. The gloss is gone, the life he's
lived, the security and authority and success that his
safe birth bought him. All the nourished, healthy blood
has drained out of it, and I see it, I see the face that
Johnny saw.

'I took a life sentence at birth,' I say, and draw back
the catch.

'May, don't.' Becca is hoarse, whispering with fear.

I look at the face of the murderer, and pull the trigger.

Parkinson gives a small, hoarse cry, and Becca gasps.
The click of the empty chamber is the quietest thing in
the room.

I look at him for a second more, then put the gun
back in my bag. 'You thought I'd do it.' I shake my
head. 'I'm not you. I wouldn't do that.'

Leo starts to cry, the pressure of his mother's arms
is crushing him. Becca is shivering, the sound of her
panting rises over her son's tears. I sweep up the pictures
and walk over to her. 'Here, let me take him.' She looks
at me, tears in her eyes. 'I'm sorry,' I tell her, and she
shakes her head. It isn't a rejection. She presses a hand
to her forehead and passes Leo over to me. Over his
head, I look at Parkinson.

'You'll . . .' he says.

'Nothing will happen to me. The gun comes from DORLA. I didn't even have to steal it, I went straight into Weapons, spoke to the man at the desk. I told him I didn't need ammo, and he didn't even bother signing it out. I'll return it tonight, and no one will ask.' Maybe some discipline will be handed down, I might lose my pay raise or have to be yelled at. It doesn't mean a thing. 'You can tell them about this, the day they come for you,' I say.

Leo is still crying in my arms. I rest his wet cheek against mine, cupping his head, still looking at Parkinson. His face has flooded red, bright under his greying hair, and I see him again, not the face of a murderer, but just a man, an ageing man who thought for a few moments that death was coming sooner than he was prepared for. I smile at him, shake my whitening hair out of my eyes. 'Now you know,' I say. 'That's how it feels on the other side.'

# 45

The day Marty comes back to work, I haven't much time to talk to him. I'm going one way down the corridor, my arms full of papers, he's going the other. His throat is wrapped in scars, and when we stop to talk, his voice is thinner than before, but his eyes are clear and he carries himself well, all six foot one of him is straight and balanced. It's an unusual look in DORLA, and it takes a moment to figure out what it is. He looks rested.

We haven't much time to chat. He's heading for the Seligmann trial; he's going to stand witness. The Harpers have already gone through the system, they're sitting in different prisons now, waiting for fifteen years to pass. Attempted murder, resisting arrest. They're in a mainstream prison, where we can't get at them any more. Seligmann, we've been saving.

I can't go to the trial. The Ellaway case, my guilty client, has been scheduled to take place at the same time, and I have to present a case. I'm safely out of the way. A very tactful piece of scheduling.

'I heard you got the bastard,' Marty says. The story is all around DORLA now, how I bravely confronted the desperate Seligmann, brought him in single-handed. This is the man who tore Marty's throat out, and there's a burning satisfaction in Marty's face as he speaks. Marty thinks I'm a heroine. I haven't the heart to disillusion him.

Ellaway has told Franklin what happened in his captivity. Franklin asked me if it was true, and I didn't deny it. I told him, when he asked me, that I was a DORLA lawyer, not much worse than most, that there but for the grace of God went he. I reckon he expected me to say something like that, and I had to give him some way of dealing with having such an unconscionable colleague. To his credit, Franklin actually thought about it. It's too bad. I'd rather liked him.

When I first met Ellaway, he was insisting that he'd been trying to get to a shelter during moonrise, that his car had broken down on his way home from work. A simple defence, a classic. Since then, I discovered how much he had lied.

I tell Ellaway the truth will make things worse, that faking evidence is a more serious crime than prowling. Of course, it's not concern for my client that makes me say this. If Ellaway tells the truth, he'll drag other people down with him, Albin, Sarah, Carla, people who've helped me. Paul.

Ellaway told me a lie the first time he met me, and expected me to build a case out of it. He can damn well stick to it now.

I look around the courtroom as I go in. This is a room I've worked in dozens, scores, maybe hundreds of times. I'd like to work in a grand court, oak panels and carved

533

docks, crests behind the robed judge, but this is just another room in our tower block, with chipped ceiling tiles and fluorescent lights, scuffed blue carpets wearing away around the door. I look around for the Marcos family, before I remember. They'll be at the murder trial next door. Whatever Ellaway did to him, it's all the same now.

It startles me to see Bride sitting on the benches. She hadn't told me she was coming back, but now Seligmann is in jail, no threat to her, I guess she figured it was safe. She sees me, gives me a grin and a wink. For a moment, I stay blank-faced, wondering at her. Gone without a word, back without a word, convinced that we can pick up just where we left off. Then I let it go. She has her sick husband to think of, her own life, her own fear of dying. And the more I think about it, the more of a relief it is. No scenes, no awkward apologies either way. I did one thing, she did another, and we can get on with our lives without looking back. I smile back at her. I need all the friends I can get.

Looking further down the bench, I see Becca. She doesn't know much about this trial, even now. She's just come to see me work. I could wish she'd come to watch a better trial, but I guess she's seen the worst of me now.

After she sat with me in Parkinson's office, we went home together. We walked in silence, block after block. My hands shook. It was a long time before I could say to her, 'Are you still speaking to me?'

She looked down at Leo. I could see her thinking of what to say, ways to make peace, ways to hurt me, ways to free herself of me for the rest of her life.

'I'm sorry,' I said.

She looked at me. Her face was pretty in the daylight. 'I'm really not happy about it,' she said. There was a pause. 'Was it true what you said about that man? Did he really shoot someone?'

'Yes, he did.'

Her hand rested against her son's chest. 'It was all true, what you said?'

'Yes. I didn't make anything up.'

She looked away from me, looked back. 'I'm really not happy about it,' she said again. 'But I guess you know your own business best.'

I reached out and touched her hand, and she didn't move away.

Some days she calls me and talks for hours, pouring out words about her son, her marriage, details and intimacies I'd never heard before and would never have expected. Some days when I go to see her she's distant, looking at Leo as he sits up and grins, not meeting my eyes. I don't know quite what to make of her. I guess she feels the same way about me. It's a queer kind of fresh start, but some day soon I'll start talking back, I'll tell her things about me. Maybe we'll find better things to say to each other.

Sitting on another bench, near the back, is a dark-haired man, on his own, speaking to no one. His face is turned away from me, but I know it's Paul.

Becca sees me first. She gives me a little wave. It's an odd gesture, strangely encouraging. My schools never went in for concerts or recitals, and my mother never attended a trial of mine, but there's something in Becca's salute that makes me think of a mother – not mine, someone else's mother, someone better – watching her child perform, applauding from the back seat. It's so

535

strange that I don't know how to respond, but in the end I just raise my eyebrows and try to smile at her.

Then Paul turns his head and sees me. My arms are full of documents, hugged to my chest, and I can't gesture. Paul looks at me and I look back, we hold each other's gaze for long seconds.

It's only when someone brushes past me that I turn my head. I go over to the table where I sit with my client, lay down my papers, pull my chair up to the desk, tidy my hands on the surface. I sit and wait for the judge to come in, ready to be a lawyer.


Nick Jarrold takes the stand. Sitting there, he tells the story of how he and Johnny came upon Ellaway, tried to arrest him, how Ellaway brought Johnny down and tore his hand away, Nick holds a packet of cigarettes he's not allowed to smoke, not while the trial is in session. He turns it over in his lap, tapping it against his knee, so that the logo on the front upends and rights itself again and again. He tells the prosecution everything he remembers about that night. I don't cross-examine him. He coughs and rasps in the stand, and I wonder how long he'll have before cancer finally comes to claim him.


Lisa Rahman, one of our expert witnesses, takes the stand. A map of the city is placed on an easel next to her. Distance Assessment is a small department; she testifies in dozens of trials every month. She studies locations, assesses how fast you could walk them, how far someone could travel over this terrain or that in any given time. People often say they were trying to get to a shelter when the moon rose. She calculates whether, if they'd been trying, they could have. In this case, she concludes that Ellaway probably could. I stand up, ask her if she's a hundred per cent certain, she says no. The re-direct asks her if she's convinced herself, she says yes.

Even though I knew it was coming, I still feel an ugly little twist in my chest when I see Ally come into the room and walk up to the witness stand. He was there, the night Johnny brought Ellaway in. He has to testify. He doesn't look at me when he comes into the room, I see the back of his head, and for a moment I don't recognise him. His ragged hair has been cut short, shaped to his skull. I remember, as if it was a long time ago, the bet we once had, that he'd shave his head the day I spoke to a lyco lawyer who didn't mention that public opinion is against us. We used to bet each other a lot, when we got too old to dare each other. I guess all our bets are off now.

He turns his head and sees Paul sitting in the benches. Paul looks back at him, implacable, untouchable. It's only a moment before Ally reaches the stand and sits down. His eyes flick over the tables, and when he sees me, his fidgeting stops, he sits still.

Under oath, he tells the judge how Ellaway was brought in with Johnny bleeding almost to death from a mutilated arm. That Ellaway was tranquillised and unconscious, and that he was still luning, but clean, there were no brambles or leaves in his hair, there was no mud on him, that he didn't look like a man who'd got lost and wandered into a park.

537

I stand up, straighten my jacket, to cross-examine him.

'Did you keep any samples of this hair?' I ask. From my tone, you wouldn't know I'd ever met Ally before.

'No. There was blood all over the floor, and we had to sterilise everything, the hair was incinerated.'

'So we have no concrete evidence for this claim of yours. We're just going to take your word?'

He looks at me, dark-eyed. 'I remember what happened.'

I know he's telling the truth, and he knows I know. 'What time was my client brought into your shelter?'

'About one-thirty.'

'Had you been on duty all night?'

'Yes.'

'What time was sunset that day?'

Ally shrugs, his shoulders roll. The familiarity of the gesture cuts at my heart. 'About four-fifteen, I think.'

'So you'd been on duty for over nine hours?'

'Yes.'

'Was he the only arrest you'd had?'

'No, there were five others in the shelter.'

'You must have been tired.'

Ally looks at me when I say this. A year ago, in another room, it would have been a stupid thing to say, he would have laughed at me, or with me. My voice is almost sympathetic, and even after everything, I still feel a tug of pain at the thought of Ally, my old friend, nine hours into the night, trying to keep awake and work through it.

'When John Marcos was brought in,' I continue, 'would you describe his condition as serious?'

'His hand was taken off, of course it was serious,'

Ally snaps. I've heard myself snap the same way, many times.

'You must have been concerned about him.'

Tired, concerned, desperate. Ally must have been all these things. I know everything he must have felt that night. He doesn't hear any fellow-feeling in my voice, though, because he knows where I'm going with this. Everything he has to say about the night Ellaway was captured is fair and accurate, but easy to raise doubts about, and that's what I'm doing. It's terrible, really, that of all the people in this trial, I'll probably do the best job discrediting Ally. If things hadn't happened the way they did, he wouldn't hold it against me, but I have a feeling he will now. It can't be helped. It's over. He won't owe me a thing any more. I've set him loose.


They raise the issue of the car, its damaged engine. No conclusive proof. I'm able to get the witness – Kevin White, the garage owner who was finally told to stop just storing Ellaway's Maserati and look under the bonnet – to admit he can't say for sure it was tampered with, not a hundred per cent. It's still a big point for the prosecution. I discovered it, this damaging point. I disclosed it to my opposite number a week before the trial, just as the law says I must.


The free-rangers, I did not disclose. I didn't have to: everyone in DORLA knew about them, all that time they were down in the cells. I could raise them, make them an exonerating circumstance, or at least a chance to spread the blame. I don't. I could call my client to the stand, too, have him tell his story. For a whole day, I was tempted. It would have given him the opportunity to add perjury to his crimes, a couple of years to his sentence. I wanted to, but I didn't.

As a result, the case I make is a thin one. Franklin works with me, calls up witnesses to refute the engine-tampering charge, finds other cases where people with similar stories were found innocent. He's very good. While he's speaking, even I'm half-convinced by what he says. When he stops talking, though, and it's quiet, after all the speeches are over, everyone knows what's going to happen.

In the pause while the judge deliberates, people stand up and walk around the room. Paul looks at me, and I take one step towards him, my whole body yearning, as if I were nothing but a hand reaching out. Something checks me, though, and I nod instead to Becca, point at my watch and raise five fingers, five minutes. She understands, nods back to me. I look at Paul, he looks at me. Then I turn and slip out of the room.

Out in the corridor, I lean my hands flat against a wall, breathing in and out. The air reflecting back off the painted surface is warm against my face. I lean for a few seconds, then I walk down the hall.

The other trial is still not finished, the Seligmann case. There's a little square of glass in the door, and I peer through it. Seligmann himself sits in the dock, a crutch beside him, bandages on his wounded leg showing thick through his clothes. His posture has changed from when I first saw him. The hunched shoulders and lupine, pulled-back neck are still there, but off to one side, curved around the place where I shot him, as if that silver bullet were the new centre point of his body.

Johnny's family sit on the benches. Peter and Julio sit side by side. Julio's face is blank; he's sitting upright and brave, keeping his eyes dry and his mouth still, not giving his pain away to anyone. Peter has one leg crossed into his lap, and it jiggles, almost too fast to see, until Sue reaches out a round, loose arm and stills it. She lays her hand on his foot, and doesn't let go. Sue is a sphere by now, the baby will be born any day. You can almost see it moving through her clothes. Her free arm rests around her daughter, who lies with her head against her mother's shoulder, a thumb in her mouth. They don't look at Seligmann much. The four of them hang close together, huddled on the narrow bench, waiting for it all to be over.

Sooner than I expect, I'm tapped on the shoulder and sent back in to my own trial. Ellaway looks at Franklin, grips his fists together as the judge prepares to announce his verdict, but I feel no tension or anticipation. There are no doubts about what's coming. I can't remember the last time I felt that way.

I thought I'd be happy to lose this case. I thought it would be a blow for our side, vengeance for Johnny, for something. When the judge sentences Ellaway to twelve years' imprisonment, though, there's no joy, no righteous anger. His face goes white, he stares at the judge, unable to believe that this is real, and then people come and put his hands in cuffs and take him away.

I don't feel like hanging around to discuss the verdict. I take off, go out into a quiet corridor and light a cigarette. I'll talk to Bride later. I'll talk to Becca later.

I'm leaning against the wall, watching the smoke coil around my hands, when I hear a voice. It's hoarse and damaged, but I recognise the polite greeting. Marty still sounds like himself.

'How's it going?' I say to him.

He smiles, baring his teeth. The scars on his neck don't move. 'Bastard's going down,' he says. 'No question about it. The judge has to give him life, doesn't he?' The question isn't savage. It's more hopeful than anything else.

I tap ash into a tray on the wall. 'Yes. It's mandatory in cases of murder. It would be the same however many murders, whatever kind he committed.' I clear my throat. 'How long he actually serves depends on how he acts in prison.'

'I thought the judge could recommend a minimum?' He still wants to know things, he hasn't stopped learning.

I nod. 'He can. Don't know how much they'll listen to it in a lyco prison, though.'

Marty looks at the floor.

'What's wrong, kiddo?' I say.

He looks back at me, shrugs. 'I don't know.' He doesn't touch his throat, his hands stay by his side. It's just a little dip of his head, his chin shielding the damaged skin. 'I just don't get it. There's all that evidence that he did it, that's all they're talking about. I – guess I

542

want to know why. What he was thinking. I don't know.'
His eyes are on the floor again, as if he was hanging
his head. But it's not a stupid question.

I inhale smoke, exhale. Grey dust rises slowly to the
ceiling. 'It's worth asking,' I say. There's only a moment's
pause before I go on. 'I don't know, really. I know
someone you can ask, though.' I take a notepad out of
my pocket, write down a number. There's no need to
look it up. I remember it perfectly. 'Give this guy a call.
His name's Paul Kelsey.'

Marty gives me a quick look.

I shake my head. 'Never mind what you've heard
about him,' I say. 'He's okay. I think he might be able
to tell you a bit about it. Tell him it was me suggested
you call.'

Marty looks doubtful. 'I don't want to just call
him . . .'

'It's okay, he won't mind,' I say. I'm almost sure he
won't. 'You should call him. He's a pretty decent guy.'


Later that day, I wander back through the building. As
I pass by the trial rooms, I hear a noise. The door opens,
and two tall men come out. Between them, hands chained
together, is a dark-haired man, limping, one leg dragging under him. He looks up. Seligmann. He looks at
me. I look back at him. He doesn't snarl, he doesn't
pull a face, he just looks at me, his eyes stay on me
until the guards walk him past me, their strong hands
clasped under his arms to hold him up.

The trial room empties. Sue Marcos walks out, her
arms around her children. There are too many people
around her for me to be able to get to her, but she sees

me, raises her hand. I sign, *I'll call you*, and she nods. Debbie clings to her hand as they walk down the corridor.

The crowd clears, until there's no one left in the room. I walk in. It's very quiet, the air still warm from so many bodies. It doesn't look like much, this room it ended in. Just walls, chairs, benches. Very likely, Seligmann never entered this room before today. I know he'll never see it again in his life.

I look at the chair he was sitting in. It's grey plastic, the legs shining black, splaying backwards and forwards to support the structure. There are thousands like it, but somehow it holds my attention, as if I'll never forget the sight of it.

# 46

Yesterday I took Leo in his pushchair and went for a walk in the park. It was one of those spring days that come before the season really turns, the sky a deep unearthly blue, the sun bright but not yet warm. The little paper mobiles I tied on the hood of his pram had been untied and re-fixed to the pushchair with neat, careful knots, and this made me want to cry for a moment. Instead I tapped them to make them spin, and Leo reached up his hands with perfect aim to pat them.

I thought of taking him to Abbots Park, where Johnny died. Or I could have taken him to Queens, where Ellaway mauled him, or Spiritus Sanctus, where Seligmann killed Nate. I could have taken him on a whole pilgrimage. I didn't. I walked with him through Kings, heading for the open spaces, and in the vernal light, the grass was golden under my feet.

It's cooler today, as I walk with him again. The year isn't ready to be warm yet. I wheel him quietly, watching from above as his small fingers curl around his jacket sleeves. The wheels of his pushchair rattle just a little, and I think about taking him to another park, but it's too cold for grass today, and I feel like a change. Leo is getting big enough to push against his straps, and he arches his back, kicking his legs out stiff, feeling too grown-up to be strapped in a buggy. I try singing to him, beginning with something soothing: 'Care is heavy, therefore sleep you. You are care, and care must keep you . . .' He cranes his neck up at me, and says, 'Bb.' When I lean down and start dancing with him, he smiles, and pulls against my hands, wanting to lead. Maybe he'll be a dancer some day, I tell him, and I lean down and give him a kiss, then stand up and carry on pushing him. He bounces a little in his chair, dancing alone.

I remember, suddenly and clearly, how much I loved music when I was a child, the few lessons I squeezed in between studying catching and curfew law, how carefully I practised the piano at home, knowing I'd be left alone as long as I was practising, free to enjoy myself, listening to the music I was making. There's a music shop only a few streets away. I pass it on my way to work, the days when I walk. Years ago, I forbade myself to stare into the windows, wishing for things I couldn't afford. I think I'd like to go there now. Maybe I'll buy Leo some maracas, something he can shake, so he can make a fine noise and let everyone know he's there. I remember how good that feels.

I have to back through the shop door to get both of us inside, but once we're in, the air is warmer, soft like dust, only the shop itself is very clean. White piano keys gleam, trumpets and flutes sit immaculate on their stands. There are some small percussion instruments, easy things to shake about, and I take down some Mexican-looking things, bright coloured with carvings on the handle, and offer them to Leo. He reaches out and grasps one, holds it, admiring it. It's only when I close my hand around his and rattle this new toy that he realises its use, and sets about swinging it from side to side, happy. He doesn't make much noise with it, he hasn't figured out quite how to make the beans rattle yet, but he'll get there.

Not wanting to deprive him of his new plaything, I take the other shaker to the till and pay for it while leaving him to enjoy the one he has. It's cheap, I won't have to forgo anything to afford it, and it occurs to me then that I'm a little richer than I used to be. The pay raise has come through, some more money every month. I wondered for a while whether to take it. In the end, I decided I would, I'd take the money and try to work well enough to justify my pay. I'm still in the habit of living cheaply, though. It means I actually have some spare money.

Leo looks curiously at the pianos as I wheel him back towards the door, and I stop, consider. I've thrown away a lot of my possessions, and I have a little extra cash. I'd always thought I couldn't fit in or afford a piano; I'd given up on playing. I'll still never run to a concert grand, but there are some electric keyboards here, quite cheap, quite small. I'd always refused to try them before, because I know they don't compare to real ones, but all the same, maybe something small would be better than nothing.

To Leo's delight, I unstrap him from his chair and set him on my lap as I sit down on a stool before one of the small keyboards. He reaches out, strokes the keys with a cautious hand, and I lay my hand over his. We press the key together. Leo grins and gives a little squeak of delight at this new sound, stretches out for another note. He hits a deep bass, and I reach around him, play a little arpeggio. My fingers aren't as awkward as I'd

547

expected. I've grown since I last tried this, the octaves are easier to span.

We play together for a while, before Leo gets bored and wriggles. I set him down in his buggy, give him the shakers and let him knock them against his lap. I stretch my hands, reach out from note to note.

To begin with, I play simply. Scales, up and down. Major for a while, then minor. It comes back easier than I anticipated. The keys sink under my fingers, a little too resilient, but the tone is pleasant, and I find I can remember some of the pieces I used to know. Music drifts around me.

The shop assistant passes me, smiles. I relax back on the stool, playing better. I make mistakes and carry on, and Leo sits beside me, happy and absorbed with his toy, as I run my hands up and down the keyboard. It's an old skill, and I'm out of the habit, but I sit and play for a long time.

Light shines in through the windows, a shaft of it falling clear on the floor in front of me. Specks of dust drift and glimmer in it, slow and bright, like a snowfall of stars. It's the most beautiful thing I've ever seen.